DATE DUE

P9-CNE-754

3/19

Necessary Changes

Necessary Changes

Mary Kay McComas

BOOKSPAN
GARDEN CITY, NEW YORK

Published by BOOKSPAN, 401 Franklin Avenue,
Garden City, New York 11530
ISBN: 0-7394-1799-1
Interior Design by Paul Randall Mize
All Rights Reserved
Printed in the United States of America

This book is dedicated to my friend,
Mary Blayney,
who knows the real story,
and that this isn't it.

PART ONE

The Early Daze

One

I F YOU KNEW at age ten what you knew at age forty-two, how much of your life would you change? A ponderous question. One she'd asked herself so often lately it had become even more important than the question of why she was alive at all. You know, what is the purpose of life?

Livy removed the thin cotton open-in-back hospital gown she wore over her slip and skirt and tossed it onto the treatment table. She could hear the doctor talking, presumably to the nurse, on the other side of the door, but she couldn't make out what he was saying. It didn't matter. They were finished with her. She'd come back in a year for a look-see, but it was over. They'd done all they could for her.

She buttoned up her blouse, taking her time, wondering if the pain had been worth it. Oh, not just the physical pain. Comparatively speaking, it was nothing. But the years of emotional pain she'd suffered . . . and the pain she was causing him now. Were they worth it?

If you believe that you are totally a product of your environment, and you're not unhappy with the way things turned out, then you wouldn't want to fiddle with your past, she decided. You'd want to experience it all again, the good and the bad, or your life wouldn't turn out the same. You'd want to know the same people, live the same experiences, cry the same tears, make the same mistakes. Wouldn't you? You couldn't even switch the sequence of events—such as marry your second husband first—because then you wouldn't know or appreciate how good you had it the second time around. Or would you?

Maybe she was still too young to answer such weighty questions. She felt as if she was just starting to get smart at forty-two. Real wisdom might take a little longer.

A pity really. Wisdom should come with gray hair, she thought, looking at her blurred reflection in the paper-towel dispenser above the sink. Beneath the concoction her hairdresser applied to her scalp every six weeks, she was salt-and-pepper gray. Prematurely, of course. After all, she had young children at home. And she couldn't run around looking like their grandmother, could she?

She used the mirror in her compact to apply a little extra blush to her right cheek. Lipstick covered the paleness the pain created—and if she smiled, maybe the Telfa dressing over her left cheek would be less noticeable. Or not. At this point, it made very little difference. In six weeks it would be gone forever. And what was six weeks to forever? Or to forty-two years, for that matter?

She studied her face in the little round mirror. It wasn't all that different.

Brian hated different, hated change. If it were up to him, time would have stopped in 1960. They'd still be ten years old and riding their bikes all over Tolford. She returned the compact to her purse and slipped her feet into low-heeled shoes. No. He'd have stopped time in 1967 so he could rediscover low-interest, no-obligation, disease-free sex. No, no, no. He'd stop it in '68. He was a basketball star that year, and Cathy Dixon was on his mind like a . . . a brain tumor.

She gave a soft laugh. Change was inevitable. He should know that by now. It was scary. And it never came easily—especially when it was a change for the better.

Why did it seem so much easier to cling to old ways, to neglect things, to let them run down and decay than to work and build and create something new and good?

Not for the first time she wondered if perhaps that wasn't man's fatal flaw, part of the curse for the original sin—his reluctance to make changes because he got burned so badly the first time he tried to change things, back in Eden. Maintaining the status quo wasn't as risky, and it was easier.

Wasn't it easier to ridicule new ideas than to embrace them? Wasn't it easier to hate than to love? Scorn than to praise? Ostracize than accept? And yet, in truth, it takes a lot more energy to hate someone for the color of his skin than it does to admire him for his character and talents. A lot more effort to fight a war than to live in peace. A lot more emotion to kill than to make love.

It was a curse all right.

There was a time when she thought she could change all that. Not single-handedly, of course. That is, not unless she was forced to act alone because of the inertia of her fellow human beings.

She shook her head in disbelief as she gathered up her purse and smoothed her hair into place with one hand. Had she really been so young and supercilious?

What a big, bad place the world had seemed in those days—and so ripe for revamping.

A new bandwagon came along every five minutes, and you could pick one or jump on them all. Black civil rights. The Vietnam war. Women's liberation. Ecology. Government graft and corruption. Endangered species. Abortion. Communist aggression. Inflation. It was a wonder she didn't break anything hopping on and off those wagons.

Of course, Brian would have been there to catch her if she'd slipped. He'd always been there. Traveling through life with her, refusing to ride on a bandwagon but walking a parallel path of his own, viewing the world from a different perspective—from a quiet, down-to-earth angle that was simple and basic.

He'd always been there, like a safe base in a game of Tag-You're-It. He was the keeper of her faith, the guardian of her innocence. His hands painted the splendor of the earth for her. She saw her own beauty through Brian's eyes . . .

. . .

Brian reached for his overcoat, shook out the wrinkles and folded it, then hung it over his arm. He did the same to her coat and filled the air around him with the scent of lilacs. Always lilacs.

He took in the familiar fragrance, long and deep, his nose buried in the soft wool. It was true red, her favorite color. Her smell. Her color. He wondered if those things would change now. He wondered if she would change.

He couldn't help it; he was scared. That deep-down, sick-at-your-stomach scared you get just before your whole life comes crashing in around you. He'd been that scared before, but not recently. Not for a long time, until now.

He glanced at the doorway, then stood, holding both coats to him. He walked to the window.

The doctor's office was part of New York University Medical Center in lower Manhattan. It was painted rental-unit tan. The furniture was covered in fecal-brown and puke-green vinyl. The nurses wore perky pink-and-white uniforms. They clashed with the decor. And the window had no view—only the outer wall of the next building, some melting snow on the ledge, some pigeon poop.

He shook his head and closed his eyes. He hated New York. He always had. Even when he lived there. Of course, that had been years and years ago. How old had he been?

That was when she first got married, so he must have been about twenty-four. They were the same age, give or take three months, two weeks and two days. He was still living there when she got divorced; that made it four years he'd spent in New York. Certainly long enough to decide whether you liked a place or not. And he didn't.

He much preferred old Tolford, the town they had grown up in. Tolford, Tennessee. Located just south of the Mason Dixon, east of Nowhere, west of Nothing. The city-limit signs weren't exactly back to back, but you could see them both from the middle of Main

Street. There were bigger dots on the map, but none better in his opinion. Good old Tolford.

When he opened his eyes, they were directed at the doorway again. Empty. He glanced at the other patients waiting to see the doctor. A dermatologist–slash–plastic surgeon who believed in the practice of innovative procedures.

The fear squirmed in his belly again. Was any other medical specialty reputed to have fewer scruples than plastic surgery? Or a higher incidence of quackery? Plastic surgery—it sounded like a game for children. Plastic surgeon—made by Tyco? Accessories not included?

He sighed. He knew he wasn't being fair. She had her reasons for being there. Livy was ever ready with her reasons for doing things. He couldn't say he fully understood them all. He tried. But he didn't always succeed.

His gaze slipped to the oversized coffee table inconveniently placed in the center of the tiny waiting room. It was heaped high with magazines and newspapers. *Sports Illustrated, USA Today, People, U.S. News & World Report.* On top was the outdated *Time* he'd tried to read earlier. A short article he couldn't finish. Something about a place called Botswana. It was one of those relatively new countries that kept popping up to remind him how long it had been since he'd studied geography in school.

Not a very stable place, the earth. There were new countries everywhere, it seemed to him. Several more in Africa, a few in Europe. Czechoslovakia was two separate countries now, and Germany was back to being a single state. Even the dreaded "Russia" of his youth, the Union of Soviet Socialist Republics was in fragments. Or so he'd heard. He didn't really bother to keep up with such things, though it did amuse him sometimes to think that whole countries could come and go, and still you could find a prize in a box of Cracker Jacks.

Some things never changed, and he liked that.

Being able to count on things was important. He'd spent most of his forty-odd years seeking solid, basic truths in his life and had managed to cling to a mere handful. He must have come to the conclusion early on that there was little truth or stability going on around him, because the world as a whole didn't affect him much.

Not the way it affected some people. Not like it affected her.

He was, by self-admission, an introverted man. Pensive. Introspective.

Maybe self-absorbed was closer to the truth.

He felt guilty sometimes, believing himself to be the only person alive at the time who didn't fall to the ground and weep buckets of tears when he heard President Kennedy had been assassinated. His vague recollection of the funeral was of how long and boring it was. The only impression he had of the first moon walk was the question of why all three channels had to televise it at the same time. And how long that guy's golf ball would be in orbit. It used to irritate him when people discussed the Vietnam war at parties and when racial equality was hotly debated as if it were a two-sided issue.

He'd taken a lot for granted in his life. His freedom. His innocence. His good fortune to be born in the exact right month, under the best of stars, with his moon rising in the luckiest of houses, so that all he had to deal with when he came of age was yuppiedom and some political turmoil in the Middle East that in no way, shape, or fashion affected his daily life.

He blinked away a small collection of recollections and glanced over his shoulder. The doorway was still empty.

It was a good thing no one could look inside his head. The confusing blur would frighten them. His memory was a nimbus of color and emotion, a thick, sometimes swirling fog dotted with distressingly few solid experiences to cling to. Facts and fragments of historical events had passed through, but they were too heavy and too detached from the moment he was living in, they simply slipped away and were forgotten.

Older but no wiser, he wasn't surprised that after forty-two years of treading life's waters he could barely distinguish one moment gone by from the next. Nor did it surprise him that his head was still above the water, even though he'd floundered and gone under so often. Somehow he'd always managed to rise to the surface once more, take a deep breath, look around.

Curious to see what *she'd* do next, he supposed, turning to look out the window again.

What he knew of the world, what he knew of his life, he knew because of her. If he had convictions and beliefs, if he had hope and empathy, it was because of her. If he'd done one decent thing in his life, taken one risk, given a single ounce of himself to better the world, it was because of her. She was his link to the rest of the world, and it was her oyster. She loved it. She cared about it. She fought for it. She protected it. She was ever faithful to the assumption that somewhere within all its ugliness, there was a beautiful pearl.

Oh, yes. If he had any memory of his life at all, it was of Livy.

Two

GOOD OLD TOLFORD.

Only Main Street had sidewalks in those good old days. The town's lifeblood flowed through three primary arteries: an electric-fan factory, a rayon textile plant, and agriculture.

There were three churches, one Presbyterian, one Baptist, and the old black Baptist church, of course. (The last, according to his mother, who still lived in Tolford, had recently been taken over by a group of Christian fundamentalists—though they weren't expected to last long.) And there were six bars. A reasonable ratio, in his estimation.

Tolford boasted two gas stations, two grocery stores, four regular restaurants, and three fast-food establishments that, to him, qualified as competitive economics. There were three public schools, one for each level—no private schools for miles and miles; a bowling alley; a small country club, which was actually a community pool and golf course that didn't require exclusive membership anymore; and one doctor—Dr. McAbey, a general practitioner whose office and small clinic claimed the four front rooms of the big old house on Walnut Street where he lived with his family.

Broadleaf forests surrounded the town. As did acres of wheat and soybeans. A few fields of cotton and tobacco had remained, but not many. Cool, calm lakes. Excellent river fishing. If you grew up in Tolford, you grew up barefoot and happy. Slow and lazy, Tolford was his sort of place. He missed it. All of it. Though he could clearly recall a time when he'd seen it quite differently. . . .

He felt again the heat of that day and the sting of the tears in his eyes. His face was burning with shame and fear. His hair was damp and curly with sweat. He wanted to run away. It was 1956, and he didn't want to live in a new house or go to a new school. He hated this new place and everyone in it. And they hated him. They were laughing at him. He wished his mother would come back for him. If he survived his first day of school, he'd never come back. Ever. No one could make him.

And then it happened. In the middle of a heartbeat.

"Next time I tell ya ta stop it, are ya gonna stop it?" he heard her yelling. Donny Moore lay crying at her feet, his nose trickling crimson. "Or do ya want me ta punch ya again?"

Donny covered his face with his hands, discovered the blood, and started crying louder—but he didn't forget to nod the answer to her question.

In utter astonishment, for he hadn't even considered hitting Donny himself, Brian slowly turned to face the girl beside him.

Granted, his knowledge of females was limited at the time. He knew they wore dresses and they didn't get crew cuts, but other than that they were just "girls" in his mind—the other half to his teacher's "Now boys and girls . . ."

But *SHE*, this girl, was magnificent. Long dark hair braided down both sides of her face and huge deep-brown eyes that were just a little too big for her six-year-old face. She had an acre of freckles scattered across her button nose and a big purple blotch on her left cheek. Her expression was still stormy with anger and mayhem as she glared down at Donny.

Then she glanced at him.

"What are you starin' at?" she asked him, glowering.

"Nothin'," he said. He lowered his gaze, taking in her red plaid dress with its white Peter Pan collar, the lace-trimmed anklets, the Mary Jane shoes, and prayed that she wouldn't sock him, too, when he asked, "How come you hit him?"

"He was makin' fun of you," she said, puzzled. "Didn't ya know he was makin' fun of the way ya talk?"

"Yeah. I knew."

"Why didn't *you* hit him?"

"You're not th-uppo-th-ed to fight at th-chool," he answered, lisping his esses. "You'll get in trouble." His mother had warned him about it.

"I won't." Her smile was smug. "I got permission."

"Permi-th-ion? To hit kid-th?"

"Well, not all of 'em," she said, walking away from the scene of the crime as if it hadn't happened. He fell into step beside her, not caring where she was going. "But my daddy says I can punch anyone who makes fun of me, 'cause they deserve it."

"That boy wa-th makin' fun of *me*," he pointed out.

"It don't matter. He still deserved it." She smiled at him.

For a second, Brian thought his heart had stopped. But, no. He could feel it pounding and growing larger and larger inside his chest. Her big brown eyes twinkled at him, taking away his breath. His mouth went dry.

"Wh-why would anyone make fun of you?" He couldn't fathom it.

" 'Cause of my mark."

"What mark?" She had a mark? He scanned her up and down once again.

She pointed to her left cheek.

Oh. Sure. He'd noticed the big purple blotch on her cheek, but it wasn't her most striking feature—not like her fists, certainly. In fact, the mark on her face was the least significant observation he'd made about her.

"Wow. How'd you get it?"

"I came with it. I was born with it," she said. "But don't stare at it, okay? I hate it when people stare at me."

"Okay." There were other things about her that he preferred to stare at anyway. "What-th your name?"

"Olivia Jane Hubbard. I sit two seats behind you."

"You do?"

"You can call me Livy, if you want."

"I'm Brian. Brian Carowack." His new dad and his mother and baby sister all had a different last name, but his was easier to say.

"I know," she said, smiling again. "I have a loose tooth. See?" She wiggled it back and forth with her tongue. "You wanna wiggle it?"

Wow! What a girl! His grandma had take-out teeth because she didn't have any real teeth at all. But he didn't know anyone in the whole world with loose teeth. And she was going to let him wiggle it and everything.

What if he broke it? What if he wrecked her smile? What if he made her look like his grandma did at night?

"Nah."

"Do you have any loose ones?"

"No." He was just an ordinary boy. Nothing special about him.

"How come you didn't come the first day of school?"

"We wa-th movin' to our new hou-th."

If he could talk like the other kids did, he might have gone on to explain about his stepfather's new job, the new bedroom he didn't have to share with his baby sister, Beth, and the fuss his mother had made about his missing the first week of first grade. He might even have told her how confused and lost he felt. But he didn't talk like the other kids did, and he preferred to keep his responses as short as possible—and with as few s-es and th-s as possible.

"Where'd you live before?" she asked, seeming not to notice the short spray of spit that accompanied his speech.

"In my old hou-th."

She looked at him. "Did you have lots of friends there?"

"No. But I had a dog. He couldn't come." His new dad didn't like dogs.

"I have a cat named Snow. But that's only 'cause she's all white. I was gonna call her Whitey, but my mama liked Snow."

"My dog was Rocky. He liked to chew on rock-th. He thought they were ball-th. He could eat your cat, I bet."

"Maybe. Or they might have been friends. Like us."

Friends? Like us? Were they friends already?

"I have a new bike," she said.

"Can you ride it?"

"Sure."

"I might get one from Th-anta Clau-th. If I'm good."

She looked at him as if she were about to tell him something important, then seemed to change her mind. "We can take turns riding mine."

"Olivia Hubbard!" It was their teacher's voice. "You've been fighting again?"

It didn't sound as if Livy had *everyone's* permission to fight.

Together they turned to face Miss Dobbs. She was young and pretty like his mother. She wore blue. A loud, happy blue. But her stern expression made his blood rush hot and then cold through his body. His heart hammered with guilt and fear. He'd never been in trouble at school before—never even been to school before. What would his mother say? What would his new dad do?

"Yes, ma'am," Livy said, her head high.

Holy smokes. Wasn't she afraid of *anything*, he wondered, full of awe.

"March," Miss Dobbs ordered, her finger pointing back to the classroom, her attitude that of a practiced referee.

Livy, too, seemed to know the routine. Without defense she started walking across the playground toward the school.

Something wasn't right. Brian felt it in his heart and then voiced it in his mind. If it weren't for him, she wouldn't be in trouble. Maybe he should be punished, too. Grappling with the knowledge that whatever they did to bad boys at Tolford Primary School, it wouldn't be half as awful as the deep Dutch he'd be in at home, he took two steps forward.

In that moment, Livy turned her head and smiled at him. Her smile could melt a flagpole.

"See ya later, Brian," she said.

"Okay," he said.

He'd owe her one.

If you were born in Tolford, Tennessee—smack-dab in the middle of the American Bible Belt—it wasn't necessarily better, but it certainly was easier, if you were born white, like Livy. It also helped if your mama, like hers, had family roots there that ran deeper than a shagbark hickory tree and your daddy was one of the two attorneys in town.

If he was the district attorney with political aspirations . . . well, let's say certain allowances would be made by certain people if you were his only daughter.

Other children, of course, proved the exception to this unspoken rule of etiquette. Kids were usually more afraid of and more eager to please their own parents than they were someone else's folks. And they rarely made allowance for your social standing. They either liked you or they didn't. No matter who you were or what you said or how you looked.

"This is wonderful, Brian," Miss Dobbs said, her soft, enthusiastic voice as clear and distinct through time as the first fat drops of rain in a summer shower.

She was looking over his shoulder from behind at the work on his desk. There was a sunny afternoon beyond the schoolroom windows, and the class was being quiet and diligent during "art time."

The assignment: Draw your best friend.

"Boys and girls, may I have your attention for a moment?" she asked, reaching for Brian's crayon drawing. "We've seen lots of friends this afternoon. Bobby's best friend was his dog, Teddy. And

Julia's best friends were her mother and father. Cathy's friend was Lisa Marie, and Arthur's was Larry. Now let's see if we can recognize who Brian's best friend is."

The class looked up.

"Are you finished, Brian? May I show the other children?"

He nodded. Brian wasn't as big as some of the kids in their class. He was skinny and shy and he didn't like to talk. Livy knew he hated being singled out in front of the others.

Miss Dobbs held the picture high, turning in a circle so everyone could see it. Livy was eager. She knew who Brian's best friend was. She saw the black x-es of dark braids along each side of the egg-shaped face and the freckles across the nose and felt great satisfaction. She waited for someone to identify her.

Her classmates looked puzzled. A few of them looked her way, then back at the picture. But they didn't say anything.

Miss Dobbs turned again. This time Livy saw the red ribbons at the ends of the braids and the brown eyes—complete with eyelashes. Brian was one of the best artists in class. Miss Dobbs always said so. Livy thought he was the very best, and she looked around the room once more. What was the matter with everyone? They all knew who Brian's best friend was—from the very beginning they'd been best friends. And who else in the class had hair as long and black as hers? And who else had to wear stupid red bows in it?

"Can't anyone guess who this might be?" Miss Dobbs asked, looking as perplexed as Livy felt. "I think it bears a remarkable resemblance to someone right here in this room."

When the picture came around a third time, Livy studied it harder. It was her, all right. She was smiling, and two teeth were missing. Miss Dobbs always remarked on what she called Brian's gift for detail, which meant he didn't miss anything like fingers or shoelaces or feathers on birds or houses made of brick instead of stone or wood. Brian liked to draw, and he was proud of his work.

Why didn't someone say something?

"All right," Miss Dobbs said. "Brian, why don't you tell us who your best friend is."

"Livy," he said.

The other children started to laugh.

"That's not Livy," they said. "There's no purple mark on her face," they shouted.

Miss Dobbs glanced down at the picture, then at Brian, then at Livy, frowning.

"That's enough, class," she said, her voice as stern as she could make it. "Please be silent. We don't laugh at other people's mistakes."

She slid the picture back onto Brian's desk and started to walk to the front of the classroom. Then she turned around.

"I'm sorry, Brian. Did you say something?"

He glanced about at the class, then stood up beside his desk. It took an act of God, or at least a direct question from Miss Dobbs, to get him to speak out in class because of the way he talked. Even Livy was surprised to see that he had something to say, voluntarily.

"I didn't," he said softly.

"You didn't what, Brian?"

"Make a mi-th-take. I drew Livy. I drew my friend, like you told u-th to."

"She's a girl, stupid," Donny Moore pointed out from across the room. To say that Brian and Donny didn't get along would be a gross understatement. Donny was the bane of Brian's existence. Bigger, louder, meaner. "Brian's got a girlfriend."

The class started to laugh again.

Brian grew pink cheeked with embarrassment, but it was the anger in his eyes that won out. He turned to Donny and shouted, "Th-ut up!"

"Now boys . . ." Miss Dobbs said, but not before Donny Moore got out another jab.

"Brian's got an ugly girlfriend with a dirty face."

Livy felt hot all over, and she was afraid she might start crying—or get in trouble for punching Donny again. She wanted to
hide her face, leave the room, disappear. But something kept her
rooted to her desk, watching Brian, his fingers curling into fists at
the ends of his skinny arms, his face a glowering mask of rage.

"*You're* ugly! Livy is beautiful!" he said, and when the class
snickered, his expression faltered with the realization that he'd gotten a little carried away. He started to blush again, but he was disin-
clined to back down. He glanced at her, then to the floor. "Th-he
i-th," he insisted, looking straight at Donny.

"That is enough. Both of you, be silent," Miss Dobbs said, leaning over her desk and writing quickly on two sheets of paper. "We
don't talk about our classmates that way. Tonight the two of you
can copy these letters a hundred times for me. They spell: No one is
ugly. And have your parents sign your papers when you're finished.
Is that understood?"

"Yes, ma'am," Donny said, making a tee-hee grimace at Brian.

"Brian?" she said, drawing his angry glare from Donny. "Is that
understood?"

He nodded.

"Are you gonna be in lots of trouble?" Livy asked him later as
they walked slowly home from school. He was always quiet in class,
but he usually had something to say on the way home. He hadn't
said a word. She could tell he was still upset.

He shrugged.

"Well, it's your own fault if you are," she said, not unkindly. He
looked at her. "It wasn't a very good picture."

"Why?" He looked hurt.

"You drew me beautiful, and I'm not. You didn't draw my
mark."

"I forgot."

"I know," she said, sympathetically. She sometimes forgot
about it, too. "But next time draw it. Then you won't be in trouble."

They walked on in silence for a few minutes. "And don't say I'm beautiful to people. Then you won't be in trouble either."

"But you are," he muttered, clearly uncomfortable in saying so but unwilling to give up his right to do so.

"I'm not. I'm strong and I'm smart and Mama says I'm pretty on the inside and that's where it counts. But my face is ugly."

"Your mama th-aid your face i-th ugly?"

"No." As if a mother would. "She says I'm pretty on the inside and that's where it counts. *I* say my face is ugly."

"You're wrong." It was a simple enough statement, but to tell Livy she was wrong about anything took a great deal of courage in someone her own size. And she knew it.

She looked sideways at Brian. He was walking along the way he always did, watching his feet, looking up at the trees, or observing the cars that drove by. She couldn't tell if he was so sure of his remark that he wasn't expecting an argument, or if he was just so confident in their friendship that he knew she wouldn't punch him for it.

Or was he simply being loyal? You couldn't punch a pal for being a pal. Did he really think she was beautiful?

"Did you throw that picture away?"

"No."

"Can I have it?"

He looked at her, then stopped to take his book bag off his shoulder and unzip it. He handed her the drawing.

Wordlessly, she waited until he was ready to walk on. And she didn't look at the picture again until she got home. She single-tacked it to her bedroom wall. Studied it. Examined her real face in the mirror. Covered the mark with one hand and glazed the focus of her eyes to see what she'd look like without it.

Not ugly. Pretty maybe.

Brian was right. Without her mark, she wasn't ugly. She looked nice. Only the mark was ugly. She scrutinized the purple blotch. Dr.

McAbey called it a port-wine stain because that's what it looked like. A stain. A smooth pooling of wine or grape juice. He'd said it was caused by having too many blood vessels or blood vessels that were too big under her skin. He'd shown her pictures of other people and other children who had the same stain over their whole face, or half their face, or down their neck and onto their bodies. He'd said she was lucky hers was relatively small.

But she hadn't felt lucky. And she didn't think it was all that small. It was about the size of her fist, an inch below her eye, and it covered most of her left cheek.

She looked again at Brian's picture. It was just an old crayon drawing, but it was her. And if she could somehow soak up the stain, Brian was right: She was pretty underneath it.

Three

L IVY SWUNG one-handed around the pole of the stop sign in front of her house as Brian hurried down the road toward her. Every morning she waited for Brian by the stop sign, and they went to school together. And every morning he wanted to feel bad for making her wait so long—but she always said he couldn't help it.

During the summer she'd explained to him that his mama was a "late person." That meant she was habitually five to ten minutes late for everything. Consequently, so was Brian. She'd said that it wasn't a bad thing to be; it was just boring sometimes.

He watched as she caught the wind in her other hand. She didn't like boring, but she was used to it. Her mama was an "early person," one who was always at a place ten minutes before she had to be, and then waited. Therefore, Livy waited, too. She didn't like being bored, but she admitted that sometimes it was a good thing. She said there were lots of things you could do inside your brain when you were bored.

She was full of this type of insightful information.

"Hi."

"Hi," she said, smiling, taking one last swing around the pole, fingers spread wide to free the wind.

"She made waffle-th," he said, explaining his longer-than-usual delay in meeting her.

"Mush again." She always had oatmeal or grits for breakfast. Alternating days.

They lived only two blocks from each other, but it could have been the whole world that separated them. Everything was different at Livy's house. Her mother didn't teach at the high school every

day like his did. She stayed home. Livy's father had a real important
job downtown and he wore suits most of the time. His stepfather
wore coveralls and drove twenty miles to Idlewild to work at a factory. It was his second new job. He hated it.

They played pretty, wordless music at Livy's house, country-
western or rock 'n' roll at his. Livy didn't have to watch her baby sister because she didn't have one. She was an only child. She lived in a
big red brick house with white pillars in front; he lived in a wooden
one-story house with a wire fence around it. All the Hubbards had
the same last name, so there was no need to explain why your name
was different from your mother's and father's and sister's. And
Livy's parents talked to her as if she was a grown-up or something,
not like she was a kid.

"Did you finish it?" she asked.

Rather than answer, he slipped a paper out of his second-grade
math book and handed it to her. She unfolded the sheet of lined
paper, studied it, then handed it back.

"She had golden hair," she said smartly. "I said it three times so
you wouldn't forget."

"I thought it wa-th dark. Like your-th."

Of all her friends, Brian knew she liked him the most. She said
it was because he liked to play ball and ride bikes and climb trees,
and he never suggested that they dress up in their mother's old
clothes—especially if there were polliwogs to be caught in Mr.
Miller's pond. He was also entirely empathetic with her attitude toward the dresses and hair ribbons her mother insisted upon. And
best of all, she said, even when they didn't like doing the same
things, they had fun together doing different things—which was
what they did mostly—because Livy liked to do different things.

He also knew that what she found most interesting about him
was the one thing she couldn't do. Draw pictures. What came naturally to him, in lines and color, eluded her completely. Even her
stick people looked crippled and diseased. Where his love of detail

came in the form of shapes and hues, hers came in words. She read them. She wrote them. She made them up.

And so, when she wanted to make up stories of her own, she did it aloud and Brian would draw the pictures to accompany them. Wonderful pictures with everything in them. Sometimes he'd draw in extra things, to make the story better, though that was usually a matter of opinion.

"Why do you always make the girl's hair black?" she asked, annoyed.

"Becau-th-th-e acts like you. Th-e-th-ound-th like you. That-th how I th-ee her in my head."

"You see her in your head?"

"Yeah."

"When I tell you a story, you see it in your head?"

"Yeah."

This impressed her for a second or two.

"Well, they're my stories, so you have to draw them the way I say. The girls always have golden hair, and the handsome man always has dark hair. All stories are like that."

"Why doe-th th-e alway-th have to die?"

"Because that's what happens. She saves the handsome man, and then she dies."

"But why?"

"Because she does."

She wasn't always so rigid in her thinking, however. Mostly she was curious. She wanted to know about everything. Bugs and leaves and where the end of the sky was. She was full of questions. And, in general, she admired that same quality in others.

Except when it came to her face.

And people were curious about her face. Lots of adults and some kids. He'd watched adults talk about the mark on her face with her mother. What caused it? Could it be treated? Was it hereditary? They would hold Livy's face in their hands, turn it from side to side, and talk about the mark as if there were no little girl behind it. Children weren't so rude. They were cruel. They'd ask if it hurt or if they could touch it. Some would ask if she'd forgotten to wash her face—and laugh.

Frankly, Brian couldn't see it. Literally. Whole weeks went by when he forgot it was there. He was always surprised and a little confused when other people commented on it. He still wasn't much of a fighter, unfortunately, but more than once he'd stayed after school with her—punished by association—and he never uttered a word. He didn't like people who talked about her face either.

They crossed Lambert Street to take the shortcut through the park. It was Wednesday. Any other day they'd be riding their bikes; they'd ride another two blocks along Lambert and cut through the parking lot behind the IGA. It was a shorter shortcut. But on Wednesdays they walked and cut through the rows of overgrown shrubs and between the trees so no one would see them.

"Here comes Chewy," she said in a whisper as she glanced about the nearly deserted park. She handed her school books to Brian. Old Mr. Shirtzer was walking his dog, Fritz, but they posed no threat. Mr. Shirtzer was stone deaf, and he couldn't see much beyond the end of Fritz's leash.

Still, they never took chances. They couldn't. Chewy was black.

Brian couldn't begin to explain or understand the danger of being black, or of being a small white boy or girl seen alone with an older black boy. All he knew was that it was dangerous. It was a secret. He and Livy had never talked about it after the initial encounter. It just happened, every Wednesday.

They knew Chewy. Charles Winston Lewis was his long name, Livy said—she'd asked him once. He worked at the BP station on Main Street. Brian's stepfather went to the Shell station, but he'd seen Livy's mother ask Chewy to change the oil in their car once, and he'd seen her father slap Chewy on the back and laugh with him and tell him to have a fine day on more than one occasion.

In truth, no one had actually told him not to be seen with Chewy. But sometimes you didn't have to be told. Sometimes you could hear a hateful sound in a grown-up's voice when he said the word *nigger*. Sometimes you'd see grown-ups do things that would make your mother cringe and look away. Sometimes you could do bad things without knowing they were bad. But then, too, sometimes you just knew when something wasn't a good idea.

And so it was on that hot summer afternoon when their path first crossed with Chewy's on their way home from the library. Livy was delivering another one of her long, elaborate tales, and Brian was concentrating to remember all the details. This new tragedy had a cast of thousands.

"Hey, Chewy," Livy said, a casual greeting in passing.

"Hey, little Miss Livy, where you been?" He was tall, almost manlike in size. Only his face, still soft and smooth and plump in the cheeks, spoke of his youth. He was sixteen.

"The library," she said proudly, stopping to talk. "I got a card."

"That so?"

"Brian's got one, too. Show him yours, Brian."

He whipped it from the back pocket of his cotton shorts and held it up for Chewy to see. He wasn't afraid of him. Chewy's smile was as big and bright as he was tall and dark, and he had soft, kind eyes. Still, he sensed something in the situation that made him uneasy, and he slipped the card back into his pocket.

"He doesn't like to read as much as me, but he wanted to get a card anyway," Livy said. "He goes to the library with me and looks at picture books."

"Doesn't like to read, you say? Why not?"

Brian shrugged. He didn't know why, he just didn't. He did know that the tension he felt in Chewy's company intensified when he was being addressed directly.

"What's that on your neck there?" Chewy asked, not touching

him but bending at the waist to get a better look at the four round bluish marks on Brian's neck.

"Nothin'."

Chewy's eyes narrowed thoughtfully, and Brian shifted his light weight from one foot to the other nervously.

"Did you fall again?" Livy asked. "He falls down a lot," she explained to Chewy. "One time he even gave himself a black eye. Didn't you, Brian?"

He nodded and looked away. There was a certain understanding in Chewy's eyes that was impossible to meet directly.

"Can you read, Chewy?" Livy asked, startling Brian. What a terrible thing to ask! Could he read? Chewy was almost grown up. All grown-ups could read. He braced himself and waited for Chewy's anger.

"I got the gift, Miss Livy," he said, grinning. "My mama made sure of that. My trouble is finding new things to read."

"Well, you got a library, too, don't ya?"

"Sure do. But it's not as big as yours, and the books are old."

Through Livy, and through day-to-day living in Tolford, Brian had surmised that things were very different for black people. Different schools, different libraries, special restaurants and drinking fountains. None as nice as the ones the white people were supposed to use. There hadn't been many colored people in rural Nebraska, where he lived before. There were town kids and farm kids just like in Tolford, but the distinctions between them hadn't been so great. Not like they were with colored people. Or perhaps he hadn't taken notice of them. That happened sometimes. He didn't see a lot of things that were as plain as the nose on his face. He noticed colors and little details, but not big things like how people lived. Either way, he hadn't been aware of the differences in skin color or lifestyles until he'd moved to Tolford. Nor had he ever been afraid of talking to someone he knew in a public place, as he was at that moment.

"What kinda books do you like?" Livy was asking.

"All kinds. But mostly histories, biographies, and autobiographies."

"What are . . . biographies?"

His smile flashed. Big, bright, and amused. "Stories about the lives of real people. Like Frederick Douglass, Abraham Lincoln, and Booker T. Washington. Good folk mostly."

"I bet my library has lots of those." They sounded like grown-up books.

"I bet you're right about that," he said. He spoke the words kindly enough, but there was a distinct edge to his voice, and he looked away as if there were something in his eyes that they didn't need to see.

"Want me to get you some with my card?"

His gaze came back to her, hard and piercing, as if he were being snookered, then softened as he considered her offer.

"You're a good little girl, Miss Livy," he said. "But you got no idea how much trouble we'd all be in if someone found out."

See? Brian knew there was trouble in this situation somewhere.

"I won't be in trouble. My daddy says all colored people should have the same things as me and him. He says separatin' things is bad. He hopes they let the colored children come to my school. He said he wouldn't put me in a private school if *they* paid *him*," she said, her young voice high and clear with conviction. "He says the National Guard in Arkansas should find somethin' better to do than keep little kids from goin' to school."

Chewy smiled and thought this over; then his dark gaze moved slowly to Brian's face.

"Your daddy doesn't say that, does he?" he asked.

"No, th-ir. But he-th not my real daddy," he was quick to add, knowing a shame he'd done nothing to deserve.

"No matter," he said, looking kindly at Brian. "I'd get it worse than both of you put together if we got caught sharin' library books."

"Then we won't get caught." This from Livy, who was always getting caught at school for something or other—and yet she sounded so sure of herself, both Chewy and Brian believed her. Instantly.

Six months later the swapping of books in the bushes with Chewy had become a routine. On Tuesday they went to the library and borrowed, along with their own selections, the book Chewy requested the week before. Every Wednesday morning they cut through the park, Livy holding the new volume in her left hand, Brian carrying her school books. Chewy walked toward them with last week's reading in his left hand, and when they passed—sometimes saying howdy, sometimes not—he slipped it into Livy's right hand, snagged the other from her left, and kept on walking without missing a step.

And they'd walk on to school.

Later they'd find the title of the next biography or history he wanted to read neatly printed on paper and folded squarely into the pocket in the back of the book. On occasion he'd squish two long red licorice sticks inside the cover to surprise them.

Livy suspected that if grown-ups ever looked forward to Saturdays, it was because of a deep-seated fondness developed during childhood. Saturdays were her favorite days, even in the summertime, when almost every day was like Saturday. There was something very special about a Saturday. No school. No church. No dresses. And if you could get up and out of the house before your parents were thinking straight, no chores.

Most Saturdays, she and Brian were free souls. They could cram a Saturday chock-full of nothing special and have a wonderful time doing it. They could travel a million miles on their bikes, set traps for the ferocious beasts in the woods down by the park. Many,

many Saturdays they spent time scouting for wood. Good wood. Plywood and two-by-fours that no one wanted, or wanted but wouldn't miss if they disappeared.

It was a Saturday idea. Building a place in the woods beside the river, beyond the park, where they could stay all day Saturday and not go home until it was dark, even if it rained. They had everything they needed there. Water. A tin can with crackers in it. A small jar of peanut butter from her mother's pantry shelf. They'd taken a three-legged stool with only two legs from Mr. Gemph's trash and propped it up with rocks, and they'd salvaged a wooden crate from behind the IGA that you could either sit on or draw on.

The problem was rain.

Livy didn't care if she got wet when it rained, but her mama did, and Brian's mama was almost as bad. More than one Saturday afternoon had had to be called on account of rain, and a dry place had become a necessity.

They'd laughed about its being like the Three Little Pigs when their first shelter, a huge refrigerator box from the trash bin behind Danworthy's Appliance Store, had not only blown deeper into the woods during a rainstorm but had disintegrated into a mushy pile of wet cardboard as well. Bricks, of course, were out of the question, so a wooden shelter had become the answer to their problem. They had three walls so far, but no roof yet. They were still looking for a just-right piece of something solid and flat for it.

"Don't you think lilacs are the best smell in the whole world?" Livy asked, her nose buried in an armful of lavender blossoms swiped from the bush beside Miss Bledsoe's garage. Miss Bledsoe was a never-been-married lady who lived next door to Brian. She had the neatest yard on the block, the most flowers, and the biggest, most prolific lilac bush in town. "When I grow up, everything will smell like lilacs."

She started laying the branches of blooms on the dirt floor of their shelter like a carpet.

"Even your food?" he asked, studying the cluster of petals she'd given him, trying to draw them in pencil.

"Maybe," she said thoughtfully. It hadn't occurred to her before, but it wasn't a *bad* idea. "Like chicken sometimes. It could smell like chicken when it has bones, but if it's boiled in a pot it could smell like lilacs. And sauerkraut could, too."

"And garbage can-th could th-mell like them."

"Okay," she said, almost out of branches. "And some people's breath. Have you ever smelled Mr. Watson's breath?"

He shook his head. Mr. Watson was the principal at their school. Brian tried never to get that close to him. He looked up in time to see Livy fall back into their partial shelter and wallow in the lilacs. Breathing deeply. Grabbing a cluster, rubbing them on her arms and then laying the bruised and fragrant blooms across her nose.

"I think lilacs are the best smell in the whole wide world," she said, crossing her ankles and using her arms like a pillow under her head. "This is a story about a beautiful, golden-haired princess who wears lilac-colored dresses, and everything she touches smells like lilacs. . . ."

That was most Saturdays.

Sometimes, on Saturdays, Brian's mother had to go to the high school to work. And for six weeks the previous summer she'd taught summer school. Those were bad times. Bad Saturdays. Jo-Jo came to watch out for Brian and his sister, Beth, and she fussed a lot.

It wasn't that Jo-Jo wasn't nice to them: she was. It was the lack of freedom they objected to. Jo-Jo—whose real name was Josephine Butler until baby Beth started talking and began calling her Jo-Jo—worried about them. She wanted to know where they were and what they were doing, and she almost always brought her two sons, Samson and Darnel, with her.

The Butler boys were a little older, but they still liked to play. It was easier to stick close to home on those particular days and not risk the discovery of their secret place if Samson and Darnel were sent to check on them.

They all played ball together. Baseball—until Darnel broke the dining room window. Brian said he wasn't sure if his dad was more angry that the window was broken or that it was broken by a colored boy, but they played kickball after that, or tag, or they ran through a water sprinkler with their clothes on.

Jo-Jo always made them wear their clothes in the sprinkler if Samson and Darnel were there. Brian couldn't understand it. He used to argue with her.

"But *why* do we have to leave them on?" he'd ask. "We took them off ye-th-terday."

"That was yesterday," Jo-Jo told him mildly.

"But it-th hotter today."

"It's best."

"But *why*?"

"It's fair."

"Fair?"

"If you boys leave your clothes on, then the girls will, too."

"What girls?"

"Silly boy. Little Beth and Miss Livy, of course."

Brian looked at Livy. She shrugged. They were both aware that they had different private parts and were supposed to keep them covered in public, but getting hot and getting wet in their underpants was an accepted practice at age seven. They looked exactly the same from the waist up. Even Beth was the same. Hadn't Jo-Jo seen that the day before?

"We'll leave our th-orts on," Brian said.

Jo-Jo went down on one knee to be on a level with him.

"You can take your shirt off, but your baby sister and Miss Livy have to leave theirs on. Now is that fair? Wouldn't it be better if everyone left all their clothes on?" Brian frowned. "Boys and girls is different."

"No, they aren't. And you didn't th-ay we were different ye-th-terday."

"My boys weren't here yesterday." Again he frowned.

Livy was a little quicker to catch on. "Come on, Brian. We'll get wet in our clothes," she said, pulling on his arm. He was more confused when he looked at her. "Jo-Jo's right. Today is different."

"Why?"

" 'Cause it is. Come on." She gave him her just-do-it look, and he followed her out the back door and into the yard. Once there, and well away from Jo-Jo's boys, she said, "They're colored. They can't look at white girls with no clothes on. Even babies, like Beth."

She could tell by the look in his eyes that he didn't fully grasp the concept, but he knew better than to ask questions. That was the way things were in Tolford. And the five of them had a grand time getting wet in their clothes.

Of course, it was people like Brian, who couldn't understand why the color of someone's skin made more of a difference than the color of someone's hair or eyes and asked why, who started to change things in Tolford, change things all over Tennessee, all over the country. Not that he *knew* he was changing anything.

One Saturday in late fall the five of them sounded like stampeding horses as they clambered up the front steps of Brian's house to answer Jo-Jo's call to lunch. It was cold, and they were all bundled in coats. They could see their breath in warm clouds as they talked and laughed. But they froze in motion when Jo-Jo stepped out onto the porch with her arms akimbo and her face a-scowlin'.

"Where you two think you're goin'?" she asked, addressing her sons. "You know better than to try and come into a white man's house this-a-way."

They simply said "yes ma'am" and turned to go down the stairs. It was Brian who took affront.

"But I don't want to eat in the yard today. It-th too cold, Jo-Jo," he said, thinking she'd made them a picnic lunch to be eaten at the table in the backyard which she frequently did in the summer. "I want to come in."

"Then ya do that. I got a real nice lunch in here for all of ya," she said, holding the door open for them.

Brian looked around to Samson and Darnel, who were trotting toward the rear of the house.

"Hey! Wait. We can eat in-th-ide today," he called to them. They stopped but didn't reverse their steps. They were watching their mother. "Come on."

"No, Brian. You come on in this-a-way and they'll go on around to the back. Everybody's gonna eat in the kitchen today," she said, waving her children on.

"But why don't they come in this way? It's clo-th-er than going to the back door."

Livy sighed. She kept trying to explain things to Brian, but he could be very stupid sometimes. She liked the way he thought—but it didn't change anything.

"They can't use this door," she said. "They're colored. They gotta go around back."

"No, they don't. This is my hou-th, and they can come in the front door if I th-ay th-o."

"Your daddy wouldn't like it, boy," Jo-Jo said softly.

"He's not here."

Livy sighed again. Didn't he know anything?

"No, but your neighbors are home," she said, impatient for lunch. "They'll tell. And pretty soon everyone in town will know you let colored people into your house."

"We let Jo-Jo in."

"That's different. She's watchin' out for you." Then it occurred to her. "And she uses the back door when she comes, doesn't she?"

He hadn't noticed.

"Do you?" he asked. And when she nodded, he asked, "'Cause you're colored? 'Cause you're different?"

"Yes." She said it almost proudly.

"Okay," he said. He turned to go down the steps.

"Where you goin'?" Jo-Jo asked him.

"To the back door. Beth and Livy can go with you, but I have to go 'round back 'cause I'm different."

"What are you sayin', boy?"

"He's right," Livy said, following him down the stairs, enjoying this particular Saturday immensely. Brian had such a strange little mind sometimes. "He talks different, and I ain't ever seen anybody with a mark like mine on their face. We're both different. We'll have to use the back door, too, from now on."

"Your daddy's not gonna like this, boy, and if your mama heard you sayin' *ain't* like that, she'd whup your bottom good, little missy," Jo-Jo said, tracking them from the porch. "You come on back here, ya hear? You ain't colored folk. No sense in pretendin' you are."

Jo-Jo was full of mercy-mes whenever they made a point of going to the back door after that. Brian started parking his bike by the garage and entering the house through the rear as a matter of course, though he never told his parents why. Still and all, their semisecret defiance of the social standards of Tolford, Tennessee, was very, very satisfying.

Four

"SHE MISSED your socks again," Livy announced as he approached the stop sign in front of her house on his bike.

It was April or May of 1958. Spring. School was almost over for the year, so Brian's pants were getting a little high-water, and his mother wouldn't be buying him new ones until fall. This meant that the mismatched socks—one white, one colored—he'd been wearing the last two months as a secret fashion statement were getting harder and harder to hide.

Secrets were big that year.

He glanced down at his ankles and grinned.

"If I don't comb my hair, th-e forget-th to look at my th-ock-th."

"How come your face is all red? Have you been crying?"

"Got th-oap in my eye-th," he mumbled, turning his face away from her.

Automatically, their right feet moved down on their bike pedals, and they were off to school.

"Did you finish it?" she asked. The question had become part of their daily routine. And so had his reply.

"Yeah." The one time he'd said "I forgot" she'd been so disappointed—not angry, but disappointed—that he always made sure he'd never have to say it again.

"You're gonna win," she said.

"I know. But you th-ould have tried, too."

"I don't draw as good as you do, and I don't want somethin' of mine hangin' up in Greely's grocery store all summer. Besides, I'm gonna win the writing contest at the library. We decided, remember?"

"I have to th-end th-ometh-in' in anyway." It was a mandatory writing contest for school; every second, third, fourth, and fifth grader had to enter. Greely's IGA art contest, however, was voluntary, which made it seem more like a real competition to both of them. He'd spent hours on a picture of happy people eating at a summer barbecue. But he didn't really like contests. He wouldn't enter any of them if no one made him. But Livy said he had to enter this art contest because he would win, and Livy usually knew.

"That's okay," she said. "It can be a dumb story. Nobody's gonna hang anything up at the library. They just tell ya who wins."

See? Livy knew everything. He didn't know anyone smarter than Livy.

Steering one-handed, she reached out and wrenched a long twig from a willow bush and sparred with the air, brandishing it above her head and singing, "Winstons taste good like a" (bonk-bonk on Mrs. Gleason's fence) "cigarette should."

Brian always kept both hands on the handlebars.

"Do you think Errol Flynn is the most handsome man in the world?" she asked. "Or Frank Sinatra? Or Henry Fonda?"

Who?

"I don't know."

"My mama says it's Errol Flynn, but she likes the way Frank Sinatra sings and the way Henry Fonda walks. Oh, and Paul Newman's eyes are dreamy." She laughed. "Daddy likes John Wayne. Who's your most favorite famous person?"

"Buffalo Bob." He could see by her expression that she wanted someone better. "Superman."

She laughed. "No. Real people." They both looked pretty real to him. "Like Elvis and Ricky Nelson. What about them?"

Something else Livy knew . . . she knew everybody. All sorts of people. She didn't always like everyone, for one good reason or another, but she knew them. And everyone knew her. Once, she wrote letters to Doris Day and Natalie Wood, and they sent her auto-graphed photos for her bedroom wall. Livy always made Brian feel special, because everyone knew he was her friend. She was about the only friend he had.

There were a couple of other kids he liked. Boys. But not like Livy. He could talk to Livy, say anything he wanted to. She didn't care if he spit when he talked or if he didn't talk very loud or if he didn't talk at all. She never told his secrets. Never said a word about them. She knew his mother had him going to special speech classes, and she never talked about that either.

Livy simply had too many other, more interesting things to say.

"It's too bad the communists are trying to take over the world. Just think what we could do if they were good people. We could go to outer space together. In Sputnik. Two heads are better than one, Mama says, and if we worked together, all of us and all the Russian communists, we could have people on the moon in no time."

She actually thought about such things! Brian could only listen with a gaping mouth. Or more often than not, barely listened as he watched dust floating in a sunbeam, examined the way leaves grew on trees, tried to remember if Mr. Phillips had any little lumps on his cheeks like his wife had or if it was all the deep lines in his face that made him look so old.

"Did you watch the *Mike Wallace Interviews* on TV last night?"

"No." Like he would have, even if he could have.

They stood on the street corner with their bikes between their legs, she looking right, he looking left for cars before they crossed over to the school playground.

"You should have."

Right.

"It-th on too late." And it sounded too dull.

"It's on too late at my house, too, but I sit at the top of the stairs, real quiet, and watch it from there. Last night it was about

atomic bomb testing. People are protesting to make the government stop."

"Why do they have to te-th-t them? Didn't they already blow
up Japan with one?"

"No, no. Sssssssss-ssssssss. Like that. Tesssssst. See? And this is the
new one. It's better. A hydrogen bomb. It's much more awful. And
with Alaska part of the United States now, and so close to the communists, you never know. We might have to start bombing the
communists, too. They probably need to know how good they
work. It's been a long time since we bombed anyone."

"My dad . . . my real dad and my uncle died in Korea. My mom
sssaid they had bombsss there. And gunsss, too."

"Your real daddy was a war hero?"

"No. He jussst died."

"Do you still miss him?"

"Maybe. I think th-o. I don't remember him much."

She was silent for a moment, thoughtful. "My daddy says if we
have another war, we'll blow the whole world up. There won't be
anything left."

It was too much to imagine.

"Then we better not have another one."

She rolled her brown eyes and made a disgusted *tsk* sound with
her mouth. Then she looked at him as if he were the dumbest thing
to crawl out from under a rock in the last two centuries. He really
hated that look.

"Of course we can't have another war. That was a stupid thing
to say. We'd make the end of the world happen."

"It wa-thn't a th-th . . . a dumb thing to th-ay."

"It was, too. Sometimes you don't know anything."

"Ye-th, I do."

"I bet you don't even know where babies come from, do you?"

"The mommie-th get them." She was such a smarty pants.

"Where do the mommies get them from?"

"Heaven." His sister, Beth, had come from heaven, and so had he.

She gave him a closed-lip I-know-and-you-don't smile and shook her head. "My granddad told me where they came from last summer. I asked him."

"What'd he th-ay?"

"Mommies get babies from daddies."

He looked at her. She sounded very certain of this.

"In the bathroom," she said, knowing he was too overwhelmed to ask questions. "That's why girls sit and boys lift the seat and stand. That's why we have girl bathrooms and boy bathrooms. So little girls can't get babies before they get married and become mommies."

Brian was stunned. "You mean babie-th come from toilet-th?"

She nodded with great knowledge. "They're like germs. Only you catch them through your bottom."

Livy was never wrong. When she knew something, she knew it. It was weeks before he could have a bowel movement without sitting on his hands, despite his mother's reassurance that no little boy ever got a baby from a toilet.

"Star light. Star bright. First star I see tonight. I wish I may, I wish I might, have the wish, I wish tonight."

She closed her eyes and drew a blank. Which wish should she wish? Richest girl in the world? Most beautiful girl in the world? Smartest girl in the world? A new transistor radio? World peace? The slow, hideous demise of Mrs. Culp, her piano teacher? Blond hair?

"What's your wish?" she asked him, as best friends weren't accountable to the rule about not telling. Once, they had collaborated, and Donny Moore got chicken pox two weeks after they had them. Brian always had good wishes, like Mrs. Fisher forgetting to give them a spelling test on Friday or so much snow they'd cancel school for a week or hamburgers for supper instead of chicken-fried steak or a Spam, macaroni, and cheese casserole. They were a little more realistic than hers and a lot more likely to come true.

"I want my dad to come back," he said softly, almost like a prayer. She opened her eyes and looked at him. It wasn't quite dark, of course, or they'd be able to see more stars. He was looking back at her. "I think we were happier with my real dad," he said.

They'd both rushed home for a quick supper and made a clean getaway, avoiding the heavy discussions of their parents' days— about the five-cent increase in the cost of a loaf of bread and having to pay $3.75 for a pair of blue jeans; the corrupting influence of beatniks on a moral society, and whether to watch *General Electric Theater* or *Tales of Wells Fargo* on TV.

Well, that's what *she* had escaped from. Things were different at Brian's house.

"Are they fighting again?"

"Yeah. Sort of. My mom was crying again."

Brian's mom cried a lot. Not all the time, but sometimes. When Brian's dad was happy, everyone was happy. He was a nice man. He liked to sit on the steps with them at Brian's house and tell them scary stories or take them for ice cream on hot summer evenings. Sometimes when they went on family picnics, Livy was allowed to come along. He laughed a lot and sang silly songs. He worked hard, when he worked. Once he brought home a baseball mitt for Brian, and it wasn't even his birthday.

But then he would get sad. Very sad. So sad he couldn't work, couldn't even get out of bed sometimes. Then Brian's parents would fight about money. They'd scream and yell sometimes. Livy heard them once. Brian would become quieter than ever, and grumpy. And his mother would cry.

Still, they had a wish to make, and wasting it on something that couldn't possibly come true, ever, like bringing back dead people, just didn't seem right to her.

"Let's wish that he gets happy again," she said. "It'll be more powerful if we both wish it."

Five

POLITICALLY SPEAKING—which he generally avoided—Tolford wasn't any more mixed up than the rest of Tennessee. And Tennessee, unlike some of the other southern states, was very mixed up, which was a good thing, he was told.

His third grade teacher said it was because of the land, that the state was divided into three separate and distinct sections, and that's why it had such a wide mix of political and social beliefs.

The eastern part, with its mountains and fiercely independent hillbillies, heavy industrialization, and strong antislavery opinions during the Civil War, tried to withdraw from the state when it chose to join the Confederacy. Gently rolling middle Tennessee, with its blue grass and tobacco, evolved from a mint-julep, big plantation, pro-slavery stance during the Civil War to a progressive trade and finance center with a conservative sensibility toward racial equality. And western Tennessee—an extension of the Mississippi Delta, with its rich valleys and black bottoms—was dedicated to King Cotton, and the slave owners fought ferociously to maintain their way of life before, during, and long after the Civil War. Soybeans, winter wheat, apparel plants, and heavier industries became its soul after the war, and abject rural poverty and a large black ghetto population in Memphis became the evidence that full racial equality and harmony would be an elusive goal in that part of the state for several more generations.

Tolford, though located in what was considered western Tennessee, had a middle Tennessee attitude, according to Livy's father. The year he ran for town councilman, in the fall of 1958, Tolford quietly integrated its schools.

"Daddy says it won't be like it was in Clinton three years ago," she said. "He says there's only a few ignorant souls left in Tolford, and they're smart enough to see the handwriting on the wall."

"What wall?"

"I don't know for sure, but he said he was real proud of our town. He said it was better to let the colored children go to our schools ourselves than to make the government force us to do it."

Brian, a color lover from birth, was fascinated by the endless variation of skin tones, from the palest white to the blackest black. He had little or no interest in the historical or social implications of this amazing phenomenon and had never been able to make sense of the wasted energy it took to maintain two separate levels of a single society. Desegregation made sense to him; he couldn't figure out why it hadn't been done before.

Still and all, if Livy was right, it was a momentous occasion, and standing outside the school waiting for the busload of colored kids to arrive, and walking into the school with them to make them feel welcome, seemed like a nice thing to do. Even his mother had agreed that it was a good idea—though she'd asked him not to talk about it at home.

"Everybody's comin'," he said, watching a group of twenty or thirty people approaching the school. "Should have got a band."

"That would have been nice," she agreed. There were a few other kids standing with them, but most were going straight into class. It wasn't the welcoming committee she'd hoped for, but it was better than none at all. "A parade and the mayor talking. We could have made it real special, like on the Fourth of July."

While they waited for the bus, Brian watched the crowd across the street grow in numbers. Mr. Curry from the Shell station on Main Street. Mr. and Mrs. Sharp, an elderly couple, who lived near the park. Bobby West he knew because the man worked with his dad sometimes. One of the ladies from Greely's IGA was there; he thought her name was Beverly. Most were familiar faces, only a few that he didn't recognize. They looked as restless as he felt, waiting for the bus, but it was nice to see them all there, supporting a good thing.

When the bus turned the corner and came into view, the crowd started cheering and waving. He watched the vehicle turn slowly into the drive and stop, cutting off his view of the crowd. He could remember thinking that it would have been better if the others had gathered closer to the school to greet the colored children, but after that his mind sort of went blank, and he could hardly register anything.

The cheering voices grew louder as the bus door opened and the first of the black children got out. Livy rushed up to one to say hello, and he moved to follow—but then one of the black children fell down. A different type of cheering rose from the crowd, and he looked around to see that they had crossed the street, and most of them looked angry, not happy.

It was then that a rock came flying through the air toward Livy, hitting her right shoulder. And another rock hit the building behind them. The boy on the ground had blood on his face, and a fourth rock barely missed his left leg. Brian's confusion joined with that of the teachers and parents and other children around him. What was happening?

"Livy, come on!" he shouted, grabbing her arm and pulling her toward the open school doors.

Tom Watt, a man who'd tried to sell his parents insurance the year before, was taking aim at a small black child cowering on the sidewalk. The rock was bigger than the man's hand. Livy was struggling against Brian's grasp, and the little boy was too far from his other hand to help.

Tom Watt took a step closer.

"No!" Brian cried out. "Don't! You'll hurt him." But the man either couldn't hear him or wouldn't hear him. Another rock landed near Brian on the sidewalk, and his confusion gave way to a terrified panic. "My way, Livy!" he shouted, pulling her, watching Tom Watt. "My way."

But when she wouldn't follow him, something other than his mind made a decision. He let go of her and lunged at Tom Watt, knocking him off balance and to the ground before he could throw the rock. For a frenzied moment he stared, shocked by his own actions—against an adult, no less. Then he turned and half-shoved, half-pulled the little boy to his feet.

"Livy! Help me. Livy!"

She was there, taking the boy's other hand as the three of them ran for the doors. Another rock broke a pane of glass somewhere. Children, white and black, were crying and screaming, tripping and stumbling on the steps of the school. Teachers were shouting orders, and far off in the distance, police sirens warned them of trouble.

Too late.

"I hate you! I hate you!" Livy started screaming just before they got inside. At the door she turned toward the crowd and continued. "Go away! Leave us alone! You're stupid and ugly and I hate you! I hate you!"

Some adult pulled at her, lifted her bodily out of the doorway. She turned and wrapped her arms around the woman's waist, sobbing.

He wasn't sure if she was crying mad, crying sad, or crying from fear the way he wanted to, but he knew he'd never forget that moment. Livy *never* cried.

By comparison, the little rock toss at Tolford Primary School that fall was nothing to what happened at other schools all over the South for the next twenty years, and yet it was a heart-shattering disappointment that Livy would never forgive.

After all, isn't it the most natural thing in the world to assume that what you have is superior to what others have? Even if it isn't true? And especially if you're young?

Tolford was her town. Its citizens were her people. Familiar faces she thought she knew and could trust. Folks she talked to almost every day of her life . . . and some of them were rotten to the core with bigotry and hatred.

For months afterward there were whispers of KKK, the Ku Klux Klan, that generated fear and anger in the hearts of blacks and whites alike, but nothing ever came of the rumors there in Tolford. No unexplained beatings, no stonings, no fires or burning crosses or explosions. And after a while the gossip stopped, the town was quiet again, and people started to forget.

People, but not Livy.

"When I grow up, things like that won't be allowed," she said. She got steamed, and resteamed, every time she thought about that day. "You'll either get along with everybody or you'll have to leave my country."

He considered the plan and determined it to be a fair solution. He nodded.

It was late afternoon, and they were walking home from the IGA. Livy's mother had sent them after a can of evaporated milk she needed for a dessert recipe. Funny thing about her mother, she was forever sending them on errands when they got too loud in the house. There was always a dime for each of them for penny candy, and dollars to doughnuts, she'd usually found what she needed in the pantry and the dessert would be done by the time they got back.

But it wasn't the bogus mercy mission that had put Livy into a snit. It was that Beverly Olmsted at the IGA. Livy had recognized her as one of the racial agitators shortly after the incident, and ever since she'd been like poison ivy to her. Livy itched just looking at the woman. Her parents, of course, frowned on being disrespectful to adults, so she would glare at Beverly all the way through the checkout line and start to fume the second they stepped outside.

"I hate being a kid," she said. "I really do. Nobody cares what a kid thinks. We can't change anything. Grown-ups can throw rocks at us and send us to the store and make us clean our rooms and go to bed early, but they never really care what we think. Daddy said we can't make those people leave Tolford because it's a free country and they can think and do what they want. But if they hurt other people, I think they should leave."

He nodded. The sun was setting and casting a very wonderful shade of pinkish purple across the sky. He'd never seen that exact color before. None of his crayons came close to it.

"Everybody should be the same. Have the same money, the same car, the same TV, the same house, go to the same schools, wear the same clothes . . ." Dreaded communism, of course, but neither of them knew that at the time. ". . . have the same bicycles, eat the same food."

"People are different," he muttered, simply thinking aloud.

"No, they aren't. People are the same, no matter what color they are. We're all the same."

"No. We're different." She frowned at him, preparing to argue. He said, "You're good at everything, and all I can do is draw. You're smarter than me."

"You're smart."

"Not like you. You should go to a really smart school, and I should go to a just-art school because that-th what I'm good at do-ing. I don't need to know about Engli-th or hi-th-tory or arithmetic because I'm good at drawing."

"You're good at other stuff, too. You're good at science."

"You're better."

She was. What he was saying was true. She sighed. They were different. And it was the differences she liked best about them. Maybe she'd rethink her everything-the-same theory.

"You were very brave that day," she said after a long silence. She was thinking of the kindergarten boy they now knew as Theo Wellman. They were almost to the corner where Brian would go on to his house and she'd turn off to hers for supper. "I cried."

He looked at her. He hadn't forgotten.

"I wanted to," he said.

"But you didn't, and you saved Theo from getting hurt. That was brave." He looked away, self-conscious. "You're a great artist, and you're very brave. That's two things you're good at."

Six

I HATE HIM. I hate him. I hate him," Brian said, chanting the words with each stroke of the rake. "I wi-th he wa-th dead."

"No, you don't," Livy said, raking, too. It was still fall, and his front yard was knee deep in dry leaves. "He can't help it when he's sad. I think it would be terrible to be as sad as he is all the time."

"I don't care if he-th th-ad."

"Ssssss. Ssssss. Sad," she said, reinforcing his speech therapy—a consummate failure in times of stress. He hated it when she did that.

"I don't care if he'sssss sssssad. He goes to bed, and we don't see him for days. I like it when he's sad," he said, finished with one pile of leaves and moving on to start another. "What I hate is when he wakes up. And all his sssstupid rules. No TV. No friends over. No talking when he's trying to rest. We can't even wear our shoes in the house because he doesn't like the sounds they make."

"Maybe he hurts," she said. "Maybe he has a headache. My mama gets headaches sometimes."

"He doesn't hurt. He's just lazy. My mom bought me a Slinky on Saturday for washin' the car and cleaning out the garage by myself, and he made her take it back. He said he couldn't afford new toys. But he could if he worked. My mom works every day. He should, too."

"Maybe his new job will make him happy again."

He stopped raking and looked at her. "Why do you do that? You're *my* friend. You always say nice things about him."

"No, I don't. I told you I never heard anyone yell like he does. He scares me when he yells. But when he's so very sad like he is, I feel bad for him."

"Well, I don't. I hate him. You're *my* friend, and you have to hate him, too."

No comment. If she thought helping him rake his yard was enough—because four hands got it done faster than two, she said—to show the depth of her friendship, she was dead wrong. She'd conned him into doing enough of her chores that he considered this payback. He wanted her to hate his stepfather as much as he did. Clearly, she needed more proof.

"Beth dropped her breakfast bowl on the floor this morning and woke him up. But I was the first person he saw. *I'm* the one he sent out here to rake leaves, not Beth. I didn't even get breakfast. Now is that fair?"

"Beth is three."

"So?"

"She can't rake leaves."

Did that have anything to do with anything?

"Beth is also his real kid, and I'm not. She never has to do anything."

"She's *three* years old."

"I hate you, too," he said, starting to rake again. "Why don't you just go home?"

"Because you don't really want me to," she said. When he looked at her he saw that she'd stopped working on her pile of leaves and was watching him with a smile on her face.

"Yes, I do. If you can't hate my enemies, you're not my friend."

"What if I have the two dollars my daddy gave me last night in my pocket? What if he told me that if it was okay with your mama we could go to the movies this afternoon? Would I still be your friend then?"

Ugh! Caught between a rock and a hard spot. Only his male pride kept him silent and ruthlessly raking the yard.

"Well, I suppose it doesn't matter," she said as if speaking to herself. She started raking again. "We wouldn't be done here in time for the matinee anyway. We'd have to wait and see *Vertigo.*"

Vertigo! Alfred Hitchcock! Jimmy Stewart! *Kim Novak*! An adult movie, *not* the matinee! Evidently, Mr. Hubbard hadn't specified *which* movie he was treating them to.

"We have to burn 'em all, too," he said, referring to the leaves, glancing at her. She was raking, her back to him. He didn't need to see her face to know she was smiling.

"We'd better hurry then."

Christmas in Tolford was nothing short of . . . magic. The weather could turn downright nasty anytime past Halloween, but no one appreciated it until after Thanksgiving, when it was considered appropriate and part of the holiday season.

Then you could walk down Main Street and observe people breathing clouds of warm air in front of their faces as they watched colored lights going up in the storefront windows. Santa Claus and Nativity scenes that you didn't see for eleven months of the year were suddenly everywhere. There were bells and singing, and not just in church. Acts of kindness and goodwill were brought to everyone's attention, and it didn't matter that the acts were performed by the same people year after year or that they went on all year long. Christmas was the time to acknowledge such things.

It was the time when everything smelled good and people had good secrets and surprises to share. Her parents called it the spirit of Christmas, the sharing and the giving and the kindness.

"I'm sorry about your train set," she said, sitting down beside him on his front steps. What was left of the snow that had fallen the week before was frozen and crunched when she walked, but the steps were shoveled and dry.

"I don't know what I did wrong. He left me a coat." It wasn't exactly coal in his stocking, but it wasn't a train set either. He'd never not gotten what he asked for at Christmas. Maybe he shouldn't have been so mean to Beth all year. Maybe he shouldn't have snitched apples from old Miss Bledsoe's tree. Maybe he should have been quieter for his dad. Maybe he should have taken the trash out twice a day instead of only once. Maybe if he'd been better . . .

"Are you talking about Santa Claus?" he heard her asking.

He frowned at her. Who else? "Yeah. Santa Claus. He left new winter coats for me and Beth and that was all. My mom got candy and the vase I made at school. That's all."

Livy sighed and studied the red rubber her boots were made of; Brian sighed and wished he were perfect.

"He didn't leave you the coat," she finally said, blurting it out like bad news.

"Yes, he did. My mom said so."

"He didn't leave it."

"Then who did?"

"Your parents bought it." He looked at her. She'd gone too far this time. He wasn't such a horrible kid that Santa wouldn't leave him anything at all. A coat wasn't a train set, but it wasn't coal, and it wasn't nothing. "I've known since I was six that there isn't a real Santa Claus, but my mama said I shouldn't spoil the secret for everyone else by telling," she said.

"You're lying."

"No. You should ask your mama. She has to tell you the truth if you ask about him, that's the rule. If you don't ask she doesn't have to tell you anything."

"Then I won't ask."

"Okay. But then don't get mad if you don't get what you want for Christmas."

After a long silence, he said, "I thought he was gonna be mad when he saw the presents under the tree this morning. My mom said something about layaway. Think that's what she meant? That there's no Santa Claus?"

She nodded without looking at him, her chin on her knees as she continued to regard her red snow boots.

It had been a rough winter. His mother had said he needed only two pairs of pants for school instead of four. She doled out pencils for schoolwork as if they were made of gold. Peanut butter sandwiches with no jam for lunch. Apples or oranges but no real desserts. Whereas they usually had eight or nine different kinds of Christmas cookies, his mother had made only two that year. She'd said times were hard with Dad not working again, and did Brian want to help decorate them?

"What did Santa Claus bring you?" he asked, feeling unusually stubborn that day.

"A new Barbie. Barbie clothes. A Little Miss Kitchen baking set. Two new dresses and three new pairs of underpants." She sat up and looked a bit more excited. "Granddad sent me new crayons and a coloring book and roller skates."

Brian wished he had a granddad. He wished there were a Santa Claus. But he was really glad he got a new coat instead of a Barbie doll and dresses.

Seven

"YOU SHOULD HAVE told me," Livy said. She was angry, but not at him. "You should have told your mama."

They were sitting in the dirt and leaves in "the woods," which was actually a stand of trees on the far side of the park. It was the first really hot Saturday in spring, and they'd been swimming with their friends in "the lake," which was actually a fairly deep and wide enough swelling in the banks of the Obion River to look like a lake to them. They'd needed to talk in private but couldn't spare the time to go all the way to their secret place.

It was 1959, one of the few specific years he'd never forget. According to Livy, Hawaii had become the fiftieth state and NASA had retrieved two live monkeys from space—*after* they shot them out there, of course. Castro was taking over Cuba, steelworkers were striking, Lunik II had hit the moon.

But none of that mattered to Brian. None of it *changed* anything in his life. In 1959 he was nine years old, and in the space of, well, it couldn't have been more than fifteen minutes—though when it was happening it seemed like a whole lot longer—his life had become a nightmare.

His dad was sadder than ever. Never happy like he used to be, not even for short periods of time. Sometimes his parents would cry together. It was frightening. Brian didn't know what to do *but* tell Livy.

Of course, her seeing the long red belt welts on his back hadn't left him with much of a choice.

"You'd better tell my mama then. She'll tell my daddy, and he'll go over and punch your dad in the nose."

"No."

"Yes. You can't swim with your shirt on all summer. And it doesn't matter if you made Beth cry, you're not a bad boy. Not that bad. Mama says you're the nicest boy she's ever met. She said she loves you like one of her own. She told Mrs. Costello that."

"I made him too mad. Usually he just grabs my arm or my neck and yells at me. Once in a while he slaps me. But he never hit me that hard before." Except for that one time when he'd gotten the black eye and they'd told his mother it was an accident and the other time when he'd been pushed to the ground and kicked in the ribs . . . did kicking count?

"My daddy will break both his arms and tie his legs into knots and pull his ears clean off his head."

Livy truly had a picturesque way with words.

"Promise me you won't tell," he said, willing to withstand anything but his mother's tears. "He didn't mean to do it. He said he was sorry."

Livy's face took on a stubborn expression he knew all too well. He reached out and grabbed her upper arm, squeezing hard.

"Promise me." She shook her head, and he squeezed harder, until she whimpered with pain. "Promise me, Livy."

"I promise."

"Let me see your fingers." She sometimes crossed them to nullify her words. And her eyes. "Look at me."

Pools of tears clouded her dark eyes.

"I'm sorry, Livy," he said, dropping her arm immediately, feeling lower than slug slime. But then he saw that the tears weren't for the pain he'd inflicted on her; they were for him. Sorrowful tears. Sympathetic tears. "Telling will only make it worse. He might even do it again."

"You have to do something, Brian. You should see your back. Doesn't it hurt? Take Beth and your mama and run away."

"Beth can't run fast. He'd catch us."

"Not if you take the car."

"He'd find us."

She thought a moment. "I wish I knew where Chewy lived. You could go there. Chewy would hide you."

They both missed Chewy. Wednesdays just weren't the same without him. He'd turned eighteen over the Christmas holidays and had graduated from high school a few weeks earlier. When he'd passed them the last library book, they found a letter in it addressed to "My Librarians."

This is the last book I'll ask you to borrow for me. I'm going to college. I want to be a great historian like Carter Woodson. Maybe I'll teach and share what I know. That seems right, doesn't it? You sharing your books with me, me sharing what I learned from them. It feels right. You've helped me to feed the hunger I have for knowledge, and for that I will be eternally grateful. Goodbye. Your friend, Chewy.

They'd gone immediately to Chewy's mother, who cleaned house for the Tuckers. They owned Tucker's Drugstore and Soda Fountain on Main Street—real nice people, but they went to church on Saturdays and had to go all the way to Union City because they were Jews. Anyway, it turned out that Mrs. Lewis had directed her son to a small state college in Colorado to further his education. She told them there weren't many blacks in Colorado, and that people in the West didn't worry so much about the color of someone else's skin. They checked with her periodically after that, asking after Chewy. Sometimes, if she'd gotten a letter from him, she made them lemonade and read parts of it to them.

Colorado, described by Chewy, was big and wide and open, and the mountains there were nothing like anything he'd seen before. He sounded lonely but determined to be educated. He said there was power in education.

"It wouldn't matter. Even if we could find Chewy in Colorado," Brian said, trying to picture Chewy's "better place" in his mind. "My dad would find us wherever we went."

"Not if you went to Ohio."

"Where's Ohio?"

"That's where my granddad's farm is. It takes forever to get there. Daddy has a road map."

Their experience with quick getaways was pretty much limited to what they saw on *The Rifleman* and *Maverick*—and hardly anyone left his horse in front of the bank anymore.

Still, it was a plan. All afternoon. The waiting for midnight. Sneaking out of the house. Livy with her father's map and some food. Brian with Beth and his mother and their clothes and toys, whatever money was in the house and the keys to the car. They had it all worked out and they were almost positive it would work . . . until they slammed into Livy's mother's kitchen, hot and thirsty and starving for cookies.

They weren't there five minutes before Mrs. Hubbard spotted the bruises on Livy's arm. And she wouldn't buy the falling down explanation. She said the pattern of the bruises wasn't right. Who knew bruises had a pattern? The closer she came to the truth, the more often her questioning gaze came to rest on Brian and the more guilty he felt.

Livy tried to defend him.

"He was a terrible looking man, Mama. A little like Brian's daddy, but mean. He was madder than he's ever been before . . . and he'd had some beer, we could smell it from his mouth. First, he was just yellin' at us cause we were throwin' rocks off the footbridge. Old Miss Bledsoe was there, she saw us. But she was gone by the time the terrible looking man came. And he was so mad and so full of beer that he scared me. I just stood there. But Brian was brave. He grabbed me by the arm, here . . . hard . . . real hard and started pulling me away from the man and then he threw rocks at the man, because we had them there on the bridge with us. One went right through his head and another one hit him in the heart and then the man just ran away."

. . .

In the summer of 1959, Brian did go to Ohio. With Livy. To visit her granddad. The driving time was closer to twelve hours than to forever.

You see, Livy was asked to repeat her fabulous story for her father—she embellished a little at the end, until it sounded as if Brian could pitch better than Bob Turley—and then things began to happen.

After the Hubbards spoke with Livy alone, they wouldn't let Brian go home. They called his mother and got permission for him to sleep on the floor in Livy's room. It was their first sleep-over. Mr. Hubbard left right after supper, he had "business to attend to." Mrs. Hubbard made popcorn and let them watch *The Twilight Zone* with her. She hugged Brian twice, really gently, as if she thought he might break—or she might hurt him—and kissed him on the cheek once, for no good reason that he knew of.

Thinking back, that was probably why he started crying in the middle of the night and why, when Mrs. Hubbard came in to comfort him, he felt so compelled to tell her the truth about Livy's arm. Wrapped in her motherly embrace on the floor, crying softly and whispering in the dark as Livy slept, that was the night he decided forgiveness was a gift.

He spent most of the next day indoors at Livy's house. Mr. Hubbard brought Beth over in the afternoon. She sat on Mrs. Hubbard's lap the whole time, rocking and sucking her thumb. His mother came for them after supper.

They sat on the Hubbards' couch together, Livy ignoring her parents' hints to leave the room. His mother said she was sorry, and she cried. She told Brian he was a good boy. The best boy in the whole world. He wasn't a bad boy. He was a good boy who was sometimes a little naughty and needed to be spanked. Then she explained that there was a huge difference between spanking a sometimes naughty boy and beating him. She said it was wrong for anyone to beat any child, but it was especially wrong to hurt some-one as good as Brian.

"Oh, he's not so good as you think," Livy said, not wanting the situation to get out of control, always willing to put things in the proper perspective. "Him and Jimmy Lowe have spitting contests at school. Show her how far you can spit, Brian."

That was pretty much the end of Brian's bruises. The rest he came by honestly and he didn't have to lie about them.

Later, he pieced together the facts of that night. His mother had asked his stepfather to leave when Mr. Hubbard went over to their house that night after supper and told her what her husband had done to Brian while she was out of the house. His stepfather had re-fused to leave and became violent. But instead of having him ar-rested, Mr. Hubbard arranged to get him into a special hospital where the doctors could help him recover from his sadness.

When school let out for the summer, Mr. Hubbard took Brian and Livy to spend the summer on his father's farm.

"It was just a *maybe*," he said.

"Maybe a divorce? She said that?"

"Yeah. *Maybe* if my dad doesn't get better, *maybe* she'll have to get a divorce. *Maybe*," he said. He wasn't sure what a divorce was, but it didn't sound good. He liked that it was only a *maybe* thing. "And I'm not supposed to worry about it."

"Well, it just means she won't have a husband anymore is all," Livy said, throwing handfuls of hay into the air above them, letting it snow down on them as they lay in the sweet-smelling grass. Granddad Hubbard had the biggest barn ever made. Huge. Livy's voice seemed to float on the air for miles. "She'll be like poor Deb-bie, sad and alone, with Eddie loving another woman." He turned in the hay to look at her. Who? "Only she'll have to be careful. She has to stay away from men from now on. Mama says divorced women have a hard time of it, especially with men. And she can't talk to married men or everyone will hate her like they do Elizabeth Taylor. You know, because of Debbie and Eddie?"

Did his mother *know* a Debbie and Eddie?

"Nobody hated her when my real dad died. Nobody hated her when she got married again."

"That's different," she said, rolling over onto her stomach and wiggling over to the edge of the loft to look down at the barn below. "When the husband dies you can't help it, but if you divorce him they think you're a bad person."

"Why?" His mother wasn't a bad person. She was already sad and alone so he figured a divorce wouldn't be that much different. But he didn't want people to hate her. She was a good mom. "Why would they think that?"

"I don't know. Mama says that once, a long time ago, you couldn't get divorced, no matter how terrible your husband was. And if you just left him no one would ever talk to you again, even if you followed all the rules. So, it's getting better to be divorced. And if you have enough money, Mama says you can change husbands or wives as often as you change clothes. Like the movie stars do. I'm hungry, are you?"

"Yeah."

She looked at him for a moment, frowning and thinking.

"Boys without a daddy have a hard time, too. You can borrow my daddy whenever you need to." He didn't know what to say. "I already asked him. He said it was okay."

In the end he simply nodded, accepting things as they were. As he always did. He was confident that his mother already knew about being divorced and the rules that went along with it. She was a teacher; she'd know to be careful.

The rest of that summer, like most of his youth, evaporated into that cloud in his mind that was his memory. There wasn't much to it before meeting Livy, and what shape and form it took after that always had her image in it. She was a constant in his life.

Like Beth and his mother and school and church and day and night and summer and winter. She defined the passage of time for him. Clarified it. When she wasn't with him, time was very, very, very slow. And when she was, she kept him so involved with living his life, challenging him, testing him, defying him, taxing him, amusing and amazing him that whole weeks, months, and years slipped away unnoticed.

Well, maybe not totally unnoticed. Livy was ever a fountain of information.

In the next couple of years lasers, the Lucy-Desi divorce, and the Peace Corps were discussed ad nauseam as he recalled, but for him they were simply words. Words that Livy and television newscasters used. After all, what did any of that have to do with him? He thought building a wall through the middle of Berlin, Germany, to keep the communists away from the rest of the world was . . . not going to work. But as long as no one was planning to build another one through the middle of Tolford, Tennessee, who cared? Bomb shelters, on the other hand, were a nifty idea—hidden, underground rooms with food in them—though Cuba on a map looked awfully small and way too far away from Tolford to seem like much of a threat. He didn't care what kind of tricks Livy said those ICBMs could do; Cuba bombing the whole United States would be like him picking a fight with Fred Springer, an eighth grader the size of Livy's Dad's garage—not very likely. He was going on ten years old and couldn't remember the capital of Argentina for more than a second and a half, but Clarabell's "Goodnight, kids" on television was a sight he'd *never* forget.

Periodically, Troy Donahue, Fabian, and *dreamy* Dr. Kildare would hit Livy's headlines, and he could at least picture them in his mind. And, of course, Kennedy. Every other sentence had *Kennedy* in it. And Nix'n became her favorite four-letter word.

This was about the time he first realized that Livy, not he, was the oddity in knowing not only who these people were, but what they were selling as well. She had a special interest in the world that few of their classmates shared. In fact, he was beginning to suspect that most everyone *but* Livy was growing up in the same innocent fog he was.

Be that as it may, if Livy was correct, Kennedy was going to take care of everything. Right all the wrongs, solve all the problems. Put an end to the increasing tension between whites and blacks, integrate everything, and guarantee basic civil rights to everyone. He was also going to take care of the hateful communists—show them up in the space race and put an end to their aggressive attempts to take over the world. According to Livy, Saint John Kennedy was going to do it all.

But before the end of 1960, after Thanksgiving but before Christmas sometime, Brian attended his second funeral in six years. It was cold, and the wind was blowing. His mother was a widow again and he'd lost another dad. But this time there was no American flag to make them stand proud and tall for a hero of war. No guns to hurt their ears and send chills up their spines. It started to rain. A dreary, oppressive sense of waste and guilt mingled with the sadness and the disbelief.

Words like *depression, hopelessness, suicide,* and *hanging* floated out of adult conversations and settled into Brian's heart like hot smoldering coals. He had a vague understanding of these words, knew they didn't add up to anything pleasant. They made him feel . . . small. Inside. How big a sadness did someone have to have to not want to live anymore? That his dad had been so unhappy, as ill with it as his mother had explained to him, made him feel . . . unkind in the worst of ways. Cruel. Heartless.

He knew wishing someone dead didn't make it so. But what about patience and understanding? If he'd wanted to, Brian could have found a way to make his dad happy. He liked fishing and baseball; they could have done more of that. He'd liked Red Skelton and Perry Mason. Brian could have woke him up when those programs came on. He could have grumbled less and told more jokes. He could have done *something*.

Livy had known all along how terrible it was to be sad.

Brian should have done something.

It became a part of all her summers to visit her Granddad in Ohio. Her parents thought it was important for her to know her father's father and she, for the most part, enjoyed going.

However, once she'd spent a summer with Brian on the farm, she let it be known how lonely and, well, frankly, dull it was with only her granddad to talk to. There was no one her own age around to play with, and she was always getting in Granddad's way, and . . .

They didn't have to ask Brian's mother twice to let him spend a whole month during the summer on a farm in Ohio.

Her Granddad Hubbard was a big, tall, heavyset man with snow-white hair and an equally white handlebar mustache. His voice carried across the Ohio plains like a sonic boom. He called her Sweet Pea, and he called Brian Hellboy.

"Hell, boy, I was pickin' up bales of hay twice that size when I was half your age."

"Hell, boy, can't you move any faster than that?"

"Hell, boy, haven't you ever seen bull balls before? Those are nothin'. You ought to see mine!"

"Hell, boy, when I was your age we ate dust for dinner. Breakfast and supper, too."

"Hell, boy, I've never seen anyone who could make a picture look as real as you do. You got a gift."

"Hell, boy, I think you've grown a yard and a half since you got here. Your mother won't recognize you."

Brian told her over and over that he thought Granddad Hubbard was just about the coolest old man he'd ever met.

"Okay, now listen to this," she said. She was sitting on a green metal lawn chair in the shade of the elm tree beside her granddad's driveway. Brian was in the sun, dripping sweat, being manly. "Brian, listen."

"I'm listening. I'm listening," he said, tired and testy, his arms aching as he practiced his hoop shots.

"Dear President Kennedy: My name is Olivia Hubbard and I am writing again to tell you that I think bomb shelters are a very good idea." She looked up to make sure he was listening. "We practice civil defense in our town. My granddad's name is Ernest B. Hubbard. He lives in Ohio. He says if Ohio gets bombed and he ends up with atomic corn in his fields, he would just as soon die in the bombing. He says he would not be able to lift the atomic corn anyway. I have been wondering how big atomic corn will get and what will happen to my granddad's cows. Sincerely, Olivia Hubbard. P.S. Please tell Mrs. Kennedy that my mama likes her hats. How does that sound?"

"Sounds fine." He was getting a little short of air.

"Fine? Just fine? What's wrong with it?"

"Nothin'." He went through the motions again. He was starting to look a little pale. "Has he ever answered any of your letters?"

"The President is a busy man. He can't answer everyone's letters. That's why I hardly ever ask questions. I just tell him what I think, so he knows, and then he doesn't have to worry about answering them."

"I see."

"What do you mean, you see? What's that supposed to mean?"

"Gee whiz, Livy. It means I see. I understand. It makes sense to me," he said, too tired to fight with her, too tired to do more than fall on the grass in the shade at her feet. "Your granddad's a maniac."

"He likes you." She smiled down at him. "You remind him of my daddy."

"Was your dad a sissy? Did he make him practice basketball this hard?"

"He's not *making* you practice. You're making yourself practice. And he didn't say you were a sissy. You did."

"He said I ought to develop my interest in sports. Pick one and get good at it. So people wouldn't think I'm so different."

"He's only trying to help you."

"Well, what's wrong with drawing pictures? I'm good at that already."

"Think about it. You're a boy who likes to draw pictures, and your best friend is a girl. You know anybody else like that?"

"No."

"Besides, I thought you liked basketball."

"I do."

"Then what are you grumping about?"

"I just don't want to be a sissy."

Eight

Y OU'RE GOING APE again, Livy. It doesn't look like a huge hickey on your face. Don't let 'em bug you like that," he said, trying to console her. She was angry. Again. Her mood swings had become as swift and lethal as swordplay. "They're just girls. And they're stupid. They can't do anything but play with Barbie dolls and talk about fingernail polish and comb their hair all the time. What do they know about hickeys anyway?"

"What do you know about them?"

He looked at her, then away. He'd heard about them, of course. Who hadn't? But he wasn't too sure he'd seen one yet.

When Brian and Livy met in first grade, he was three months, two weeks, and two days older and a half a head taller. And he was a boy, of course. Seven years later, things were pretty much the same between them.

He bounced the ball twice as they stood under the net at one end of the basketball court at the junior high school. He was hoping she'd reach out and steal it from him the way she usually did. She kicked the pole instead.

"They're jealous, Liv. That's why they give you a hard time. You're smart and you're fun. You're like one of the guys. Your birthmark is the only thing they can find wrong with you."

"Why'd it have to be on my face?" It wasn't the first time she'd asked him that question. "Why not my back or my butt, someplace less obvious?"

It was always sort of a pleasant shock to hear Livy say a word like *butt*. She did it a lot. It was part of her way with words, saying exactly what she meant. A butt is a butt, she'd say, and there isn't anything wrong in saying so. And, of course, it wasn't anything like when she'd talk about penises, but still, it was something of a surprise . . . coming from a girl.

Brian sighed. He didn't think her birthmark was anything to get shook up about. But she was hurting, and he didn't like that. He tucked the ball under his arm and leaned against the pole with her, their dark heads barely inches apart.

"You want me to hit 'em for ya?" he asked, teasing her.

She gave a soft laugh. "You can't hit girls. Your mother'd kill you."

"Then you hit 'em. It'll make you feel better."

"Can't. Now that Daddy's running for mayor he says I have to grow up. Be a lady. Find some other way of dealing with it." She raised her gaze to his and gave him a tiny smile. "How do *ladies* deal with anything?"

They were silent for several uneasy minutes.

At thirteen Brian had, shyly but naturally, taken notice of some very hot girl-type "chicks" strutting about. There had even been a few rare moments of awareness to Livy's being above-average cute. Pretty even. Sometimes. Sort of. But boy-girl stuff was very tricky. And lately, when he had taken notice, it was weird trying to talk to her. She was still his best friend, still the best person to talk things over with, and certainly the easiest girl to talk to, but still . . .

"Liv?" She looked at him. Her eyes were still big and brown but her face had grown to fit them better. The port-wine birthmark had grown with her face as well, starting an inch or so below her left eye and covering a space about the size of a baseball along her cheek. What amazed him was how anyone could look into her eyes and see anything else.

"What?"

"I know it's easy for me to say. I mean . . . I don't lisp anymore and nobody . . . It really doesn't matter. People who really care about you don't even see your mark." It felt truly bizarre to be telling her that he cared about her, but sometimes a guy had to do uncomfortable stuff. "I never see it. Unless you're talking about it."

"I know. But you don't count."

That made him feel a little strange inside, but he knew what she meant.

"No. I do count. It's gotta hurt when people stare and when they tease you and all, but *those* people don't count. They don't care about you."

"And the ones who do . . . pity me."

"No, they don't. They just don't see it. There's so much more of you to look at . . . well, ah . . . we just don't see it."

She was thoughtful. "Do you think Steve Donovan will ever not see it?"

He shrugged. "Who cares?"

"I do."

He looked at her, frowning. Steve Donovan? It was weirder than weird. There was a tightness in his belly, like just before he threw up, only worse. They'd talked about guys, like they talked about chicks, but she'd never singled one out before. Too weird.

He pushed away from the pole and started dribbling the ball, scanning his brain for something to say.

"If he sees it and it matters to him, then he's not the guy you want," he said, thinking it was something his mother would say. Something wise that didn't provide a solution or help the situation at all but that was probably correct in a general fashion.

"Well, who said I wanted him?" she asked, lashing out as quick as a whip to snatch the ball from him. She moved out toward center court, turned, dribbled twice, and pitching the ball in a perfect arc, swished it through the hoop. A three-pointer. Brian groaned with envy, and she grinned. "He's cute, but he doesn't play basketball any better than you do, Carowack."

·   ·   ·

They dismissed school early that particular Friday in 1963. The teachers were crying.

Livy could hardly speak—wouldn't speak to him except to say that she didn't believe it. She ran all the way home, insisting that her mother would tell her the truth.

Saturday was interminable. Livy refused to come out of the house, and there was nothing to watch on television but the endless replays of the shooting in Dallas. Seeing it once had been more than enough for him. Sunday wasn't much better. They watched the long procession with the casket from the White House to someplace called the Capitol Rotunda, again and again. People crying, everywhere. For a while it was all about a man named Oswald getting shot, over and over, by a man named Ruby.

The new President—the *old* Vice President, Lyndon Baines Johnson—looked nervous and scared when he talked to the reporters. Brian didn't blame him. Who knew who was going to shoot who next?

Monday, no school, but he had to sit in the Hubbards' living room with Livy and her parents, Beth and his mother, and watch President Kennedy's funeral on TV.

It was sad, all right. Really sad. He felt sorry for Mrs. Kennedy and the kids. He could barely remember his own father, but his death had left an impression. And of course, his stepdad's death . . .

Well, four years was a long time. You forget a lot. You remember once in a while. You feel tight inside, sort of sick, then it goes away. But mostly you learn that the world doesn't stop. Not for anyone.

And to tell the truth—which he wisely kept to himself on this occasion—Wilt Chamberlain and Bobby Pettit had a bigger impact on his life than John F. Kennedy. At least they moved around on TV; you could dream about breaking their records someday and you could listen to them talk and know what they were saying.

President Kennedy usually talked about crisis, aggression, and embargoes, and who cared about that stuff?

No, the President's death was shocking and terrible, but the country had switched presidents thirty-five—no, thirty-six—times already without skipping a beat.

Brian figured it would be business as usual on Tuesday.

And it was.

It was the first time she was ever truly frightened. Frightened to the point of despair. It was the first time she took a good look at how much evil there was in the world, what a cruel place it was, and realized that even she was vulnerable.

The day Lee Harvey Oswald shot President John F. Kennedy, it was as if the whole world had turned upside down. The citizens of Tolford walked around in slow motion, floundered in a quagmire of confusion. Every time she saw pictures of Mrs. Kennedy in that blood-soaked pink suit, she cried. She tried to emulate the First Lady's brave composure, but she couldn't. She cried. She was heartsick and scared. She couldn't help it. Most everyone was frightened, and no one knew what to think.

Except Brian.

"How could it happen?" she asked, more of herself than of him. It was dark out. Their parents were still inside, mourning with the rest of the nation in front of the television. Brian had silently followed her out onto the front porch and taken the seat beside her on the porch swing. "How could anyone kill the President? It doesn't seem real, does it? I keep thinking it's a dream and I'll wake up soon and everything will be back to normal. What will happen to us now?"

She didn't expect Brian to have the answers, but anything he had to say would have been better than the ominous silence left by her unanswerable questions.

"I just don't understand it," she said, looking at him as if to say she was sick of talking to herself.

"Maybe you're not supposed to," he said, looking away from her into the night that was as deep and obscure as their lives seemed to be. "Maybe things just happen and you're not supposed to understand why." He was silent for a moment, then added, "Maybe that's how things change, and sometimes good things happen because of it."

"That's the dumbest thing I ever heard." She should have left him alone. He was always saying stupid stuff. "What good could come from President Kennedy's death? It's the worst thing to ever happen to this country."

"Maybe."

"What's that mean? Maybe. You don't know anything," she said, almost as angry as she was heartsick and sad. "Nothing good happens after someone dies."

"Sometimes it does," he said, his voice soft and sure.

"When? When has anything good ever come from somebody's death? Tell me that."

He looked at her then. "When my real dad died, we moved here and I met you. That was a good thing."

She stared for a second, then relaxed her spine against the back of the swing. Okay. His father hadn't been John F. Kennedy, but their friendship was a good thing—most of the time.

"I used to wonder why my dad had to die. All the time," he said, his voice soft, sounding older than usual. "And why my mom had to go and marry my stepdad and why he got sick. You don't figure out the answers to everything right away. Sometimes it takes a long time."

Well . . . maybe. She'd give it some time and see.

Nine

"HORSE!" he bellowed. He stuck his face in hers and grinned with great superiority. "You lose, Livy. Again."

She wiped the perspiration from her brow on the hem of her T-shirt and gasped for air. "You're taller than me. It's not a fair match anymore."

Being a healthy fourteen-year-old, Brian wasn't impervious to the flash of smooth bare skin he got when she raised her shirt. But he was careful to remind himself that it was Livy's stomach—not the warm, naked, raw flesh of a real girl. Which isn't to say that it didn't send his hormones hopping. It did. But then, so did just about everything else in those days. Half-dressed girls on TV commercials, the steamy fragrance outside the girls' locker room at school, the *very idea* of topless go-go girls dancing somewhere, underwear ads in the Sears catalog!

Sometimes, not always, but sometimes . . . once in a while, his hormones just plain embarrassed him. But Livy didn't need to know that.

"Hormones, Livy," he said, hoisting himself up to sit on the retaining wall along his mother's driveway, quickly downing a third of the Miller beer he'd left there thirty minutes earlier. It was warm, but that didn't matter; it was wet. "You got those wimpy girl hormones that start to peter out at thirteen, while I got *male* hormones that'll be good for at least another two years, maybe three."

He could boast now, but he hadn't forgotten the whole year that Livy was a good three inches taller than he. He'd died a thousand deaths that year.

"Oh, God," she groaned. She liked to use swear words—for effect, she said. She pulled herself up to sit beside him on the wall. She was tall for a girl. Five-eight and three quarters. But he was taller. "Three more years. Will that be the end of it then? I won't have to listen to any more of this crap?" She flopped back on the grass behind them and stared up at the intensely bright and infinitely empty blue summer sky. "You used to be such a sweet, shy little boy," she said wistfully. Then she scowled at him, saying, "Now look at you."

He did, and he liked what he saw. One hundred percent prime U.S.D.A. Grade A male. Ready for high school. Ready for women. Ready for a driver's license in eighteen months. Ready for more women. Ready for anything. He sighed contentedly and looked back at Livy. He liked what he saw there, too. Her hormones might not have been as satisfying as his own, but they hadn't done a half bad job on her. She had great long legs and breasts he'd kill to touch . . . if they belonged to some other girl.

Well, truthfully, he wouldn't have minded touching them on Livy, except that something inside him told him he'd regret it if he did.

She was his friend, the best he'd ever had, and he never wanted that to change. He'd rather die of chronic hormonal overload than do anything that might jeopardize their friendship. Great breasts or no great breasts.

His gaze followed the softly rounded female curves of her body until it reached her face. He was a man now, but deep inside there was a lot of the first grader who still loved Livy's face. How many times had she sat perfectly still, an action against her nature, while he'd tried to draw that face? he wondered. And how many times had she told him that he was getting better and better, when it was plain to him that he never got it quite right?

"I suppose if the coach asks you to play forward on the varsity team next year, there'll be no living with you," she said, her eyes closed, a smile on her lips. He'd thought about kissing her, too. She had a great mouth. Soft, full lips.

"You got that straight," he said, lowering himself down beside her so he wouldn't have to look at her. "But they almost never ask freshmen to join the varsity team, so I might have to settle for being the star junior varsity player this coming year and the lone sophomore on the varsity team after that."

"You're an egotistical idiot."

"And when I do make varsity," he said, ignoring her, "the first thing I'm gonna do is ask Cathy Dixon for a date."

She groaned. "Cathy Dixon?"

"Yeah," he said on a sigh of pure, unadulterated lust.

Livy sighed, helpless and hopeless of his salvation. "Well, if you're going to college with me, you better be careful. You know, get some of those rubber things Miss Crawford told us about in P.E. Remember, I told you? They keep girls from getting pregnant?"

He chuckled. "Loverboy Larry bought me a carton of 'em."

She gasped and rolled up onto one elbow. "You're kiddin' me!"

"Nope." He grinned. "My Mom found those magazines I showed you. She made Larry go back to the drugstore after supper and then have a little talk with me."

They snickered and laughed. Adults—you just had to love them sometimes. He sat up and finished off his beer while she watched.

"Does he know you're drinking his beer?" she asked, more curious than concerned. It wasn't as if drinking your parents' alcohol was a big deal anymore. Not really. Practically everyone they knew had at least tried it. Livy had been one of the first. It was no big deal.

He shook his head and grinned at her. "He brings a six-pack every time he comes over. He drinks two. Mom has one. I think he thinks she drinks them when he's not around. Want me to get you one?"

She wrinkled up her face. "How can you stand the taste?"

"You get used to it," he said with a shrug. He'd liked the taste from the beginning. "And it's great for my free throw. One or two of these, I'm all relaxed. Nothing but net every time."

"Do you think she'll marry him?" she asked. The courtship of Brian's mother by the new pharmacist at the drugstore got more publicity in Tolford than the new TV series *The Addams Family*. Apparently, it wasn't loathsome enough that your own mother taught at the high school where she could actually speak to you in the hallway between classes in front of your friends—it now looked as if he'd belong to the only family in town that possessed three last names.

He shrugged. "Don't know."

"You like him." It wasn't a question.

"He's okay." He wasn't the problem. "Beth hates him."

"Why?"

"She likes the way things are, I guess. She's eight. Who knows why she thinks anything?"

They were quiet for a moment, remembering Beth's father.

A year ago, Brian might have told Livy that he wasn't too keen on the idea of changing things either. He didn't like change. He didn't know why, he just didn't. He didn't even like the idea of growing up. However, now that he had the muscles and the height and the fascinating patches of hair appearing on his body, he thought it somehow less manly to talk about feelings he couldn't begin to explain. Even to Livy.

"I can't believe your mother," Livy said, starting to chuckle again. "What kind of woman would turn someone like you loose on the female population with a whole carton of rubbers? What could she be thinking?"

"That it's useless to fight the inevitable?"

"Are those extraordinary hormones of yours ever going to kick in with some humility?"

"I hope not." Then he remembered. "Gary Wymer wanted me to find out if you were going to Debbie Richie's swimming party."

She shook her head slowly. He saw disappointment and pain in her eyes before she lowered her lids to hide it from him. His eyes automatically fixed on the cause.

She'd taken to covering her birthmark with makeup. It was still visible. True deep purple was a hard color to cover with commercial makeup. But she'd toned it down a bit and seemed pleased with the results—except that it washed off with water.

The makeup had worried him at first. She'd argued that people weren't staring as much and teased her less when she covered her birthmark. And he'd held fast to the notion that their peers, like them, were maturing and growing more sensitive and didn't feel the need to razz her about it anymore. Everyone at school knew she had it; covering it up was silly.

His concern had finally taken him to his mother, who wisely advised him not to be concerned. She'd told him that for Livy, part of growing up would be experimenting with her hair and clothes *and* with her birthmark until she found the right combination, until she accepted what she looked like and who she was.

His mother had gone on to say that he was doing the same thing in his own way. He'd yawned and turned off. He hadn't wanted a human-development lecture from her, just some reassurance that what Livy was doing to herself was okay.

At the moment, however, it was his opinion that refraining from summer water sports and swimming parties down at the lake was unhealthy and not at all okay. There were all those female forms in tiny wet strips of cloth to be seen and touched and . . . well, it was mind boggling. And he didn't want Livy to miss any of it. But all he could do, it seemed, was to hope that his mother was right, again, and that Livy would someday come to her senses.

She did.

By the time they went to visit Granddad Hubbard in August,

Livy was back to normal and, for Brian, *"the long hot summer of '64"* began—not in the ghettos of New York, Philadelphia, and Chicago, where television newscasters were telling of riots, fires, and looting. Or even in Memphis where more of the same was reported almost daily in the newspaper. No, it all began in Granddad Hubbard's clover field.

". . . and poor Patty Coleman hasn't even had her period yet."

"What? Her what?" Brian's whole body felt sunburned, though only his torso was exposed to the light.

"You know. Her period."

"Livy!"

They were walking back to the house through a field of clover after delivering lunch to Mr. Hubbard and his hired hand, Walt Lippman, in the fallow field the men were tilling for fall planting. They'd only just arrived the day before, and they were soaking in all the warm sunshine and sweet earthy smells they could. Most everywhere they looked corn stood tall and green and almost ready for harvest.

"Well, no one would call her Pancake Patty anymore if she'd start having her period. Then she'd start to develop like the other girls, and the boys would stop laughing at her," she said, in both her own and Pan . . . Patty's defense.

"I wasn't laughing at her. You asked me to give you a list of girls I wanted to take out next year. And I did. Then you asked if I wanted to ask Patty Coleman out, and I said no. I didn't laugh and then say no. I just said no."

"Well, why not? She's a nice girl, isn't she?"

"Nice enough." *Really* nice. *Too* nice. *Very*, very nice and he wouldn't get anywhere with her.

"Then why won't you ask her out?"

"I don't know." Because her body was as flat and sexless as a pancake.

"I know why," she said, using a manner she had of sounding intellectually unparalleled in her present company. She walked ahead of him.

"You don't know anything," he said to her back. He brutally flicked a ladybug off his bare chest with his index finger. Women! "Maybe I just don't like her."

She stopped and turned to face him.

"What do you think of me?" she asked.

"What do you mean, what do I think of you?"

"Well, look at me." He did. He saw Livy. "What do you think?"

"About what?"

"About me. How do I look?"

"You look fine."

"No, no. I mean *really* think of me," she said, scanning the stupid look on his face. "Pretend you're not you. Pretend you're just a regular boy."

"Okay." He pretty much was a regular boy, ah, man.

"Now, look at me." He did. He saw Livy. "What do you think?"

"About what?" He held out his hands in frustration.

"My body."

"What?"

"What do you think of *my* body?"

"Livy!"

"I'm serious. And you're just a regular boy. You don't even know me."

She put her hands on her hips and waited for him to answer. She was wearing white shorts—short shorts—and a pink middy shirt that buttoned up the front. Her movement raised the middy up to reveal the smooth, tanned skin above her navel and pulled it tight across her breasts.

Now, among the many things that a fourteen-year-old boy has no control over are ocean tides, an eclipse of the moon, the national deficit, Halley's comet, and the wild thing in his pants.

"Well?" she asked. He couldn't breathe, much less speak. "Do you think I'm too fat?"

"No."

"Do you think I'm too skinny?"

"No."

"What about my butt?" she asked, turning sideways. "Does it stick out too much?"

"No." Was he sticking out too much?

"Do I have bird legs?"

He shouldn't have looked, but he did. "No."

"My waist looks okay, doesn't it?"

"Sure." But what did it feel like?

"What about my breasts?"

He tried to swallow, but his mouth was too dry.

"Well?" she asked.

"What about your . . . them?"

"Are they too little?"

"Livy! I don't know." He had a sudden urge to pull out all his hair.

"Are they too big?"

"I don't *know*."

"Can breasts ever be too big?"

"No. I mean, I don't know. Why are you asking me this stuff?"

"Because I want to know. You're a boy. And you're my friend. I want you to honestly tell me what you think of me."

"Livy, I can't."

"Why not?"

"Because."

"Great answer."

"Because . . . I don't know what to tell you." *And* because his heart was beating so fast he thought he was going to have a heart attack.

She stared at him for a minute and then slowly lowered her gaze to the ground.

"It's my face, isn't it?"

"What?"

"There's nothing really wrong with me except my face. Isn't that right?"

Oh, God.

"No, Livy. That's not it. There's nothing wrong with you *or* your face." He could tell she didn't believe him. "It's me." She looked at him. "I . . . oh, man . . ."

He turned and walked away. He needed some space—and a lot more air. Was this the hottest day ever made, or what?

"It's all right, Brian," she said in a soft, comforting voice. "I understand."

He turned to look at her.

"No. You don't understand." He sighed as if resigned to walking on the hot coals of hell. "Livy, sometimes I want to touch you so bad I could die." She watched him without speaking, and he would have given anything at that moment to know what she was thinking. "I know. We're like brother and sister . . . only better. It's sick. I know. But . . ."

"Is this one of those times?"

He could barely nod his head.

"When you and Cathy Dixon met at the movie that time, did you touch her?"

Damn. He'd never lied to Livy before, but he sure wanted to now.

"No." Old habits were hard to break.

"Did you want to?"

"Yeah, I guess so."

"Yes or no?"

"Yes!" Okay. Enough. "I'm sick of this. Let's go."

"No, wait." He stopped and turned back. "You can touch me if you want to." He felt dizzy and sick. "No, I mean it. You can practice on me. I want to know what it feels like, too."

He looked from one corner of Ohio to the other for a rational excuse not to do it. Trouble was, he had his irrational glasses on and couldn't see a thing.

"This isn't like practicing basketball, Liv. It's . . . different."

"Not so very. You want to score with some girl without looking clumsy and stupid, you practice."

Okay. She had half a point there.

"It's more than that. She has to want to be touched."

"I do. I told you that. I want to know what it feels like." There was only the slightest hesitation before she glanced down at the front of her shirt, her fingers making fast work of the buttons.

"Livy," he said when she stepped before him, his voice a breathless whisper. "I don't think . . ."

"I know," she said, cutting him off. "But I've gotten used to that in you." She laughed. "Come on, Carowack. It's me, Livy. Relax. You've touched me a thousand times. Maybe two thousand times if you count all the times you've hit me playing basketball." She pulled the front of her shirt open. "Take your best shot."

First he looked at her forehead, between her eyebrows. Then gradually into her eyes. They were as warm as the sunshine on his back; they seemed to soak in the light and shine like molten gold. They were so familiar and trusting and frank. There was an expectation that he didn't want to disappoint and a . . . a certain dreaminess, an illusion he was reluctant to shatter.

He was about to refuse, tell her no, start to cry . . . when he felt her left hand close around his right. Something in her eyes changed, a reflection from the pit of her soul perhaps. He watched it, mesmerized, as she placed the palm of his hand over her breast.

And then there was fire. In him. In her eyes.

He snatched his hand away and looked down.

Her brassiere was so white against her summer sun-darkened

skin, it almost blinded him. It was plain, not silky and lacy like the ones he'd seen in the magazines he had rolled up behind the towels under the sink in the bathroom. Not a huge bazooka like his mother's. Smaller, simpler, less intimidating—and much more inviting. And under it was the smooth, soft-looking flesh that he *did* recognize from the magazines.

As if his hand belonged to someone else he watched it mold itself to Livy's breast. Soft. Full. Consuming. Enthralled, he discovered the warmth and texture of her skin on the gentle curve with the pad of his thumb, and he imagined the whole of it, bare, in the palm of his hand, what it would taste like, what it would smell like.

"Were you telling the truth when you said you haven't kissed anyone yet?"

He looked at her. Then focused on her mouth. He'd always liked Livy's mouth.

"Yes."

"Not even Cathy Dixon?"

"No." And a guy would *never* lie backwards about something like that, you know. Pretending to be more inept than you really were didn't even make sense. This was kissing, after all. Was there another fourteen-year-old boy alive who hadn't kissed a girl yet? He doubted it. But if she was even half-thinking of . . . Oh, God. His hand slipped from her breast. "Liv."

"Shhhh," she said, moving closer. He felt the front of her against him in several different places, and his hands went to her waist. "We drink out of the same pop bottle sometimes. Sometimes we eat off the same fork. Our germs get along. And I want to know what it's like. Don't you?"

"Yeah, but . . ." He knew Livy. She wasn't a cruel person. She was fair and honest and caring. Clearly, she had no idea what she was doing to him.

"Please. Just once."

For crying out loud! He did it quick and got it over with.

"Not like that, Carowack. I can kiss my dad like that. Do it like Sean Connery in *From Russia With Love* and *Goldfinger*. Like Cary Grant in *Charade*. You know."

He didn't know, but he was getting the pictures in his head. Sean Connery and Cary Grant? Hard acts to imitate. Why didn't she like those old movies where no one really kissed, they just sort of cheeked each other when the film was over?

"You better not laugh if I do it wrong."

"I won't. Cross my heart."

He was feeling so strange. As if he were going in to have a cavity filled—and couldn't wait to get started.

He took a better, firmer hold of her and readjusted his stance.

"Mama says it all comes naturally, like it's built into you already, but you just don't know it," she said, reassuring him.

"What?"

"Sex."

"What?" He stepped two feet away and pretended not to know her.

"Kissing and sex," she said, showing a little of her exasperation with him. "She said that there's no right or wrong way to do it. It just comes naturally, and your body knows what to do."

"You talk about this stuff with your mother?"

"Not all the time. But that one time. When I started my period last year. Remember?"

"Livy! Don't talk to me about that stuff. I don't want to hear it. I told you that."

"I'm just telling you what she said. Kissing and sex are easy. Now are you going to kiss me or not?"

He glanced down at her open shirtfront, at the shallow valley between her breasts.

"Not. This is crazy. You're my friend. It's like trying to kiss Beth or my mother. It's worse than that. It's like trying to kiss Jimmy Lowe."

"Fine," she said, shrugging as she looked down to button her shirt from the top down. "I'll find someone else to teach me how to kiss. Jimmy, maybe. I don't think he'd mind."

Mind, hell! Jimmy never talked about Livy; she was part of their gang, one of the guys, a pal. *However,* more than once he'd noticed Jimmy watching Livy walk away, seen him glance down at her chest.

They were both surprised when Brian grabbed her. Surprised and determined to get the damned kiss over with. She flung her arms around his neck and pulled his head toward hers.

"Close your eyes, stupid," he said, all but growling at her.

She did—another surprise, as she rarely responded to that name. She must really want to be kissed, he thought, softening a bit. If he did it right, he'd only have to do it once. And he was . . . well, a little curious.

He lowered his face to hers. Her lips were parted, and he could feel her breath on his own. He brushed against them softly. And again because it felt nice. He applied a little pressure and a little suck like he'd practiced on Beth's plastic hand mirror. That felt nicer.

This must have been where the "natural" kicked in. His mind began to spin and he felt like he could eat her alive. His mouth pressed harder against hers; he could feel her teeth against his, touch them with his tongue. Her tongue came out to meet his, and every nerve in his body stood up and screamed.

Her breasts. He touched them once more. Squeezed and pressed. Pushed the bra up and liberated them. Stroked and caressed them. He marveled as the soft nipples grew hard. He felt her pelvis pushing hard against his. Her mouth was warm and wet and sweet. The whole lower half of his body was pounding for a release, and the rest of him didn't seem to be there at all. In a slow, detached frenzy he lowered his mouth to her breast. He licked the nipple to taste it, took it into his mouth because . . . because . . . he wanted to.

The sound that came from Livy's throat was like nothing he'd heard before, and yet he knew it, felt it, rejoiced in it. She trembled in his arms, and he sucked a little harder—and just a little harder until she went almost limp and he had to hold her tighter.

Their lips came together again. He pressed her hips tight against him. He wondered if she could feel him throbbing. Wondered if she had a pulsing need in her. Wondered if he could feel it if he touched her there. There in that secret place of hers. That secret place he hadn't allowed himself to think about until now. The only secret he and Livy had from one another.

His hand slid from its new home at her breast and drifted down her belly. She pressed it between them, stopping the progression. Like a baby taking his first steps, one after another, without intent or clear direction but simply because he could, he pulled back a bit and slipped his hand into the top of her shorts. And a little lower, until the tips of his fingers felt coarse hair.

She rocked in his one-arm embrace and suddenly pushed away from him with all her might. They stared at each other, eyes wide and frightened beyond belief.

"Maybe . . ." she said, trying to catch her breath and arrest an entire body blush at the same time. "Maybe you were right this time." A concession rarely made. "Maybe this is different."

Maybe?

"I'm sorry, Livy."

"No, no. God, don't be sorry. Don't ever be sorry. I'm not sorry."

"You're not?"

"No." She looked away, then back. "I just . . . don't think it's for us."

"Me either." Wow. What a relief. Sort of.

"Well, good then. We won't do it anymore. Okay?"

He nodded. "Okay."

"Okay. Let's go." She pulled her bra down over her breasts and finished buttoning her shirt.

"Um. You go ahead. I, ah, I think I'll just hang around here a few more minutes."

Mercifully, she didn't ask any questions. She nodded and said she'd see him later. She walked perhaps thirty feet before she started running back toward the farmhouse. Brian fell onto his back in the clover, wishing a swarm of bees would come along and sting him to death. He was miserable. Even his hair ached. The sky was blue and empty, like him.

He lay there a long time, thinking about what they'd done, thinking about everything and nothing. When he felt he could face Livy again, he walked back to Granddad Hubbard's house to find her. To say he was sorry. To make it all right between them.

He couldn't find her. Not for hours.

When she showed up for supper with a few stray pieces of hay in her dark hair, he knew where she'd been—and why she hadn't answered when she heard him calling her.

Things between them had changed. He knew this. He felt it. Neither of them spoke of it.

Everything was as before. And everything was different.

Livy was bold and outspoken and determined. She was motivated and idealistic and a pain in the ass sometimes. And Livy was fragile; she made mistakes. She was susceptible and trusting. She needed him to protect her.

They didn't talk about that day in the clover field for years and years and years. But it was always there. Standing out, bold and ever fresh, among the many memories they shared.

Whoever coined the phrase "Sweet Sixteen" didn't know Livy. By the time she turned sixteen, she wasn't sweet anymore. Certainly not if sweet meant dewy-eyed and romantic. While some of the girls in her class were beginning to experiment with sex, she had already come to the conclusion that it was vastly overrated.

It had to be.

Two years earlier, on her granddad's farm, she'd kissed Brian on impulse, a crazy, self-indulgent whim she wasn't likely to favor again. People were very immature at fourteen. Even she was a little overly dramatic at that age. Imagine, believing she'd probably die before she was kissed by a boy, believing no boy would want to kiss a girl with a purple stain on her face. Consider, thinking she might be in love with Brian. Not that she *loved* him—that was never an issue; she did, always had, always would, she couldn't help herself—but was *in love* with him because of the way he'd made her feel that day.

Immature and dramatic.

Two years later, she knew differently. Boys would kiss slugs if they thought they could have sex with them. And she'd kissed enough boys by then to know. Frankly, she didn't get what all the fuss was about. She thought she did, at first. That kiss with Brian had turned her inside out. She'd staggered away to hide in the barn until she stopped trembling and the ache inside her, in private places she didn't know could ache, had diminished to a strange hollow sensation.

The rest of that month she'd done everything, short of tying him down, to get Brian to kiss her again. She touched him whenever she could make it seem accidental. But he wouldn't have anything more to do with it. He wouldn't even sit close to her when they were alone. And he spent an awful lot of time with her granddad that summer, avoiding her as if he thought she might attack him or something.

Immature and dramatic.

By the time they got home, just before Labor Day and the beginning of school, she wanted so badly to be kissed again she could hardly think straight—which explains why she let Jimmy Lowe kiss her behind the bleachers after the Tolford-Christmasville football game a couple of months later, which they lost. No surprise. Tolford didn't win at anything.

She'd kissed him over and over again, waiting for the leg-bending thrills she'd experienced with Brian to kick in. She even let Jimmy touch her breasts through her shirt, in the hopes of jarring loose some of the same excitement.

Nothing. She got bigger chills kissing pictures of Paul McCartney.

After a while, she tried it again. Larry Estes conjured pictures of fat-lipped fish, and Gary Wymer had a tendency to gag her with his tongue. Charlie Monroe was too shy to kiss her like Sean Connery and Cary Grant, but his little pecks weren't unpleasant.

The most telling kiss was probably Steve Donovan's. Instead of watching him covertly as she had since junior high school, she mustered the courage to smile at him, to stand in his line of vision whenever possible, to be where he was and engage him in senseless conversation—he was drop-dead gorgeous but not too smart.

Over and over again she managed to be caught alone with him. Outside the drugstore, in detention; once she rode all the way to Nashville with him on a field trip to the state capital. No easy thing. It was a challenge to make the seat next to her appear to be taken until the kids who smoked cigarettes in the bushes on the far side of the school finally got on the bus and were forced to take what seats were available—like the one next to her, suddenly.

It took a while—nothing great coming easily, you know—but a few tutoring sessions was all it took. He was failing English, her best class. So when their teacher approached her with the idea of helping Steve pass the final exam, she had magnanimously agreed to fit him into her busy schedule.

Three afternoons a week they stayed late in the school library under the watchful eye of Mrs. Elman, the school librarian. She was a large, gray-haired, no-nonsense type of woman who generally had a pencil sticking out of the tightly wrapped bun on the top of her head. And she was tall. You could always tell where Mrs. Elman was by following the pencil-speared bun of hair above the racks of books.

The first couple of weeks were nerve-racking. All they did was diagram sentences and punctuate paragraphs. They sat close, heads bent over the same book. Habit always seated her on his left, so he didn't have to look directly at her birthmark every time he turned his head. Sometimes their shoulders and arms brushed, by accident or by design, and they'd smile at each other. Once, when she was writing out a sentence for him, she would have sworn he tried to smell her hair.

The scent of lilac did that to people.

But by the third week, Mrs. Elman had clearly surmised that they were trustworthy students and could be left alone in the library for up to twenty minutes at a time. Twenty-minute windows of opportunity, to Livy's thinking. The week before the final exam, she took one.

"Okay, now in this sentence, is worn-out used as a verb and preposition or as an adjective?" she asked Steve in a whispery library voice, watching Mrs. Elman's bulk waddle out the door. She glanced back in time to see him frown and shake his head. Then he looked to her for the answer. She hesitated. "You know, you have really nice blue eyes," she said, as she'd been planning to for some time. Her heart was pounding like jungle drums in a Tarzan movie. "I don't think I've ever seen any quite so blue."

"Oh, yeah?" He looked surprised, then scanned the room for Mrs. Elman. Relaxing, a lot, he gave her a cocky smile.

"Yeah. They're a very distinct blue."

"You like this stuff, don't you?" he said, motioning to the English book. "You're real brainy, huh?"

"Not so very. But I like school, so I guess that makes it easier for me." Her hands started to tremble. She hid them under the table.

"What do you like about school?"

She shrugged and smiled. He glanced at her mouth.

"Everything, I guess. Learning. Being with people my own age. Experiencing new things."

"What kind of new things do you like to experience?" he asked, scanning her mouth again.

"All kinds. I'll try most anything once."

"Is that so?" he asked, moving his head a fraction of an inch closer to hers.

This was it! He was going to kiss her at long last. She could see the intent in his eyes, feel it in the pit of her stomach.

"Oh, sure," she said, afraid that she'd start to babble and say something stupid when his face came closer. "Experimenting and experiencing new things is the best teacher of all, they say."

"They who?"

"People," she said, fidgeting into a straighter position for a better alignment. She didn't want this kiss to miss its target.

"Experimenting." How he made a sterile, scientific word like that sound like a detailed account of the faded-out part of a love scene, she'd never know. But he did. It was the sexiest word she'd ever heard. Thrills ran up and down her spine.

She sat perfectly still as he came close, afraid that the tiniest movement would make her jump out of her skin. Her eyelids lowered as she watched his lips draw near. She closed them and felt the first gentle, tentative touch.

Nothing.

She leaned into the kiss, parting her lips by a breath. The tip of his tongue tested her lips, and a great swelling of anticipation rose within her. The warm palm of his hand touched her left cheek and neck when their mouths met open and inviting. She touched his tongue with hers.

Nothing.

She wrapped her arms around his neck and pulled him tight against her. He was . . . enthusiastic. He fondled her breasts.

Nothing.

She pulled away. Something was horribly wrong. Where were the bells? The thrills and chills? She glanced around the room. Maybe it was the setting. How conducive to excitement was a dull old library?

She smiled at him nervously.

"This probably isn't the best place for this," she said.

"Elman's out having a smoke in the parking lot," he said, locking his mouth to hers.

"She smokes?" she asked, ignoring the broken suction sound when she freed her lips. "I didn't know she smoked cigarettes."

"Baby, there's a lot you don't know." The way he made a sweet, innocent word like *baby* sound dirty and nasty confused her.

He was eager to continue but . . . well, the library was closing in on her and she was nervous that Mrs. Elman might return and catch them and . . .

"Would you like to come over to my house tonight?" she asked, holding him off with one hand.

"What for?"

"Ah, well, we could study some more. Or watch TV or listen to music or something." She was picturing the swing on her front porch, stars, a big full moon.

He did think about it, but with an expression that indicated that it seemed like a lot of trouble for nothing.

"I don't think so," he said, turning away from her and back to the book on the table.

"What about Friday? Maybe we could go to a movie or something?" It was generally understood that a boy and a girl didn't go to the movies together just to see the movie.

"No, thanks."

Maybe he had plans.

"Saturday then. We could do something on Saturday."

He looked at her as if it were just then occurring to him what she had in mind, and in the blink of an eye he broke her heart. He took a quick peek at the stain on her cheek.

"Look, Livy, you're a nice girl and all . . . You're real smart, and I appreciate you helping me out . . . but . . ."

She laughed and looked away long enough to blink the tears from her eyes.

"Relax, Romeo. I was kidding. I have to edit all the articles for the school newspaper before Monday, and I promised to stuff envelopes for the Young Democrats League. I don't have time for a movie," she said, forcing herself to smile into his dull, ordinary blue eyes. "But if you change your mind about coming over for an extra lesson or two, I won't mind. I'll squeeze you in somewhere. Finals are coming up fast, and we could use some extra time, so . . . well, think about it. Okay?"

She nursed that blow to her pride for a long time. Kept it a secret. Attended to it frequently. She also contemplated giving up kissing altogether, attributing Brian's kiss to a weird fluke of circumstances—the first kiss, the overexcitement of a new discovery, a little fear of the unknown, that sort of thing. And if kissing left you feeling flat—or in pain—then it stood to reason that sex couldn't be much better. So what was all the fuss about?

Brian, on the other hand, had clearly enjoyed their kiss far more than she, for he seemed determined to rekindle those emotions with everyone he met. He kissed anyone who came near him. He had an attraction to a new girl about every fifteen minutes. He was shameless.

"That's why guys are guys and chicks are chicks," he said simply, grinning proudly, all but strutting as they walked to their next class together. "It's hormones, Liv. Great hormones." Oh, not those again. "They get guys stirred up faster than girls. I read an article about it in one of Loverboy's magazines. Girls get too emotionally involved with it. They can't relax and enjoy it like we do. It always has to mean something."

"Like what?"

"Like you want to get married or you want to have a baby or you want the guy to do something."

"Like what?"

"Like take you somewhere special or . . ."

"You mean, to get him to do what I want."

"Yeah."

Her mother had told her sex was special and wonderful, that it felt good most of the time. It didn't feel all that good or special or wonderful to her. Of course, her mother had said all those things and added "with the right person," so maybe Mr. Right would make a difference.

Or maybe not.

In the meantime she'd kissed everyone in Tolford she'd cared to kiss, and it wasn't a big deal anymore—or so she told herself. She concluded that with sex being what it was, and with her birthmark being what it was, her greatest asset was still her brain, and her key to the future would be . . . brainpower.

Ten

IN 1965 BEATLEMANIA was hot and getting hotter. But it didn't start the fires that burned for five days in Watts or cause draft cards to spontaneously combust when the draft calls doubled. All it did was make your hair grow and Brian's country-lovin' mother shudder.

"Well, how far do you think it is from Tolford to Selma?" she wanted to know. She had her daddy's road map out again.

"Oh, only about three hundred miles. Why? Think we oughta hoof on down there and march to Montgomery with Dr. King?"

"Yes, I do. But Daddy won't drive us. He says I've got no business there."

"Good for him. Come to think of it, I don't have any business there either. We'll both stay home."

"Brian Carowack, I'm ashamed of you," she said. "It *is* our business. It's everyone's business. All they want to do is vote. Black people have a right to vote. They were whipped and tear-gassed, and Governor Wallace didn't lift a finger to help them. He's a terrible man. Daddy says it's a wonder someone hasn't shot him yet."

"Maybe Ginsberg should share some of his LSD with him. They could chant together till dawn. It worked with the Hell's Angels in California."

"That's not funny."

Nothing was anymore.

"What do you think two white kids who aren't old enough to vote themselves, who can't even get there unless they ride their bikes, can do? Other than get beat all to hell. Or killed."

She frowned, stymied. She sighed. "There should be something we can do."

"Chewy said it would happen no matter what," he said, re-minding her of Chewy's visit a month earlier. He'd stopped to see his mother on his way to New York, where he'd gotten a job at City College of New York teaching an experimental class in black history. Mrs. Lewis invited them, Brian's mother, Loverboy Larry, and Livy's parents to "tea" one afternoon. The Reverend Mr. Oates, from the Baptist Church, his wife, and Chewy's uncle, Mr. Hughie Potts, came too—it was quite a sight.

Informally, he and Livy had been to Chewy's house plenty of times, and no one seemed to notice. But when the minister, the mayor, their wives, another white couple, and two white kids showed up at Chewy's house to talk, most everyone in the all-black neighborhood stood in the street outside to watch.

Brian felt very grown up that day. Chewy was all grown up. He was twenty-four now. He put a hand on Brian's shoulder and shook his hand, man to man. He and Livy sat and listened to the adults talk, understood what it meant when Chewy explained that the time had long passed to *give* blacks their due because they were now prepared to simply take it, and they were proud they knew him.

"I know what Chewy said," she went on. "But I want to do something to help. Make it happen sooner."

"Write to President Johnson again."

"No."

"Why not?"

"He answered me last time."

"He did?"

"Well, not him. He pawned me off to some secretary or assistant or something. It wasn't even his real signature. It was stamped on."

"What, you think the President should sit down and answer your letters personally?"

"No. That would be worse. He'd be wasting his time. That

would mean he wasn't paying enough attention to what's been happening in this country," she said. "But I'd just as soon he didn't answer me at all than pawn me off on some stranger."

Lyndon Johnson should have known better, but let's face it, he
was no John F. Kennedy.

Brian couldn't blame Livy for being frustrated. Her little world
where people were either good or bad was all mixed up. A well-
deserved punch in the nose didn't settle much anymore. Right and
wrong glared at them daily, but neither side was winning. And her
old two-heads-are-better-than-one theory was moot. No two heads
ever agreed anymore.

By the time they were seventeen and their junior prom rolled
around, there was no ignoring it anymore. She was clearly living in
two different worlds. Television and Tolford.

Nightly, between *The Flying Nun* and *Ironside,* her television
brought the riots in Newark and Detroit and 127 other cities across
the nation directly into her living room. She sat spellbound as gruesome snippets of the Vietnam war and the protests against it were
covered almost like sporting events—with the casualties and injuries from both reported at the end of the piece. Still, all she had to
do was turn off her TV set or step out onto her front porch to see a
different sort of reality.

Close enough to the hydroelectric facilities and the waterways
along the Tennessee River to attract textile and chemical companies, Tolford was slowly and quietly growing. Yet it remained rural
enough to have a county sheriff who hadn't drawn his gun in almost thirty years of service and to have Sunday afternoon picnics
in the park along the south fork of the Obion River with your
neighbors. Lazy and peaceful, Tolford allowed its citizens to feel
safe and cut off from what was happening in the rest of the world.
And most folks liked it that way.

But then Livy wasn't most folks.

To most American adults, a summer of love on Haight-Ashbury as seen on television was just plain horrifying. Social suicide. In Tolford, to most of the young people, love-ins were one of the few newsworthy events that made any sense.

"Can't you do something about her?" Cathy Dixon whispered in his ear. She nipped at his earlobe, then stuck her tongue inside. He hated it when she did that. He didn't like having someone's tongue in his ear. What if it was dirty in there? He was always careful to clean them for just this reason, but who knew what went on in your ears between washings?

"Like what?" he asked, turning his head toward her, hiding his ear in the grass. It tickled—a much nicer sensation. Almost as nice as having Cathy's warm, curvaceous body—nearly naked because he'd cajoled her into the water a while back—pressed close and wrapped tight to the left side of his body. Which was almost as nice as knowing that he wouldn't have any trouble lowering the top of her two-piece swimsuit to fondle her breasts or sliding his hand into the bottom half to get her excited. Which was almost as nice as being confident of his ability to go all the way with her—if there weren't so many people around. "You want me to stick a sock in her mouth?"

"Would she let you?" she asked, looking hopeful.

"No." He grinned at her disappointment. "And even if she would, I wouldn't."

"She's going to ruin everything," she said, speaking of Livy.

It was a warm, lazy Saturday afternoon in spring of 1967. Brian liked spring. And summer. Fall and winter were seasons to get through, too busy with school and holidays and things to do, to be enjoyed. Spring and summer were slower, lazy even. You had time to think and paint things in your mind so you wouldn't forget them. It didn't get cold. You could wear fewer clothes. All in all, he probably should have been one of the Beach Boys.

It was getting late, maybe six or six-thirty, but he hadn't been there long. He worked at the BP station, doing lubes and oil changes from eight to four-thirty on Saturdays and for a few hours every day after school. He had a car to support, a black '57 Chevy with gray interior, a six-pack, and four hundred cubic inches of engine under the hood. A gas hog. He was tired. He wanted beer, food, sex, and bed, in that order.

"All those petitions weren't enough," Cathy was saying. "Now she wants us to boycott the junior prom."

He chuckled and drained the last few drops of his third beer.

"It isn't funny. She'll ruin everything," she said with a soft, pronounced southern accent that he found delicious. "Who's going to care if some little girl from Tolford, Tennessee, thinks the government isn't doing enough for colored folks? Who's going to care if she thinks the war should end?"

"Nobody. Which is why she's so mad."

"Can't you talk to her? What if she actually convinces a few kids to listen? I've already got my dress. My mama took me all the way to Jackson to get it. She'll ruin everything."

He sighed. Cathy was—always had been—hands down the best-looking girl in their class. Popular. He knew for a fact that he was the first to have sex with her. Generally, she was pretty cheerful. She hardly ever complained unless he messed up her hair—and even after their swim her hair was long, dry, and straight as a board, the ends cut equally as straight across the bottom. His only criticisms of Cathy were that she had traded in last year's bikini for a two-piece swimsuit that covered up her navel—and she was a selfish airhead.

Crushing the beer can between the palms of his hands—once a game, now a habit—he came to a sitting position. He glanced over his shoulder to where Livy sat on the rocks, deep in discussion with Jerry Levitts, Susan Crawley, Junior McDunn, and a few others. The lake by the park had long ago become too public a place for this crowd to hang out, kick back, and let it all hang out. However, even moving a mile or so down river to a quiet little cove where the boulders broke away and left a small cozy beach with not too many rocks on it didn't allow for everything to hang out—which was why he decided to take another beer and go check on Livy, deal with Cathy later.

They still shared their love of sunshine. Livy's long, slim body never got sunburned, just darker and darker as the summer wore on. And she always got her hair wet when she went swimming. She frequently declared that the greatest boon to women's fashions was the current trend to long, board-straight hair—like hers. (Cathy, it was reported, had to resort to extremes—to the point of pinning and drying her hair around orange juice cans to get "the look.") Silly girl stuff. He was surprised Livy cared. Heck, he didn't care if she wasn't quite as fashion conscious as Cathy and still wore a bikini; he didn't care if she wanted to boycott the junior prom. But he *did* care that she might be getting a little carried away.

You see, Livy had a power. She wasn't the prettiest girl at school or the most popular, but she was smart and there was . . . something . . . a presence, a charisma about her that demanded people's attention, that made whatever she said believable. It was never more evident than when her father got her a part-time job campaigning for Albert Gore in the Senate race the year before. She'd been like a Pied Piper to young and old alike. It hadn't mattered if they were of age to vote or not; they'd followed her to the polls just to make sure he won.

"We're going to dress like wounded soldiers, blood everywhere," she was telling her companions. "Coral's helping me make wounded dummies with missing arms and legs to lay in front of the doors. People will want to think twice before stepping over a dead body to go to a party, don't you think? The TV station in Jackson said they'd think about coming if we could get enough supporters, and who knows? We could end up on the six o'clock news in Memphis or Nashville, and once we do that, we could very well be heard in Washington."

"Aha!" he said, sneaking up behind her, standing tall above her with his hands on his hips. "Plotting to overthrow the government again, I see."

Now, there were times when Livy could turn and look at him, and it was simply Livy, turning to look at him. But on occasion, she'd turn and look at him with a sort of happiness to see him in her eyes that would clutch at his stomach muscles for a second or two. It was an odd sensation, a nice sensation, a sensation he didn't feel he wanted to explore and one he'd come to accept as part of the special feelings they shared as longtime close friends.

"Carowack, you idiot," she said, laughing at him. "There's a huge difference between overthrowing a government and exercising your right to participate in it. If you could think with any organ above your waist you'd know this," she said, grinning as she glanced across the cove at Cathy Dixon.

He glanced back, too, then squatted down behind Livy to whisper in her ear, "Make love, not war, Livy. You should try it sometime."

"I will," she whispered back. "If I ever meet someone with a mature, responsible attitude toward world peace and racial equality. *Mature* and *responsible* being the key words here. I'm going to save myself for a *real* man, not just some boy with hot pants."

"Ugh," he groaned loudly, grabbing his chest. "Stop. You're killin' me." However, in the blink of an eye he was cured. "But that brings me to why I came over here. Can I talk to you for a minute?"

"You had your minute, and you wasted it."

"Then give me another one. We need to talk."

Despite their growing up and despite the expansion of their social obligations, they always had time to talk to each other. They were still best friends. But it was rare for anything in their lives to require immediate private consultation between them.

"Is something wrong?"

She looked worried and ready to help in any way she could. He smiled inside at her reaction. It was so . . . Livy.

"My mom's planning to reenact her wedding," he said, sober-faced, sending everyone within listening distance into whoops of laughter.

The whole town knew his mother's wedding had been a small intimate disaster through which his sister sobbed hysterically; at which Mrs. Shoop, the church organist, took a direct hit between the eyes from a stray champagne cork; and during which the entire gathering, including the bride and groom, got deathly ill on bad spiced shrimp.

But that wasn't the half of it, and as embarrassing incidents went, he much preferred referring to the wedding than to the fact that his mother turned up pregnant a few weeks later. He cringed every time he thought of his mother and Loverboy Larry having sex in the room next to his—he wanted to die now that there was ab-solute evidence of it and the *whole town* knew they were doing it.

If a third marriage was charmed, he couldn't help but wonder in what way.

"Oh, no," she said, laughing. "We can't let her do that. My dad was in the hospital for a whole week, and your mom's sick enough already."

More laughter—but morning sickness was no joke at his house.

She stood and told the others she'd be back directly, then fol-lowed him down the beach.

"So?" she said when he stopped, glancing over her shoulder to make sure they were alone enough to speak privately. "What do we need to talk about?"

"You." There weren't many bushes to beat around when you'd been friends as long as they had.

"One of my favorite subjects. What about me?"

"Livy, take a look around and tell me what you see."

Confused, she did. "You mean besides the sand and the rocks and the water and the trees?"

"Yeah." He took a long draw on his beer while she took a second look.

"A bunch of kids?"

He nodded. "Kids, Liv. Not a bunch of congressmen or senators. Just a bunch of small-town kids who can't even vote yet. A bunch of kids—nobody important—and all they want to do is go to a dance."

"So? Who's stopping them?" she asked, bristling immediately. She was used to opposition from certain quarters, but she hadn't expected it from Brian. Ever. He wasn't always as politically active as she thought he should be, but he'd always supported her thinking. "I'm not stopping them. They can go to their stupid old dance, if that's what they want to do."

"You're not making it easy for them."

"Easy? Why should it be easy for them? You think it's easy living in a ghetto? You think it's easy being black? You think it's easy going off to war and maybe not coming home?"

"No, but what difference is a junior prom in Tolford, Tennessee, going to make to any of that?"

"The difference has to start somewhere. Even the smallest difference counts. If we don't do something now, some of these kids won't be here next summer. Look at Billy Vaughn and Steve Rollens. They left last year right after graduation. Samson Butler, too, and now Darnel's been drafted. They'll be taking kids from our class next."

Aha! The chink in her armor.

"Then they should go to this dance, don't you think? While they can."

"If we can put an end to the war before—"

"We're not going to put an end to the war," he said, cutting her off. "Five years ago, McNamara said Vietnam would be a cakewalk,

and we're still there. They're sending more troops. The war is escalating. It's nowhere near the end."

"But if we—"

"Livy," he said softly. "We can't. We should be kids for as long as
we can."

She fell silent. Seeing his point, but not wanting to.

"You, too, you know," he said, smiling. "Sometimes I think you
were born all grown up and fighting for what's right. Would it kill
you to be a dumb kid, like the rest of us, once in a while?"

She looked away. "It would make me really sick, but it wouldn't
kill me, I guess."

"Then pick some unsuspecting victim and ask him to the
prom."

"Mama says nice girls don't ask boys to go out. It's too forward." Like she cared.

"Ha. They do and they don't, believe me." His vast sexual experience and blatant knowledge of the inner workings of the female
of their species was beginning to annoy her.

"Well, it's supposed to be the other way around, and I don't exactly see anyone beating a path to my door."

"That's because you're never there. You're too busy editing the
school newspaper and campaigning for senators and student-body
presidents and picketing the post office and . . . and what not. Slow
down. Act like a kid. Do something for *you*."

"It is for me. And everybody else." He gave her a bored look, as
if he'd heard it all before. "All right. Like who?" She was far from
giving in, but it couldn't hurt to hear him out.

"I don't know. Steve Donovan, maybe?" The most obvious sug-
gestion as he knew there was still something between her and the
big blond football-playing farm kid from years gone by.

"Alice Rice asked him two weeks ago."

"I don't think so. He was at the garage this morning, and he
didn't have a date then."

"Well, don't look at me," she said. "I wouldn't invite Steve Donovan to a hog toss."

"Then come with me and Cathy," he said simply.

She glanced at Cathy who was brushing her very long, very straight hair. "I'd rather have my appendix removed."

"Well, find somebody and come. Or don't come. But . . . don't wreck it for everyone else, okay?"

She looked at him. "I don't want to wreck anything. I just want them to pay attention to what's happening to our world."

"I know. And some of them will. Some won't, no matter what you do. But either way, there's not a whole lot a bunch of seventeen-year-old kids can do about it. They should grab their happiness while they can."

He took her silence as agreement, and they both watched her toes curl and dig a small hole in the sand. "Do you really believe someone as young and dumb and insignificant as me could wreck anything for anyone?" she asked finally.

It wasn't a did-she-have-the-heart-to-do-it question; it was more a did-he-think-she-had-the-power-to-do-it inquiry. She was wondering if anything she did made a difference or was she simply shadowboxing?

"Yes, I do. With all my heart, I believe you could."

Eleven

EXPECTATIONS. They're hard to live with, harder still to live up to.

Expectations. Where did they come from? Your parents? Their parents? Society? From deep within yourself?

Sometimes you did what was expected of you and things turned out fine. You're glad you did it; you didn't mind doing it. Other times, instinct tells you that acting on other people's hopes and desires will be disastrous, or at the very least a waste of your time. Still you do it, taking the path of least resistance, aiming to please, granting more credence to the wishes and dreams of others than to your own heart. The expectations of others versus your own instincts—it can be a tough call sometimes.

Take a teacher's kid for instance.

Everyone was expecting Brian to go to college. Just like they'd always assumed that a teacher's kid would be brilliant—which they aren't—they assumed a teacher's kid would want to go to college to further his education—which he didn't.

"It's too bad art schools don't have basketball teams," he said, only half joking as he popped the top of an ice-cold beer, catching the foam in his mouth without wasting a drop. "I'd have it made in the shade."

"You have it made in the shade anyway," she said, declining her share of the six-pack with a shake of her head. Actually, they both had it made—and they knew it. She kicked at the dust in the road in shameful discontent. She knew that she was getting her life handed to her on a silver platter. Alice Rice would have given her right arm *and* leg to be going off to college in the fall. Hell, half their senior class would. Still, deep in her heart she was coveting a gold plate, and she hated it.

Tennessee back roads are infamous for being quiet and desolate. And they are. They are also multifunctional. You can drive on them to get from one place to another or to feel the wind in your hair on a warm afternoon. You could race them for the title of hottest car in Gibson County. You can also park on them to get drunk with your pals on the beer you bought illegally in Idlewild, or have a private talk with your oldest friend . . . or scream at the top of your lungs till you're blue in the face without anyone hearing you.

"Made in the shade. Yeah, I know," he said, picking up a rock and throwing it far into an empty, newly planted wheat field. "I feel like I'm cheating."

She looked at him. "Cheating?"

"Like I'm getting something I don't deserve. Like I didn't work for it. Like I got something someone else needs more."

"That's crazy. You deserve that scholarship. You worked hard for it. You need it as much as anybody else. What are you talking about?"

"Remember when we went to that art gallery in Nashville? To see the Robert Morris collection?" he asked, turning toward her. She nodded. It was just last year. His oil painting of Chucker's Bend and the old rickety footbridge had won First Place in the Tennessee Arts Council Statewide High School Competition for Multimedia Art. A watercolor and ink of his sister's profile won an honorable mention, too. His mother had taken them to Nashville to see them displayed in the lobby of the National Life Building. The Robert Morris collection had been a bonus treat for Brian. "Remember that guy, the artist who was making sketches of every piece, to study the detailing, he said? Remember him?"

"Yes."

"Remember him telling us that there was no such thing as an

art teacher for an artist? That true art came from the heart and the soul and the mind of an individual, not from a method or a technique or a textbook?"

"I remember."

"That's what I should do. Just do it. Go off somewhere and draw and paint. What do I need to go to school for? To play basketball? All the real classes would be wasted on me. They always have been."

"That's not true. You got good grades. You learned."

"I showed up and turned in homework. I learned by osmosis."

"Come on, Carowack. You don't mean any of this, do you?" She hesitated. "You're not planning to do something stupid, like turn down the scholarship."

"It's an athletic scholarship, not a . . . scholar scholarship. I love basketball, but I'm not good enough or even dedicated enough to go pro, and I can play it for fun anywhere. Who'd miss another basketball player at Memphis State?"

"All the cheerleaders?"

"I'm serious."

"No. You're crazy," she said, pushing her rear end off the black Chevy and walking to the middle of the road to stand beside him. It wasn't that she didn't understand what he was feeling; she just didn't want him to do something stupid. "Do you know how lucky you are? Do you know how many kids would give anything to be in your place?"

"Yes. And I think they should be. Give the scholarship to someone who really wants to go to school, and let me go paint. It doesn't make sense for me to go to college."

"So, what makes sense anymore? You have to go. They're not going to give that scholarship to someone more deserving. They'll give it to someone who can't play basketball as well as you can, number one. Number two, your mom and Larry are expecting you to go to school. You'll break their hearts if you don't. And number three—NUMBER THREE in capital letters—if you don't go to school next year you'll lose your deferment and you'll end up in the army. Is that what you want?"

Well, no.

His cheeks ballooned as he looked out over the wheat field and sighed deeply. He was silent a moment, then . . . angry. Slowly, like a bubble from the bottom of a jar of honey, the frustration rose up inside him. With all his might he dashed the half-empty beer can in the road and got a foamy explosion. He let out a wail of rage that pierced the emptiness—briefly—before it was swallowed up again in the silence.

Livy watched him wide-eyed, but said nothing. An emotional outburst from Brian was like hearing that a circus was coming to town.

"Where's all the control you're supposed to have over your life when you turn eighteen? Where's the independence? The freedom? You look forward to graduating high school because you think things will be better, and they're not. They're worse. Our parents can still put the screws to us to get us to do what they want us to do. My mother has this look she gives me . . . you know?" She nodded. Her mama had that same look. "The draft board can track us down like dogs and send us off to fight a war. We can finally buy our own beer and drink like adults, but we can't make adult decisions about our own lives?"

"Well, we could," she pointed out. "But then we'd have to live with the consequences."

"Right. So what's the point?" he asked, looking at her.

She stared back. "What? Are these real questions? Do you think *I* know?" So, they were both lucky to be going to college, and they both knew it. If everyone around them still considered them children, then a little whining—in private—when things weren't *exactly* the way they wanted them, was okay. Kids whine, right? And if Brian wanted to spend their afternoon together, out in the middle of nowhere, bellyaching about his not-so-perfect good fortune, then far be it from her to be stoic and spoil his party.

"Maybe you've forgotten that I'm the girl who's been stuck in Tolford, Tennessee, her whole life. Where nothing ever, *ever* happens," she said, exasperated. "I finally get a chance to go where the action is, to go out and touch the real world, to go to Berkeley or Columbia or at the very least Tennessee State. *But, no.* I'm going to Southwestern at *Memphis* because both my parents graduated from there. What kind of crap is that? Don't ask me. I don't know anything. I'm as powerless as you are." She took a deep breath; she had a full head of steam now. "We're both stuck in a society that places a greater value on a preestablished, set-in-cement social structure of higher education than in individual talent and aptitude, with the added threat of military servitude or imprisonment for noncompliance."

He stared at her for a minute, as he often did when she strung more than ninety-six syllables together in one long sentence. He shook his head and raised his dark brows in resignation.

"At least we'll both be where we don't want to be, together," he said. "In the same city."

It was a consolation.

He could remember people constantly telling him to enjoy his senior year of high school. They'd take on a wistful expression and say he'd never forget it as long as he lived; it would be one of the best years of his life, that once it was gone you could never get it back; after high school nothing would ever be the same.

They were right, but he didn't realize it then. He focused on the enjoyment part and simply assumed his senior year of high school would last the rest of his life . . . or something. An eighteen-year-old's perspective on life is limited and boundless at the same time. It was too simple to grasp, too complex to decipher twenty-odd years later.

At the time, if he chanced to give his future much thought at all, it seemed fairly well mapped out and not worth thinking about, he supposed. Graduation. College. Some sort of commercial art job while he established himself as a professional artist. Wife and kids. Rich and famous. Dead of old age.

At the time, it was more important to live each moment, to see every cloud in the sky, every color in a sunset; to feel every zing in a kiss, the fuzzy buds of a pussy willow, the heat in the soil. For him, it was a wasted moment not to savor the sweet smells of freshly mown hay, his baby brother's recently bathed neck, springtime after a rain, Cathy Dixon during sex, his mother's fried chicken after church on Sunday.

At the time, it would have been a crime not to experience the elation and veneration of scoring the most points at nearly every basketball game that season and helping to take your undefeated team all the way through regionals and division. Not to be in on the planning of Senior Skip Day; not to steal mean old Mr. Camden's outhouse for the homecoming bonfire, or not to paint a bright pink penis on the statue of the Confederate soldier, Elias Tolford, that stood proudly in the park.

At the time, the future seemed inconsequential compared to the strange, sad ache in his chest every time he heard that Huey Sheridan and his old nemesis, Donny Moore, had enlisted in the Marines. To the pity he felt as Cathy Dixon who, without college to look forward to, tried to hold him tighter and tighter as graduation drew closer. To the confusion he knew as he watched some of his peers grow suddenly old and responsible before his eyes.

At the time, it was more important to simply be there, in that moment. That moment that had never been before, that would never come again. . . .

He'd arrived late that night because of work, and alone because it was easier than bringing Cathy. They weren't officially "broken up," but their relationship was too rocky to be called steady anymore. She made him uncomfortable.

It was a perfect night early in June the year they graduated. 1968. There was a full moon and plenty of stars, and the world felt like a new place. Fresh and clean. He had serious things on his mind—a new carburetor for his car; what to get his brother, Bobby, for his first birthday; having to clean out the garage the next day; Cathy; extra money for college in a few months—and he was looking to be distracted.

Still semisober, he was sensitive to the noise of "Soul Man" blaring from someone's car radio and the shouting and laughing of a party well under way deep in the woods that bordered the old Trell farm, about eight miles outside Tolford. It was a wonder no one had heard them yet. He didn't have to turn around to recognize the giggles and squeals coming up behind him. But he did. Just in time to hold his quart bottle of beer away from him before Livy plastered herself to his chest.

"Help me. Help me," she said, laughing. He smelled beer on her breath before she slipped under his arm to stand behind him as Gary Wymer emerged from a stand of bushes and trees in search of her. He felt her hand in his back pocket. "I beat him fair and square. He's a poor sport. Don't let him kill me." She peeked around his chest at Gary. "I can't help it if women are superior to men."

Now, Gary Wymer didn't pose much of a threat to someone Brian's size—to someone Livy's size, for that matter. He was maybe six foot but rail thin and as slow and good-natured as a snail. However, from experience, Brian knew that even the most saintly individuals could get riled in Livy's company.

"She cheated," Gary said, clearly vexed. "Make her give me my ten bucks back."

As if he could. It always amazed him when people acted as if he had some sort of magical power over Livy, when it was so apparent that it was the other way around.

"She doesn't cheat," was all he could say, while he tried not to laugh at her antics behind him—a raspberry and a neener-neener to Gary. Of course, that didn't mean that the ten dollars weren't ill-gotten. "What'd she do?" he asked, his speech beginning to slur with alcohol, as was most everyone's in the clearing that Saturday night.

Keggers, as they called their informal gatherings in an abandoned field or deep in the woods beyond some old dirt road, were almost weekly events since ninth grade. Brian rarely missed one. Livy came occasionally, got drunk once in a while, and always vowed never to do it again—until the next time.

"Hold on now," he said when Gary advanced several steps toward them. "What'd she do?" he repeated, unwilling to give her up without at least hearing the reason.

"She cheated," Gary said again.

"What'd she do?"

"She took my ten bucks."

"We know that," he said, indicating the twenty or thirty other kids in the clearing. "Why'd she take it?"

"Because she cheated, that's why." He swayed back and forth, but it took nothing from his righteousness.

Livy was giggling uncontrollably by now. She made a snorting sound and crossed her legs with a certain urgency as she wrapped her arms around Brian's waist.

"I beat him fair and square," she said.

"At what?" he asked, craning his neck to look down and back at her.

"Ch-ch-chugging," she sputtered. "For riddles. He threw up, and I didn't spill a dro-p." She could have blown out a safety torch with that last *p*, but her knees buckled and she started giggling again. He had to lock his free arm around her from behind to keep them both from falling over.

Their schoolmates cheered her swilling skills, and she raised her arms in victory. "Good night, Mrs. Calabash, wherever you are!"

"She's a cheat," Gary said, reaching for one of her fisted hands, thinking his money was inside. "I want my money back."

"Hey, now." Brian stepped sideways, pushing Livy back behind him. "Fair's fair. If you threw up, she won."

"But it isn't fair if the riddle's too long."

"What?"

She giggled harder.

Gary was as drunk as she was, and completely frustrated. He took a moment to glare at her and clear his head, then tried to explain.

"We were doin' riddles, ya know? Riddles? Like kid stuff? And if you didn't know the answer you had to chug a beer." Clearly the rules had seemed simple enough to him. "Whoever downed ten beers first had to pay the other person ten bucks."

"And you lost," Livy said, sniggering.

"You cheated," he said, dismissing her to go on with his story. "She doesn't do regular riddles. Like . . . like . . . like she did the black and white and red all over one? The one that's either a newspaper or an embarrassed zebra? And you know what she said it was?" They were all waiting to hear. "A skunk in a blender. She makes up her own answers, so even if you answer right, it's not the answer she wants."

Livy collapsed into a gob of giggles at Brian's feet. Gary grew red-faced as everyone else enjoyed Livy's creative answer.

"She wanted to know how come golfers don't use clubs anymore, and when I said I didn't know, she said because they're long enough. Does that make sense to you?"

With quizzical expressions, they agreed it didn't. They looked at Livy, sprawled spread-eagle on the ground looking up at the stars, who raised a finger skyward and said, "The riddle was, why are golfers not using clubs any *longer?*" Gradually her audience started to chuckle. "I rest my case."

"They were all like that . . . and she didn't even give me a chance to answer the last one. She just said I'd never guess it, took my money and ran," Gary said, using his last and best example of her chicanery.

"It's a good one," she said, extremely self-satisfied.

"Livy, get up," Brian said, bending over to help her. "You're going to get dirty down there."

"I'm already dirty down here," she said, then laughed. "Man, I'm hot tonight, aren't I?"

He laughed, too. She could hardly stand, her reflexes were shot, but her mind was still sharp. Parts of it anyway. And it was fun to see her apply it to something as silly as riddles instead of overworking it on the solutions to all the world's injustices.

"You are hot. Now, get up."

"What about my ten bucks?" Gary said.

"What about 'em?"

"Well, it's not fair to make up stupid riddles that no one can answer and then run off with their money."

"It's not a stupid riddle, it's a good riddle," she said, on her hands and knees, contemplating standing.

"The hell it is. I never heard a stupid riddle about a king and a monkey and a kid before. You made it up."

She got to her feet, climbing hand over hand up Brian's tall frame. Then she leaned against him, as if he were a lamppost.

"Okay. Here's another one for you, Gary," she said. "If an ignorant fool in Tolford, Tennessee, hasn't heard something before, does that mean it doesn't exist?"

"Hey, hey," Brian said, familiar with the tone of her voice and recognizing fighting words when he heard them. She was so unpredictable lately. Dr. Martin Luther King, Jr.'s death in April and now Bobby Kennedy's had really rattled her. She hadn't been able to shake off the memory of Darnel Butler's flag-draped funeral either. She'd told him that the image of Josephine—Beth's long-ago JoJo—clinging desperately to Samson's arm, still sheathed in a uniform at his brother's funeral, would haunt her forever. Her friends and heroes were dropping like flies, and as hard as Livy tried to maintain her faith in the human cause, she was angry, disappointed, and bitter. "Let's get back to the real riddle. Give Gary a chance to answer it."

"I like the new one," she said, tipping over almost sideways, to look up at him. "We'll keep it simple for him. We'll make it a true or false question. Give him a fifty-fifty chance at it, huh?"

"Livy . . ."

She shook her head. "Okay. What's the difference between a king's son, a monkey's mother, a bald man, and an orphan?"

Otis Redding's "(Sittin' on) The Dock of the Bay" wafted through the clearing with the buzz of the crickets, the quiet of the night . . . and not much else.

"See?" Gary said. "There's no answer. She made it up. Nobody can answer it. It doesn't even make sense."

"It's a riddle. It's not supposed to make sense," she said. "Can I help it if you're stupid?" She glanced around. "Can I help it if you're all stupid?"

"Livy!" Brian tried to silence her but she went on.

"Look at you all. Lying around. Getting drunk every chance you get. Do you have any idea of what's happening outside Tolford? What's happening to your world? Don't you care? Can't you see? Aren't you scared?" Otis went on singing. It was the only response she got. She looked from face to face, shaking her head sadly.

Brian couldn't tell what the other kids were thinking. The party had taken a sudden nosedive. As it stood, they might chalk her outburst up to alcohol and her well-known political passions and shrug it off as . . . Livy being Livy. But if she said any more, she was going to have more enemies than friends in the morning.

"Liv?" he said softly, touching her shoulder.

"I know. I know," she said, shrugging him off. "I should get to the point. I should get to what's really important here, get to what really counts. These kids need to know the truth, and if I don't tell 'em, nobody will." She took several steps forward. "A king's son is an heir apparent. A monkey's mother is a hairy parent. A bald man has no hair apparent. And an orphan has nary a parent." She stopped for a second to review, to make sure she got it right, then added, "And I don't cheat."

Infinite seconds ticked by before members of the gathering started to chuckle. She made a formal bow from her waist and stuck her tongue out at Gary.

"If you'll all excuse me," she said, peremptorily, "I need to find a bush."

Sighing in silent relief and wonder, Brian looped an arm around her neck and pulled her to him. "Come on, you lush, the bushes are this-a-way."

Wordlessly, she fell into step with him, slipping her hand into his back pocket and pulling the ten dollar bill out of its safe hiding place. She threw it at Gary as they walked past him.

"Have another beer on me," she said, and a few steps later she muttered, "peckerhead."

"Livy," he said, chuckling, glancing back to make sure Gary hadn't heard. "Gimme your socks."

"Wha-for?"

"I'm going to ram 'em down your throat before you get us in trouble here."

"Trouble?" He turned her face (and mouth) against his letterman jacket and made her walk sideways until they'd gone by several small groups of merrymakers. "Trouble? Me? I'm only trying to make them see what's happening."

"They see."

"Then why aren't they doing anything? Why aren't they all screaming their heads off for justice and peace?"

"They don't have to. Not with people like you around to scream for them. How's this one?" he asked, with a general motion toward any number of available bushes well away from the crowd. When she didn't scurry off right away, he squinted to get a better look at her in the dark. "What?"

"Was that supposed to be funny?"

"What?"

"That thing about having me around to scream for them. You didn't really mean that, did you?"

Actually, he had.

"That's the way it is, Livy. If the whole country was screaming, you wouldn't be able to hear anything and there'd be no one around listening. So a few brave screamers, people who are comfortable screaming and yelling and fighting—like you—get together and scream out your opinions. And the rest of us let you, because we agree with you."

"That's the dumbest thing I ever heard," she said, stepping high into the bushes. "The apathy in this town . . ."

"It's not apathy. We care. We just do things different than you. If there's somebody somewhere screaming out our opinion, then that's good enough for us. We're simple people. The day-to-day living of our lives should be simple, but it's not. It takes all our energy to get from one day to the next. That's not apathy, that's life, and without it there wouldn't be anything worth screaming about."

"People, *all of the people,* should stand up for what they believe in."

"They do. We do. We . . ."

"Turn around."

" . . . stand up. We just do it different than you."

"Do you mind? Turn around."

"Why? Girl stuff doesn't bother me anymore."

"Well, it bothers me. Turn around."

He sighed, turned, and rolled his eyes heavenward.

"It's darker than a stack of black cats out here," he muttered.

There was some thrashing and crashing in the bushes before she spoke again.

"You know, sometimes I feel . . . all alone. Different. Like I don't fit anywhere," she said in a voice that had a 0.8% alcohol-depressed tone to it. She started zipping up her blue jeans as she waded out of the bushes to stand beside him. "I look different. I act different. I think different. My zipper's jammed." Her arms fell loose at her sides. "I'm a mess. I'm too different. No one will ever want me."

The darkness of a stack of black cats was now a blessing as he grinned and laughed silently. The full moon was at his back as he reached for the top of her unzipped jeans and pulled her closer. He could see the hopelessness in her expression and the moonlight imprisoned in the shadows of her dark eyes.

"You're wasted," he said before turning his attention to fixing her zipper.

"Do you think so? I feel like that sometimes. I don't know why I was even born."

He shook his nearly clear head and tugged the front of her jeans together.

"You're wasted as in drunk, Livy. That's all. Tomorrow you'll go back to being the most unwasted person in this town. Suzie Citizen. The girl most likely to succeed at anything she sets her mind to. You know, if you think it's hard being you, you should try being your friend sometimes. It ain't easy," he said, comparing himself to her and coming up extremely short.

Her forehead landed with a thud against his breastbone.

"You are my friend, aren't you, Brian." It wasn't a question. "You're the best friend I ever had. The best friend anyone could ever ask for."

"I'm a saint. Hold still, I think I got it," he said, blindly dislodging the zipper, the backs of his fingers grazing soft abdomen, the tips touching panties. He clenched his teeth and tried not to think.

"I love you, Brian," she said, wrapping her arms around his neck, pulling him close to hold him tightly against her.

Taken off guard, he released the front of her pants, his hands floundering in the air uncertainly for a second or two before he touched her, his arms curving easily around her body.

He was awash with sharply wonderful and strangely disturbing feelings as he embraced her. He'd been needing to hold her for a long time. He felt comforted, content. He fought the itch to let his hands wander, to palm her nice little ass, to fondle her breasts, to kiss her . . . kiss her as he had that day in the clover field.

"I love you, too, Livy," he said softly, meaning it more than when he said it to his mother, who was the only person in the world he'd ever said it to before that moment. "You're the best thing that's ever happened to me."

She lifted her head from his shoulder to look at him, then nodded. "We'll always be friends. No matter what. Won't we?"

"Always," he said. If he were making this deal with another man, they might shake hands. But he was making this deal with Livy, and it felt like the most natural thing in the world to want to secure it somehow, to write it in blood, carve it in stone, seal it with a kiss.

He reached out and placed the palm of his hand against her left cheek. Her hand shot up automatically to stop him, then hesitated. Slowly she relaxed her hand over his as it covered the mark on her face, the mark that had become part of the night shadows and couldn't be seen by anyone but her. She leaned into the warmth and gentleness and closed her eyes.

"You're the only one who does this to me," she said, as if in awe.

"Does what?"

"Touches me like this."

There was a tightness in his muscles that went beyond sexual tension, beyond anything he was accustomed to—like anger or rage—but it was neither. Pity, maybe, in its most extreme form for those who would forgo any opportunity to touch Livy, to feel the silky softness of her, to get close enough to smell the muted scent of lilacs on her skin—because of the port-wine stain on her face.

"You're easy to touch," he said. "Anyone who can't touch you like this isn't worth shit."

He felt her smile against his palm. Her lips tickled his skin when she muttered, "Now you tell me."

He frowned. "I've been telling you that for years. Since we were kids." He slid his hand to the center of her face and gave her head a playful shove—as if it might shake something loose inside. "You're not as different as you think, Livy," he said, turning to get his bearings in the trees.

She was silent and pensive, her hand still covering her left cheek, as if she were mulling over a new riddle.

He shook his head. How anyone as smart as Livy could be so dumb, he'd never know. She allowed her birthmark to influence so much of her life that it was like a . . . a shadow that followed her everywhere she went. It was her silhouette, her self-image, and only she had the power to make it disappear—by shedding less light on it, by giving it less importance in her life, by not letting it influence the choices she made.

But she did. And so much of what was Livy was because of it. Her empathy for the underdog, the humiliated, the victimized. Her fighting spirit. The disdain she had for physical beauty and the value she set on intelligence, wit, and cunning. She motivated, pushed, browbeat others into doing good and great things, taking none of the credit, staying well away from the front of the room, out of public view. And yet her efforts would have been so much more effective if she'd stepped from the shadows and done them herself.

"Maybe it's you. Maybe the difference is you," he heard her say softly, as if confused—as one might be with a beer-marinated brain.

"Me? Different? You kiddin' me?" he asked, swinging an arm around her shoulders and starting them back toward the party. "Hell, I'm not just different, I'm an original. Larry says I'm just plain weird, which is true enough, I suppose, but personally I prefer to think of myself as unique. Artists should be thought of as unique, don't you think? Weird has such a . . . weird ring to it."

PART TWO

The Hazy Phase

Twelve

S HE WAS FOREVER ribbing him about being late for his own funeral, and he couldn't deny that time had a way of slipping by. But he'd done his share of waiting, too. Sometimes it felt as though he'd wasted half his life waiting for her, twiddling his thumbs while she was off changing things.

He stared out the waiting room window as if there were a view—not the outer wall of the next building, snow melting on the ledge, and pigeon poop. He stared with his mind's eye, into the past, beyond the fog that collected to block out the mundane; that obscured the intensity of a moment; that cast good and bad, laughter and sorrow, in oblique shades of remembrance. Somehow, those early years seemed . . . not so bad, pleasing . . . comfortable maybe.

Of course, not all his reflections were as clear as those formed in good old Tolford. Time seemed to speed up and days disappeared faster after high school. The fog that clouded vast portions of his life in routine humdrum getting-from-one-day-to-the-next living was, for a while, thick with heavy drinking as well.

A shame really. With a great portion of his life already spent, and with life being so short, a man should have at least one outstanding memory for every day he lives. His time should be marked, not just spent.

Finally, a movement in the doorway.

He turned his head to look, realizing in that moment that *she* marked his time. She scribbled on it, defined it, notarized it, catalogued it. Time without her never felt real. It was more like fragmented dreams, long nightmarish episodes that came back to haunt him now and again, but it never felt real.

She was still tall and shapely; time and childbearing hadn't changed that about her. She wore her dark hair short—had now for several years. A matter of convenience, she'd said. She was heavily into convenience these days.

Her eyes were the same. Clear. Deep. Quick. You couldn't see the tiny lines fanning the outside corners unless she smiled.

And when her gaze met his, she did just that. She smiled, scrunching the Telfa dressing taped to her left cheek, deepening the laugh lines he teased her about, telling her he hoped they'd be forever under construction.

There was a softness about her that had come with the intimate understanding of disappointment and heartache. Maturity maybe. Tolerance perhaps. She wasn't as quick to judge anymore. Black and white were still the primary colors of her thinking, but she had also accepted gray as a legitimate tone of consideration. It took less and less to make her happy. Her world was smaller. The battles she chose to fight were carefully selected, achievable, and she led from the front, no longer pushing from behind.

And yet, she was still Livy. Still opinionated, stubborn, and determined. Still deeply empathetic, energetic, and enthusiastic. Still an intelligent, willful pain in the ass. Still his best friend. She was the same . . . but different.

Was he? The same, but different?

He clearly recognized his time impersonating Richie Cunningham—seeking his thrills on Blueberry Hill like everyone else—and he could vaguely recall dropping out, getting laid back, and doing his own thing as a . . . a student of the sixties. But when vast numbers of his generation decided to jump on the fast track to Yuppieville, he had somehow neglected to pick up his ticket. Was there some pivotal point in history when everyone but him switched from drinking beer and smoking Maui Wowie to sipping designer waters and pumping beta endorphins? He couldn't remember. When had it become more fashionable to ban cigarette smoking in restaurants than to ban nuclear weapons? Had he missed the vote to outlaw iceberg lettuce and polyester?

He hadn't changed; everything around him had.

It was as if he'd gotten drunk one night and passed out to whiny sitar music. And when he woke up, everyone had a cellular phone, a Gucci briefcase, and an investment portfolio. Everyone except him, that is.

Of course, Livy was always there. Awake during the whole thing. Living it. Taking it very seriously. Coping. She knew all about it. How and when it all changed. And why. That was her bag, changing things.

That, and coming back to drag him through the next obscure pinhole in time. . . .

She'd thought about closing the door when she left the treatment room, as a symbol of finality; then she left it open.

It wasn't really over. Was anything *ever* really *over*? Done? Finished? Gone? She didn't think so.

In the hallway she passed a nurse, followed by a young woman, a teenager, going in the opposite direction—back toward the treatment room. The girl looked nervous and frightened. The port-wine stain on her face was twice the size of Livy's and involved her right eye.

She fought a peculiar impulse to hug the girl, smiled at her instead. She wanted to tell her not to be afraid, that everything would turn out beautifully. And did she know how *lucky* she was not to have been born thirty years earlier?

She knew better. Pain and fear were difficult to evaluate in other people. Some people suffer every day of their life, while others can't bear the thought of being uncomfortable for more than a minute. Some suffer silently, while others share their pain and fear with anyone who'll listen. And who's to say which man's pain is

worse than another's? Or which is more intense, the lifetime of suffering or the suffering of a lifetime in an isolated moment?

His back was to her when she entered the waiting room. He was
always so easy to spot in a crowd. So tall. So handsome. So quiet
and peaceful.

Well, that's how he looked. Quiet and peaceful. In truth, his appearance and manner were deceptively simple. He was one of those
still-water people. People with unseen currents that run deeper
than anyone who knows them could imagine. Private people with
private joys, private pains, private fears. Personally, she preferred
common folk who let you know who they were, what they were,
and how they felt in no uncertain terms—like herself. But if you
were looking for someone to love you hard and fast; to raft the river
rapids beside you; to be there whether you need him or not; to support you whether you're right or wrong . . . well, then you'd need
someone like Brian.

He turned from the window expectantly, as if he knew she was
standing there. In the few micromoments before he smiled at her,
she identified the look in his eyes. She'd seen it before.

Responsibility with the anticipation of retribution, she called
it.

Damn. She returned his smile, and in her heart she cursed the
devils that plagued him. He'd never traveled calm seas, didn't know
they existed, she supposed. Growing up with three fathers, a step-
sister, a stepbrother, and a small collection of caretakers while his
mother worked; coming of age in the late sixties; surviving the early
seventies and narrowly escaping a bout of disco fever later that
decade. He was then swept away with the rest of the baby boomers
into the world of Young Urban Professionals whose holy grail was
something called The Best. The buying of it, the owning of it, the
using of it, the watching of it, the wearing of it, the cooking of it,
the growing of it, the eating of it, the driving of it—and if you

didn't instinctively know what The Best was ... well, then your boat rocked. A lot.

She had long suspected that it wasn't the constant rocking and bobbing of his boat, the constant changing of Brian's life, that frightened him as much as the not knowing which wave, which change would tip him over again, throw him back into the murky waters of uncertainty and precipitate another struggle to save his own life.

Sometimes the waiting is worse than the trial. She'd heard that somewhere. But only twice in all the time she'd known him had the anticipation and anxiety really gotten to him, causing him to fling himself overboard *before* his boat could be overturned.

Thirteen

FUNDAMENTALLY, what is now called the "youth movement of the sixties" was exactly that. The movement of nearly sixty million Americans from adolescence to adulthood. And when was the last time a large group of Americans did anything quietly?

"Don't say a word," she warned him, crashing against the heavy metal outer door of the Memphis police station as if it were paper, the sound echoing across the chilly stillness of that early morning. It was fall 1968. "Not one word."

"Okay." He skipped down the concrete steps ahead of her. She could see that he was as put out as she was—he didn't feel like talking to her anyway. So, she'd make him talk.

"And don't look at me like that. I hate it when you look at me like that."

"Okay," he said.

Could he tell that she'd gotten up on the wrong side of the jail cell that morning?

"If my parents find out about this, I'll know who told them," she said, the threat in her voice as conspicuous as a mobster's violin case.

He cast her a derisive glance.

Since Dr. Martin Luther King, Jr.'s assassination in April, Memphis had become a hotbed of hippies and hostiles. Livy was in heaven. It wasn't San Francisco, Chicago, or New York, but she was becoming aware that there was enough abject poverty, local government graft, and festering bigotry to walk the legs off a dead mule.

And, of course, there was always the war to shout about.

It was mid-November and she'd already been arrested four times since their parents waved good-bye and sent them off to college. She'd been protesting everything from the cold war and the threat of nuclear annihilation to contaminated air and water, inflation, unemployment, and the double standard between white American males and every other sex and nationality in the Melting Pot.

She and Brian called home once a week to report on their excellent health and the benefits of their fine study habits—and not much more. And adults thought kids were naive!

"Why would I tell your parents? They'd tell my mother and we'd have them *and* Loverboy Larry down on us like sheets at a Klan rally." And as it occurred to him, he added, "Somebody else'll tell them. The cops. Your school. Wait till somebody finds out your old man's a mayor. What if he does decide to run for the state senate?" He shook his head at the thought, then grimaced at her. "I don't think I'm the one you should be worrying about here, Liv."

She made a disgusted noise as she looked about for his car. "Man, I can't believe this town," she said, throwing her safari pouch bag over her shoulder. "They'll arrest you for anything."

"Burning draft cards isn't just anything. It pisses people off," he said, leading her to the parking lot across the street. The sun was just beginning to dawn; the sky was gray and threatening rain. "Not that you had a draft card to burn in the first place," he muttered.

"I will. Someday I will. It's a male-dominated society for now, but not for long. You wait and see." She all but shook a finger at him. "I'd have burnt yours if you'd have given it to me. You should have come and done it yourself."

"Who'd have bailed you out then?"

"Very funny. You've got to stand up for your rights, Carowack. You don't want to go to Vietnam. Make yourself heard. It's not our war. It's . . . ?"

"Yeah, yeah. It's the military-industrial complex and the capi-

talist establishment and . . . whoever. We've been over all this before. It doesn't matter whose war it is. If my student deferment
doesn't hold and I get drafted, I'm the one who's going to have to
decide between going to prison and going to war. Not you. And not
those fast-talking brainiacs you hang out with. Me." He frowned.
"Yesterday, this kid on my team got his notice to report to the draft
board because he wasn't showing up at any of his classes, and he's
failing them all. He says it was because he's been arrested six times
for protesting the war. I'm not giving General Hershey any reason
to go messing around in my files. And I'm not wasting what time I
have left sitting in a jail cell. I've got better things to do."

"Really. Can you remember this one's name?"

"Dorcas," he said, pleased to tell her. Flashbacks of the night before sent enthusiasm growing in his voice—and between his legs,
no doubt. He grinned. "We went at it *all night long,* Livy, I swear to
God. I don't think she even knows the word no."

"You're lucky you didn't kill yourself," she said absently, looking
for his car once again, pretending it was any other Friday morning
and she hadn't just spent the night in jail.

She was wearing a black turtleneck and tights with a short,
thick-belted plaid miniskirt. A long red scarf was tied about her
forehead, the tails hanging long with her hair down the left side of
her face. Very mod. Less fashion conscious, Brian generally stuck to
his bell-bottom jeans and any shirt he could find.

"Well, for a few minutes there, I did think that I'd died and
gone to heaven," he said, motioning to the end of the row of parked
cars, grinning like an idiot. Suddenly he was less annoyed, more
charitable toward her. Clearly, this Dorcas had a way of making him
feel . . . charitable, all over.

She sighed and *tsk*ed her disgust. "We all have to die sometime,
I suppose. I guess I'd rather have you die that way than in Vietnam."

"What way?" he asked, a sly grin coming to his lips. He flung an arm across her shoulder and bent his head to her ear. "In the throes of passion? During hot, wet, screaming . . . *sex?*"

He knew she had a certain . . . disdain for this act she hadn't yet experienced. She sometimes felt like the last virgin on earth—and depending on the day, that made her vastly superior or incredibly inferior as a woman. But for some strange reason, and no matter how she was feeling about it, his constant yammering about sex irritated her like an itch she couldn't scratch. He knew that, too.

"Ya know, Livy, sex is a lot more fun than going to jail. It's cleaner. It's cheaper. It makes you feel fantastic . . . *and* it doesn't go on your permanent record."

"Get away from me," she said, pushing at him. "You've probably got some social disease already. And what if you get some girl pregnant? That'll be pretty permanent, won't it?"

"I'm *very* careful," he said, still grinning.

"Yeah, right. Could we move a little faster, please. I'm going to be late again and Huckaby is a fascist war monger who accuses everyone who's late for his morning class of being in jail the night before . . ."

"I wonder why?"

". . . then wastes the entire period quoting Spiro Agnew and preaching nationalism as a way of life," she said, parting from him to stand on the rider's side of his precious Chevy.

"And what do biology profs know about life anyway, huh?"

He was smirking at her over the hood of the car. She grimaced and rolled her eyes heavenward.

"Can we just go?" she asked, opening the car door—to find nearly every inch of the interior cluttered with partial or complete drawings, art books, an easel, a basketball, painting supplies, and generalized junk.

He shrugged and got in, reaching immediately for one of the two beers he had under a towel on the seat.

"Beer? For breakfast?" she asked, disapproving, clearing out a place on the front seat to sit—part of the ride-with-Brian routine.

He gave a short laugh before tipping the can back and taking the long, quenching drink he'd mindfully postponed until after he'd talked to the cops inside the police station.

"Listen," he said. "While you and your pals get tanked up and wired on coffee or Coke or weird Asian tea some guru recommends, so you can go out and agitate the hell out of the rest of the world, I'll be drinking this for breakfast, lunch, and dinner to insulate myself from *all* of you." He made a broad sweeping motion with the can. "I drink just enough to keep a happy little buzz on all day so *no one* can ruin it for me."

They'd talked about this before, a few weeks earlier, when she commented on the fact that she rarely saw him anymore without a beer in his hand. She knew he'd been . . . experimenting with some of the illegal drugs floating around campus. Most everyone was. And they were everywhere. Even she'd tried smoking a little pot. But Brian didn't enjoy them. He said they were dangerous, that they couldn't be controlled. They scared him. He said there was no telling how much of a drug you were taking in—in smoke, in a pill, or into a vein—nothing you could do once it was in your system but hang on for the ride until it had run its course. He could titrate alcohol—that was the word he used, titrate, like in a chemistry class—and he could tell when he was getting too much and when he hadn't had enough, when to stop drinking and when one more wouldn't make him lose control. Plus, it was legal, he'd added.

At the time, she'd agreed with him and had felt a sense of relief, not knowing for sure how some of the experimental drugs they were being exposed to would affect people. And when Brian said he could handle something, he usually could. But the idea that he was using the alcohol to . . . insulate himself from the rest of the world, when he seemed so isolated already, bothered her, a lot.

She tilted her head to one side and studied him, loving everything she saw in him, wondering if and how she could ever break through to him—or if she should even keep trying. She watched as he fished the keys from his pocket, then hesitate, turning to look at her with a solemn expression.

"Livy, what you're involved in is good. It's right. I admire you for that. But it's also really dangerous. This isn't Tolford. Nobody knows you here. No one's going to cut you any slack. You're going to get hurt." He glanced out the windshield for a second or two before he continued. "And those kids, those people you're hanging out with, they won't care. They'll offer you up as a martyr to the cause if you happen to get shot, and they'll go on without a second thought if you get your head bashed in."

What he was saying was probably true. There was nothing peaceful about the peace rallies or peaceful demonstrations for civil rights in Memphis. During the riots after Dr. King's death, the authorities lost all patience with the First Amendment. They had no understanding and felt no mercy when students or blacks gathered in groups of more than five or six at a time. And if you happened to be both black and against the war—well, it was usually best *not* to be seen alone.

On the other hand, if you were picked up in a police sweep and arrested, and if you were *white*, there was a chance of being bodily removed from the site, possibly hit now and again. But you were rarely beaten senseless and you could feel relatively safe inside the system. For white females, it was even easier. It was no big deal at all. A tense moment or two if a male officer had to search you, but for a worthy cause it was tolerable. Later, your best friend could pay the fifty dollar fine and you could be released into the adult custody of any twenty-three-year-old linguistics student who happened to be in your acquaintance. Simple.

And, of course, all the things your parents didn't know couldn't possibly hurt anyone.

If you hung out with the right people—and she did—free love

and defiance were the order of the day. Mind blowing was the idea that you could be both free loving and violently defiant without being hypocritical. In fact, militant hippies were the ideal in certain factions of the under-thirty population. And if you listened to the news reports every evening, the country was teeming with them.

In reality, they were few and far between, she supposed.

She smiled at Brian. Maybe he was paying more attention than she thought. Maybe he wasn't as insulated or isolated as he liked to pretend. "You worry too much, Carowack. Frankly, I don't know how you can stay uninvolved, but you don't need to worry about me. I'm not going to get hurt."

"How do you know this?" he asked, more than a little frustrated. "What makes you so smart? I have nightmares about having to go out and buy a new black suit for your funeral. One with lapels as wide as my shoulders, and a new tie about ten inches wide."

"Here we go . . ." she said, turning to face the front of the car, which wasn't moving.

"I look like Bozo in this dream. I wake up and my life is still a nightmare. I have to ask my mom for more money, and you know how freaked old Larry gets about the money. He refuses to understand that the scholarship doesn't cover basic living expenses. And as a man, I have certain responsibilities. There's the black suit, of course, and one of those water beds would be real nice. I need a little beer money to relax me enough to broaden my mind . . . a little beer money for two when I'm studying with someone." He grinned briefly at that and went on. "I'm constantly running out of paint and canvas, and let's not forget bail money for . . ."

"Don't I always pay you back?"

". . . Livy who, instead of studying, is out burning draft cards . . ."

"Oh! Look who's talking."

". . . and inciting riots and pissing off every cop in Memphis. They know who you are, you know. They call you 'the one with the mark on her face,' " he said, looking at her, letting her know that her situation was no joke.

"I know. Isn't it great?" She laughed. "It's my hallmark. Finally, it's good for something," she said, wishing again that he'd start the car and take her back to her dorm. She'd lick fire before she ever admitted to hating every second of her night in jail, but if she didn't get a bath soon she'd have to tear her skin off. "It makes organizing so much easier. People come to me now because I'm easy to pick out in a crowd. No more running all over campuses to track people down. They come to *me*."

"Groovy. And think how easy it'll be when the feds come to arrest you. The dean of students will be coming to you too, no doubt, with dismissal papers. It should be interesting to see how you keep your parents from hearing about that one."

"Jesus, Carowack, what is your problem?" she asked, turning on him. "If you're mad because I interrupted your date with . . . with that *Dorcas* person, I'm sorry. Next time I'll use my dime on someone else and you can save your lecture . . . and *that* look."

"What look?"

"The one on your face. Right now. Like you're responsible for me. Like you're going to get in trouble for what I've done. Like you weren't baby-sitting me well enough. I'm not your problem, Brian. I'm my own woman. I can take care of myself."

"Okay. Fine." He jammed the keys into the ignition. "Take care of yourself. Do what you have to do, but next time leave me out of it."

"Fine. I will and . . . I will . . . and I will. Can we go now?"

Livy always did what she felt she had to do. It was part of what made her special to him. It was part of what made her a pain in the ass, too.

Livy. She was as busy as a moth in a mitten that school year of 1968–69. So was he. As official bailsman to the repeat offender,

Olivia Jane Hubbard, he soon began to suspect that he was the only person she knew who had elevated the act of calling home for more money to an art form. He could have taught a level-one class on Basic Creative Lying.

Of course, there was more to Memphis than the police stations. Compared to Tolford . . . well, there was no comparison to Tolford. The size of the city alone was mind numbing and confusing at first. The buildings, the traffic, the masses of people. Elegant mansions and hovels worse than any seen in the countryside around Tolford. Brian loved the museums and the music—great music that could drown out the rock beat of The Doors, Led Zeppelin, Creedence Clearwater Revival, and Blood, Sweat and Tears, on any given night with the slow, moody strains of the blues. Not that he didn't love rock 'n' roll and, of course, the country music he'd grown up with, but the blues were something special. Hell, you might even say he was developing an *eclectic* taste for music. Very educational.

The Mighty Mississippi *was* Memphis and it became part of your life's blood whether you worked its docks or not. Elvis too, you venerated, whether you liked his music or not. He was a home-grown boy who'd done better than good; the only king America had ever recognized and claimed as its own and the biggest single tourist attraction Memphis had. Brian counted himself among the millions who preferred to dream of their son or daughter becoming another Elvis, instead of President of the United States.

Memphis, unlike Tolford, was exciting. There was a dark side that reached far into the daylight hours if you were interested in exposing yourself to it and, on occasion, Brian dallied on the fringes of it.

Nothing he did, however, was as alarming as Livy's activities. Sit-ins and walkouts. Moratoriums and the seizing of public buildings. Marches and strikes. Next to the sort of things Livy was doing, filtering college life through seedy bars, shady acquaintances, and several pitchers of beer was more like child's play.

Livy. She was so serious. So dedicated.

She was absorbed in a list of carbon-based chemicals she needed to know by the next day. Shortly after Christmas, they were well into their second semester.

"So, how's your roommate?"

"Recovering nicely," she said, with a sidelong glare in his direction. He pretended to be engrossed in a drawing of the intersection of Goodlett Street and Southern Avenue—detailing, his favorite part. "And I'll thank you not to date her again. Or any of my other friends either. Girls talk, you know." She squirmed in her chair a little. "I admit, I gossip as much as anybody but I don't think it's necessary to discuss, to death, certain things about certain people, and I'm sick of getting blow-by-blow descriptions of *your* dates from *my* friends."

There were so many chinks in Livy's armor she could have used it as a sieve. But it wasn't every day that a body found one that was as irrational and unfounded as the one she had about sex. If she hadn't been the one to explain it to him in the first place, he might have thought her shy about it, or embarrassed maybe. But it wasn't the general topic of sex that made her squirm—it was *him* having sex that made her uncomfortable. And so, of course, he teased her with it every chance he got, which was whenever they were together.

"I'll bet you are sick of it." He grinned broadly. "But at least it's not me telling you how great I am all the time. Maybe now you'll believe me."

"You're such a *pig*." She endeavored to put a feminist sting in the tone of her voice, but it came out amused, affectionate and . . . a lot like a compliment, this time.

He laughed. He was having altogether too much fun at college. Big city. Campus life. Beer and like-thinkers everywhere he turned. Livy had no idea what she was missing.

"Have you even opened a book this semester?"

"Sure." He tossed the sketch pad aside and picked up a basketball with one hand, then started to spin it on his index finger. "I was reading a book when you called."

"Right." She studied him with narrowed eyes. She knew him too well. "Did the center page have a colored fold-out?"

The ball slipped off his finger. "I met this unreal girl from one of the sorority houses yesterday, but I couldn't remember which one." He glanced at her. "I was . . . refreshing my memory."

"You're going to have to study more than the campus phone book if you're planning to keep your scholarship and stay in school, Carowack." A pause. "You know, women aren't the suckers they used to be for a guy in a uniform."

"Yes, mother," he said, turning his attention back to the spinning orb.

"I'm serious."

"I know, and despite the damper you tend to put on things, I'm really glad you called. I've missed you. Have you got so many snooty new friends now that you don't need me anymore?"

Again, they found themselves living in completely different worlds, separated by a remarkably short distance. A ten minute drive through town was all it took to get from the devoutly academic, very highbrow, preppie-infested private institution of higher education—Southwestern at Memphis where Livy worked up a brain-sweat over every little quiz and question—to Memphis State University where you could obtain an excellent education . . . or not, depending on your propensity to party.

Brian's propensity was off the chart.

The first few weeks of school had been hard, confusing, and lonely for them both. Coed and open dorms were more the thing on the freer-thinking Memphis State Campus, and Brian had quickly adjusted to Livy's frequent evening visits to his room. At first they had talked, compared their experiences, shared their feelings. As they became more comfortable, they talked less and simply spent the time together—Livy studying ardently, Brian daydreaming over an open book or sketching furiously.

By midterm they were introducing each other to new friends, double-dating on occasion—in Livy's case, it was more like running an escort service for one. Brian. But they began to meet people they had things in common with, certainly more in common than they had with each other. Athletes and activists. Artists and writers. Party people and political science majors.

They were, as always, home-safe for one another—a familiar voice a phone call away, a trusted face when they needed one. But Memphis was a big place; the rest of the world was even bigger, and for the first time ever, they were truly free.

"My snooty friends aren't as snooty as you think and what makes you think I *ever* needed you?" she asked. A fatuous question since they both knew the answer. They ignored it.

"You were the one who said they were snooty. I was amazed at how many of them were pretty. I was the one who figured they'd all be rich little bow-wows, remember? Doesn't seem fair, does it?"

"Doesn't seem to bother you much, either."

He chuckled. "No way. Why should it? Soft talkin', sweet smellin', sex wantin' stunners have a right to be as rich and as smart as they want to be. It's the American way."

She shook her head. He was hopeless. And he liked it that way. Whenever he could manage it, he was completely carefree and unconcerned.

"Brian." She closed the book and slid it into the mess of debris that covered his rarely used desk.

When she turned to face him, he smiled at her and sighed. Her face never changed. It was one of a handful of faces that he loved and trusted above all others. It was a beautiful face.

"Spit it out, Liv," he said when she hesitated. "I got practice in half an hour."

"Well, I was wondering how you'd feel about living off campus next fall."

He laughed. "After I flunk out of school, you mean? Your faith in me is inspiring, but if I get kicked out of MSU I won't be hanging around." He bounced the ball off the wall a couple of times. "I'll bum around the country for a while, like I should have done in the first place. Europe, too, maybe, and paint."

When he glanced over to catch her reaction, she was staring at him.

"You have it all planned out, don't you?" He could tell she was a little stunned. "You're not really flunking out, are you?"

"Maybe not this semester, but it seems inevitable. School just isn't my bag, babe." He paused. "You look surprised. I thought you were expecting me to drop out."

"Of course I'm not expecting you to drop out. You're smart. You can do anything you set your mind to. I . . . well, I just didn't think you'd be setting it to flunking out of school, is all."

"Then what's this about living off campus?" He gestured about the cramped and cluttered 11×13 dorm room he shared with another basketball player. "Why else would I want to give up such splendor?"

"I can see where the choice might come to a flip of a coin, but I was actually thinking of taking a house off campus. If you and I and a couple other kids pool our money, we could afford it."

"What other kids?" he asked, skilled at sensing when something was too good to be real.

"It's a big house. Five people live there already, but two are leaving. There'll be room for us next semester."

"What other kids?"

"Alben Hollender. He's MSU. You met him a few weeks ago, at that Dixie place with the blues music? On Beale Street? Remember? We went in for a beer and . . ."

"And you didn't have your ID with you and had to leave. Was he the black dude with the eight inch Afro and the glasses?"

She nodded. "And Stephanie Pence. She's a junior at Southwestern. She practically runs SCAW single-handedly."

"SCAW?" It rang a bell, but there were so many abbreviations to remember in college. NAACP, FSM, CIA, NLF, FBI, KKK, UN, LSD, VDC, AFL-CIO, SNCC, HUD, SLA, SCLC, VC, BPP, GOP, and Ho Chi Minh. Nobody was speaking basic southern English anymore. Except for the NBA and the NFL.

"The Student Coalition Against War. I told you about the national network it's setting up to unify our strength? Like National Turn In Your Draft Card Day? Remember?"

Vividly. He'd been with . . . ? when Livy called from jail. What was that girl's name? A forty-six-inch chest and blond hair. D something. Doris? Daphne? Darlene? Dena?

"And the Free Huey campaign?" she went on. "We need solidarity. The bigger we are, the louder we are and the sooner someone will listen to us."

"In other words, this Stephanie isn't my type," he said. Dolores? Dinah? Dodie? Darcy? What the hell was that girl's name?

"Well, no. She has a brain and a flat chest so you wouldn't really be interested, but that's the beauty of this place. It's purely platonic. No messy love affairs. No sex. Just five people sharing a house."

"No sex, huh?" To annoy her, he made it sound discouraging. "So who's this fifth person?"

"Oh." She pretended to feel foolish at the omission. "Richard. Richard Kerrigan. He's . . . Brian, he's so wonderful. He put together the *Freedom Express*, the *un*authorized campus newspaper I want to write for. Remember? I showed you a copy. The administration is calling it an *underground* newspaper," she said, like a true conspirator. "Wait till you hear him speak. He has . . ."

"Short blonde hair and thick black sideburns?"

"Yes."

"Does he know how weird that looks?"

"It's the sun," she said, a bit impatient. There were so many more interesting things to say about Richard. "It bleaches his hair in the summertime, takes almost all winter to grow out. By spring his hair will be closer to the color of his sideburns, but then it'll bleach out over the summer again. But it's so much more than the way he looks. He has charisma."

"Charisma? Is that what you call it?" He dropped the basketball on the floor and sat up on the edge of the bed to finish off his near-warm beer. Smuggling alcoholic beverages into the dorm was a huge drag, so he never wasted a drop of it. "Isn't he the one who was screaming and yelling in front of *our* Ad-building, about the CIA secretly funding certain organizations in education and . . . law, I think he said, and journalism, too, for their support of the war? He looked a little crazy to me. And why doesn't he do his screaming on his own campus?"

"There are more kids over here and he's not crazy. He's passionate. He's deeply committed to civil rights and putting an end to the war."

Brian nodded. "Great. That's really great, but I don't think I want to live with anyone that passionate or that committed. I might have to tie him up and gag him if he talks like that all the time. He might not think I was very . . . platonic."

"But everything he says is true. There's proof."

"Okay. But he still doesn't have to scream and yell. Couldn't he just state the facts? Calmly. It made me nervous just watching him. Wouldn't more people listen if he acted a little less crazy?"

She leaned back in the chair, looking at him.

"You know, I thought so too, at first. But Richard says there's too much apathy. He says he's like an actor, that he has to be outrageous to get people's attention."

He stood up and started looking for his coat. It was almost time to leave.

"He's outrageous, all right." He zipped up the front of his jacket and then looked at her. "Trading Bubba Du Bois for your friend Richard feels like a step down in roomies to me, Liv."

"But if you don't do it with me, I won't be able to," she said. "Sophomores have to live in the dorms unless they have permission from their parents. I don't think mine will go for it unless I tell them you'll be there with me."

"Livy . . ."

Fourteen

THE TWO-STORY HOUSE on Highland Street was conveniently located about halfway between the MSU and Southwestern campuses. That was probably the only good thing about it.

Talking Brian . . . well, nagging, really . . . okay, badgering Brian into that move was a huge mistake.

"Please stop calling Richard dickhead."

"Is asshole better?" He slammed his bedroom door in her face. The windows rattled. She sighed, took another deep breath, and quietly let herself into his room.

Brian's room was . . . so Brian. Everything he owned was scrambled and tossed around the room. She could feel the blush in her cheeks every time she entered it—and it had nothing to do with the mess. He'd been painting the walls since the day they'd moved, almost two months earlier. Not baby blue or sunflower yellow or fanatically fuchsia or deeply depressed black. He'd been *painting* them. There were nude women everywhere. Most were charcoal renderings of MSU girls, but there were several acrylic portrayals she recognized as classmates at Southwestern—and two she knew by name! Coyly looking over their shoulders, draping themselves in chairs, lounging suggestively all over his walls—images *she* didn't need in her head when she sat next to them in class.

Irksome was the fact that it had become something akin to winning a Nobel Prize to have your body rendered on Brian Carowack's bedroom walls that year. Well, that and his talent for detail were both infuriating.

She crossed the room silently and sat down on his rumpled bed. The whole place smelled like turpentine and Brut cologne. He watched her, rocking backward on two legs of his chair, never hitting the wall behind him.

"I hate that guy."

"No kidding. Any specific reason?"

He glanced away. "No. I hate everything about him, equally."

If this clash were between anyone but Richard and Brian, she could have ignored it—might have enjoyed it as she'd rarely seen Brian impassioned about anything but art before. But it was Richard whom she felt in her bones, and in her heart, was destined to become one of America's great leaders, and Brian who hadn't truly disliked anyone since Donny Moore in first grade. Something about it felt very wrong.

People person described them both. Richard reaching out with his words, stirring minds and hearts with his beliefs, instilling the courage and the strength to fight for their convictions. Brian quietly taking them into his heart, cherishing their spirit, admiring their form, loving the expressions on their faces.

"Richard likes you," she said, appealing to his conscience. "He thinks you're extremely talented."

"He thinks I'm an idiot. He thinks he can use his vocabulary of fancy four-syllable words to talk in circles. He thinks he can say anything he wants and people will believe him. And the sad thing is, some of them do."

Moments ago he'd said pretty much the same thing to Richard's face, only he'd been more accusing and his language had been far more colorful.

"We're all entitled to an opinion, Brian."

"Do not," he said, standing up, "condescend to me. That's his trick. Talk to me like a person, like you used to. Tell me you believe all that shit he's serving about the government using the war as a means of black genocide. Tell me you believe him."

"Statistically . . ."

"Not statistically. Sincerely. Do you believe in your heart that it's true?"

She lowered her eyes to the floor. "I don't know. I hope not."

He was silent for several minutes. Hoping, too, she supposed.

"America isn't perfect. Nothing's perfect. The government sucks sometimes. But it's the people in this country that make up the government, and aren't there more good people here than bad?" He paced two steps forward and back again. "Hasn't it done some good? Ever? Anywhere? Where else in the world can you tell the government when it's gotten off track, when it's doing things we don't approve of, and hope for change. *Expect* it to change. God, Livy, what happens if we stop believing? What happens if we really think that the people who run this country are capable of the mass murder of thousands and thousands of black men?" A horrible quiet. "If you believe it's possible, then there is no hope for this country. Blacks will never be equal. The war will go on forever. The environment will be destroyed. We'll starve and die."

Brian was no speech maker, never had been. But when he had something to say, he really said it.

"I'm sorry, Livy," he said, sitting down in the chair once more. "I know you think he might be another JFK, but I think he and his newspaper are full of shit."

No one could be another JFK, but Richard was unquestionably someone special. People listened to him. They read what he wrote in the *Freedom Express,* quoted him all the time. Given time, Brian would see it, too. Her smile was small and lopsided.

"Think we can set up a DMZ in the living room where nobody discusses politics or religion?"

He looked at her, amusement warming the chill in his eyes.

"Like we talk politics in the kitchen only, civil rights in the dining room, ecology in the front foyer, equal rights for women in the big bathroom downstairs, and . . . we plan sex in the living room?"

"No sex in the living room."

"Movies and music then."

She laughed. "He really does like you, you know."

"He really pretends to . . . for you. If he thought he could swing it, he'd stick a bow on my nose and present me to the Marines."

"Oh, Brian." She would never believe that.

It took some time, but a strained agreement to cordially disregard one another was as friendly as Brian and Richard ever got.

Brian and Alben Hollender were another story. Not only were they both MSU students, they shared a deep appreciation for college nightlife and the sexual revolution.

Alben, however, was also closely involved with Richard's antiwar activities. He knew people. All sorts of people. Brian said he could charm the scales off a snake. Much of what he did for Richard had to do with money, for the newspaper mostly, and Alben didn't talk about it much—which was fine with Brian—but it also made him something of a mystery.

By his own design, Alben slept in the only bedroom on the first floor. For quick escapes, he'd said. She'd thought he was joking at first, but as time went by she came to believe that he did feel safer close to the ground.

As for Stephanie with her wire-rimmed glasses and toothy smile, she was indeed not Brian's type, but he seemed to have a certain fondness for her.

"Steph! Spell resipsaloquitur," he'd call from wherever he was at the time.

"What?"

"Res ipsa loquitur. Three words. Latin." A pause. "You know, somehow it seems fitting that the American legal system still adheres to a dead language."

She'd try to spell his word-of-the-day—painstakingly chosen from a legal dictionary he'd stolen from the law library specifically for this game—and sometimes succeed, pleasing him entirely.

But if she couldn't . . .

"Good try, but it's r-e-s i-p-s-a l-o-q-u-i-t-u-r. Got it? My mom used to make me write my misspelled words twenty times each. That worked pretty well. And you should keep a list for quick reference. If you're going to law school, you're going to need to know this stuff. They say presentation is about 99 percent of it. Here, I wrote down the definition, too."

His calling her Steph had made her shudder at first, but she got used to it, and if the truth were known, Livy always had the feeling that Brian was exactly Stephanie's type, despite his lack of ambition, old family name, and money.

Long into the night she would hear the two of them talking—God only knew what about, they had so little in common. And shortly after Valentine's Day that year, he painted her portrait—with clothes—as an anniversary gift for her parents later that summer.

Stephanie's function in the house was clear. To use her brilliant mind to advise Richard on local, state, and government legalities involving his antiwar activities; to explain procedures; to keep him updated on issues he may have overlooked, and in general, to be his second brain.

The house on Highland Street could have been a campaign headquarters. In fact, it reminded her a lot of her days as a volunteer with Senator Gore's campaign. Lots of planning. Lots of busyness. Lots of tension. Between school and the house on Highland Street she often felt like a cross-eyed boy at a three-ring circus—and she loved every minute of it.

But (and it was a big *but* at the time) she couldn't help wondering why she had been invited to move in.

"Are you kidding?" Brian was amused by her ignorance. He'd wandered into her room looking for a pen—as if he might study if he had one—and caught her deep in thought. Janis Joplin was playing on her eight-track stereo tape player; she loved that hoarse, raspy voice of hers. "Livy, people follow you like a tail on a comet.

Your enthusiasm for a cause is contagious. It always has been. Your eyes . . . the way you talk about it . . ."

"In Tolford, maybe. But I'm a lowly student here, like everyone else. A nobody. No one listens to a sophomore journalism major."

"They listen to you. You know they do. Every time you say something about Richard, one more person will listen to him. And if they get tired of his ranting, they'll still come back to hear what you have to say. Hell, every time he opens his mouth it's almost verbatim from the articles you write for the paper—on the war, on racism, on . . ."

"I don't write them alone. Stephanie and Alben . . ."

"Stephanie and Alben are like . . . like reference books. Brilliant and street smart. You're the one that makes sense of it. You string the words together. The words are yours, Livy. The sincerity is yours. The energy is yours. I'm here to keep your parents happy. You're here because Richard needs you."

She laughed. "Richard doesn't need me. Richard's . . ." She stopped to search for eloquent words.

"Richard's a hot-air balloon. Without you to fill him full of gas, he'd fall flat."

"No. I . . . don't be so . . ."

"Yes." He looked her straight in the eyes, his certainty as clear as his concerns. "Watch him, Livy. Listen to him. Think about what he says. Don't . . ." He stopped and looked away.

"What?"

He sighed. "Don't let what you want to see cloud what really is."

She leaned back on one elbow and drew her legs up on the bed. She considered him for several moments before saying, "You know, Psych 101 has made you very insightful. Higher learning is rubbing off on you whether you want it to or not, isn't it?"

He sighed and gave her a closed-lip grin. Their long friendship shone deep in his eyes.

"Just be careful. Richard isn't the only one around here who needs you." He stood to leave, offering her one last endearment. "Smartass."

She watched him snag a pen from her desk, walk across the hall, and close his bedroom door.

The very idea that someone like Richard could actually need someone like her was . . . well, pretty damned thrilling. Of course, there was a vast distinction between needing someone's thoughts and ideas, and being attracted to her as a person. As a woman. But if one were possible . . . the other wasn't *impossible*. Right?

Platonic. Platonic, she reminded herself, falling back on the bed. Her relationship with Richard thrived on a higher cause. Right?

Come to think of it, Richard hadn't had time for any personal, intimate relationships either. She'd have noticed if any of the girls he had long discussions with spent the night. Lots of girls fawned over him, perhaps he was too preoccupied to notice. Then again, he didn't need other girls the way he needed her. What was it Brian said? "Without you to fill him full of gas . . ."

Maybe Richard needed her more than she'd realized. She wasn't the sharpest knife in the drawer when it came to picking up on these things. God, she'd actually thought herself in love with Brian once! Maybe that's what Brian was picking up on and reacting to— he'd never been too happy with the guys who showed an interest in her or the guys she choose to date. He was worse than a big brother.

What if Richard was as attracted to her as she was to him and she hadn't noticed?

Historically, the Age of Aquarius came to light with the discovery of the planet Uranus in 1784. The Industrial Revolution was taking place in Europe and drastic changes were affecting essentially all spheres of life. Astrologers say Aquarius rules Uranus, that its key word is change (usually disruptive or sudden), and that the planet is frequently associated with dramatic, unexpected events. They

said the coming of the Age of Aquarius would be a time of great scientific expansion and of humanitarian deeds, that it would be an
astronomical phenomenon related to the complexities of the
earth's motion, and that it would have an effect on every member
of the zodiac.

Brian figured that was as good an explanation for the state of
world affairs as any he'd come across so far. The Fifth Dimension
was right on, man—a little idealistic perhaps, but as far as phenomenal explanations went, how far off could they be?

"No. It has two *i*'s," he told Stephanie, handing her the correct
spelling and the gruesome definition of the words, *disjecta
membra*—scattered remains or parts or limbs. "It's pretty gory, but
the way things are going you'll probably need that one. A lot."

Livy, making a sandwich, turned from the counter to read the
definition over Stephanie's shoulder and grimaced. She looked at
him, narrowing her eyes.

"Are you growing a beard?"

"And a mustache," he said, preening.

"That might be a mistake, you know," was all she said. She
turned to finish making her meal.

Being the sole jock in the house, the only thing he had in common with the preppies from Southwestern—like Richard and his
pals—was unfashionably short hair. He was aiming to nix that sim-
ilarity right away. Despite his coach's objections, and the unfair
rules against it.

"Larry's not going to like it either," she added, shaking her
head. She'd been with Brian when he saw the sign posted in the
drugstore window over Christmas vacation. It read: *Keep America
Clean. Get a Haircut.*

"I know," he said with a devilish grin. "I've been thinking about
asking for a hair dryer for my birthday. Or maybe a mink coat like
Joe Namath's."

Larry wasn't an all-bad guy. Actually, he was pretty okay. He was good to Brian's mom and to Beth. He and the new baby Bobby shared this thing for fire engines. And he kept *trying* to understand Brian. He wasn't an all-bad stepdad. He was just so . . . uptight.

"I like your hair," Stephanie said, her voice soft and shy, extremely unlawyerly. That was what Brian liked best about her. She was the most unlikely prelaw student ever born. Small, quiet, mousy. Clever and thoughtful. She was going to be the most lethal criminal attorney in the country someday—or the world's greatest failure. Either way, he liked her.

He grinned and winked at her for the compliment, then watched her blush. It was the rare woman, indeed, who wasn't fall-down stupid for him.

"I do, too. I like it," Livy said, also watching Stephanie turn pink, but with much less appreciation. "You look like one of the twelve apostles. Next thing we know, you'll be walking on water."

His brows rose in astonishment. "You mean you haven't heard about that yet? Last Thursday night. After the supper." Stephanie giggled. "No one was more surprised than I was."

"What were you on?" she asked, close to enjoying his blasphemy, but reluctant to miss an opportunity to point out his faults. She had one hand on her hip, the other hand clasped about a mustard-coated knife.

Livy wasn't what you'd call a real drinker. She'd drink a few beers now and again to mellow out, but no more. Anything powdered, pilled, or crystallized made her nervous and she wouldn't even try it, which was fine by him. She didn't like that he drank so much, though, but she rarely said anything if he did. To do so would have been very uncool, what with everyone doing their own thing and all. However, she did, on occasion, read him articles on the permanent physical damages caused by alcohol—and now that he was smoking cigarettes, nicotine. Clip them out of magazines and tape them to his door—just to keep him abreast of things.

"Straight incense and holy water. I was practically sober," he said, taking the knife from her. He spread mustard yellow on whole wheat brown and finished the sandwich. Picked it up and ate it, too. Livy punched him.

"What? It's Friday night. Relax. Fix yourself some real food for a change. Try eating in a sitting position. What's your hurry? You got a boat to catch . . . or another hot all-nighter with the *Freedom Express*?"

"It shouldn't be all night," she said, her thoughts already on the article she wanted to finish. She took two more slices of bread from the bag and started another sandwich. "Richard needs the article I'm doing on Kleindienst and his repression of 'ideological criminals.' Can you believe that guy? 'When you see an epidemic like this cropping up all over the country—the same kind of people saying the same kinds of things—you begin to get the picture that it is a national subversive activity,' " she quoted the assistant attorney general. "If he'd take another look at the picture, he'd see that the same people saying the same things are the same people who have to go fight a war that has nothing to do with them. If it's epidemic, maybe someone should listen."

"Isn't she cute when she's mad?" Brian mumbled around the sandwich to Stephanie, who giggled on cue. "My favorite is her Betty Friedan speech about defining human personality and destiny in terms of sex organs." He swallowed. "Brings tears to my eyes every time."

"Don't laugh at him, Stephanie," she said, slapping her sandwich together. "He's pathetic. He sees women as good for only one thing. He uses women. And he's going to be so sorry one of these days."

"What are you talking about? I love women," he said, his eyes twinkling merrily.

Livy rose to the bait every time. It never seemed to matter that he'd spent the greater part of his life listening to her, respecting her opinions, believing in her capabilities, supporting her interests, and

regarding her not only as his equal, but in many ways vastly superior to himself. He enjoyed sex with females who enjoyed sex;
therefore he was a chauvinist pig.

He could live with it.

"Love women? You?" She made a sputtering noise, saw the
laughter in his eyes, and closed her mouth tight. She flipped her
long hair over her shoulder with a movement of her head that was
nothing if not scornful, and grabbed up the leather bag she carried
her life around in. "I am not going to discuss this with you again,
Brian Carowack. You don't take the women's movement seriously.
You don't take anything seriously. Not even your art. You are so talented, and you take it for granted. It's just something you can do.
Something else you're good at. Well, take a look around, pal. This
isn't high school anymore. It's not going to be basketball and getting laid forever. It's time to grow up."

He watched her stomp off, heard the front door slam seconds
later. He glanced at Stephanie, who couldn't or wouldn't meet his
gaze, and slouched back in the chair, disgruntled. Mostly with himself.

He hated it when Livy was mad at him. More, he hated that she
thought he didn't care. He did care. Well, not about the women's
movement perhaps, but other things. Huge things that he felt he
had no control over. Terrifying things that were threatening to suck
him in, chew him up, and swallow him. Little things that seemed
far beyond his reach. Noble things he was afraid would never be
his.

And so he laughed, when he should have been crying. He drank
when he should have been shrieking at the world. He floated down-
stream like a leaf on a current, making no waves, causing no trouble. He pretended to be invisible, slipping from one day to the next
without being seen, trying to go unnoticed by the dangers that
awaited him, praying they'd move on without him.

He read somewhere that a moment of insanity was all that separated a hero from a coward. He called his madness surviving.

No social disorder in the world could affect college parties. But even better than a party was *hanging out.* Hanging out was a party for no special reason, without a theme, without invitations, with no preparations necessary, no time limits observed, no etiquette expected. You could hang out alone, but for party purposes, two or more was better. You could hang out at one place for a while, leave, hang out somewhere else, and come back. As far as Brian knew, there never were any set rules to hanging out.

And so it was that night, late in March of 1970, almost spring but still bitterly cold at night. He returned to the house on Highland Street to find a few more people than he'd left there two or three hours earlier. Somebody had *Switched-on Bach*—Walter Carlos with a Moog synthesizer—and neglected to open any windows. He could have gotten high on the second-hand smoke—if he hadn't been in flight already.

It was still early, a little after midnight maybe. He was sleepy but still willing to hang out if anyone else was so inclined, which didn't appear to be the case at first. He roamed through the dining room and kitchen first, spotting sleepers in dark corners and a small group of serious-minded political types deep in discussion. Yawn.

He took a cold beer from his hiding place in the wood bin on the back porch and continued through the house, looking for a familiar face. By the time he slouched down beside an unattended brunette on the couch, he'd come to realize that he knew only two or three people by name, and half a dozen more by sight. The rest were strangers . . . including the brunette.

"Hi." One syllable, and she slurred it.

"Hi."

"Far out."

"Yep."

"Man . . ."

"I know."

Ordinarily, he might have considered a dialogue on lost civilizations and attempted utopias with this girl, but he wasn't in the mood. He slid to the floor, his back against the couch, and closed his eyes, his mind ambiguously associating danger with the burning candles all around the room.

The music had changed. Something bluesy. Something W. C. Handy, he thought. He revered the man's talent and let his music carry him into the shadows of life, where souls speak and hearts listen. He grew peaceful and drowsy, his mind slipping below the music, catching bits and pieces of murmured conversation around him—a soft laugh, pleasured throaty noises, the unmistakable sounds of a love struggle . . . and Livy.

He opened his eyes, but he didn't move. Richard came first, picking his way carefully around and over their languid guests, leading Livy to the center of the room and the coffee table littered with empty bottles and overflowing ashtrays and a small array of pharmaceutical party supplies that could be had for the taking.

"Whoops! Sorry," she whispered loudly to an inert form at her feet. She giggled, through her nose. "Where did all these people come from," she asked in the same soft-loud voice. "I don't think I know any of them. Hi! Who are you? Whoops!"

Livy was lit. He hadn't been around for a few days, so it was good to see her. They hadn't talked about the night she blew up at him, but he knew she wasn't mad anymore. She never stayed mad at him.

"Richard," she called faintly. "Do you see any Coke in here? I could sure use a Coke. I'll drink anything, but I sure could use a Coke. Do you see any in here? Whoops! Sorry. Do I know you?"

Richard hushed her, pulling her down to sit on the floor beside him—six or eight feet from Brian. They kissed.

That's when he should have gotten up and ripped Richard's

head off, but he didn't. He couldn't. Stone-drunk had taken on a dual meaning. He was stoned and he was a stone. He felt like a stone. Through the slits of his eyes, he watched. Disgusted and fascinated at once. He knew what it was to kiss Livy; his body remembered. She looped an arm around Richard's neck and Brian's heart skipped erratically. She pressed herself against him—Brian could feel that, too. Richard murmured in her ear and Brian's mind filled with the scent of lilacs.

His body grew hard and taut as he watched them. Richard's hands inside her sweater, Livy feebly halting their progress.

If for one second she appeared frightened or angry, Brian was sure he could have broken through the heavy, stony paralysis to kill Richard. But she didn't. She kissed him again and again. Held him close. Smiled at him.

She pulled his hand out from under her skirt and whispered something in his ear. She laughed quietly in response to his reply, then let him pass the open end of a Jack Daniels bottle from his lips to hers.

With the eyes of a man who had been there before, Brian watched as Richard helped Livy get fried to the gills. She became more and more relaxed, babbled cheerfully, kissed passionately.

In a moment he would regret forever, he faked sleep when he heard her say, "Wait. Wait a second. Is that . . . is that my Brian there? Pisssssst. Pissssst. Brian?" Richard shushed her, trying to kiss her again. "Out cold," she determined, then giggled. "Have I ever told you how much I love that guy?" She sighed happily as he laid her back on the floor. "Did you see those way cool posters he made for the Earth Day celebration next month? He *hates* doing that kind of stuff. But he did it. Without me asking him to . . . even. He's the best friend I ever had. The very best. I love him," she said between Richard's kisses. "More than anybody in the whole wide world." Her arms flopped wide to demonstrate the present size of her world, and Richard promptly filled the space with his body, covering hers, blocking her from sight.

Brian felt cold all over. Nausea pooled at the back of his throat and still he didn't move. Couldn't move. His body began to ache from the tension. His chest felt tight around his lungs; he could barely breathe. His mind drifted deeper and deeper into the stone-like state, refusing to acknowledge the pain and anger he had no right to feel, attempting to dull the tremendous sorrow in his soul. He closed his eyes tight, wishing for the past, wishing for the time when he was the closest man to her heart.

He couldn't look at them anymore. Wouldn't. He could tell by the sounds they were making that Richard was already spent. Livy was no longer a virgin and a heart-shattering wail rose up within him. He pressed his lips tight, biting down on them with his teeth. His chin quivered. A tear rolled down his right cheek.

It was in the silence that followed, with only the sweet, sad music to cling to, that his wretched soul finally spoke the truth and his miserable heart listened.

He loved her. He'd always loved her—from the very beginning. He began to tremble as if shivering with cold. Chills ran riot over his body. His mouth was full of saliva, he swallowed hard, and it was full once again. It was salty. He really was going to throw up this time.

He rolled to one side, staggering to his feet, tripping once or twice on his way to the bathroom.

He was in love. With Livy. He'd always been in love with her. She was everything to him. He hurled food he ate before Christmas into the toilet, then wished he could die. He was in love with Livy.

Ah, man, couldn't he ever do anything right? Just once? Would he ever be normal? Why was he continually picking the impossible roads to nowhere? Plumbers were normal—a regular paycheck, a house, a wife, 3.5 children. That was normal. Whoever heard of a normal man falling in love with his best friend? Normal men had men friends and fell in love with strange women . . . well, women they hadn't spent their entire life with anyway. Livy would never love him . . . not this way . . . not like this. Ah, man, he was really screwed now.

It was difficult to tell how long he lay there, talking to the toilet, feeling like the biggest fool in the world. But there he was when the doorknob rattled and there he stayed to watch Livy peek inside at him.

"Oh. Hi," she said. "Sorry. I didn't know anyone was . . . are you all right? You look pale."

"Too much fun."

Her smile was small. "Me, too," she said, stepping inside and closing the door. He made an effort to move and give her room at the commode. "No, no. I'm not sick. I . . . wish I was."

This time he lifted his head off the floor to look at her. She too was pale, and she might have been crying. He scooted into a sitting position, resting his back against the wall.

"Are you all right?" he asked, his heart twisting painfully.

"Sure. Just tired," she said, wetting two washcloths with cold water. She wrung them out, tossed him one, and applied the other to her face. "Got a headache."

"Me, too," he said. And a heartache she'd never believe, he thought. He had a deranged moment of amusement at the thought of telling her. Not only would she laugh at him, she'd carve his chauvinist ass into pork chops—fry him up and serve him at an ERA meeting.

There was no way it could ever work out between them.

"How, ah, how long have you been awake?" she asked. She couldn't look him in the eye, he noticed. Did she think he'd see in her eyes that she was different? Would she care if he could? Did he care that she was?

Yes.

Ironic, wasn't it? He could have sex with a thousand women

and she wouldn't care. She makes love once and it feels like the end of the world to him.

"What's so funny?" she asked at his chuckle.

"I feel like I've been asleep forever."

She nodded, staring at the linoleum floor. Her legs and feet were bare. He wondered about her underpants, where they were, then squeezed his eyes closed, feeling shame. She didn't look happy. He'd only been with one virgin, Cathy Dixon, and couldn't recollect much of what happened afterward. He wasn't sure about a girl's first time. He'd been ecstatic as he recalled.

"I'm as dry as a wool sock," he said suddenly. "Wanna Coke?" She looked up and nodded at him. "Got any money?" She shook her head. "Okay," he said, using his feet to push himself up the wall. "Get your shoes and a coat and meet me at the front door."

Knowing where she'd have to go to get her shoes, he took the stairs two at a time to the second floor to use the phone extension Richard had hot-wired into his room. He checked the rest of the bedrooms for sleeping roommates, found none, and returned to the first floor. Livy was waiting at the door.

He rolled his eyes like the village idiot and told her his coat was in the living room, and it was. So was Richard, passed out cold. Without ceremony, Brian rolled him face down on the carpet and removed the wallet from his back pocket.

"The least you could do is buy the girl a Coke, you dumb fuck." He took a fiver, and a second look at Richard convinced him to help himself to the remaining twenty as well. "I'm going to need gas, too."

Dropping the wallet, he hurried away to get Livy out of the house.

Funny thing about that night . . . While Livy might have taken her Coke home and to bed, Brian still had some hanging out to do. He took her to meet what he called "some gentle souls"—back-to-nature hippies who were intense in their efforts to return to Mother

Earth, weaving and sewing their own clothes, growing their own food, educating their own children, creating their own barter system. They listened to the planning of a commune in the Pacific Northwest until nearly dawn, when Livy fell asleep with her head on Brian's lap.

Meanwhile, back at the house on Highland Street, not fifteen minutes after they had left, the police arrived. They walked straight in the unlocked front door and arrested everyone inside.

Fifteen

I T'S DIFFERENT NOW, isn't it," she asked him, sounding too young to have distant memories.

"Yeah. A little." He followed her into Granddad Hubbard's huge old barn, seeing the old man everywhere. Not for the first time, tears stung at his eyes and he blinked them away. It was the manly thing to do. Granddad Hubbard would have . . . encouraged him to be manly.

"Hell, boy, no sense cryin' over spilled milk. Never planned to live forever, no how, no way."

"What's going to happen to this place now?" he wondered aloud, rambling across the dirt and straw floor, packed concrete hard from a hundred years of use.

It was spring break. The Hubbards had put this trip off for nearly a month after Granddad died. No one wanted to see that he wasn't there anymore. Livy's parents came to "settle the estate," remove a few family heirlooms from the house, and make sure old Walt Lippman had somewhere to go. Livy and Brian came to mourn.

"Daddy will sell it, I guess." She hated the very idea of it. She breathed in the sweet earthen scent of the barn, laced with that distinct "farm odor" that only country people loved, and resigned herself to leaving a big chunk of her heart on the plains of Ohio.

"Think he'd hold me to a loan? If I quit school and get my old job back at the BP station I could pay him forty-nine dollars and sixty-seven cents a week for the rest of my life." He turned to look at her. "I could ask Larry for the money, I guess, but he'd probably just stand there and stare at me, like you are."

She smiled. "I was trying to picture you as a farmer."

"No, no. I'd hire someone to run this place, and just come here when I want to be happy." She nodded her approval. It was a good plan. A nice dream.

"Could I come visit?" she asked. It wasn't a facetious question. She needed to know. Emotionally, her life was going up and down like a well bucket and, frankly, it was beginning to frighten her.

She'd always assumed that if she walked that straight solid line between good and evil, right and wrong, it could take her through a minefield, unharmed. It always had before. But lately . . . sometimes that line was so thin she could barely see it. And sometimes, honest to God, she couldn't find it at all.

She was about to make the Dean's List at school; that was good. The student strike they'd organized at Southwestern demanding a Third World Studies department was a bust; that was bad.

Astronaut Neil Armstrong, an American, was the first human to walk on the moon. Very good. Her father had been asked to run for state senator. Really, really good. (Even better if they had to move to Nashville.) But then there was Woodstock, not good—a bummer really—but only because she was stuck in Tolford last summer and missed the whole glorious thing!

There was Richard. Unbelievable and wonderful. And sex, a thin confusing line between good and not so good. There was Mayor Wayne Chilton of Memphis. Bad, bad, bad. Just as short-sighted as his predecessor, Harry Lever. He was a good administrator, but deeply prejudiced against the blacks. He wasn't healing any wounds in Memphis; he was rubbing salt into them.

"You can come visit whenever you want," Brian said. "But leave the dickhead in Memphis."

And then there was Brian.

"I wish you'd stop calling him that." He shrugged, as if any name was as good as another for Richard. She gave too much attention to an empty horse stall and asked casually, "Why can't you like Richard?"

"He's a jerk."

She caught his eye between the slats in the stall. "He likes you," she said, convinced of it. "Why can't you give him a break?"

"He doesn't deserve one." He roamed off as if something unusual attracted him.

"I think he does. I think it was sweet of him to come all this way for Granddad's funeral. He didn't have to do that."

There was fresh hay in the stall and she was tempted to lie down in it, close her eyes, sleep—block out all the thoughts in her head. She remembered hiding from Brian in one of the stalls once. A long time ago. After they'd kissed in the clover field.

She remembered that kiss . . . and crossed over the thin confusing line again. Not that making love with Richard wasn't a good thing. It was. It was great. It was fine. It was just that she had vague recollections of feeling something so different once. Something finer. Something grand. Something she wanted so much to feel with Richard, but hadn't yet.

He was everything she could wish for in a man. Socially conscious. Motivated. Principled. Ambitious. Brilliant and handsome. She was nuts about him . . . she loved him . . . and yet. . . . Besides, she was an emancipated woman of the seventies who read the magazines. Gongs and whistles don't last in a relationship; it was the meeting of minds, the mental mating that counted. Right? And it wasn't that sex with Richard wasn't . . . pleasant enough. It was. Pleasant. And being responsible for your own orgasms was very . . . liberal and liberating. Right?

"Of course he had to come to the funeral," Brian said. She couldn't see where he was or what he was doing—she didn't have to, to dislike the tone of his voice.

"No, he didn't. He's been very busy all spring. He's been trying to get low-rent housing desegregated, and there's been talk that once they start busing kids to different schools, church-sponsored private schools will crop up like mushrooms. It'll destroy the public school system. So, he's been talking to . . ."

"You didn't happen to mention to him that the Democrats approached your old man about running for governor in '78, did you?"

"Of course, I did. I've been bragging about it for weeks. State senator in '72. Governor in '78. United States senator . . ." she said, letting the last office hang in the air like the dream it was. "He's as proud of Daddy as I am. He even offered to help out with the campaign. He'll be out of school by then and . . ."

"And dating the next governor's daughter can't hurt his own political aspirations."

"What?" Okay. That was it. If Brian wanted a fight about Richard, she'd give him a good one.

He appeared suddenly in front of the stall with both hands up in front of him.

"Sorry," he said, shaking his head. "I shouldn't have said that. I take it back."

"I should hope so," she said, her head of steam slowly dissipating. "That was a terrible thing to say."

"I said I was sorry."

"Okay," she said, wanting to forgive him. They hadn't been alone together for so long and there was so much she wanted to discuss with him. "Does . . . does Richard have anything to do with you're being . . . standoffish lately?"

"Standoffish?"

"I hardly ever see you anymore."

"Larry's been pretty pissed since he got that letter from the dean, the one about me losing my scholarship." Some fool had left a pitchfork leaning against a beam, spokes up. He turned them to the ground automatically—the way Granddad had taught him. "And about the money I've spent this year. He wants me to spend my own money next year, so I've been looking around for a job."

"No," she said, stepping out and closing the gate on the stall, turning to face him. "It started before the letter. Sometimes you're gone for days. And when you're home there . . . well, we don't talk much."

He chuckled. "No offense, Liv, but I'm pretty much all talked out about the war."

"That's not all we used to talk about."

"And civil rights and government corruption and social change and environmental suicide . . ."

"What about our feelings and what we're dreaming about? We don't talk about anything, anymore."

He stopped and made a point of studying her. "I'm here now. Tell me what you're feeling."

Her smile was filled with relief and forgiveness.

"I've missed you," she said, looking self-conscious. "I've missed bumping into you every time I turn around. I get . . ."

"What?"

"Lonely, sometimes."

His expression was dubious.

"For you," she explained. "For our friendship. We've been friends a long time. I feel . . . lost when you're not around."

He opened his mouth to say something smart, something like *Teach Richard to draw maps then* or *Get a compass*. But then he changed his mind.

"You're not lost," he said, looking away, gravitating to the small door on the east side of the barn. He leaned against the jamb, looking out at the green fields beyond. "You'll never be lost. You're one of those people with a built-in sense of direction."

"Not always."

"I, on the other hand," he said as if she hadn't spoken, a hand over his heart when he turned to her, "could get lost in my own closet. That's why we've always gotten along so well. You're a leader, I'm a follower. I'm an Indian, you're a chief."

"That's not true." Oddly enough, his words hurt. "I'd follow you anywhere."

"That's because you know I'm not *going* anywhere."

"What are you saying?" Her chest was uncomfortably stiff. She could feel her heart speeding up and working harder. "What's going on with you?"

He laughed. "Nothing. There's nothing going on with me. I'm the same old Brian I've always been. Happy-go-lucky dreamer, that's me."

"Brian," she said, then hesitated. "If . . . if there was something wrong, would you tell me?"

"Sure."

"I mean, between us. You and me. If there was something wrong between us, would you tell me? Could we talk about it?"

"Absolutely."

"We've been friends for so long . . . I . . ."

"Livy, Livy, Livy." He closed the distance between them with long, slow strides. "Nothing will ever change the way I feel about you. Not Richard. Not time. Not the world. Not anything."

For half a second, she was prepared to hear him say he loved her. She could see it in his face, feel it in the air around her. All was as it should have been, as it always had been. She closed her eyes to hold back her tears and wrapped her arms around his chest.

"Oh God, Brian," she said, her voice wavering. "I was so afraid. You seemed so far away from me, even in the same room. And then Granddad . . . I . . . I was afraid. I thought I'd lost you, too." She held him tighter. "I don't think I could stand that. I really would be lost without you."

She felt his arms come strong and safe about her. Felt the tender kiss in her hair.

"It'll never happen, Livy," he said. "We may wander away, but we'll always know how to wander back when we need each other."

He didn't say he'd always be at her side, didn't say their relationship wouldn't change, didn't say he wanted it any other way. She wanted to hear those things, but she was glad he didn't say them. It would have been a lie.

They weren't kids anymore. They couldn't sit in the woods, telling stories and drawing pictures. They weren't speeding down country roads on their bikes. They couldn't pretend they were two halves of a whole, or a perfect pair of misfits, or that they had common interests. It simply wasn't true any longer.

For a long moment they rocked in each other's arms, until Brian took a deep breath and set her firmly away from him.

"I can't live in that house with you and Richard next year," he said, as if the decision was last minute, but final. "I'm sorry. I'll tell your folks whatever you want me to tell them, but I can't stay there."

She nodded her understanding, wishing things could have been different between him and Richard.

"Will you go back to the dorms then?"

He gave her a strange I-don't-think-so look and shook his head. "I met this guy who teaches art classes at one of the elementary schools. He's getting divorced and says he could use some help with the rent. There's a studio. He said it wasn't very big, but the light was good and he'd be teaching most days anyway. I thought I'd try it. As soon as we get back from break." He chuckled. "He can't be any worse than Bubba Du Bois." He grinned. "Or Richard."

"Will I still see you?"

"Of course. I'm moving to a new apartment, not falling off the end of the world." He sat down on a bale of hay, stretched out his long legs, and spread his arms and back against the bale behind him as if he were sitting on a couch. "Remember when we built forts out of these things and bombed each other with apples?"

She laughed and sat down beside him. "Remember Granddad making us pick up all those apples before they spoiled his hay?"

"God, there must have been a thousand of them."

"Remember the wild barn cats out here?"

He snorted a laugh. "Remember the time you finally caught one and it shredded your chest?" He made an awkward hand gesture toward that area of her body, looked embarrassed, then away.

"There was blood everywhere. Granddad thought I fell on a pitchfork."

"No, no, no. He thought I'd finally stabbed you with a pitchfork. He said he knew all along that someone had to do it, and he was glad it was me and not him. Remember?"

"Aw, that's right! He said I was the noisiest kid to ever die on his farm, and then he started telling us all those awful stories about the dead children."

"Your cousins. The ones you didn't know about. The ones you'd never meet," he said, using his spookiest voice.

She sighed in happy remembrance, leaning back into the hay and the circle of his arm. "Every uneven piece of ground was a grave that summer."

"And the cats lived happily ever after."

Why is it, that even the saddest times are better when you have someone to share them with?

To Brian's broad streak of creativity, the expression *handwriting on the wall* took on graffitilike dimensions. Bold, bright, and telling.

The draft, the skeleton, the strong black lines of the art work—specific and limiting—were his feelings for Livy.

He doubled his efforts to meet women. His mission: to fall in love with anyone but her. He dated airheads and intellectuals—sometimes it was hard to tell the difference. He tried ugly girls. Some were kick-ass tough; some were gentle wallflowers. He laughed with funny girls and took the boring girls home early.

Hip'n jive chicks were a challenge. Innocent girls reminded him of his sister, Beth. Bossy women he ignored. Whiny women, too. Easy girls were still his favorites, but he just didn't trust them. Country girls and sophisticated women were so much alike, narrow and fixated. And none of them were Livy.

Inside the lines of the doodle he saw an abundance of red. Anger and fear and war.

"You know," Richard said, his tone suspicious. "Sometimes you talk as if you'd really go through with it. Like you'd go."

He shrugged. He'd come to see Livy and, of course, Richard was with her. Old-Knoxville-family-old-money-old-never-had-to-do-anything-for-himself Richard. Naturally, the topic of choice was the war—you couldn't go anywhere without talking it into the ground. As a rule, he let other people do all the talking but . . . well, Richard irritated the hell out of him.

"If I get drafted, I will go," he said plainly enough. "America's the only country I've got. I won't run to Canada and I can't spend the rest of my life in prison. I'll take my chances in Vietnam."

"You're crazy. Did you know this?" Richard asked Livy, who lifted a shoulder and looked away as if she might have guessed it. He turned back to Brian. "They're killing women and children over there. They're murdering civilians."

"And no civilians ever got killed in any other war in history, is that it? It's a war, not the selective killing of military personnel only."

"So that makes it all right? To kill women and children?"

"Nothing makes it all right, Dickhead. There's nothing good or righteous about any war."

"It's not even our war. Those killers shouldn't even be over there."

"Oh, Richard." Livy started to protest his choice of words.

"That's why you're a dickhead, Dickhead. It's so easy for you to sit on your butt and call kids you went to school with killers. Sign up for a tour over there, why don't you? Walk in their shoes for a while. If you live to talk about it, you can set yourself up as judge and jury and call them anything you want."

He wasn't advocating the war. He wasn't saying it was right or wrong. All he was saying, had anyone asked him outright, was that *he* didn't want to fight it. Personally. He wasn't a killing kind of guy, and he sure as hell didn't want to be killed. It was just that simple. Which isn't to say it was that simple for everyone. Nor was it saying that those who did go and did fight were evil or bad. Hell, it wasn't even saying that if he got drafted, he wouldn't go. Only, simply, that he wasn't going to *volunteer*.

He knew a few guys on campus who'd been over there, who'd fought in the Vietnam war and come back to try and pick up where they'd left off in their lives. They weren't horrible people. They weren't even much older than him, just two or three years. But you could tell by the look in their eyes and the way they tended to group together for support that they'd been to another world and were seeing the situation from a whole different perspective. Some felt used and were angry, others were proud and unapologetic, but most simply wanted to forget and go on.

It was times like this when he'd wish he could have known his real father better. Had he wanted to fight in the Korean war? Had he been proud to go and serve his country in a war on foreign soil? Or had he been . . . sort of sucked up into it and terrified the whole time? Had he been killed marching forward, advancing into battle, or shot in the back running away? He didn't know, and his mother rarely spoke of him except to say that he was handsome and sweet and good with his hands—he'd planned to build houses after the war, she'd said.

Brian liked to imagine his father as a regular guy, like himself. One who knew he wasn't Superman, and prayed he wasn't a coward. Definitely someone smart enough to know when he had a good thing going, living in America, where he was free to do most anything he wanted to. A fair man. An honest man. A fellow who was wise enough to know he had duties and responsibilities, to his country, his family, his future. Mostly, he hoped that whatever he was called upon to do . . . he wouldn't discredit that image.

The war was escalating. There were reports of secret bombings of Cambodia. The first draft lottery was instituted and student draft deferments were being canceled. His chances of being put to the test were getting pretty tight.

There was a drab brown on the wall behind the graffiti, which was the boredom he felt in college classes he couldn't relate to, couldn't envision as useful in anyone's life much less his own, and couldn't justify attending when he could be doing something else. Anything else.

Several hues of blue in the garbled message was the confusion he felt as he tried to find a place for himself in the world. He used to dream of being grown up. Why? What had he planned to do when he was grown up? *For the rest of your life* seemed like an eternity, and what was he going to do with it? Paint? Play basketball? He was a dreamer; he wasn't delusional. If he wasn't in school, he'd have to get a job and support himself—Larry said so. Work. At the same job. Every day. For eternity. It blew his mind. Marriage. Children. A house. He needed a new car. Oh God, food. He'd have to be buying food all the time.

A golden yellow highlighted his fanciful epigraph. It was hope.

There were whole days when Memphis was the most beautiful place on earth. The sky, the trees and flowers, the river, the architecture, the people. He'd inhale the air of a fresh spring day and wonder at all he hadn't yet seen. The world pulled at him. His soul ached to wander away. It wasn't all war and anger and confusion out there. Couldn't be.

There were dabs of green here and there in the etchings he saw covering the walls of his heart. A sense of urgency. A yearning. Restlessness. No one he knew was guaranteeing him a tomorrow. All he had was today, and he was wasting it.

That there was handwriting on his wall was undeniable. What it was trying to tell him was a puzzle until May 4, 1970.

"Come with us then," Livy said, rolling a pair of jeans into something the size of a loaf of bread and stuffing them into a satchel. "There's plenty of room in the van, and if you'd rather not go with me and Richard, you can follow us in one of the other cars. Come on. It'll be fun. Two days on the road and we'll be camping out in sleeping bags. And once we get to Akron you can party with us or go off on your own. The rally is in Kent, where the college is, on Monday. We'll be home by Wednesday. Come on."

He shook his head. "It doesn't feel good," he said. It was the only way he could express the strange feeling he had about traveling all the way to some university in Ohio to listen to Richard guest-speak at a protest rally against the invasion of Cambodia. He didn't want Livy to go either. "Don't they have their own campus big mouth up there? Why do they have to import ours?" He shrugged at her frown. "And why Richard anyway? He's not exactly Abbie Hoffman. He's as loud as a fart in church, but I find it hard to believe they can hear him all the way up in Ohio."

Her torpid expression told him how amusing she thought he was. "It was the *Freedom Express*. Someone up there got a copy of it, liked what Richard had to say, and called him."

"What Richard had to say? Or what you wrote for him?"

"Don't start."

His sigh ruffled the long hair around his face as he watched her sort through her cardigan sweaters, pick out a red one—always red—and ram it into her full bag.

"Man, I could use a change of scenery, but somehow Richard in Ohio sounds like a bigger drag than Richard in Tennessee. I pass."

"Suit yourself," she said, then tempted him with "Alben and Stephanie are going."

He shook his head once again. "If he's got them, why do you have to go?" he asked sullenly, knowing full well why she was going, wishing he had even the slightest chance of getting her to stay home.

She gave him a look that made him feel even more like a sulky baby and said, "Aside from the good cause and the bad case of spring fever I've been nursing lately, I'm going because Richard asked me to go. Any other stupid questions?"

"Are you using some sort of birth control with that guy? Junior Dickhead sounds like a comic strip from *Mad* magazine."

"Cute. But it'd be Richard IV if I weren't being careful."

An indelicate snort. "Okay. It would be a Shakespearian tragedy then. I was close."

"Not that close. It's King Henry IV or King Richard II or III, to be specific," she said, with that same know-it-all look she'd used on him since they were seven.

He couldn't win.

May 4 was a Monday, though after the blitzed-out weekend he was lucky to know it was Monday, much less May 4. It might have been fate or merely coincidence that he was dragging himself from class to class that day. But being a fairly well-known friend of the well-known Livy Hubbard and company made him one of the first to hear the rumors of a shooting at Kent State University just outside Akron, Ohio, that day.

Wasn't that where Richard and Livy had gone? Had he heard from them? Had they released the names of the four victims yet? Had the National Guardsmen really opened fire on unarmed college students? When were they supposed to be home? Was he going to Ohio to be with them? Did he know anyone there he could call? Had he talked to Livy's parents yet? Didn't he have any information at all?

No. He didn't. And the pit of his stomach lodged in his throat as his mind grew frantic in its search for some news. He was on the phone with the dean of students at Southwestern and then the local cops as he sat on the floor in front of the TV, flicking from channel to channel to catch the news broadcasts of the shooting, again and again, scanning the crowds in the background, looking for a familiar face, walk, jacket, body type . . . anything.

He finally called his mother, his heart heavy and aching, and asked her to casually inquire after Livy at the Hubbards' house and call him back. She advised him not to go to Ohio in case he missed them in the traffic coming home, told him it would be better to man the phones in Memphis. Great. He could twiddle his thumbs, too.

He stayed at the house on Highland Street and asked his roommate, Jordan, to relay any messages he might get at the studio apartment. It took the second hand on the clock an hour to travel from twelve to twelve as he roamed the rooms and hallways, waiting, listening, watching. Tuesday was interminable. There was a nationwide student strike protesting the extension of the war and the killing of the students at Kent State that day, and no one mentioned the names of the wounded. His stomach was so tight he couldn't eat, couldn't sleep. Wednesday was worse. Nothing happened.

He sat in Livy's room to feel closer to her, to smell the lilacs, to castigate himself over and over for letting her go—for not being there with her. It was shortly after midnight when the sounds of cars pulling into the driveway and stopping woke him from a light, restless sleep. He caught himself falling down the stairs twice on the way to the front door, but he was out on the porch, barefoot and bare-chested, before the vehicles were completely empty.

The front porch light flooded the yard. When he couldn't see Livy right away he went down on the new spring grass, across the walk, and halfway to the drive before he stopped in his tracks. Not from the van she'd left in, but from one of the other cars, Alben was helping her out of the back seat.

The first thing Brian saw was the cast on her left arm; the second was his fist in the middle of Richard's face.

"You stupid, self-centered son of a bitch!" he screamed as the others came to pull him away from the nose-bleeding Richard. "She coulda been killed. You coulda got her killed."

"Brian. No." It was Livy, but her voice seemed to be coming all the way from Ohio.

"My nose! He's crazy. Get him away from me. He's crazy. You're crazy, Carowack!"

"I'd rather be crazy than stupid, you parasite. Don't you ever think of anyone but yourself? Don't you ever *think?* She coulda been killed."

"We all could have been killed," Richard said, holding his nose, getting slowly to his feet with help from the others. "But that's not really the point here, is it? You can't stand it that she doesn't give you all her time anymore. You can't stand it that you have no control over her anymore."

"What the hell are you talking about? I've never had any control over her. Never wanted any."

"Oh, right," he said, removing his hands from his face. His nose was broken all right, and his eyes were going to be black and blue. "If it were up to you she'd be chained to a kitchen sink in that dingleweed town you come from. She'd be crawling with babies by now and her brain would be as dull as yours."

"Richard! Brian!" It was Livy again.

Brian struggled to get free, but couldn't.

"Her life isn't up to me, it's up to her. It always has been. And no one ever tried to shoot her until she met you."

"You dumb hayseed. She wasn't shot. She got caught in the crowd. She tripped. She fell. She broke her damn arm." He palpated his nose again, wincing with pain.

Brian felt a little better, but not well enough to forget what he'd been through the last two days.

"It doesn't matter how she was hurt. She shouldn't have been there in the first place—wouldn't have been there if you hadn't made her go."

"He didn't make me go," she said, but Brian ignored her.

"If you were even half as smart as you think you are, you wouldn't need her to tell you what to say. She wouldn't have to tell you what's worth fighting for and what isn't. She wouldn't have to plan your speeches or write most of the articles in your paper. Without her you wouldn't be anything but another fanatic screaming in the wind."

"Brian, please," she said, putting her free hand on his bare chest. "Please stop. It was all my fault. I was clumsy. I should have called you. I'm sorry you worried. I'm fine. Brian, I'm fine." He looked at her then as if for the first time. "Really. I'm fine. It wasn't Richard's fault. It wasn't anyone's fault, it just happened and . . . and I'm a lot better off than the ones who died."

No, she wasn't dead. He went limp with the realization, and the hands that were holding him began to loosen and let go.

"I'm sorry," she said again softly. "I should have known you'd worry. I should have called."

"You shouldn't have been there," he muttered, his voice nearly gone. He couldn't stop the hand that reached out to smooth her soft hair from the crown of her head to her shoulder. Nor could be help saying, "It just didn't feel right. I should have tried harder to stop you."

"Right on, man, you should have tried to stop her, like you usually do," Richard said, stepping closer. His adrenaline had kicked in and he was ready to do his song-and-dance routine. "Well, she's with me now. She knows who's going somewhere and who isn't. She knows we need each other, that we're a unit, a team. We're solid," he said, shaking his fist. "We're going to change things. Together. There's no telling what we could do if she didn't have to drag you along behind us all the time, slowing us down by holding her back."

Brian looked over Livy's head at him, but didn't speak.

"That's enough, Richard. You have it all wrong. Brian doesn't hold me back. He holds me up. He's my closest friend. We don't always agree on things, but he supports what I do."

"He's a loser," he said, reaching for her. "He doesn't understand your drive or your dedication to bettering the world. He wants to party and pretend everything is going to be fine, and he's wrong. You know he's wrong. Nothing's going to change unless *we* make it change. All of us. He isn't one of us. He's a deadbeat."

"No. You've gone too far this time. I . . ."

"Livy." She stopped and looked at Brian. "You don't need to defend me to anyone." He stared into the depths of the honesty and goodness in her eyes and loved her until his heart ached. Maybe part of what Richard was saying was right. Maybe it was time to let go—for both of them. There were things she needed to do, things he needed to do, that they could never do together. Maybe Richard, with his old southern family background, his money, his connections, his Roman numerals after his name . . . maybe he was what she needed.

"I want to talk to Livy alone," he said finally, glancing about at their friends . . . and his foe.

Richard looked as if he might put up a fight at first—at least a verbal contest as he couldn't possibly win a physical confrontation with Brian because of his size—but when the others moved away and when Brian's stare didn't waver, he went inside, too.

"I'm sorry," she said again when they were alone.

He shook his head and smiled. "Don't be sorry. You're a big girl. He's right about that much."

"Let's go upstairs and talk. You'll freeze out here."

"Actually, I'm still pretty hot. Let's stay out here."

"Okay," she said, pulling her red sweater closer over her shoulders and around the cast on her arm.

"Does it hurt?" he asked, touching the cast lightly with the tips of two fingers. She shrugged, shook her head, no.

There was a long, uncomfortable silence as they both sensed a change in the air around them. A necessary change that was neither good nor bad. An indefinite change—without a specific beginning, the outcome of which was unknown. An inevitable change that had already occurred.

"I'm gonna split," he said.

"I thought you wanted to talk."

He laughed softly. "I'm trying to say good-bye, Livy."

"Good-bye." She repeated the word as if it were the first time she'd spoken it aloud. "But what about school?"

"What about it? It was never for me, Livy. I came here for my mom, for you, because of the scholarship . . . because I didn't know what else I was going to do."

"But you know now?" Her voice sounded tight, strained. "What will you do? Where will you go?"

He held his arms out wide. "Anything I want, anywhere I want. I thought I'd check out Chewy's Colorado first. Remember how we used to want to do that?"

She nodded. "And you'll paint," she said, making it sound like the right thing for him to be doing. "And someday you'll be rich and famous and you won't recognize me when we pass on the street."

"Are you kidding?" He smiled at her. "You're the one who's going to end up as some big political hotshot. You'll probably have me arrested for being a mere commoner."

"You couldn't be a mere anything, it's not in you. You'll be a . . . a unique commoner and I'll favor you with a pardon because of your many wonderful talents."

"You are too kind, Your Highness."

She watched him bow low before her.

"And you are too wonderful, my friend," she said, her voice soft, her eyes suddenly filling with tears. "What will I do without you?"

He looked at her, his throat constricting from the pressure of a hundred emotions. He shook his head once. If he had the answer, he'd have given it to her.

He didn't know if he could survive without her. All he knew was that it was killing him to stay.

"Brian," she said, an unnamed fear in her voice. "Don't go." She wrapped her good arm around him as if she were heavy enough and strong enough to keep him restrained.

"Livy." He held her close and buried his face in her hair.

"Okay, go," she said, crying. "But come back." She sobbed against his bare chest and he decided not to leave, for a second or two. "See what you need to see. Do whatever it is you have to do, and then come back. Don't stay away. Don't disappear. Don't leave me forever."

"I won't," he said, his voice thick with pain. "I promise. Livy, I love you."

"Oh. I love you, too," she said, lifting her head to look at him, tears rolling down her cheeks. "You're more than my friend. So much, much more."

He nodded, wishing she knew how much more than a friend he truly was, how much more he wanted to be.

Sixteen

BRIAN DIDN'T FINISH his sophomore year. He didn't say
good-bye again. One day he was just gone.

*Chewy was right about the Rockies. Come see them as soon as you
can. Love Brian*—came on a postcard from Colorado six months
later.

Amazingly, Livy's life went on—though she couldn't count the
times she'd look up, expecting to see him, and feel again and again
the ache of disappointment in her heart.

It was a difficult adjustment. She likened it to losing an arm or
a leg, certainly not life threatening but it made one feel freakish and
alone in a crowd; it was an obstacle that one might frequently feel
was impossible to overcome.

She felt . . . out of step. When she could have told Brian everything in a single glance, she had to explain herself to Richard. Her
rationale had to be clear and logical for Richard, and not the recur-
rent just-a-feeling she had about things that Brian accepted so
readily. Her witticisms had to be cutting and complicated, urbane
even, to make Richard laugh. Brian found humor in trivia, and he
loved a good Arkansas joke. She couldn't draw a straight line or
hum a tune in key, but she admired and enjoyed those who could—
Richard had no interest. There were things in her life she was too
embarrassed to set before Richard, things she wouldn't hesitate to
mention to Brian—girl stuff, Livy things, that Brian was used to
and Richard wouldn't understand.

She missed him. Missed him a lot.

On the really rotten days she made herself happy imagining
how much worse their separation was for Brian. After all . . . he was

Brian. She'd pretend he spent most of his time working on schemes to come back to her. He was miserable. Everything he painted was gruesome and dark. He was so unhappy he couldn't make love to the dozens and dozens of women who passed through his studio.

In the end, the circumstance that brought them together again was not of his making—in fact, he hadn't even called to let her know he was coming home.

It didn't make sense that a hospital that dealt with people's minds should smell just like the hospitals that dealt with their bodies. The odor of blood and alcohol spiked with Pine-Sol was a component of every memory she had associated with hospitals.

She thought of lobotomies and frowned, of electroshock therapy and closed her eyes. She was tired. Her brain felt like mush.

She'd had classes all day, reviewing for finals. Graduation was less than a month off. She drove two hours, all the way home after her mother's call that afternoon. Brian had come home suddenly, to see Beth, and Livy wanted to be there.

She knew Beth had been acting strangely for some time; her mother had kept her informed. That she was acting strange enough to provoke a visit from Brian worried her.

When she found Brian's house dark and empty, she drove another thirty miles straight through to Spring Gate House, the closest private facility to Tolford. She'd never been to Spring Gate before, and she couldn't remember if Brian had ever come to visit his first stepfather, Beth's daddy, when he was there.

It didn't matter really, she supposed; it wasn't the sort of place that spawned cherished memories anyway.

"Wibby!"

Four-year-old Bobby was the first to spot her when they came through the front doors into the main lobby of the small hospital and found her sitting there, waiting. It was after nine o'clock. He looked as tired as she felt.

"We've just been out getting something to eat. Hasn't Brian

come out yet? He'll be starving," Brian's mother said, after expressing her pleasure at seeing Livy and commenting several times on the sweetness of her loyalty in standing by the family at such a distressful time. Larry mumbled something under his breath and she hushed him, saying, "If he were disturbing anyone, they'd ask him to leave, Larry. Not everyone's a stickler for rules the way you are, dear. And it has been almost two years since Beth's seen him. Maybe she's talking to him. She doesn't talk to us, you know," she told Livy, who was helping Bobby climb up her leg and into her arms. "Bobby just loves you, dear. He asked and asked about you after you went back to school last summer. Where's Wibby? he'd say. Wibby. Is that darling?"

Brian's mother wasn't usually what her own mother called a prattle-puss, but she did have a tendency to pretend nothing was wrong when she was most stressed. That she was sick with worry for Beth was very plain in her eyes. Livy reached out and gave the woman a one-armed hug.

"If you'll watch Bobby, Larry and I can go back and find Brian. Tell him you're here," she went on, abruptly sighting and picking invisible lint off her green wool coat. "We have such a time with Bobby. He's not allowed to go into the wards until he's seven, so he can't really see Beth yet, and he pitches the most awful fits when we try to leave him with someone. He's so young. And he misses her so much. He doesn't understand. But you draw sissy beautiful pictures to make her feel better don't you, honey?" she asked him, smoothing back fine brown hair from his face. "Will you stay and be good for Livy while Daddy and I go . . ."

"No," Livy said, stopping her. "That's okay. I'll wait until Brian's done. Beth needs to see him more than I do."

"You are the sweetest girl." She patted Livy's shoulder. "And such a good friend to my Brian. He's missed you. He stopped in to see your mother just this morning."

"I know," she said. "She told me."

Her mother also told her that Brian had changed some, and to be prepared for a difference in his appearance. Nothing shocking or bad, minor changes really. Her assurances had left Livy feeling uneasy, making the trip home to see him all the more necessary.

"I want to go back and say good night to Bethy before we leave. Larry? Do you want to come?" He shook his head and lowered his eyes to the floor. "Well, um, watch Bobby and talk to Livy for a minute. I'll be right back."

He watched her walk away, then watched his fingernails grow for a few minutes before looking up to catch Livy watching him.

"Saddest thing I ever saw," he said, looking away. "That little girl in there. Breaks your heart."

He didn't see it, but she nodded her understanding, remembering Beth's daddy and how sad it was to see him unhappy. There didn't seem to be anything to say, so they waited. She sat in a chair with Bobby on her lap and listened as he recited his birthday wish list for her.

"Livy?"

The deep voice was so familiar and so dear, it detonated a powerful assortment of emotions inside her. She turned, helping Bobby off her lap, and smiled at Brian as he walked across the lobby toward her.

"Brine!" Bobby shouted, running at him.

Livy felt her smile falter a bit and forced it to stay in place. Her mother was right. He was different. And it wasn't the long black ponytail that hung down his back, or the close-cut beard and mustache. It wasn't as obvious as the black leather jacket he wore with his T-shirt and jeans, or the biker boots. It had more to do with the baby fat he'd lost in his face and the new lean muscles he'd acquired. The difference was in the way he walked and in his eyes. Clearly, Colorado wasn't the only place he'd been; the mountains weren't all that he had seen.

She stood as he scooped Bobby up without breaking stride, carrying him under one arm like a sack of potatoes, much to the little boy's delight. There was a moment of panic when he didn't slow down, and she thought he might charge right through her, but he didn't. He looped his free arm around her neck and held her so tight she was afraid her head would pop off . . . so, she did the same to him.

"Oh, man, it's so good to see you," he said, still holding her, Bobby squirming to get out of the crush. After another second or two he released her and set the little boy on the ground. "You look great."

"So do you," she said, feeling the pressure of tears on the back of her eyes. "So do you. You look . . . great."

He grinned and his eyes lit with his particular humor.

"That about covers it for looks, I guess. How've you been?"

She laughed. "Fine. I've . . . how's Beth?"

"Depressed," he said. He frowned and shook his head. "I'm sort of surprised there isn't more activity with manic depression. You'd think she'd be wildly unhappy from the sound of it, but she just lies there. Sleeps a lot. Cries some. . . ."

His words trailed away, but Livy could read his thoughts as if they were flashing in neon across his forehead.

"It's easier to recognize now, Brian. People are tuned into it. They have medication for it. It won't be the same for Beth."

There was a look in his eyes as if he'd forgotten how easily they could get into each other's head. Only Livy knew how guilty he felt when his stepfather committed suicide so long ago. He looked a little surprised and then intensely happy.

"God, I've missed you," he said, smiling broadly. "I haven't met another know-it-all since I left Memphis. At least, not one as sure of everything as you are."

"How confusing for you," she said, trying to emote sympathy when all she felt was the extreme happiness of seeing the mischievous sparkle in his eyes.

Larry muttered something, and Brian's mother, who had silently followed her son out of the ward, responded.

"Leave him alone, Larry. He doesn't need a haircut, for goodness sake. A little trim would be nice but that's how they're wearing it these days. To tell you the truth, I think he has beautiful hair."

"He does. It's disgusting, isn't it?" Livy said, grinning. It was thick and dark, shiny clean and full of body. "Life is so unfair."

"Oh my, you should have seen him this morning, after his shower," his mother said proudly. "It was hanging loose, down past his shoulders and he didn't have his shirt on yet, and I told him he looked just like one of those pictures of the young American Indian braves you see sometimes, so handsome and noble and dignified."

"Handsome, noble, dignified. That's me," he said, smiling fondly on his mother.

Larry grumbled again.

"Will you stop? Please? He hasn't been home in so long, and he says he can't stay. Let's not waste his visit, complaining about the way he looks. Okay?" She turned her back on him. "Why don't you two go back to Tolford together. Oh, Livy honey, you should be so grateful Brian came with us in Dad's car. When he showed up on a motorcycle the other day, I nearly had a heart attack, I swear. Big brutish thing, all black and silver. Wait till you see it. Dad and I'll take Bobby back and get him to bed, and you two can stay out and talk for a while. I imagine you have a lot of catching up to do."

She kissed both Brian and Livy on the cheek before she herded Larry and Bobby away to the doors.

"Some things never change," Brian said, watching them go.

"Some things do," she said, looking at him again, seeing secrets she didn't know about, feelings she couldn't share, knowledge he'd acquired independently that she'd never find in a book. "You have."

He tried to laugh off her seriousness.

"Not me. I am Brian the Unchangeable. Son of the denying, stepson of the unbelieving, brother to the manically depressed, and the very young and unknowing." He slouched into the vinyl-covered couch and ran his hand across the surface of the seat next to him. "Jesus, this is a funky yellow color, isn't it?"

"It's not your fault," she said, sitting on the seat where his hand had been.

"This color?"

She continued to looked at him. He looked away.

"No, I know it's not my fault. Not her illness. But . . . if I'd been home or calling more often, they might have gotten Beth some help sooner. I'd ask about her and Mom would say she was a little out of sorts. And what fifteen-year-old isn't? Hell, I didn't even know that stuff could be hereditary. I never dreamed it could happen to her, too."

"Who would?"

"I should have."

"God, Carowack, you're right. You haven't changed a bit. Everything is still your fault." She flopped back against the seat, defeated.

"Livy, she sleeps for weeks at a time. If I'd been here, I would have seen it. I would have remembered from before. I would have brought her here sooner."

"But you weren't here. And when you started to suspect that something was wrong, you came home. You forced your mother to bring her here. You did everything you could."

"Not soon enough. What if she'd . . ."

"She didn't."

"But she might have."

"Come on, Brian. You can't live your life on mights and ifs and buts. You'll make yourself crazy." Poor choice of words. She laid a hand on his shoulder. "Sorry. What I'm trying to say is that if I had a brother, I'd want him to be you."

He turned his head to look at her. Whatever he was feeling he kept hidden from her, but he smiled a little, amused and self-mocking at once.

"If you had a brother, *he'd* be manic depressive. Don't you ever let anyone else win an argument?"

"Nope."

"At least tell me you didn't bring the dickhead with you."

"All right. I didn't bring Richard with me. Happy? Can we go now?"

They stood to leave and it was almost as if they were something of a rubber band. They'd been apart so long, stretched their friendship so far, pulled at their emotions until they were thin with deprivation. Together again at last, they snapped together with satisfaction.

She looped an arm around his waist and he dangled one across her shoulders as they left the building. They were together again and it felt good. It felt right.

"Tell me every single thing you've done while I've been plowing my way through sociology books and English papers and journalism classes."

"Every single thing?" he asked loudly, laying his head on the back of the seat as they drove through the night. She had become the owner of a dull-green and dirty-white Volkswagen van that her parents bought for her used. It was the thing to have if you hauled a lot of people and stuff around all the time, she said. It also rattled and the wind whistled through it like an air tunnel.

"Everything."

He frowned and shrugged and was silent for several minutes before telling her, "Nothing."

"Nothing?" She glanced at him. "You've been gone almost two years and you haven't done anything?"

"Nothing that matters."

"Okay. Then what have you been doing that doesn't matter?"

"Hanging out mostly. A little work here and there. Drawing. A little painting now and then. Nothing to write home about."

"So I've noticed," she said pointedly. "One postcard in two years? I spend my childhood raising you and you send me one post-card?"

He laughed, knowing full well how she'd spent her childhood.

"What can I tell you?" he asked, as if asking himself what he could tell her and what he shouldn't mention. "Colorado is beauti-ful."

"Your mom said you moved to California."

"I did. I'm starting at the beginning. Colorado was beautiful. The mountains are something else. Unbelievable. The people are . . . earthy. Nice. Clumps of rednecks . . . they loved my hair, too."

"I bet. I got one of those road atlases from a gas station and I've marked every town you've called your mother from. You've done some traveling."

He chuckled. "I'd love to see it sometime. It'd be nice to know where I've been."

Another glance in his direction. "It isn't what you thought it would be, is it?"

"No," he said, closing his eyes and letting his newly honed de-fense system slip away. What he'd seen of the world was its beauty and its incredible ugliness, its kindness and extreme cruelty. It was back-breaking labor for gas money and pocket change; sharing scraps of food with strangers; getting ripped off, beaten up, thrown in jail and ignored. The prize at the bottom of the box was a friendly smile in a pack of strange faces. The country was bigger than he imagined, and lonelier, too.

"Are you sorry you did it? Sorry you left?"

"No," he said, and he wasn't.

His first night home he'd thought that sleeping in his old bed was like going back to the womb—being with Livy was even better. It was . . . hard to explain. It was knowing he belonged somewhere. It was knowing there was one person he was completely free to be himself with, free to admit his mistakes to, free to show his disappointment to. He was even free to cry in front of her—that is, if he'd had any tears left. He was safe with Livy. There was nothing she could take from him that he hadn't already given her, nothing she wanted from him but his friendship.

"Brian?"

"Hmmm?"

"Have you been hurt? Has someone hurt you?" she asked. Her voice was riddled with guilt and shame as if he might have been hurt in some way she shouldn't ask about, hurt in some private way that would only cause him more pain if he spoke of it.

He opened his eyes and tipped his head in her direction.

In his mind she came eager into his embrace, they kissed, he made love to her until she purred with the contentment he felt, they slept warm and safe in each other's arms.

"No," he said. "I'm not hurt. Tired. Sad. But not hurt."

Did losing his innocence constitute being hurt? What about disillusioned? Probably not. Not in any way that mattered. Not so it showed anyway.

Or . . . maybe it did show to Livy.

"I can't believe you're still with Dickhead," he said, changing the subject. "What did he think of you coming home suddenly, just to see me?"

"I don't know." Their gazes met briefly. "I didn't hang around to get his opinion. I left a note and took off."

He whistled long and duly awed, and she threatened him with a pointed finger.

"Don't start," she said. "Richard's been really busy and he needs me right now. He's working with the local Vietnam vets who are protesting the war. He went to Washington with sixty of them last April. We really thought things were turning our way, you know, with Ellsberg leaking the Pentagon Papers and the eighteen-year-old vote and George McGovern running for President. But the guy who shot Wallace picked a lousy time to do it," she said without much remorse for the incident—George Wallace having been on her personal hit list longer than Nixon even. "Not that he should have done it at all, I'm still opposed to violence, but if he *had* to do it, his timing was lousy. Wallace might have divided the Republican vote for us, but I doubt he'll run now. And if Nixon's reelected for a second term it'll be a real blow. To all of us. You should have seen Richard the night we heard that Nixon had ordered the increase of air attacks on North Vietnam." She shook her head in recollection.

"Don't tell me. He screamed and yelled. More than usual."

"And broke things and threw things all over the house. Stephanie wasn't there. Alben and I finally left him there, alone in the house. There was no consoling him and . . ."

"And what?"

"He was scaring me."

"Did he hurt you? Did you think he might?" As always, Brian's instinct was to protect her. He was on red alert.

"No, no. I just didn't know how to help him. I'd have stayed, but Alben said it was better to let him cool off alone."

Alben. Alben was smart. He had a sixth sense for trouble. The highways and byways of America had scraped the same sense raw in Brian. Violent overreactions were generally an omen of things to come.

"He was fine the next morning," she said defensively, responding to the new and varied and not-at-all-nice names Brian had for her boyfriend.

"I heard about your dad," he said, quietly changing the subject. Richard and the war had been talked to death years ago. And besides, her dreams had taken several, less publicized blows lately.

"I heard about your calls to the hospital while he was there. The nurse told us." She smiled her appreciation.

"I'm sorry he had to drop out of the state senate race because of his ulcers. I know you were excited about it."

"A temporary setback. If he's feeling better in '76, and the doctors say he should be fine by then, he can run again. Who knows what'll happen in the next four years."

Her words were lighter than the tone of her voice. He could hear the fear of the next four years—without the people she believed in running the country—and what could happen in that time.

They drove several miles without speaking. The slow sad strains of *Ain't No Sunshine* played on the radio, and in the back of their minds, reminding them of how happy they'd been as kids. Blind, sheltered, together, and full of dreams. How sunny their lives seemed when they were with each other, how much they missed each other.

"Skiing," Brian said unexpectedly.

"What?"

"Skiing. I took up skiing last year," he said, glad to have one thing to account for his time away. "You gotta try it. It'll blow your mind."

"Skiing?" She laughed.

"Yeah. And I want you to see the West. Montana, Idaho, Oregon, Washington. Utah was a trip. Oh, and I was in San Francisco when the Indians gave up Alcatraz."

That was two things. Maybe he had been busy.

"You were? I'd forgotten about that," she said, her mood buoying, just as he'd hoped it would. "What finally happened? Did they get to keep it as a culture center for Native Americans?"

"No."

"Oh."

He did a quick mental head scratch. "But, well . . . I was a reading tutor for six weeks on the Hoopa Indian reservation. They got that," he said with a laugh. "Summer school, you know, eight kids for an hour every day."

She laughed—and almost drove off the road. "You're kidding. No. Really? That's great. Brian, I'm proud of you."

He shook his head. "Don't get too excited over there. That was the first time my Chevy died. Right there on the reservation. I didn't have any money to get it fixed. The guy at the gas station said his wife was running this summer tutoring program for some of the younger kids in Hoopa. A government-assisted thing with not enough funds and too little help. Said he'd fix my car for free if I stayed the whole six weeks. I didn't have much choice."

"Was it so awful?"

He hesitated, then spoke slowly. "No. Well, at first it was a little weird, a little different, the people, some of the food, the Indian art all over, being an outsider, you know? But it was always beautiful. The Klamath River and the salmon runs and the red woods . . . and the kids were cool." A pause. "Everywhere you go it's like that at first, a little weird, but you get used to it. After a while it's the weirdness of a new place that you look forward to. You know, what's different about this place? It's a big country and everywhere you go there's something new or different or unusual. I have drawings and sketches of everywhere I've been, and they don't even come close to showing everything I've seen."

He glanced at her and caught her glancing back, a smile on her face. She was always so easy to talk to.

"What else did you do? Your mom said you were doing odd jobs. How odd were they?"

He grinned. "The jobs weren't odd, just me doing them was." He laughed. "I was a waiter in this really funky health food restaurant in San Francisco for a while. Couldn't wait for my dinner breaks. I'd walk down the street to McDonald's, bring a Big Mac back and eat it out front in the parking lot. I got fired from that place. Then I painted this house in Astoria, Oregon."

"Painted it? Like with nudes?"

"Worse. I painted it magenta." He laughed. "Magnificent magenta. The whole outside of it. Stuck out like a really sore thumb. For room and board. For this little old lady who raised white rats for science labs . . . hundreds of 'em."

They laughed. And everything was okay. Everything. They would feel pity and sorrow for Beth tomorrow. They could feel betrayed and let down and shake their fists at the world any day of the year. That night they were together again. Brian and Livy. There were happy times to remember, some catching up to do, stories to tell, personal alterations to discuss—and time was short.

"I heard somewhere that the ratio of men to women in this country is 95 to 100. That makes someone for everyone, and five women for me." She groaned. But it was a fair fact in the game they were playing. For every fact he knew about the world at large, she'd feed him a fact about their little world, about the people they knew and about Tolford. Maybe it was her way of making sure he was keeping up with current events, maybe they were simply trying to please each other with subjects the other was interested in. Truth be told, the topic didn't really matter to either of them. "Oh, here's a good one you'll like on . . . the EPA."

"The Environmental Protection Agency? It's a government agency . . ." She sounded skeptical.

"But it's a beginning. If we assume from the start that they'll rob the taxpayers blind, we won't be disappointed. And anything they do to make it look like they're doing something will be a step ahead of where we are now. Think positive."

Again she laughed and Brian laughed with her. There had been too much for them to talk about, and neither of them could face going home or ending their time together. They stopped at a bar outside Tolford and bought a six-pack of beer, a pint of Jack Daniels, and a pack of cigarettes, then found one of those convenient Tennessee back roads, parked and proceeded to get high as kites.

It had gotten chilly and the windows were rolled up, blocking out the night noises, the rustle of leaves, and the steady din of the bugs. The van was cozy and quiet as the sound of their laughter faded.

"Alice Rice got married." They were both leaning with their backs against the doors of the van, facing each other. He took a sip of the whiskey and waited for the details. "Well, she had that job over in Idlewild, working for some lawyer. Secretarial stuff. I guess she met the guy there. Mama says she's met him and that he's a real nice guy, a salesman, I think."

"Weren't you invited to the wedding?"

"Oh, sure. But I . . . couldn't make it." He was grateful for the dark of the night and the shadows inside the van. Ten to one, if he'd asked: *Because of Richard?* she'd have answered: yes. He forced himself to say nothing at all, a great effort on his part to keep their conversation lighthearted and friendly. "I hear she's pregnant already," she went on, "I don't know how many months yet, so I can't do the math, but wouldn't it be interesting to know? Alice was always such a prude in school."

He chuckled softly, and she must have suddenly recalled that she too had been something of a . . . well, not a prude certainly . . . but maybe a moralist at the time. She hurried to speak before he could remind her.

"I suppose you heard about, well," she hesitated, "Donny Moore and Jimmy."

He felt suddenly restless and squirmed in his seat. "Yeah. I heard."

"Donny was on his second tour over there," she said, meaning Vietnam. "I keep thinking that if he'd just done his year and then come home . . . if he hadn't . . ." She couldn't say it. "I hated that guy. All through school. He was always such a bully and a big mouth." Silence. "It still hurts . . . it still makes me sad . . . so sad."

"I know," he said quietly from his little corner of their world. "Remember when you punched him in the nose, in first grade?"

"Yeah."

It was like yesterday for him, that day they first met. Was it for her, too?

"I went over to Jimmy Lowe's right after I saw your mom this morning. Jimmy's doing okay. I mean, it was weird seeing him with only one leg, but we laughed and stuff. He seems pretty excited about getting an artificial leg and going to school and . . . his head doesn't seem too screwed up, you know? He seems . . . hopeful."

"I saw him, too. A couple months ago. He was doing all kinds of therapy. For his legs. For his head. I'm glad it's working."

"Me, too." Taking hold of the conversation as if it were a steering wheel, he made a hard right turn. "I saw Gary Wymer, too. God, he hasn't changed at all. He hasn't even asked poor Susan to marry him yet. They'll probably go steady forever."

"Not if Susan has anything to say about it. I talked to her last time I was home. . . ."

They talked until their voices got tired and raspy, until the cool night air chilled their bones. They crawled into the back of the van—an intoxicated whim Brian felt he could handle, at the time—covered themselves with blankets and sleeping bags, cuddled close, and talked in whispers until their eyelids grew heavy and closed, until their respirations became slow and deep.

But they didn't sleep.

Well, Brian couldn't sleep and Livy wouldn't shut up.

"Oh God," she groaned hours later, cuddling closer to him under the blankets to stay warm. "That isn't the sun coming up, is it?"

Supremely distracted, his mind and body running hot and cold with the idea of seducing his best friend, he opened his eyes and peered at the light shining through the small windows at the back of the van.

"Don't think so. Passed right by us," he said, half-glad he was too whacked and too weary to do more than hold her in his arms and enjoy the feel of her snuggled against him.

"You know," she said as if having a lofty thought. "I can understand what women see in you."

"Hmmm."

"I don't mean the obvious things like the way you look and . . . and how funny and smart and talented you are. But this . . ." She bent her left leg over his and adjusted her head on his chest for comfort, sighing contentedly. "This is so nice."

He opened his eyes and stared at the black space between him and the roof of the van. Opportunities to learn meditation and find inner peace would no longer be scoffed at by him. That kind of stuff could come in handy at moments like this.

"Snuggling with Richard is like trying to cozy up to a washboard, he's so thin and bony."

He was feeling somewhat bony himself. Uptight and feverish as well.

"You're comfortable. Big and soft and cushy. I bet you make them feel safe and cared about."

His boniness shriveled away to nothing.

"You were right about him, you know. Richard. He does need me," she said. Brian held his breath. He'd often thought it would be easier to keep his feelings to himself, if he knew Richard was out of the picture. Even he, as her oldest friend and the nearest thing she had to a brother, would be a preferable mate to that big-mouthed, egotistical, pompous . . . "In fact," she went on. "I think maybe that's what I'm attracted to most in him, his need for me. No one's ever needed me before."

If you've ever been drunk and dumbfounded at the same time, you know what a horrible sensation it is. There are thoughts in your head, but they're tangled up like fishhooks. There are emotions, but they're as scattered as a mad woman's wash. You want to speak but your lips flap like bird wings.

What about me? I need you. I've always needed you. I need you more than anyone else in the world. I am the neediest person you know. I have needs with needs. I have needs I don't even know about yet. Let me need you.

"I really think he's going to do great things someday," she said, confiding in her truest and best friend. "I can help him." He closed his eyes to stop the spinning of the van and took a deep breath to calm the sick feeling in the pit of his stomach. "He's not you, of course, but I like him as a friend, too. We talk. We share things. It's nice."

Nice? Just nice? There's still hope if it's only just nice. Terrific, great, spectacular would be serious . . . but nice?

"It's better than nice really. It's . . . fulfilling. He makes me happy. Brian?" She dropped her voice to subwhisper. "Brian? Are you asleep?"

He could have listened to her talk for the next thirty years, but not about Richard. He'd missed the sound of her voice, the scent of lilacs, but not the strain of feeling wedged between hell and a hot spot.

He knew from the past that his bad-mouthing Richard increased her loyalty to him. To blurt out his own feelings for her was either too obscene or too ridiculous to consider for more than a moment or two.

And so he remained silent, letting her think him asleep, enduring the kiss she placed on his cheek, suffering the movement of her body as she drew him closer to her warmth and settled in to sleep next to him.

Seventeen

TWO YEARS LATER, *brunch* was so California she could hardly stand it.

She squirmed in the padded metal chair, feeling conspicuously alone at one of the eight or ten empty tables on the sunny patio. It was early summer of 1974. She was so excited she could hardly stand anything, really. The silly-looking palm trees. The incredible beauty of the early summer morning made her feel as if she had a good chance of living forever. The pink and yellow and white blooms spilling over pots and cascading the rockery that surrounded the cozy patio. The ocean. The seagulls. The air. The sunshine. The California people walking by with their singular attitude and manner. The stylishly casual outdoor restaurant in Santa Monica where Brian suggested they meet.

And seeing Brian, of course.

She had so much to tell him, so much she wanted to hear.

He'd been better about writing to her. Christmas and birthday cards, typically late, as he was now. But there always seemed to be more news left between the lines, unwritten, than what actually got scribbled on paper.

She released some of her tension with a silent laugh and a smile, thinking of the brouhaha she'd gone through getting dressed that morning. Lord, you'd have thought she had an audience with the Pope.

No world class traveler she, there were two suitcases full of clothes and more to pack when she finally came to the conclusion that a Tennessee girl couldn't be expected to know how to dress in California. She'd had piles marked California casual dress-up, Cali-

fornia casual business, California casual-casual, and California ca-
sual-very casual. The distinction between the latter two being new
jeans with creases and old comfortable jeans with holes. Hemlines
were another minor controversy.

On the off chance that Archie Bunker was right, and "Men are
men and girls is girls and that's the way the good Lord made'em . . .
ever shall be. Amen," she packed two outfits from each pile for three
days and hoped she could make the best of them.

The first day she did. Business. However, meeting with Brian
on the second day was an ambiguous occasion—in the sense of
what to wear only. She wanted to impress him, but not overwhelm
him. She wanted to look well employed but not . . . Republican. Up
and coming but not too ambitious. Like a woman, liberated but not
radical. Excited to see him . . . but not as excited as she really was.

She smoothed out the already smooth skirt of the polyester-jer-
sey T-shirt dress she'd decided on at the last minute, and hoped she
looked somewhere between California casual dress-up and California casual-casual—of course, looking around, most of the natives
were wearing jeans. Very casual jeans. She sighed. She was probably
overdressed and looking too excited.

"Man, are you a sight for sore eyes."

"Brian," she said, happy, flustered, anxious all at once as she
recognized his voice and found him standing in the doorway across
the small patio, watching her.

His physique was entirely familiar, but somehow she'd forgotten how tall he was, that he was remarkably good-looking. He
seemed to fill the double-wide door space with . . . with a presence . . . an interesting new composure . . . a subtle energy she
sensed was better off left on a leash, regardless of his cordial manner.

He was wearing an old white T-shirt under an open-down-the-
front red and gray striped sport shirt that needed ironing, with

threadbare jeans and sandals. Very-very casual. California indifferent.

"Welcome to California," he said, walking loose-limbed and lazy toward the table. "It's a trip, huh?"

"A trip? Yes." She laughed. "I love the palm trees."

He shook his head with one better. "There's an orange tree growing in the parking strip out in front of my apartment building."

"Really? With real oranges?"

"No, plastic oranges, but I eat 'em anyway," he said, stopping next to her chair to give her a California-casual kiss on her cheek. "You cut your hair."

"Yeah. I did," she said, feeling—irrationally—as if she ought to explain her actions. She watched him take the seat across from her. He was thin in the face and not altogether healthy looking, in spite of his wonderful tan. Living on bachelor food too long, she decided. She twisted a swag of her chin-length, pageboy-styled hair behind her right ear and left the other side free to swing forward, covering most of the birthmark on her left cheek. It was a great hair style—and she didn't need to explain anything, to anyone. "I got sick of trying to make it look like yours," she said, feeling defensive, not knowing why and not liking it at all.

"Well, it looks really great." He chuckled, as if he too were a bit on edge. "*You* look really great. All grown up. College grad. Big-time *career* woman." He grinned at her.

"I'm not exactly big time . . . yet," she said, warming to the familiar lights in his eyes. "I'm having a lot of fun, though."

"Sounds like it. Between your letters and my mom's, it sounds like you'll have the world shipshape and under control in no time."

"Don't be silly. That'll take some time, a lot of time. So, I'm starting small. Tennessee first, then the whole United States, *then* the world. I'm only one person, you know."

"Yes. I know. But you are Livy Hubbard." He chuckled, a sound so well known to her, she forgot about being nervous.

"Oh, Brian," she said, reaching out impulsively to cover his hand with hers. "It's so good to see you. You can't know how much I've missed you. You wouldn't believe how often I've asked myself 'Now what would Brian think of this or that.' I miss talking to you."

His smile was self-conscious. "I've missed you too, Livy," he said. His gaze faltered and he looked away.

Her hand remained over his, but suddenly he was miles and miles away again. Untouchable. When he glanced back, he was the same—smiling, jovial, eager—but different. It was as if he'd encased himself in a thin protective coating, like the shell of a peanut that protects the tasty tender meat inside.

"So, tell me how you've been. How are your folks?" He laughed. "How are my folks? You're still living in Memphis, right?"

"For now."

"How often do you get home?"

"Everyone's fine. My folks, your folks. I get home every couple of months or so, depending on what's going on with my job. Bobby's great. He loved first grade . . . your mother probably told you," she said, speaking too fast—there was *so much* to tell him. She made an effort to slow down. "Beth, you know, is out of the hospital again and she's in therapy and she's gone back to school and all . . . they held her back that one year, but still, it's hard to believe she'll be graduating from high school in two more years." She hesitated. "But . . . it hasn't been as easy for her as your mama may have led you to believe."

"What do you mean?"

"Well, I don't know what she tells you, but when I ask after Beth your mama says she's fine, but . . . well, technically I suppose she is, but when I go home to visit, I sometimes see her around town. I've tried to talk to her a couple of times and she's . . ." She waved her hands vaguely.

"What?"

"I think she's sad. Not like before," she said hurriedly. "It's different. I . . . I don't think she has many friends." She faltered again. "I don't think she has *any* friends. Mama says she thinks the other kids are a little afraid of her maybe. Like they could catch what she has or she might do something . . . weird. I don't know. I just keep getting the impression that she's alone and lonely."

He rubbed his hand over the light stubble on his chin, looking concerned. It was then she realized that he'd shaved the beard he'd sported the last time she saw him, and her memory floated back to a time when his face was as soft and smooth as her own.

"They should move out of town, leave Tolford. But I can't see Larry giving up the pharmacy," he said. "She could hang out here with me, I guess, but . . . hell, what would I do with her?"

"Mama says she thinks it'll take time. It hasn't been all that long really. A couple years, and she was in and out of the hospital so much of that time. She thinks the other kids will come around when they see Beth is back to acting normal, and she's going to stay that way."

"Can't be easy," he said, slowly shaking his head. "What is she? Seventeen? Poor kid."

They sat in unresolved silence for a few minutes. She could see he wanted to do something for his sister, kiss her boo-boos and make them all better for her. Then abruptly and unexpectedly, he set it aside.

"Well, you didn't come all the way to California to get depressed, and I didn't get out of bed and shower and shave and get all dressed up to come down here to watch you get depressed. Tell me all about Seirs and the campaign and your job and . . . tell me everything."

After a second or two, she did, reasoning that it would take more than they could accomplish over brunch to change Beth's plight. More, perhaps, than anyone but Beth herself could accomplish, given the time.

She was aware, too, that Brian could have asked about her parents next, that he had purposely skipped over her father's change of heart regarding the senatorial race in the fall, and gone directly to her new interest in James Seirs. It was so like him to already know how disappointed she was. Also typical to be so very willing to support her father's decision, without question, to remain a political force within the Democratic party alone, and not run for an office—and that it wasn't necessary to discuss it to death the way Richard needed to.

Her father hadn't bounced back to full force after the surgical removal of his ulcers—and a good part of his stomach. He didn't think he could handle the strain of a political office and only she, Brian, and her mother seemed capable of understanding that it had been just that simple a decision to make. But then again, nothing was ever just that simple with Richard.

And so she started her tale with the deplorably slow and myopic intelligence of the people of Memphis in reelecting Wayne Chilton as mayor once again and her turn toward state government in '73 as a means of dragging Tennessee out of post–Civil War thinking and into the twenty-first century.

With Senator Brock, the candy heir, beating her very outspoken antiwar hero Albert Gore in the 1970 election, and with Senator Howard Baker, Jr., firmly entrenched in his seat for a while longer, she had directed herself to the 1974 congressional election of Henry E. Fuller. As one of the few whites campaigning for the black owner of funeral homes that year, she was in the way of meeting Democrat James Seirs, senator wanna-be in '76, who was also lending his support to Fuller's election.

She liked Seirs and his ideas of stamping out oil-pricing fraud, wasteful government spending, and abuse of political power—so aptly demonstrated by her longtime antagonist President Nixon the year before during the Watergate cover-up. She also liked the idea of ousting Brock from her hero's chair.

Seirs had apparently liked her, too. Green and still learning the ropes, barely graduated from school, she was invited by him to join his campaign management team. He'd said he was impressed with her writing, that the short campaign ads for television that she'd written for Fuller were bright and imaginative, but that what he needed most from her was the enthusiasm she showed for a good, honest campaign. Press Liaison would be her official title.

It had been a tough decision. Albert Gore, Jr., would be running for a House seat in rural Middle Tennessee that same year—and she thought he had some potential.

"It's public relations really," she told Brian. "Writing press releases on everything from where he stands on a specific issue to rebuttals of campaign slurs; attending fund-raisers for campaign money; scheduling public appearances in places that will generate *more* good press or demonstrate his views on the issues, that sort of thing. You know, like setting up a visit to an elementary school so he can show his support for better education, talk about increasing the funds for higher wages for teachers in the national budget . . . and so on," she said, with a roll motion of her hand—it went on and on. "I've written a couple short speeches for him, nothing big or important, but it's a start." She laughed and splayed her hands across the sky. "Speech writer for the President. Who knows where I could go with all this."

It wasn't the telling of the story that excited her, as much as it was the telling of it to Brian—even though he knew most of it already from her letters. It was the pride in his eyes, the interested questions he asked, the knowing smile as if he'd assumed all along she was destined for great things. She had his undivided attention again, and it made her feel like Queen of the Mountain.

"A direct link from your brain to the President's mouth," he shuddered violently in jest as if it were a frightening idea, and they both laughed. "Yeah, well . . . if anybody can sell this guy Seirs, you can," he said—and he was serious.

A waitress had come and gone several times while she'd talked. They'd eaten something with water chestnuts and bean sprouts sticking out all over, but for the life of her she couldn't have said what it was called or how it tasted. Drinks came, then disappeared and came again—a little more frequently for him than her.

"Oh, we won't have to sell him. He'll sell himself. He's a good man and he cares. We just need to get him out there over the next two years, so other people can listen to him, hear his views, make up their own minds that he's the best man for the job."

"Spoken like a true politician." He smiled his smile at her, warming places in her heart that had been empty too long, like un-used rooms in a huge house, closed off and neglected for many years. "It's that way you have with words, Livy. It's your talent."

"No. It's just the truth about the man," she said, basking in his praise anyway. It was a big job, a scary job. When the campaign be-gan in earnest there wouldn't be time to turn around. What if she screwed up? It meant a lot that Brian was so confident. "And now that I've bent your ear out of all recognition about me, tell me about you. What you've been doing. Where you've been. Are you . . . seeing anyone? Special," she added, guessing he *saw* plenty, but only someone special would be worth discussing.

"Not really," he said, skipping nimbly over the first two ques-tions. "How about you? Have you dumped the . . . Richard yet?"

"Thank you," she said, smiling at the price he'd paid in resisting the name Dickhead. "And no, I haven't dumped him. As a matter of fact, he's with me on this trip. Jim gave Richard a job, too. Personal assistant." In less than a split second, she saw in his expression the questions, the anger, the accusations, the disbelief, and the disap-proval. "*Temporary* personal assistant. Just for a few months, until Jim can find someone who wants the job permanently."

Brian shook his head and closed his eyes.

"Tell me where you've been," he said, opening his eyes, ignoring the subject of Richard altogether. The omission emphasized his contempt for the man. "My mom mentioned New York, I think."

"Just for a weekend," she said mildly, with a shrug, then all that changed. "Oh! Oh! But wait! Guess who I saw!"

"Don't make me guess. I hate it when you make me guess."

"Chewy." She leaned back to watch a slow, sweet, sentimental grin cross his face. Their eyes met in a memory. Her hand slid into her purse and pulled out her wallet as she said, "*Doctor* Lewis now that he has his Ph.D. in History. He wanted me to be sure and give you his number"—she handed him a card—"and to tell you to call him if your travels ever took you to New York. I told him about all the places you'd been to . . . oh! And, get this . . . his wife calls him Charles." A hoot of laughter. "I got to meet her. She's beautiful. I called Mrs. Lewis in Tolford before I left, got his number, called him. They picked me up at my hotel and we went to dinner at this wonderful Italian restaurant nearby. It was easier that way, I guess, although I would have loved to have seen how people can actually *live* in New York with all that traffic and all those people and no place to move around in, not even a front yard . . . oh! They have a little boy. William. Gorgeous little boy. He's four. I think he's going to look just like *Charles* when he grows up." Another giggle. "And she was pregnant—I should call when I get back and see what they had. . . ."

She went on to tell him that Chewy and a few other like-minds had parlayed an experimental class on black history into an entire department of black studies at NYU and that Chewy was heading it. She then went on to tell him about Theo, whom she'd heard about through Chewy, actually. It was hard to think that that small boy, getting off the bus amid a storm of rocks and angry words that day so long ago, heading for kindergarten . . . was now heading for NYU on the recommendation of a certain history professor from his hometown. But there you were.

From there she moved on down the list, noting the birth of Junior McDunn's second son and the marriage of Jerry Levitts to . . . none other than Patty Coleman, the skinniest girl ever to be born in Tolford. They laughed and reminisced, and by the time the sun started to settle in the west, staring its fading brightness directly into Brian's eyes across the table from her, they had come full circle and were talking about . . . her . . . again.

"Only in this case, he isn't just any old politician. He really does deserve the respect. He's a good man," she said, speaking once again of Jim Seirs. A bright idea. "Why don't you come meet him. Yes. You have to. I'm not ready to say good-bye to you yet, and besides, you've let me do all the talking and . . . please, Brian. We spent all day yesterday meeting and interviewing reps from half a dozen large campaign management firms. Jim wants an advisor to work with the smaller management group he's worked with for years, out of Nashville, which was great for local campaigning but—and this will impress you—Richard suggested that a bigger campaign would probably do better with a bigger management firm."

He looked vaguely interested, but not the least bit impressed.

"Anyway, we're down to two firms and they're both wining and dining us while we're here. There's a barbecue at one of the vice president's homes tomorrow afternoon. Come and meet him for yourself. You'll like him."

He smiled and tipped his head to one side, saying, "You're a long way from draft card burning and sit-ins, aren't you?"

She chuckled. "Not so very far," she said. "It's . . . it's just a new approach to the same old stuff. What?" she asked, when she caught him studying her.

"Same old stuff and you're still pushing from behind," he said. "You should run for office. It'd be the cheapest campaign ever. You could do your own thinking. You wouldn't have to hire other people to do it for you."

"Oh, Brian," she said, flattered and appalled in turn. "You love me too much. It's not like that at all. First off, Jim Seirs does do his own thinking. I believe in what he stands for, so I want him to succeed. I want to do what I can to help him, that's all. Secondly, I'm not running material. I haven't got a big enough personality. I'm better backstage. And thirdly, if I did run, I would never win."

"Why? Because you're a woman? That crap won't float anymore, Livy. Remember the Equal Opportunity Act? Women are starting to take over the country."

"We're not taking over; we're taking our share," she said.

"And *you'd* have a great chance of taking any office you wanted."

She lowered her eyes to the table, shook her head, then looked up smiling. "Jesus, Carowack, you never change. I thought you had, but I must have been wrong. You still can't see it, can you?"

"What?"

"My birthmark. It's like you'll always be in first grade, painting pictures of me without it. I love you for that, but everyone else in the world *can* see it. And Age of Enlightenment or not, there are still plenty of people out there who think it's connected to my brain or even my soul. You don't have to be beautiful to run for office but you have to have an honest face. Mine attracts superstition and mystery, as if I've been cursed or touched by the devil. They think I'm hiding behind it. This is not a face that inspires confidence."

"Has someone told you this? Or are you making it up as you go?" he asked, stupefied. "Compared to your eyes and your energy and your words and . . . and to the blind faith you have in the rest of the world, that mark on your face isn't much more than a pimple. It's nothing. You have so much more to offer the world than a purple blotch on your cheek. And I'm not the only one who sees that. Seirs must see it."

"I know. I didn't say I didn't have anything to offer. I know what I'm capable of, but the fact remains, I'm capable of much, much more behind the scenes than out in front."

"I will never agree with you," he said, rarely stubborn, but stubborn beyond belief when he wanted to be.

"And I will never run for public office," she said, as if to say, so there! "That brings us back to my invitation to the barbecue tomorrow."

Okay. So maybe it wasn't a great idea to get a little drunk . . . or a lot drunk on the ride up the coast from West L.A. to Malibu that day. And maybe he should have borrowed a car for the occasion, instead of tooling up to the huge two-story brick mansion on his motorcycle. And maybe he should have guessed that casual attire in political circles wasn't what the proletariat thought of as casual. And, all right, so maybe he did know that when Livy said he could bring a date, she was assuming he'd bring one with a brain. But he'd discovered that half-lit was the best way to have intercourse—with girls and with life in general, and he hadn't wanted to go to the damn barbecue in the first place, and in the second place, what the hell difference did it make how he got there or who he was with? Okay?

Besides, he liked Jenna. She made him laugh, and he had a feeling he'd be needing a few that day. And if Seirs was truly of the people, for the people, and all that, he was going to have to get used to people like Jenna—people who walk into antique stores and ask what's new.

Anyway, Jenna's humor wasn't her only good feature. She also happened to be a California fantasy girl—tall and tan and young and lovely—and . . . he didn't know if she was from Ipanema, didn't know if she even knew where Ipanema was, but he was pretty sure no one would ask and who cared anyway?

The doorman at the beachfront estate, who led them through the house to lawns overlooking the ocean, should have been his first clue that it wasn't going to be the type of barbecue he was accustomed to. You know . . . blankets, charred hotdogs, a six-pack of beer.

His second lead came when his companion suggested that the other guests might have cornered the market on white cotton and polyester. White linen suits with pastel shirts and bright wide ties. White flared slacks with bold-colored, broad-collared shirts. Creased white Bermuda shorts and polo shirts with designer emblems. Expensively simple white sundresses. A few white sun hats. Billowing white caftans and wide-legged pant suits. She said if she'd known the party had a white theme, she'd have worn her white hot pants instead of her red ones.

About the only correct assumption he'd made—and counted on—was that Jenna would draw more attention than he. She wasn't shy or clingy, so he'd be free to eat his dogs and drink his beer in relative obscurity, almost immediately. Comfortable-Anywhere was her middle name.

"Well, when I heard it was a party for a congressman . . . or is it a senator? I can't recall. A political party, let's say," she said to the first man she caught looking interested in her red hot pants—a tall distinguished-looking gentleman with graying temples. "Anyway, when I heard it was a political party, I just assumed the theme colors would be patriotic, you know, red, white and blue, flags and stars and such. Who would have guessed they'd be plain old white? That's why I wore these red shorts—and this halter top I actually bought for the Fourth of July but . . . well, that's patriotic too, isn't it? Besides, it's a cute outfit, don't you think? Course, I lost the top button on the ride up here," she then whispered to him. "Bri and I stopped to make love, but it doesn't matter cuz I have my swimsuit top on under. . . . Is there a pool here?"

"Yes, miss," he said, presenting his tray to her and Brian at the same time. "Wine?"

"Is there something stronger at the bar?" he asked, nodding at the setup a few feet away. The waiter nodded.

Jenna took a glass of wine, drank it, set it down, and took another before turning to the next man she caught looking interested in her red hot pants.

"When I heard this was going to a political party, I just assumed the theme colors would be . . ."

Brian faded into the crowd.

The dogs turned out to be pigs . . . in blankets, and pâté on crackers with green olive slices on top. The employees of the catering service were considerably more friendly, interesting, and talkative than most of his fellow guests. He struck up a conversation with every hors d'oeuvre waiter that came his way, to at least *feel* a little less out of his element, even though he obviously was. You can take the boy out of Tolford, you know, but . . .

Thirty minutes went by without a sign of Livy, and he began to worry that he'd brought Jenna to the wrong party, to the wrong address, on the wrong day, in the wrong year. With his usual resolve, he decided they'd leave if he didn't see someone he knew by the time he was finished at the buffet table.

Not seeing Livy that day would have been something of a blessing, he supposed. Two seconds with her the day before had been enough for him to know that nothing had changed. He thought they had, he had hoped . . . he was convinced that seeing her again would be the end of it, that he'd be over her, that he'd be able to see how foolish he'd been for so long and go on with his life. One look in her eyes was all it took. He still loved her—and no matter how many other women he kissed in distraction, no matter how much alcohol he consumed to dull the ache, no matter how many miles he put between them, he always would.

During his second pass over the ham and turkey and spiced shrimp, past the array of iced salads, hot and cold vegetables, hard and soft breads, and the fruit display, he thought of taking Jenna a plate of food. She, at the time, was entertaining a small horde of gentlemen—with her opinions on color schemes for parties, no doubt.

He smiled when she looked up and wiggled her fingers at him in greeting. She didn't appear to need or want to be rescued; she was having a good time. He was glad one of them was.

"I see it was you who brought the entertainment for the afternoon. I should have known. You always were a thoughtful person."

"Hey, Dickhead, how's it hangin'. Care for some cheese, or fruit?" he asked, curbing a strong urge to spill his plate of refills down the front of the white sleeveless sweater and slacks he was wearing with a light patterned shirt. He looked like Robert Redford in *The Great Gatsby* and he was tempted to shoot him.

"No. Thanks. But feel free to help yourself," he said, gesturing to Brian's plate, which looked as though it had been loaded with a backhoe.

"Nice day, huh?" he said, turning back to the buffet table because it was easier than looking at Richard. He was feeling pretty much Teflon-coated by now, so anything the dickhead had to say wouldn't be sticking in his mind for long anyway.

"Definitely. It's hard to believe it's almost always this beautiful here. Olivia says you're thinking of giving all this up and going east for a while."

Olivia?

"I'm thinking about it," he said, picking up his third drink and turning toward his isolated seat at an umbrella-covered table.

"It must be nice to drop whatever you're doing, whenever you want, to go where the wind blows you."

It wasn't what he said as much as the way he said it that had Brian glancing at him cautiously, preparing for an attack.

"It is nice," he said. Then thinking to beat him to the punch he added, "It's one of the few benefits to being a lazy bum."

He smirked. His eyes were humorless. "Interesting outfit for . . . a bum."

He'd been waiting for that one. The clothes he was wearing—
purchased just for the occasion, just hours before arriving—weren't
exactly gettin'it-on, you know? The Salvation Army down the street
from his two-room apartment over a liquor store wasn't what you'd
call designer conscious, but they were good about spraying for bugs
and their prices were right. He'd been glad to find a black sport
jacket that fit him, already pressed, not too smelly, and only six or
eight years out of fashion. He'd worn his best jeans and his whitest
T-shirt with it for a *Six-Million-Dollar Man* look.

"Thanks," he said, walking away with his plate of food.

Richard followed him.

"So, what else have you been doing with your life? Besides
building up your wardrobe and being a bum. Oh! Here she is now,"
he said, all brightness and good cheer as Livy crossed the lawn toward them. "Look who showed up after all. Brian was just filling me
in on his California lifestyle."

"Was he?" She sounded doubtful, but willing to believe almost
anything to keep the conversation happy and light. "Hi, you," she
said, taking Brian's free hand, going up on tiptoe to kiss his cheek.
"You made it, huh?"

"I said I would," he said, leading the way to the shaded table.

"And you look so handsome," she said, her eyes shining with
happiness, and maybe pride, too. "See those women up near the patio? They were tittering about you when I walked by—wondering
who you were, where you came from. One of them thinks you're a
rock star."

"Cool. I'll give her my autograph later, see if she wants to be my
new groupie."

She laughed. "I'm so glad you decided to come," she said, taking
the chair next to his at the table, while Richard took one across
from him.

"You mean I had a choice?"

"Well, no, you didn't, but I'm still glad you came," she said, grinning. "Jim Seirs and I were talking this morning and I told him all about you. He said . . ."

"Brian was just about to tell me what he's been doing here all this time," Richard said, breaking in. His masque was enthusiastic, as if he were truly interested.

There was a challenge in his eyes that Brian couldn't refuse. Should have perhaps, but couldn't.

"There's not much to tell. Odd jobs here and there. Painting, drawing."

"What sort of odd jobs?"

"Bartending. Construction. I picked oranges for a few bucks once. On weekends I sometimes sit on Santa Monica Pier and drew caricatures of tourists at two dollars a head. It's good practice. I even sold a painting. Once. To a woman from Virginia, for fifty bucks. I'm not in the market for an investment broker," he said, looking Richard in the eye. "But I'm staying alive."

Truth? Well, the Virginia woman and the painting were a lie. Weekends on Santa Monica Pier were contingent on the severity of his hangovers . . . but the rest was true. He made enough to keep him in rent, gas, beer, and cigarettes. What else was there?

"How interesting," he said, as if stifling a yawn. "Not exactly Fortune Five Hundred material, are you?"

"Richard!" Livy looked embarrassed—for him or for Richard? "How dare you? I can't believe you'd say something like that. It doesn't . . ."

"Livy. Livy. It's OK. It doesn't matter. Really. Because whatever I'm doing, I'm doing on my own. I don't have to ride around on someone else's shirttail."

"Brian . . ."

"No, that's a fair assumption, honey," Richard said, a calming hand to her forearm. "You may have forgotten to mention to Brian that this is a temporary position until I go back to graduate school in the fall." For Brian's edification, he mentioned, "Yale. Business."

"Congratulations," he said, taking another mouthful of pasta salad, hoping he wouldn't choke on it. He swallowed. "Who's paying? You, your rich parents . . . or Livy?" Livy gasped and Richard opened his mouth to answer, but he held up his hand first, waving him off. "Forget it. It's none of my business."

"Damn right," Richard said, glaring.

"With me on the campaign trail with Jim next year, there won't be a lot of time for us to be together," Livy jumped in, nervous and prattling. "Richard and I. That's why having him with us this summer is so great. Because then in the fall, Congressman Druet has offered Richard a part-time internship in his office. It'll be a heavy load for a while, but Richard's always had so much energy. . . ."

"Congressman Druet? Isn't there a Senator Druet who's a friend of your dad's?" he asked, recalling the name from somewhere, and having very little contact with Connecticut politicians, there could be only one *somewhere.*

"He and Daddy went to school together. Christopher Druet, the congressman . . . is his son," Livy said, realizing too late how the connection sounded—not that it sounded any different from the truth. She didn't miss the accusing stare he aimed at Richard, who dodged it by looking away.

"Lucky for you, huh . . . Richard?"

"Brian, it isn't like that at all. Daddy didn't do all that much to . . ."

"I am a lucky man, indeed," Richard said sarcastically, cutting her off once again and meeting Brian's gaze with a renewed confidence. "Of course, after the wedding there'll be no end to the nepotistic opportunities available to me."

"Richard!"

"Well, he's always making those insinuations and . . ."

"What wedding?" Brian asked, his stomach starting to coil and churn.

". . . I'm sick of it. And you know what else? I don't care what he thinks. He's jealous."

"What wedding?" he asked a little louder, feeling a whole lot nauseated.

"He sees us climbing to the top while his life is going, literally"—he motioned to the neat shot of Johnny Walker Black in front of Brian—"up in fumes and he can't stand it."

"Don't be ridiculous. He has no interest in politics. His life's road is in a completely different direction."

"Straight to hell, I'm sure. And he'd love to drag you down with him."

"What wedding?" This time he shouted it loud enough to get their attention—as well as the curious regard of most everyone else at the gathering.

"Olivia and I are getting married in the fall," Richard said simply.

Brian didn't believe it, of course. He'd gotten too drunk. It happened sometimes. He'd passed out and this was just another horrible nightmare, that's all.

"Damn it, Richard," Livy was saying. "I told you I hadn't had a chance to tell him yet. And I asked you not to say anything."

His gaze traveled slowly from Richard's devilish expression to Livy's seraphic countenance. Was she in on this ridiculous joke, too? Had she heard what Richard said? Why wasn't she denying it? He was going to be sick—all that whiskey, all that food—all over them.

"What difference does it make who tells him? It's not like we need his blessing."

"He's my best friend," she said, scowling at him, her mien softening to compassion and worry as she turned to Brian. "I wanted to tell you. I was waiting for the right time and yesterday you . . . I'm sorry you had to hear it like this." She smiled a little. "Actually, you're the first person who's looked the least bit surprised."

Surprised? He didn't look crushed? Ripped to shreds? Twisted as a nest of snakes?

"Holy cow! You two talk alike," Jenna said, approaching the table just as Livy finished speaking. They all turned to look at her in her patriotic hot pants and halter top. She wagged a finger between Livy and Brian and said, "You could be brother and sister, you sound so much alike. That sweet southern accent is one of the things I love best about Brian. You must be his friend Livy. Hi," she said, taking the last chair between the two men. "It was really nice of you to invite us. If I'd known about the white color theme and all, I'd have worn something different. Well, not really different but another color, for sure."

Brian sat with his mouth open for several more moments, stunned, feeling angry and betrayed, desperate not to embarrass himself by being sick. The sound of Jenna's voice continued to buzz in his head, like a bee caught in a jar. Part of him wanted to break Richard in half. Part of him wanted to shake Livy till she came to her senses. Most of him wanted to cry.

He kept looking at her, hoping she'd burst into laughter, ending the hoax.

She looked back at him, her warm brown eyes full of concern, pleading for his understanding and best wishes.

". . . and he's so quiet! Doesn't that drive you crazy some-times?" Jenna was asking Livy. "You never know if he's home unless you knock on his door. He's the quietest one in our building. He never talks much about his family . . . but he has mentioned you. Well, not really mentioned you, just said your name once or twice. He's got these drawings of you, of your face, from different angles, you know? They're real nice. I like looking at them, they're . . . spe-cial . . . sort of . . . you know? But I keep forgetting your name, and every time I ask, he says Livy. So when he asked if I wanted to meet you, I said sure. Of course, then he told me this was a picnic put on by a PR firm for your boss who's in politics so I just assumed the color theme would be patriotic. . . ." She looked beyond Richard's shoulder and started to wave furiously. "Jim. Jim. Hi."

James Seirs, candidate for the U.S. Senate, waved his campaign wave and smiled his campaign smile as he walked slowly across the lawn to their table.

"I see you found your friend," he said, smiling kindly at Jenna.

"And he found his friends," she said, beaming back at him as she spread her arms wide to present the friendly gathering—as it were. "I was just telling them about Brian's pictures of Livy. I would have known her anywhere from them."

Seirs smiled, directing his gaze to Brian.

"Jim Seirs," he said, extending a hand to him. "I'd love to see your work someday. My wife's been after me for years to have a family portrait painted. Livy says your detailing is incredible. She says she holds her breath, waiting for your pictures to move or say something, they're so real."

"Livy's a loyal friend, sir," he said, standing to take the man's hand and giving his own name. "You won't be sorry she's in your camp."

"I have that same feeling, Mr. Carowack," he said. For a second or two Brian wasn't sure who Mr. Carowack was. Then he looked for traces of sarcasm or condescension in Seirs and found none. "She tells me you've been friends since first grade. It's a shame more friendships don't last that long."

Friendship. Friendship. Friendship.

God, how he was beginning to hate the word! It put impossible limitations on a relationship—it regulated the amount and the type of love you can give someone; it impeded the intimacies you can share with her. It restricted what you can say and feel and think about her. It was the strongest bond two people could have, as well as the most fragile. Without it, even the ties between husband and wife, brother and sister, parent and child were more easily severed, and yet to Brian, it was extremely confining.

He looked down at Livy, her anxiety almost audible. Are we still friends? Can we still be friends? I need you to be my friend.

It wasn't her fault he felt the way he did. She wasn't feeling the limitations, only the boundless affection, trust, and understanding she'd always felt for him.

His smile was sincere, but an effort nonetheless.

"It is a shame, sir," he said, addressing Seirs, but speaking to Livy. "I wouldn't trade one second of my friendship with Livy for anything in the world. And I suspect I'll always feel that way."

Inside, he was screaming.

Eighteen

Mr. and Mrs. Geoffrey L. Hubbard
request the honor of your presence
at the marriage of their daughter
Olivia J. Hubbard
and
Richard T. Kerrigan III
Saturday, the eighteenth of September
Nineteen hundred and seventy-four
at four o'clock in the afternoon
Downtown Presbyterian Church
Nashville, Tennessee

Brian bought a plane ticket. He planned to go to the wedding. He would have preferred to spend the time having his eyes plucked out, but he wanted to be there for her. He really did.

Nineteen

I F WE'D HAD the wedding in Tolford, he might have come," she said, peeved. At Brian. At Richard. At herself. At the world. "You know Daddy didn't care where the wedding took place."

It was the day after New Year's Day, January 2, 1975. It was a cold, dreary day in Nashville. Cold and dreary outside, but colder and drearier inside the two-bedroom newlywed apartment on 12th Avenue, where only *one* newlywed resided full time.

"Your father is a . . . nice man . . . and he spoils you," Richard said, holding up and comparing two conservative dark suits that looked almost identical. "He never would have told you how important it was to him, politically, to have the wedding in Nashville. He's the party rep for his district, for Christ's sake. He has obligations. You can't expect him to rearrange his life for the convenience of someone like Brian Carowack."

"Tolford is our hometown. Daddy was mayor there before he was district chairman. He has obligations there, too. He didn't care if every Democrat in the state came to our wedding; *that* was you." She frowned over an old tweed jacket. "A small wedding in Tolford and a reception at my folks' house would have been perfect. We didn't need to invite all those strangers. I didn't know half of them. Are you sure you want to pack this tweed jacket?"

"Yes. I'm going to have leather patches put on the elbows. And all those strangers were friends of your father's . . ."

"Acquaintances."

" . . . who happen to be very powerful people in this state. Not one of them could have been left off the list without repercussions. And your father knew it."

They'd been over this before, of course. Over it and over it before the wedding and several more times over the four months
since. It wasn't the only thing they fought about as young newly-
weds, but it did seem to be the most recurring. Maybe that was because she still had a number of thank-you notes to be written to
people whose names she didn't recognize. Or because she was still
sorting the candid photographs of the reception with so many un-
familiar faces in them. Or maybe it was because she still resented
the absurdity of Richard insisting the wedding be held in a town
where she had lived for barely a month and knew no one, when
Tolford or Memphis where her family and most her of friends
were—or even his hometown of Knoxville—would have been more
practical, made better sense, and would have *meant* more to her. It
was hard to tell. So many things seemed to trigger a fight these days.

The constant packing and unpacking over the past several
weeks wasn't helping her nerves either. In August, along with all the
preparations for the wedding, she'd packed up her apartment and
moved from Memphis to Nashville because of her job with Jim
Seirs—then she unpacked. She packed up all the wedding and
shower gifts from both Tolford and Memphis, took them to
Nashville—then she unpacked them. She packed up everything in
Richard's seldom-used apartment in Memphis because he was too
busy at graduate school, hauled it all to Nashville—then unpacked
it. Now she was packing the things Richard would be taking back to
school with him . . . and wanting to unpack it.

She didn't want to spend what little time they had left bicker-
ing, she really didn't. She just couldn't seem to help herself. Something was terribly wrong—and their time apart was only making it
worse. She wanted to quit her job and go with him.

"This doesn't make any sense at all," she said, placing a half-
dozen pressed shirts in the suitcase beside his underwear. "It was
bad enough last summer trying to plan the wedding with you gone.
But you fly in for the ceremony and our weekend honeymoon,

leave me here high and dry until Thanksgiving, fly back to Yale, come home for Christmas, and now I won't see you again until spring break. I hate this! A husband should be with his wife. I should be going to New Haven with you."

"We've been over this, too," he reminded her, dumping three or four pairs of shoes on the bed for her to pack. "We're not the first couple to get married under these circumstances. We're young. We're both working on our careers. And it's not the quantity of our time together that counts; it's the quality."

"Yeah, well, I don't think the quality of our marriage has been all that great so far, Richard. We saw more of each other and were happier when we were single."

He turned from the bureau to look at her, sighing as if he were dealing with a child. Smiling, he drew her gently into his arms.

"We agreed on this before the wedding, remember? We have an agenda. I get my MBA and find out everything I can about Druet's operation. You stay here in Tennessee, get Seirs into the senate, and by the time your father's ready to run for governor, the two of us will manage his campaign. A couple terms here in Nashville, then we'll take him to D.C. Ten years tops. We can do it, if we stay focused on our goal."

"Daddy hasn't even decided yet if. . . . If he's not well enough . . ."

"He will be. Seirs is ready now, but the history books already have your father's name all over that seat in the senate. He's a shoe-in. The party leaders love him."

"He's not your puppet, Richard. He's getting older, and Daddy has definite . . ."

"Of course he's not my puppet, dear," he said, cutting her off as he frequently did, forcing the endearment he only used to cajole or placate her. Just once, she wished he'd called her sweetheart or honey or babe . . . and mean it. "He's a reasonable, rational, intelligent man. He listens to his constituents and advisors—that'll be us someday—and he makes the best possible decisions."

"I don't know, Richard," she said, letting him press her head to his chest and hold her tight. "Working for Jim now, setting Daddy up to challenge him . . . it feels like cheating."

"Don't be silly. It's politics. Seirs knows the game. He knows who you are. You're giving him your best effort *now* . . . that's all we promised him. No one's cheating anybody." And then to pacify her, he added, "I'll try for more weekend visits, I promise."

She sighed. If she could draw this same picture for Brian, she was sure he'd shade it differently, define it better, make it clearer.

With his hands on her shoulders, he kissed her brow and bent his knees to look into her eyes, smiling. "Feel a little better now?" he asked. "Our time apart is only temporary. Remember that. And we'll both be so busy for the next few months, it'll go by in no time at all. You'll see. Do you know where the red striped tie your mother gave me for Christmas is?"

"Dry cleaner. I'll pick it up this afternoon."

"Thanks." He gave her shoulders a reassuring pat and started to leave the room.

"Oh, yes," he said, slowing to a stop at the door. Against the door was propped a portrait they'd received as a wedding gift. A portrait of Livy. A gift from Brian. "If you're going to insist on hanging this somewhere, do me a favor?"

"What?"

"Hang it behind a door that stands open most the time, will you? Or at the back of a full closet or something."

"Richard." She was cut to the quick.

"Now don't misunderstand me, dear, it's an incredible rendering of you. It is. But it's . . . it's like a portrait of your beautiful twin—the one without the birthmark, you know? It doesn't even look like you without it."

"The angle's wrong. You can't see it from that angle of my face."

"Of course you can. Come here." She stepped in front of him. Using her chin, he tipped her head to match the angle in Brian's portrait. "Oh, sure. See. I can definitely see it at this angle. It's not a true likeness. He probably painted you beautiful because he couldn't paint your brain into the picture, and for me, your intelligence is your beauty."

That stung her pride, even though she knew what he meant by it. There had been times when he'd said he liked her eyes or her smile or some other physical attribute—as any good lover would, she supposed—but he'd always made it abundantly clear that he was most attracted to her mind, and that how she used it determined her real beauty in his eyes.

At least he was honest.

He went off in search of something else he wanted to pack and left her standing there, staring at the portrait. She was having one of those weird déjà vu moments, as if she were reliving a memory . . . the memory of another portrait she had been proud of, another portrait that wasn't of her after all.

She thought of the note that came with it: *I think I finally got it right this time. Be happy. Love, Brian.*

No *Sorry I have to miss the wedding, I have other plans.* Not a *Can't come to the wedding because I hate Richard and think you're making a huge mistake.* Nothing. No explanations. No excuses.

During the first few weeks after the wedding, she'd tried several times to call him—to ask why he didn't come, to chew him out, to make sure he was safe, to end their friendship, to plead for forgiveness for whatever wrong she might have committed, to tell him about the wedding, to curse at him—but his line had been disconnected.

His mother was her only firm link to him now, and she believed he was on his way to New York.

New York.

She couldn't remember ever feeling more alone.

She turned the portrait to the wall.

"What am I doing here?" Brian asked.

A large, overweight man in his fifties with graying brown hair and hands the size of bear's paws rattled the newspaper he was reading impatiently and answered mechanically, "You have been subpoenaed by Judge William Ogden Asher and the State of California to appear in his courtroom on . . ."

"I know *that*, but why?" Brian asked. Though the man was wearing a plain, off-the-rack brown suit, he had cop written all over him. Cops made him nervous. Guilty or innocent, it didn't matter, he always felt deeply in trouble when they were around. "And why can't I use my crutches instead of this wheelchair? I can get around pretty well with my crutches. They're easier than this thing." He smacked the arms of the wheelchair and felt a familiar frustration. He was on the mend, he reminded himself. He'd left the wheelchairs behind him, in the hospital. All those weeks of physical therapy meant he'd never have to sit helpless in a wheelchair again. But he hadn't forgotten how it felt. The loss of freedom, the lack of control. A swift, staggering wash of fear consumed him whenever his mind touched on the realization of how close he'd come to losing it all. His legs. His hands. His life.

"If Judge Asher says he wants you wheeled into his courtroom, that's what I'll do," the big man said. "I'll wheel you in." His voice was deep and sort of booming, as though he was talking through at large hollow pipe. He closed the paper, folded it in half, then tossed it on the table between them. There was a sad emptiness to the man's eyes, as if he didn't really care about anything one way or the other; he was just . . . there, putting in his time.

It was almost Christmas. Brian hadn't been out of the hospital two weeks yet. He didn't have gifts to send home for Beth and Bobby. His collect calls to his mother had been cheerful and reas-

suring and had contained nothing about the accident or the hospitals bills or . . . anything. He hadn't made it to Livy's wedding,
hadn't heard from her. He couldn't work. The last thing he needed
was cop troubles. What he did need was a drink.

His companion's name was Cooper; it was the only name he
gave. They were sitting in a waiting room with a table and four
chairs—five if you included the wheelchair. Brian was barely conscious after the accident when Cooper showed up at his bedside
with a subpoena, and to inform him that he'd be contacting him
again after his release from the hospital—to make sure he didn't
forget to show up and to make travel arrangements if necessary.
Maybe he should have talked to a lawyer, he thought. Too late.

He glanced up to find Cooper staring at him, considering him,
as if trying to determine his species. Finally, he gave in a little and
said, "Judge Asher always has a good reason for what he wants
done. I don't ask questions."

Obviously. And obviously Brian wasn't going to get any answers to his. He shook his head. "You'd think cops would have better things to do than to haul people all over L.A. just to make sure
they show up in court . . . traffic court, no less," he said with some
derision, referring to the fact that Cooper had insisted on picking
him up and delivering him to the courthouse in person—since
Brian's right leg was still weak and he couldn't yet drive himself.
Even Brian's promise to hire a taxi or bum a ride from a friend
hadn't fazed him. "Nice waste of taxpayers' money."

"You pay a lot of taxes, do ya?" Cooper asked, giving Brian's old
jeans and older flannel shirt a smooth, amused once-over before
adding, "I'm not a cop anymore anyway. I'm retired. I do this for
fun."

"For fun?"

He shrugged. "More for a good cause, I guess. And because
Judge Asher is my wife's uncle, and I like the way he does things."

He shrugged again. "And because it's part time, so it doesn't inter-fere with my other job."

"Which is . . . ?"

"I teach driver's education in West Hollywood. Used to be a traffic cop."

"I'm beginning to see a connection. Basically, the driving of cars has been pretty much your whole life, huh?"

Cooper stared at him for several seconds. "Let's say the stupid, reckless, irresponsible, and dangerous driving of cars has pretty much been my whole life. And let's say, too, that . . . people like you and your friend *still* give my life meaning."

He said it so slowly and softly that Brian might not have known he was serious or exactly what he meant if he hadn't seen the look in his eyes. He lowered his own from the stark pain and anguish and fury he saw in their gray-blue depths. And he remembered. Clearly, he was one of the luckier people this guy had had to deal with in his long career—and Brian knew it.

When he could look at Mr. Cooper again, he said, "I figured this had something to do with the accident I was in, but what does he want with me? I wasn't driving."

He smiled with closed lips. "He'll explain it to you soon enough."

Brian went back to the doodle he was working on, on the back of a bail-bonds flyer with a not-so-sharp pencil left by some other unfortunate wait-ee, no doubt. It was sort of a self-portrait actually, of his own hand holding the dull pencil.

"You're pretty good," Cooper said, leaning forward and to the right a little to see better.

"Thanks." Almost without thinking, he added, "For a while af-ter the accident I didn't think I'd ever be able to do this again. One of the doctors thought there might be some nerve damage with the broken wrist but . . . I was lucky." A pause. "It's funny the way you take something for granted until you think you might not have it anymore, isn't it?"

Remembered fear and panic rolled through him; it nauseated him.

When Cooper remained silent he looked up. The big man met Brian's eyes straight on and he said, "There's nothing funny about that, son. Nothing funny at all."

Not long after, a female police officer poked her head around the door and told Cooper that the judge was ready for them. She waited at the big double doors under the sign that read Traffic Court, then held one side wide for them to pass through.

It was packed. It didn't seem as big as some of the courtrooms he'd been in, but it was big enough to be impressive, to look like a place where some serious business was done. There were enough pewlike seats to cram a hundred, maybe a hundred and fifty, people into it. Why they were all staring at him he couldn't imagine.

"Ah. Mr. Carowack, there you are," said a faraway voice. "I hope my summons today hasn't been too inconvenient for you. A little closer, Coop, if you please." A small, mostly bald man in the black robes of a judge was directing the room from high atop the podium at the front of the room. "Officer Green, please hold the gate open for them. That's it, good. Thank you. And thank you for coming this morning, Mr. Carowack," he said—as if Brian had had a choice.

Cooper had parked him about halfway between the court reporter's desk in front of and below where the judge was sitting, and the two desks where the lawyers and defendants sat—right in the middle of everything, really—and then he'd gone off to sit in the crowd somewhere. Brian had a quick glimpse of his pal, Issy Jordon, with a man he assumed was Issy's lawyer at the table to his left. But he kept his attention pinned to the judge. To tell the truth, the whole truth, and nothing but the truth, he was scared spitless. Cops were one thing; judges were another. His mouth was dry, his heart was pounding, his hands were sweating—and he hadn't done anything illegal.

"I would imagine that you're wondering why I asked you here today, Mr Carowack," Judge Asher said with a friendly enough smile. He wasn't an unreasonable-looking man. Maybe not very tall, and thin, but with a certain presence that made him seem bigger than he was.

"Yes, sir."

"If you will bear with me for just a few more minutes, I promise to make it perfectly clear to you." Brian gave a slight nod. The judge read his name and address and asked if they were correct. Then he told Brian that he was not under arrest, that there were no charges pending against him, and that he was not being called as a witness in the case against Mr. Isaac Jordon, *at this time*—did he understand?

"Yes, sir."

"Good. Then, first, will you tell this court whether or not you were with one Isaac Loyd Jordon on the night of Thursday, September 16, 1974 of this year?"

He knew the date, and he figured Issy's real name was Isaac. "Yes, sir, I was."

"On that night were you a passenger in a 1967 Ford Mustang driven by Mr. Jordon?"

"Yes, sir."

"And have you, Mr. Carowack, spent the greater part of the last three months in a hospital, unconscious and/or recovering from very serious, even life-threatening injuries sustained as a result of that 1967 Ford Mustang crashing into a retaining wall on Jefferson Boulevard, just off the Pacific Coast Highway, with Mr. Isaac Jordon behind the wheel?"

He turned his head and looked at Issy. He wasn't sure what was going on but it didn't feel like anything good. Issy's expression confirmed it.

Obviously, the wheelchair was to make him seem more of a sympathetic character to the people in the room—the judge notwithstanding.

"Answer the question, please, Mr. Carowack."

He took a deep breath. "Yes, sir. I was in an accident that night, in that car, with Issy . . . ah, Isaac . . . Jordon. I got out of the hospital about ten days ago."

"Can you tell me, Mr Carowack, what exactly took place that night and how the accident happened?"

"No, sir." The judge's expression switched from judicious to hostile in a blink of his eye. Brian stammered. "I mean . . . I would . . . if I could. I don't remember much. I know it was raining."

"Had Mr. Jordon been drinking anything alcoholic prior to driving the car that night?"

Again, he looked at Issy. He hardly knew the guy, really. They worked construction together sometimes. A fast-food place once and then the bank building just before the accident. Brian had taken the bus to work that day. The gas tank on his bike was leaking from somewhere; he'd taken it into a shop to have it worked on. He'd hoped to get a lift home from someone, and Issy had volunteered. He was a nice guy, friendly, did his job, didn't ask too many questions. Brian liked him. He could remember being soul-sick at the thought of leaving for Tennessee the next day to attend Livy's wedding. All summer long his heart had felt like stone in his chest, heavy and sore. So, when Issy mentioned wanting a beer or two before going home to face his wife and kids, Brian offered to keep him company—eagerly, gratefully, needfully.

"Was Mr. Jordon drinking alcohol, at any time, prior to driving the car that night, Mr. Carowack?"

"I think so. Yeah. Maybe." This just wasn't looking good for Issy. He didn't want to be the one to rat the guy out, or make things worse for him. Hell, that could just as easily have been him sitting there next to the lawyer.

The judge sighed loudly and narrowed his eyes at Brian. He looked as if he had only a few drops of patience left in his bottle, and when that was gone, even he wasn't sure what he'd do next. After a long moment he spoke quietly and calmly.

"For the record, Mr. Carowack, and just so you know where you stand here. This case has been thoroughly investigated, first by the California State Patrol, then by the L.A. Police Department, and most recently by my personal aide, Mr. Aloysius Cooper. This court already has all the facts. About Mr. Jordon. About you. It knows exactly what happened that night. Telling us anything but the truth as you know it will have serious repercussions for you, personally. Is that understood?"

"Yes, sir," he said, and it was. He felt dread in the pit of his stomach.

"Was he drinking that night?"

"Yes."

"Thank you." He lowered his head as if reading something in front of him. There was an eerie silence in the courtroom, especially since there were so many people there. It was as if they were all waiting for a bomb to go off. When the judge finally looked at him again, he thought for sure he was going to be told to light it. "To be perfectly frank with you, sir, I hate people who drive drunk. If it were up to me, anyone caught drunk behind the wheel of an automobile would go to jail for at least a year, whether it was the first time they were stopped or their tenth time. And they would *never* drive legally in this state again." He leaned both arms on his desk and raised his body a little higher and forward over his desk. "However, it is not up to me entirely and so I am forced to use whatever means allowed me, within the law of the State of California and the Constitution of the United States of America, to see to it that people like Mr. Jordon, who drink and then endanger the rest of us by driving, are stopped." A pause. "Mr. Carowack, this court requests that you file a formal complaint of attempted vehicular manslaughter against Mr. Isaac Jordon"—a low murmur broke loose in the room, but the judge went on—"who knowingly put your life at risk by allowing you to be his passenger in a car he willfully drove while intoxicated." In what appeared to be an afterthought, and more for the benefit of the audience than for Brian, he tacked on, "I, personally, would have you file on a more serious charge—attempted murder perhaps—but this is all the district attorney will concede to for now, as it is all that he thinks he can legally prove and win judgment for in a court of law. A sure win is what I believe he called it."

Brian was stunned, couldn't think, couldn't move. The bomb was lit and he was suddenly holding it. He didn't know what to do with it. Throw it back at the judge? Throw it to Issy? Let it blow up in his lap?

"I don't think I understand, sir." Stall for time.

"Of course you do. You speak English and I don't stutter," he said. Then, as if he was going to make the situation easier on everyone, he said, "I will tell you that the defendant has already admitted to knowing how dangerous it is to drive a car while intoxicated. I am asking you to file a formal complaint against this man for disregarding that knowledge, and for acting in a negligent manner, thereby placing you in harm's way, when he allowed you to get into the car with him. I am asking you to put him in jail for the next one to three years and in doing so, make the streets of Los Angeles safer for the rest of us."

One to three years in jail was all he heard. Issy had a wife and kids. He was an okay guy. He hadn't had any more to drink than Brian. Hell, any other night it would have been *him* driving. Everyone drove home a little drunk sometimes—if they got stopped they got tickets, or fines, or their license suspended. They didn't go to jail, for God's sake.

And yet . . . somewhere, deep down inside him, in the place where his darkest fears ruled, he knew the truth. How close to dying did he have to get to accept and respond to it? Yes, his drinking had given him a certain amount of control over his life—numbing pains he didn't want to feel, blurring thoughts he didn't want to think. But without feeling, without thought, there was no control at all—of his heart, of his mind, of his body . . . of his drinking. He'd poured so much of his time and his money and his life into a bottle that he lived there now, inside that bottle, without freedom, without control, without . . . a life outside of it. And there beside one truth lay the other—a drunk in a car was a lethal and dangerous weapon.

"Sir? Do I . . . do I have to do this? What happens if I don't press charges?"

The judge stared down at him for . . . forever it seemed; the look of disappointment and disgust on his face left Brian with no doubt as to what he was thinking. Brian couldn't blame him, but he couldn't leave Issy hanging either, not alone.

"If you fail to carry out your responsibility . . . your duty in this case, the Assistant District Attorney for the City of Los Angeles, Mr. David Westfield, sitting there behind you, has agreed to file formal charges on behalf of the State of California, and you will be called as an eyewitness to the incident. Should you refuse to do even that much, you will be subpoenaed again and forced to testify against Mr. Jordon. And should you refuse to do *that*, Mr Carowack, *you* will go to jail."

"But you can't force me to testify about something I don't remember. I'm pretty sure you can't," he said, twisting in his wheelchair to look back at the prosecutor. "I was unconscious for thirteen days. I had a head injury. I don't even remember leaving the bar," he told the man, sitting quietly with his hands folded on the table in front of him. He wheeled himself backward to sit next to him at the table. "Can he do this?"

The man sighed and took pity on him. He looked up at the judge. "Your honor, may I have a moment?" With his consent, they turned away from the judge, then kept their heads down to avoid the crowd behind them. David Westfield kept his voice low. "He can do everything he says, and he will, if you don't cooperate. He's not messing around. He lost a niece last year in a car accident. The driver was drunk . . . and he survived."

"A niece?" Brian scanned the gallery, his eyes locking with Al Cooper's. His wife—the judge's niece. The sad, empty eyes . . .

"He's not the only judge cracking down on drunk drivers these days," he was saying. "But he is the most aggressive. He's backed up his whole calendar today so that all these people would be here to see this. Probably half of them are repeat DWIs like your friend, but *he's* the one who's going to be made an example of, one way or the other. He has nine DWIs, man." Brian's stomach rolled. He had six, eight if you counted the ones from Oregon and Colorado. "Fines and suspensions aren't stopping guys like him. All the judges are getting fed up with seeing the same people over and over . . . and the statistics of drunk driver–related accidents and the fatalities from them are . . ."

"I know. I know. I listen to the news," he snapped at him. He was terrified. He didn't want to go to jail. "I'm sorry, but I honest to God don't remember leaving the bar that night. For all I know I could have been driving. Maybe Issy was too drunk and I decided to drive. That could have happened. I do it all the time." His mouth and eyes snapped shut on his last few words.

"Records state you were pried out of the passenger's seat," Westfield said, his tone no longer helpful and informative, but flat and unsympathetic. "And just as a warning, the judge had Cooper check you out, too. He's got your driving record, so watch your step."

He stood then and turned to address the court.

"Your honor, the People are inclined to believe that Mr.

Carowack is unable to give clear testimony regarding Mr. Jordon's physical condition at the time of the accident, and without it we feel unable to pursue this matter in a higher court. However, should the witness regain full recall of the night in question . . ."

"What! You think he's going to run in here and let us know?" the judge broke in, his voice loud and angry. His face was red as he tried to control his breathing. He looked from Brian to Issy and out over the crowd of people in his courtroom. "Very well. I admit I am disappointed but I am not done yet, nor will I suspend my efforts to bring these criminals to justice. For criminals is exactly what I believe them to be." He adjusted himself in his chair and took a bead on Issy. Brian started to sweat. He'd seen hatred like that before, knew the pain it could inflict. "Mr. Isaac Jordon, in light of the fact that this is your ninth conviction of Driving While Intoxicated, and that eight other arrests have failed to produce a punishment significant enough to cause a change in your behavior, I am imposing the maximum sentence allowed me under the law, which is six to twelve months in the county jail. Effective immediately."

"Your honor." Issy's lawyer was on his feet. A police officer was heading for Issy with handcuffs. "My client would like to humbly request work-release privileges. He has a wife and two children."

"I am sorry for his wife and children, but your client should have thought of them before he had a drink, and before he got behind the wheel of his car."

"Yes, your honor," he said, dejected. He said something to Issy and started to pack up his briefcase, as another attorney and client moved through the gate to take their place.

"I am not finished." The judge's words stopped everyone in their tracks. Brian, assuming he was now on his own with the wheelchair—being the memory-lapsed second party again and not a potential plaintiff—was half-turned toward the gate when he felt the judge's gaze boring through the back of his head. He turned the chair slowly to face him.

"You're a disappointment, Mr. Carowack. To me. To all of the victims of all the drunk drivers in this country. To your parents. To your loved ones. And whether you know it or not, to yourself. Do you suppose that one of the reasons you don't recall the incident, the incident that very nearly put an end to your life, is that you were as drunk as Mr. Jordon that night? In fact, according to your hospital records, your blood alcohol level was actually higher than his at the time." He didn't seem to really want an answer from Brian. Didn't really care what Brian had to say for himself. He was setting another example for those nervously awaiting their turn before his bar, and Brian was his target.

"If aiding and abetting a drunk driver was a crime, I'd nail you to the floor with it," he said, his expression sad and serious . . . and threatening. "However and unfortunately, it's not. So, I must lie in wait for you, young man, to reappear before this court as you most surely will because, according to your DMV records, it is your habit to drive while intoxicated, as well. So it's just a matter of time. In fact, you might say that I am now gunning for you, Mr. Carowack. My advice to you, then, is either stop drinking or get the hell out of Dodge. The choice is yours."

Twenty

NEW YORK was as she remembered it in the early spring of 1978. Vast. Crowded. Dirty. Exciting. Potentially wonderful.

She liked that word, potential. As a kid, she had instinctively tried to live up to it, but it was different now. As an adult it took on new connotations like . . . the anticipation of, could be, maybe, hopefully, very likely. A subtle promise of something good to come.

She could use something good in her life. In fact, she longed for it.

For several months now she'd been feeling . . . a little dead inside. A lot dead actually. She was lower than a beetle's belly button, as Granddad used to say. Lost as yesterday. Glum as the undertaker. Lonely as a duck in a desert. Sad as a . . . well, and so on.

Her life was falling apart at the seams and there didn't seem to be anything she could do about it, anywhere to hide from it, anyone to share it with . . . except Brian.

So dumb.

She'd hemmed and hawed over this trip to New York for so long, you'd have thought her a veteran politician. It was like her new mantra. Hem. Haw. Hem. Haw. Her mind was a muddle, overloaded with what-ifs and if-onlys and whys. The worst of it was that she couldn't . . . step outside of herself, couldn't move beyond a certain point that wasn't totally self-absorbed. And it wasn't as if she didn't know or couldn't see how messed up the rest of the world was; it was just that her life, her own little world, was so screwed it was sapping all her energy. She was aware of all the changes taking place—beside her, around her, over there, everywhere. She just couldn't move—move on, move past, get around, be there, get involved.

While she watched from afar, American men who didn't want to look like John Travolta in *Saturday Night Fever*—whether they liked to dance or not—were thinning their ties and lapels and going conservative; women were getting padded shoulders and going double breasted—so to speak. She spent most days in her pajamas.

Better than anyone, she knew the job market was tough and that finding the right people for a job and getting them into it was a totally different thing from *keeping* them there. For instance, between the time President Ford took the country's reins from President Nixon and handed them over to President Carter two years later, he survived two assassination attempts—just part of the job description? Even the Roman Catholic Church had three popes in less than two months—unforeseeable complications? But it was Senator Seirs asking *her* to resign when rumors about her husband's connections to certain shady Tennessee businessmen rocked his office, during the construction negotiations for a state-funded water treatment facility, that really brought it home.

When rumor became truth, and Jim Seirs was forced to defend himself, to prove he had no knowledge of the money taken or the promises made in his name . . . well, something withered and died inside her. Her pride maybe. Or her ability to blindly believe in someone. Maybe just her innocence.

She supposed that in a time of occupational *persons* and bionic men and women; a time of factions of terrorist factions of terrorist groups in the Middle East taking political hostages; a time of the necessary 100 million dollars' worth of security at the Summer Olympic Games in Montreal that year—the little *no-fault* divorce she was considering seemed pretty tame. Adultery, no big deal. And yet, these were the things that consumed her.

Livy's "misery index" was not just the sum of her unemployment and the inflation rates. It went far deeper. She felt her life was merely another drop of water in the bottom of the communal com-

mode, going round and round and round . . . and she was drown-
ing.

Which is why it made no sense whatsoever to drop everything
she was doing—napping between job interviews, mostly—to track
Brian down after four years of minimal contact with him, just to
talk. What was she expecting him to say? I told you so? If he even
looked as if he was going to say it—she'd punch him.

Such a fool.

What made her think Brian had any answers for her? He'd
washed his hands of her long ago. What made her think that their
friendship still existed? She'd made other friends over the years.
What was it about Brian that made her yearn for him. To see his
face. Hear his voice. Listen to him laugh. Her mind knew better, but
her heart was convinced that a single word of encouragement from
him would see her through any crisis.

What an idiot.

And yet, there she was, hailing a taxi in New York City. Giving
the driver the numbers and street names Brian's mother had given
her over the phone. She fussed with her denim skirt and jacket, fid-
dled with the hoops in her earlobes, and wondered how much
longer her heart could pound the way it was before she had a
stroke.

She'd been to New York several times before on business, but
never saw more than the inside of a taxi cab. She had assumed, as
she assumed most tourists would, that Greenwich Village—the bohemian birthplace, battlefield, and testing ground of American literature, art, and theater—was *still* the bohemian birthplace,
battlefield, and testing ground of American literature, art, and theater.

It wasn't. Hadn't been for nearly forty years.

To keep the taxi ride short, it was in a hodgepodge of modern
skyscrapers, warehouses, large apartment buildings, run-down ho-

tels, shops, open markets, and a constant stream of traffic that they found the four-story building they were looking for.

The street level was occupied by Eugene's Eatery. It looked like one of those deli-café-liquor-grocery stores that seemed to sprout up and bloom all over the city. Through the unpainted parts of the big, high window she could see people eating at tables inside, others leaving with bags of carry-out. Sort of your all-purpose place of food, she surmised, noting a strange combination of odors from within. Not a bad or unappetizing smell, to be sure, but strange, oddly interesting.

She walked past the door to the upper floors twice before she paid it any attention, a simple unmarked door in the wall of the building. A steep stairway took her to the landing of the second floor and a door marked B. Another set of steps took her to C on the third floor and stopped.

There was no nameplate on the door, no familiar sounds from within, nothing but the numbers over Eugene's Eatery to indicate she even had the correct building.

Eugene's unique odor was about eight months old in the stairwell and not nearly as interesting, she noticed. The palms of her hands were numb. She examined the crack in the plaster wall, trying to decide if she should knock on the door or go back to the hotel. She wondered what name Brian had given the color she was looking at—dead gray, perhaps.

Well, hell. She couldn't come all this way without at least knocking on the damned door, could she? Her knock was so soft she could barely hear it. Okay, what was the worst that could happen? Wrong apartment? Or right apartment, bad idea to have come?

She was debating this when she rapped on the door a second time, louder, as if she meant it. A lifetime ticked by in the seconds before she heard movement from within. Footsteps. Chains and bolts rattling against the other side of the door. She gasped, surprised to find that she was holding her breath.

A young girl answered the door. Or perhaps she wasn't as young as she was small and frail looking, pale as the white T-shirt that hung, miles too big, from her thin shoulders to her bony kneecaps. She had long, straight black hair and huge, sunken brown eyes. She could have been the poster child for a nation of starving refugees.

"Oh, I'm so sorry I disturbed you," she said, sure she'd gotten the girl up from her deathbed. "I must have the wrong apartment."

"No. You don't," she said, her voice so soft Livy was sure she'd misunderstood her. The girl's appearance had shocked her so, she hadn't noticed that she, too, was being observed and studied. "This is the right apartment."

"I don't think so . . ."

"Then you think wrong. This *is* the apartment you're looking for," she said, her voice growing stronger with use.

"I'm sorry," she said again. "Should I know you?"

She was sure she didn't, and the girl confirmed this with a single shake of her head.

"But I know you," she said, opening the door wider. "Come in."

No way was Livy going in that apartment with this very strange-acting, near-dead-looking young woman—who should be in a hospital anyway.

"Brian'll be back with lunch soon," the ailing girl said, noting her hesitation.

"Oh. Well. Um. Okay." She stepped inside and the girl closed the door—an unnerving act. Livy felt trapped.

The apartment was a big, gloomy L-shaped room with a high ceiling and long shaded windows the length of the longest wall. And it was a mess. Not filthy, just cluttered. It smelled of paint thinner and chalk, and of Eugene's, and a little like illness.

"If he isn't working, he pulls the shades in the morning because the light hurts my eyes," the girl said, sorrier about the dimness than the clutter—not that she needed to be sorry for either.

"How, ah, how do you know me?" Livy asked. It was the first of the many questions that were, by now, begetting questions of their own.

By way of answering, the girl led her into the main part of the room. It was longer than she had at first perceived, and more open. The fourth floor had been removed, so the ceiling was two stories high. The upper windows, aligned with the lower ones with wall space between them, also had pull shades drawn against the late morning sun. Had all the shades been up, the natural lighting would have been phenomenal. Perfect for painting.

The distal end of the L was decked with what appeared to be a series of temporary walls, six or eight of them in a row, about five feet apart. Along the far wall was a long workbench—heaped high with . . . stuff. Ladders. Canvases. Spotlights. Cameras. Gallons and tubes of paint and painting supplies. Tarp. Ropes with pulleys. Wooden frames in assorted sizes.

Evidence of Brian. Lots of it. Serious evidence of a serious artist.

Her heart beat a little faster.

There was what likely served as a living area with a big tan couch, two brown chairs, and a couple of tables in the middle of the space. A kitchenette with a separating bar and stools lay beyond that. All of it was littered with clothes and newspapers and empty food cartons. Soda cans, paper coffee cups, dirty paint rags . . . and a basketball hoop on the wall between two windows.

More evidence of Brian; it made her heart smile. She couldn't wait to see him again. And that would be enough, she realized; just to see him would be enough.

On the wall that cut the room into an L shape, there was a double door to a second room with a bed in it. She imagined a bathroom in the space as well. But it was the pictures on the wall beside the door that captured her attention.

Among the many, many drawings that papered the entire wall—whole or partial drafts of landscapes, flowers, insects, faces, particular body parts, like hands and bent elbows, of birds and benches and vending carts—was a grouping of sketches of Livy. Some large, some small. Not only were they drawn from different angles, but at different ages as well. Charcoal and pencil. Long hair and longer hair. Eyes open or lowered, as if reading from a book in her lap.

Her hand reached out to touch one in which she couldn't have been more than sixteen, and the closest sketch, resembling the portrait he'd sent her, was done . . . probably the first or second year of college.

"So much talent," she said, her voice a whisper.

Walking along the wall, she tried to pretend that she was seeing all he had seen in their time apart—the places, the people. What if she couldn't catch up with him? What if their paths had led them too far apart, so far apart they didn't recognize each other?

It was like coming home and finding it changed. Familiar but foreign. What was familiar was greatly loved, without a beginning or end. What was foreign, she found . . . intriguing.

"I wish I could see the portrait he did from these," the young woman said wistfully, still studying the sketches of Livy, her head tilted to one side.

"It's . . . reality perfected. Reality made perfect, when reality isn't perfect at all."

The girl looked her way, but didn't speak.

"He's doing murals now. Come see."

Livy followed her to the far wall; the temporary walls were facing that direction. They turned the corner to look at the first huge canvas.

She stepped into the middle of a forest, into a clearing, cool in the shade of the towering green-leafed trees, warmed by shafts of sunlight. She could almost hear her feet rustling in the underbrush as she approached a low, flat boulder near a clear, rippling pond. She was tempted to put her hand in the water to test the temperature.

"The water looks . . . wet. How does he do that?" she asked, more of herself than the girl.

"Beats me," she said, turning another corner to look at the next mural. "This is my favorite."

If you were a child lying on your belly with your chin on your hands in a field full of wild flowers, the mural was what you would see. Mostly sky and the field beyond, the grass in front of your eyes would tickle your nose. The bees would buzz in your ear. The riotous array of spring flowers would make you smile and your heart would feel too big in your chest. You could smell them and the earth and the sunshine, see minuscule particles of pollen and dust dancing along the rays of the sun. You'd be holding your breath to see if you could hear the wings of the butterflies not two feet away.

"My God," she said in awe, a shiver of . . . of unrealness passing through her body. "It seems so . . . so real, but . . ."

"Too perfect?" she asked. "Reality perfected?"

In a blink, she was out of the picture and back in Brian's apartment, shocked to have her own words thrown back at her.

For the first time, the girl smiled. "You're right. It is too perfect to be real. That's the first thing that grabs at you. All that incredible detail, but no wilting, dying flowers. No broken blades of grass. What's scary is that Brian really sees things this way, at first. Perfect. Like a child. Beauty in its purest form." She looked back at the picture. "He sees how it really is, though, too, after a while. The not so perfect, the flaws, the decay. But his first impressions have the biggest impact on him. They're what he prefers, what he wants to believe is possible, so he paints them." She took a deep breath, as though she wasn't used to talking so much. "I've never seen anything like these, but they actually have a name for this kind of art, you know. Surrealistic. Idealized vision, I heard someone say once. I like both names." She narrowed her eyes and shuddered, looking at Livy. "Gives me the creeps every time I wonder what these would look like if he painted what was ugly in the world with this much clarity."

The ugly would be as shocking as the beauty was breathtaking, she imagined, feeling an odd attraction to this slip of a girl with so much wisdom and insight into Brian's paintings. An odd attraction, and something more. . . .

"I'm Livy Kerrigan," she said, holding her hand out in friendship.

"I'm Eve."

"May I co-chair the Brian Carowack fan club with you?"

"Sure," she said with another smile. "Want something to drink?"

"No. Thanks," she said, feeling suddenly more awkward than before. Brian had a life here. Had she dared to believe that he'd put it on hold all this time? He had a home, a girlfriend, a routine to his life. If she'd left any sort of void in his life, he'd filled it. He might not appreciate her intrusion. That thought was almost more than she could bear. "Actually, I can't stay. I should have called first, I guess. I acted on an impulse and . . ."

"If you leave, you'll have to take me with you."

"What?"

"Brian'll kill me if I tell him you were here and I didn't tie you up or something, until he got back. I would," she said seriously. "But I don't think I have the strength today."

Livy smiled, feeling uneasy. It was too obvious that she could blow Eve over with half a breath. She wanted to know about her illness but couldn't bring herself to ask about it.

"How long have you known Brian?"

"Not as long as you have. About two years, I think, maybe less."

She walked away from the murals toward the living area. Livy glanced at each painting as she followed her. Ocean beach, one that looked as if you were gazing out of Granddad's old barn door at miles and miles of Ohio farmland, a penthouse window view of New York, a couple of others. Each looked so real that hopping from place to place made her a little dizzy.

"Are you an artist as well? Is that how the two of you met?"

"Nope. I used to work down at Eugene's with him. That's how he pays the rent on this place, working for Eugene. Cooking, waiting tables, working the counter, you name it. He and Eugene get along pretty good."

"I see. I . . . didn't know Brian could cook. I don't think his mother knows he can cook. She'll be relieved." She gave a weak laugh. She was nearly out of small talk. "Has . . . has he sold any of his . . . walls yet? His murals?"

"He did a couple baby nurseries for friends. You know, like bunnies and clouds, but he wouldn't take money for them. He has an agent, though. She's interested."

"An agent? That sounds impressive, and encouraging. How interested is she?"

She shrugged a bony shoulder and collapsed on the couch, sitting on one leg. "Beats me. She seems pretty interested to me, but Brian says she's just after his body."

Livy laughed. "Well, I see some things haven't changed. He still has a galactic ego, I see."

Eve frowned as if she didn't agree. "No, she probably is after his body, but I think she likes his work, too."

"Oh. Well, that's good then. But . . . well, doesn't that bother you? That his agent wants him, his body, I mean?"

"No. Why should it?"

Because it bothered Livy. It bothered her that Eve wasn't bothered, and it bothered her that Eve was there in the first place, and *that* bothered her because she had no right to be bothered by it.

"Sorry. I guess I assumed . . ."

"You assume a lot of things, don't you?" Eve's expression was bland enough to make the question seem guileless, but the light in her eyes told of a power that her physical appearance camouflaged.

"What?"

"I'm making an observation, is all. Lots of people assume things, and it's okay . . . if that's the way they want to live their lives."

"You don't make assumptions, I take it."

"Not about important stuff. I ask questions. Then I know for sure."

"Then, in other words, I haven't been asking the right questions."

"He said you were sharp."

"Just how sick are you?"

Eve laughed out loud, then started to wheeze and cough.

"Are you all right? I'm sorry. That was stupid of me."

Eve waved her hand back and forth to stop her as her coughing subsided.

"No. That's okay. You just surprised me. I didn't think that would be your first question."

It wasn't that her personality was stronger; it was because her body was weaker that Eve seemed to have control of the situation, and Livy thought it an unfair advantage—even though she didn't want an equal share of whatever the ailment was to even the odds.

"Why don't we make this simple then. You tell me what questions to ask, and I'll ask them," she said, feeling defensive.

"Okay. Ask me how long I've been living here."

Livy sighed. The awkwardness was hardening into irritation.

"How long . . ."

"Seven months. Now ask me . . . why I moved in here."

"Why did . . ."

"Because I have tuberculosis and I can't get a job that exposes me to the general population, so I'm broke. And because Brian's a soft touch who said I could move in here with him, if I didn't spit on him." She smiled sweetly. "No spitting and no illegal drugs. Those are the rules."

Taken back by her bluntness, it was a few seconds before Livy could ask, "What about family? Your parents."

"They kicked me out when I was thirteen—ten, no, almost eleven years ago, on the occasion of my very first visit to a pawnshop. I hocked some of my mom's jewelry for drug money. Oh." She held up an index finger. "You better ask me about my drug problem, too."

"Why?"

"Because you're probably *assuming* that I met Brian at Eugene's."

"But you didn't." Livy was getting better at the game, and feeling less competitive.

"Nope. Met him at an AA meeting. You know, Alcoholics Anonymous."

"Yes, I know. I mean . . . I see," she said, trying to take it all in. Brian at an AA meeting? No one ever said anything about AA meetings. Not Brian, in his few short Christmas notes. Not her mother. Not his mother when she stopped to visit during her trips to Tolford. What was this girl trying to do? Insinuate Brian was an alcoholic? Scare her off? Frighten her?

"No. You don't see."

"What?"

"You don't see at all. You're sitting there making more assumptions."

"Am I?" Well, maybe. "What should I ask then?"

"Ask me if we're more than friends. Ask me if we're lovers."

"Are you?"

"Nope. He's never touched me except to put me to bed when I couldn't get there on my own."

Livy nodded, looking away. She didn't know what else to say. Didn't know what to ask. Didn't know if she wanted to know more. But if it was true . . . God. Brian an alcoholic? Her mind flashed back through a thousand and one shots of Brian drinking over the years. Her heart knew the truth even before her brain could admit it. What had she been thinking all that time? That he could control it? Had she really believed that? Why hadn't he told her? Why hadn't she suffered her pride and come sooner to find him?

She felt small. And miserable. A lousy marriage, her career goes belly up, and he's the first person she runs to. What about him? Her eyes filled with tears. What if he hadn't felt he could come to her, couldn't tell her anything? What if he'd wanted to, but didn't, because she was married to Richard, or because he thought her job was more important to her, that she wouldn't have time to listen to him? What if he didn't know how important he was to her? What if he didn't know how much she loved him? What if . . .

"I think it's my turn to ask you a question," Eve said.

"I hope you don't want me to tell you which one to ask."

"No, that's okay. You're not very good at questions."

"Clearly," she said in a self-deprecating manner, slapping at a tear that had slipped away from her.

"No, don't beat yourself up about it now," Eve said in earnest. "Like I said, assuming things is okay. Sometimes it's safer. It's better sometimes. It's just that I don't assume anything anymore. I ask questions."

"Well? What is it?"

"How come you never told him you're in love with him?"

"What?"

"You *are* in love with him, right?"

"I love him. Yes," she said—although she couldn't believe she was actually answering this nosey person's impertinent, highly personal, and extremely ludicrous query. "We've been close friends since we were children. Of course I love him." She swallowed.

"But . . . you're asking if I'm *in* love with him?" No reply. "I'm . . . ah . . . I'm married."

"And you're here because you're positive you didn't marry the wrong man, right?"

"What?" A strange sort of panic let loose inside her.

"Well, I just want to make sure I've got this right, do you mind? See, I know all about you. Brian and I do the Twelve Steps. . . . Do you know about those?" Livy nodded and shook her head at once. She did and she didn't. God, did she know anything anymore? "It's part of our rehab. Drunks and addicts are basically the same thing, you know, so we all go through the Twelve Steps set up for the AA program. Anyway, one of them is that you have to ask forgiveness of all those you've hurt because of your addiction. Brian feels he has to ask you to forgive him for missing your wedding to, ah, who was it . . . ? The dickhead, right? He really hates your husband, you know."

He wasn't the only one anymore.

"Yes, I know. And he doesn't have to ask my forgiveness . . ."

"Oh yes, he does," she insisted. "If he *feels* he does . . . though . . . well, I told him I didn't think it was his fault that he missed the wedding because he was in a hospital recovering from a car accident that he didn't cause. But he says if he hadn't been drunk that night he'd have made it to your wedding. So, see? He has to ask, then he can forgive himself for hurting you. See how it works?"

She nodded again. "I forgave him a long time ago. I . . ."

"Maybe, maybe not."

"What does that mean?"

"I suspect you haven't really talked to him in four years, to punish him," she said, as if she'd gotten a degree in psychology from a book of matches.

"I've talked to him," Livy said, feeling totally guilty and very uneasy. "I've sent him cards. I thought he was avoiding me because he hated Richard. And because I married him."

"No-no, you assumed that. He never actually said anything like that, did he?" Livy shook her head. Eve went on talking. "See, the way I have it figured, and you can correct me if I'm wrong, but the way I think it went was that you always *assumed* that he knew you were in love with him, even when you were kids," she said. "And he never did anything about it . . . because he didn't really know, see? So you dated the dickhead all through college to make Brian jealous—because Brian hated him, and when he *still* didn't do anything, you married the guy. Are you following me?"

"This is ridiculous." Her heart was racing and her palms were starting to sweat.

"Is it? When Brian didn't try to stop your marriage, you gave up. You figured Brian didn't love you, not the way you loved him. And maybe you weren't punishing him . . . maybe it was just easier to steer clear of him than to have to face what you *assumed* was the truth."

"Are you feverish?"

Eve's smile was smug. "I bet you wish I was." Her eyes narrowed as she studied Livy. "Are you divorced yet?"

"What? That's none of your business. As a matter of fact, none of this is your business. I can't believe he would talk to you about me this way."

"He doesn't."

"He doesn't? You know all about me, or at least you think you do. Some of the facts anyway. He shouldn't have told you all that."

"He didn't. I asked."

"Well, he shouldn't have answered."

She hesitated. "Actually, he didn't very often, which forced me to make up my own answers."

Livy stood up. Plainly, Eve's disease was affecting her mind. Poor thing.

"Look. I think I was right to begin with. I'm in the wrong apartment. If you feel compelled to tell him I was here, tell him I waited for a while, then had to leave. It's been . . . a unique experience meeting you, Eve. Good luck. Don't get up, I'll let myself out."

Eve burst into laughter and wheezes and coughing again.

"No-no, I'm fine," she said toward the end of a bronchospasm that had Livy looking for the telephone, repeating 911 over and over in her head. "He was right about you. I do like you. But if we're going to be friends, you're going to have to learn to take helpful criticism with a little more grace."

"Helpful criticism?" It really was time to leave. Livy was quaking inside, not with anger, but fear. Eve had the facts twisted in knots to create a completely different story that made some sense . . . but it wasn't the truth. Brian would laugh his head off at the very idea of it. *She* wanted to laugh, too. Hysterically. "This isn't helpful criticism. This is . . . this is . . . insane."

"I'll do what I can to help from this end, but you really should get your head straight before you start messing with his again."

"Now what are you talking about? Forget it. I don't want to know. Good-bye."

"I was only going to say that I think you're right, about leaving, I mean. You need time to think this through. I won't tell him you were here today. You can come back and surprise him tomorrow, or next week, or whenever you have things figured out."

"Tell him whatever you like," she said at the door, hesitating briefly before she opened it. "*Except* what you've been telling me today."

"Okay." She slouched down in the couch as if preparing to take a nap. "Hey!"

"What?"

"You forgot to ask, so I'll tell you that he's fine. Healthy, you know? But if you want to make sure, instead of just assuming that I'm telling the truth, he'll be coming down the street with my lunch pretty soon . . . I hope. You'd be able to see him if you were sitting at one of the window tables at that little Italian restaurant across the street. Or at one of Eugene's, if you want to chance him seeing you, too."

"Thanks. Have a nice day."

"Hey!"

"*What!*"

"If you see him, and if there's a leggy blonde draped all over him, don't worry. That'll be Celeste. She's just the flavor of the month. Next month he'll have a leggy redhead or brunette draped all over him."

"Great!"

Eve started to laugh again. Livy closed the door, waiting until the coughing stopped before she went down to the street to hail a cab.

She was halfway back to the hotel, wishing she hadn't come, wishing she'd crawled under some rock back in Nashville and just stayed there . . . when she suddenly begged the driver to take her back.

She stayed in the little Italian restaurant Eve recommended for nearly twenty minutes—more than a little afraid that she'd missed him—before she spotted his long, loose walk among the pedestrians across the street.

She smiled and blinked tears of relief from her eyes.

His hair was shorter, but not much. The ends were straight and even and hanging well below his shoulders, billowing away from his clean-shaven face as he strode past, tall and confident, with a white paper bag in one hand. No leggy blonde. Her smile got broader. He'd put on a little weight since she'd seen him last. His standard jeans and T-shirt with a plaid flannel shirt were All-American. He looked . . . healthy, robust even, as he stopped and did some sort of silly shenanigan through the front window of Eugene's for someone he knew inside. He looked happy.

Happy, healthy, and so much a part of her still that parts of her felt complete at the sight of him. Mended. Parts of her that she hadn't realized were fractured and disintegrating were soothed. Pieces of her that she had neglected, ignored, and scorned as weaknesses felt consoled and validated.

She called herself a failure, at her marriage, as a woman, in her career. But Brian would never believe that. He would never allow her to believe that, either. She watched him disappear through the unmarked door in the wall of the building across the street and knew exactly what he would have said to her if she had waited for him upstairs.

Richard refused to let you have a baby because he was afraid it would be marked, like you? Then get rid of Richard.

Richard's unfaithful, you say? Then get rid of Richard.

You lost you job with Senator Seirs because of Richard? Then get rid of Richard and find yourself a new job.

Brian had an eye for beauty. He also had an eye for simplicity. He would have boiled all her problems down to the simplest solution.

She sat at the table a while longer, feeling stronger and . . . and more like Livy than she had in months. Years. So much so that she felt a little sick inside as well. Not because she now knew what she had to do to get her life back, and that it wasn't going to be easy. But because it had slipped through her fingers so easily, so unnoticed, piece by piece in the first place, until she'd had almost nothing left. Nothing but Brian. She lowered her head and covered her eyes with one hand as she acknowledged the distinct possibility that Eve had been right about her.

"You are in love with him, right?"

PART THREE

Braving the Maze

Twenty-one

HE WALKED across the doctor's waiting room to stand beside her while she took care of the bill. Still holding their coats over his arm, he leaned against the wall behind him, looking low to get a glimpse of her face.

She was in pain—it always hurt afterward—but when she glanced up at him, it wasn't in her eyes.

Over the years, he'd seen so much in or through her eyes. He smiled at all he knew without ever having heard it or read it or experienced it firsthand.

For instance, at a party, he knew exactly which guests he didn't want to talk to if Livy's eyes became fixed and glazed in their company. Childbirth is frightful, painful, and pure elation—she felt it, he saw it, there was no debate. He knew to haggle for a bargain if she cast a suspicious eye at a salesman. He was being selfish or unreasonable when she wouldn't hold his stare—hard on her to see him that way, he supposed. He knew she was tired when her eyes didn't sparkle. And when they flashed his way in anger, he was in deep doo-doo.

They talked like that now, deep doo-doo, dog-gone-it, holy smokes. Livy had cut her vocabulary in half—it was almost laughable. He, on the other hand, had set himself up in the position of having to set a good example for others. Him, a good example. That was laughable, too, and yet it was one of the few things in his life he took seriously. Had *ever* taken seriously.

Well, that and loving Livy, of course.

He only half-listened as she and the nurse talked for a few minutes, his mind stuck in a backward groove, slipping into the past.

He was born with a talent many people envied. He was lucky. He never had to wonder about what he wanted to do with his life, or where that would inevitably take him. All he ever had to do was use the gift he was born with, be the best he could be . . . and follow where it led him.

Strange the way it's always the simplest lessons that are the hardest to learn. For him anyway. And Livy, too, he supposed. It was weird the way the world got smaller, the older you got. And the way you start out ready to conquer the whole thing, and settle contentedly with half an acre to call your own. Life was funny in so many ways.

Once you thought you had it figured out, it changed. That was the only guarantee it came with, actually. Eventually you learned that it was best to turn all corners with caution, expect the unexpected . . . and never take anything for granted.

She was still talking to the nurse when she reached out for her coat. She could have gotten into it herself—usually did, in fact— but he held it for her this time. Mostly, because she *wasn't* expecting it but . . . well, also because he had an unexpected, engulfing urge to be near her.

That's the way it was with them—and perhaps it was the strangest of all the strange phenomenons in life—that no matter how long or how well you think you know someone, she is bound to do the least expected and the most surprising.

She slipped her arms into the coat, covering her mild astonishment with a grateful smile, then asked the nurse to repeat the last of her instructions.

He smiled. It had taken him a long time—over half his life—to finally realize that he was just as startling to Livy as she was to him. He was. Although he couldn't imagine anyone less startling than himself, she frequently said he was a constant amazement to her. Of course, that generally involved something he'd forgotten to do or something he'd done that was dumber than an average child would do, but sometimes it was something terrific. Something that made her happy, awed her speechless, made her giggle and laugh. Then she'd say that together, their life was an adventure.

An adventure. He was afraid it was more like skating on thin ice most of the time, but in a way—a crazy, convoluted, capricious way, he supposed that could be called an adventure. Besides, he liked the sound of it. Life as an adventure.

Livy said good-bye to the nurse and slipped the strap of her purse over her shoulder. She turned to him smiling, expectant, and she held out her hand to him.

He remembered another time she reached out to him. Another time, another day. An adventure or so ago. . . .

She needed to pay the bill. She turned away from the concern in his eyes as he crossed the room to join her. There was nothing she could do to stop his worrying.

Except to prove him wrong, perhaps.

That wouldn't be hard.

She could feel him trying to get her attention, sliding down the wall he was leaning on, to get a better look at her face, to see some reassurance. He was like a child that way, taking the tone with which to deal with a situation from the expression on her—the mother's—face. Men and babies were very similar, she'd discovered, and not in a derogatory fashion. They just were.

What was it the novelist Ellen Glasgow said? There wouldn't be half as much fun in the world if it weren't for children and men, and there ain't a mite of difference between them under their skins.

To prove this once again, she glanced up at Brian and winked at him—his relief was a tangible thing.

Another example was . . . oh, say, Christmas. Men, like children, have a tendency to believe that Christmas simply happens once a year. They have no idea of what it takes to maintain a single family tradition. You badger them to string lights and put up trees and then the holiday, like snowfall, happens. Women, the mothers, create and maintain all the magic in the world. It's true. Christmas, the Easter bunny, the tooth fairy.

She was never too sure if that was a good thing or not, though, spreading tales of jolly fat men in red and elves and flying reindeer with bright, glowing noses to children, only to have them grow up to the disillusionment of it all—and the discovery that their most trusted adults had been lying to them since birth. Still, when they grow up, they fill *their* children's heads with the same outrageous and wonderful tales.

Go figure.

Besides, what would life be without holidays like Christmas and Halloween and Easter? Without the magic and the supernatural and the beyond belief? Most of the time she contented herself with the idea that making magic for children wasn't an all-bad thing. There was plenty of time for them to grow up and find out that reality wasn't so nice. And maybe a hard-core foundation of *magic, could be,* and *what if* served as a basis for hope, for believing against the odds, for faith in miracles. Who knew?

All she did know for sure was that it took a really long time to grow up and figure out what in the world was really worth living for . . . and that most of it involved something closely akin to magic and miracles.

Nature. Love. Babies. Friendship. Kindness. All magic. All miracles. All rare. All worth living for. And somewhere along your lifeline you discover that you can't change what's wrong with the world until you change what's wrong in your own backyard. It's okay to send twenty bucks a month to starving children in Africa, but if you can't give a bag of groceries to the people next door or the family down the street, what's the point?

She wasn't sorry or ashamed of the changes she had fought for in the sixties and seventies. Or of the money she had made in the eighties. She'd needed to learn that time was swift and change was slow . . . and that some things were more important than others. She'd needed to learn that making more money didn't make happier children or better marriages, that it didn't have anything to do with love, and that those drab, old humdrum middle-class family values her parents believed in weren't so far off base.

She had no regrets—notwithstanding the fact that she was such a slow learner.

But that was okay, too. She was happy with what she had and who she was—and maybe wouldn't be if she could go back and change things. She was lucky—more of that magic stuff.

The nurse was almost finished with her instructions. They were exactly the same as all the other times, except she wouldn't have to come back for a year unless something went wrong.

She reached blindly for the coat she knew Brian was holding and was pleasantly surprised—even flustered a little like a teenager—when he held it open for her. She smiled at him, appending her previous thoughts on men and children.

Another thing they had in common was that they were a constant wonder. Children could be extremely independent and wise sometimes. And men could be incredibly brave and tolerant and insightful. Both could perform acts of daring no woman would consider—although sometimes that was just plain old stupidity. Both could love limitlessly, trust completely, and . . . well, both were made of that magic stuff that made her life worth living.

She said good-bye to the nurse, slipping the strap of her purse over her shoulder. She was ready to leave, to walk away from a part of herself that she wanted to forget and knew she never would, or could.

It was time to prove him wrong . . . again . . . a constant mission in her life, it seemed. And it was always *so* satisfying to see the look on his face when, once again, he realized she was right.

She turned to him, smiling, and reached out to take his hand.

He learned best that way, if she took his hand and led him through the process one step at a time. His expression was wary, just like all the other times, and she couldn't help but recall the last few times she had difficulty getting him to place his hand in hers. . . .

Twenty-two

IT IS ENTIRELY POSSIBLE to put too much faith in fate, which is why one should always be looking for ways in which to help it out a little.

For four years, ten months, and three days, Brian had been dry and sober; it was 1979.

He was trying to live his day-to-day life the best he could, one day at a time, and leave the rest to his higher power—a stronger, wiser, more forceful and godlike entity—to contend with. He couldn't please everyone, so he settled on simply pleasing himself. He couldn't make the world right for anyone else, so he did his best to make it right for him. He was responsible for only one life, his own, and that's where his responsibilities ended. He could love someone all he wanted to, but he couldn't *control* anyone but himself.

That was the hardest lesson to learn, that no matter what he did or didn't do, said or didn't say, was or wasn't, he wasn't responsible for the actions of others. Not his father's. Not his stepfathers'. Not his mother's or Beth's or Livy's or Chewy's or Donny Moore's or Granddad Hubbard's or Eve's or Jimmy Lowe's or Bobby's or . . . or anyone's. A very hard lesson to learn.

However—and isn't there always a however?—sometimes you can just tell when your higher power is . . . stressed, say. Overworked and falling behind, maybe. Focused, but unable to see the *big picture* when an incredible opportunity arises, but isn't taken full advantage of, or is overlooked altogether. That's when you have to help yourself. You realize you still have no control over the situation, but you put yourself in the way of an opportunity and *hope* that your higher power kicks in and takes over before it's too late.

And so it was, when his agent called to tell him that he'd been invited to join a national art tour sponsored by Lucent Vollini—of Vollini's Gallery of Modern Art, better known just as Vollini's in thirteen major cities across the U.S. and in Europe. He was ecstatic. His work, his name, was to be included with the likes of Christian Safian and Jeri Kett in a traveling exhibit entitled "Six New Artists: Six New Visions," going from New York to Washington, D.C., Minneapolis, Houston, and San Francisco. He could hardly stand it . . . except . . . well . . .

He found himself casually asking Mr. Vollini's art director why it was six new artists, six new images, and only five cities and wasn't Chicago big on modern art? He thought he might have read that it was somewhere. That's all he said, that's all he did. He wasn't trying to control anything; he was merely using one opportunity to put himself in the way of another opportunity. There was still plenty for his higher power to orchestrate.

So, he went home and prayed like hell.

Three weeks later the show was called "Six Cities: Six Artists: Six New Visions."

He was a nervous wreck in New York. More than anything else he wished he were drunk or in some other way there, but not there. It was one thing to tell yourself to paint to please yourself, but anyone who wrote, painted, or acted out in self-expression knew that pleasing yourself didn't always buy food . . . nor was it always as completely gratifying as receiving praise from others.

Each artist was to show ten works in each city, and was advised to have at least double that in reserve, in a separate, huge moving van, to replace any pieces bought and removed from the show during the tour. There was a private, by invitation only, opening the night prior to each public showing at which they were asked to make an appearance and mingle with the potential buyers. It was like trying to sell his soul.

Another 8- × 10-foot mural and two of his smaller paintings

sold in Washington, D.C.—the private parties were getting a little more palatable. However, it was the public showings he enjoyed most, passing among the scattered viewers anonymously, listening to their comments. The "public" was less critical and seemed to simply enjoy the art more than the so-called collectors and critics and experts. Selling was important, but seeing your work appreciated was far more satisfying.

By the time the show got to Chicago, he could almost pretend to look calm and collected at the openings. He had the tux he'd bought thirdhand from a buddy in New York cleaned and pressed again. The haircut he'd gotten before he left town had grown out to near perfection. He slapped on the cologne that Eve swore, on her oxygen tank, would turn a woman's knees to Silly Putty. Then, he had an invitation hand-delivered to Livy.

He saw her the moment she came in; she was one of the first to arrive. Tall and dark in a ruby red skirt and jacket, simple and elegant. No more of the chic chin-length pageboy hair that she'd worn five years earlier. She'd layered it to give it more life, let it grow to her shoulders and pulled it away from her face.

She showed her invitation to the guard and he directed her to the open bar, but she didn't go that way. Instead, she went straight for the first painting, an Elgin Kelly titled *Two Diagonals with Curve 6*. If she continued, she'd pass by the impressionist work of Jack Deal and landscapes by Jennifer Barrett before she got to his—he didn't think he could wait that long.

He did, but only because he wanted to see her first impression, and only by reminding himself of what a pain in the butt she was viewing art. She always had to study each picture whether she liked it or not—and why stand in front of a picture trying to decide why you don't like it, if you just plain don't like it? He never could figure that one out. He could get through a museum twice as fast and get ten times more out of it. She didn't even know that much about art.

What she liked and didn't like was about it, and you could tell that at a glance, for crying out loud.

It was worth the wait, though. She turned the corner, saw the first picture, and didn't have to look at the nameplate before she smiled and pressed the tips of her fingers to her lips as if she might cry.

That was all he'd needed to see. He started toward her as she stared at the painting of a wrinkled old bag lady on a park bench with a yellow plastic flower in her hat, wearing scruffy old brown shoes with bright new orange shoelaces—he'd bought the shoelaces and paid the old lady fifty bucks to let him sketch her that day. She was no ordinary bag lady.

A glance turned to a gaze when she saw him, her eyes as warm and welcoming as they ever had been. Five years vanished in a blink.

"She looks like a wealthy woman," she said, pointing to the bag lady. "Like she feels wealthy."

"I'm sure that's exactly how she felt that day," he said, trying to speak lightly around the lump in his throat. He could barely breathe. "Those designer shoelaces cost me five bucks."

She laughed, and he thought he was going to fall down. He'd missed her laugh, her smile, the sparkle in her eyes.

"Did you let her keep them?" she asked, teasing him.

He shrugged. "I figured she could trade them later for food, or a drink to keep the chill away."

She nodded, watching him closely. "You always were a sucker for a pretty face."

Looking at the pruny old puss, he nodded, conceding the truth, then looked back at Livy.

"I've missed your face something terrible," he said.

There was an awkward moment in which she looked as if she thought she might have too many arms, before she sort of cast it off and curved the two she had around him.

"It's so good to see you," she said, holding him tight. "I was so excited when I got the special invitation yesterday, I got here an hour early and finally went across the street to have a drink." She leaned back, still holding him at the waist. "I was still too early when I came back. This is so exciting for you. For me. I . . . I'm so proud of you, Brian."

She babbled on and kept touching the front of his tux as if to make sure he was really inside. These were good signs. She was as excited and nervous as he was.

"These are incredible. I want to see them all. I want to see everything and hear everything. I can't believe you're here. I was planning to come to New York in a couple of months. I was going to look you up. Then I heard you were coming here . . . your mama told my mama . . . and I watched the papers for the ads. Oh, why didn't you get in touch with me sooner? When do you have to leave? Will we have time for dinner or something? Time to talk?"

"If we don't stand here too long, we will. Come on," he said, taking her hand, making up his mind not to let go of it at any time during the next decade or two or three. "We'll take a quick look at the rest of these, see if there's anyone here worth meeting, then shake this place off. How's that sound?"

"Perfect." Her dark eyes studied him a few seconds longer, as if she couldn't bear to look away, afraid he might disappear. He was actually beginning to feel a little self-conscious.

"This, ah, this one sold to an attorney in Washington last week," he said, trying not to sound too boastful, feeling like a peacock. "He wanted to leave it in the show till it's over. Said he wanted the world to see what now belonged to him. You can sort of see where lawyers get their reputations, can't you."

"Absolutely. That was Washington, D.C., then?" He nodded. "How wonderful. Oh, Brian. Have you sold any of your walls yet?"

He frowned, wondering how she knew about his larger pieces,

then looking down the aisle at them, he decided that they would be a little difficult to miss.

"They only had room for two in this gallery. A doctor bought one for his new office space and a dealer friend of mine in New York sold one to a dentist for his office. I'm hanging in doctors' and dentists' offices, but I guess that's better than not hanging anywhere."

"Are you kidding? There's nothing else to do in places like that but look at the walls. If nothing else, it'll be good advertising, not to mention the pleasure the patients will have getting lost in them."

"Getting lost?"

Her gaze darted away; she looked flustered. "Well, if they're all as supersensory as these, I can see where someone might feel like they're inside the picture, can't you?"

"Is supersensory a real word?"

"Of course." As if she'd use imaginary words. "How do you get the water to look wet like that?"

He leaned closer to the picture, squinting his eyes. "Beats me," he said, using one of Eve's favorite responses.

The arm of the hand he wasn't holding looped around his as she laughed, then said, "Never, ever again."

"What?"

"Will we let so many years come between us."

"I promise."

"Me, too."

"Let's spit in our hands and shake on it, like we used to," he said, turning to her.

She started to giggle, but that died in her throat when she saw him getting ready to spit.

"Here? Now? No," she said, looking around, holding his hands together between hers. "You haven't changed a bit."

Not a bit, a hunk, but he was glad she hadn't noticed yet.

"Then we'll seal the deal with a kiss," he said.

"A what?"

"A kiss?" He laughed. He couldn't help it. She had the strangest look on her face. And she was blushing.

"Oh. Sure. Good. I mean, better . . . than spitting."

The kiss was dead on the mark and very quick; then she moved away. Hell, that kiss wouldn't hold paint to a wall. They'd have to fix that later, he decided.

He followed her from picture to picture with his hands in his pockets, answering her questions, relishing her delight, and trying to convince himself that what he was seeing wasn't a trick of the heart.

Was this his Livy with . . . lust in her eyes? No, no, no. He'd been celibate too long. Too busy getting ready for the show, no time for fun lately. He was imagining things. Wishful thinking. Hm-mmm. There it was again.

She looked great up close, barely a day older but . . . different somehow. Stronger, if that were conceivable. Weaker, too, if that made any sense. Vulnerable, although he could have been imagining that, too.

He knew what she'd been through these past few years, how tough the last year must have been on her. The gossip, the publicity, her divorce—the move to Chicago to start over, to start new. The grapevine from Tolford came his way, too, and his mother had indicated that even Livy's father had suffered a few repercussions over the incident with Richard, though nothing his solid reputation couldn't withstand. Seirs, cleared of all charges and as shocked as everyone else at what had been going on in his own office, had also decided to remain where he was and go on with his worthy career. But none of it could have been easy for her to deal with.

"I wanted to call . . . or just be with you somehow, when I heard what was happening," he said, so abruptly it startled her. He had the tact of a mad rattlesnake, he knew, but he didn't want any more time to go by without telling her how sorry he was. "Last year. I wanted to be there. I just didn't know what to say to you."

" 'I told you so', didn't cross your mind?" She turned away before he could see the expression on her face.

"No. God, no." How could she think that of him? He hurried to close the distance she was making between them as she went on with her study of his work. "Livy, I had no idea. I hated Richard because he had a big mouth and because . . . well, because I didn't like him in general, but I never dreamed he'd end up taking bribes and paying off government officials and . . . whatever else he was doing. If I'd known what he was going to do to you, I would have . . ."

"What?" She stopped but didn't turn to face him.

He was stumped. He wasn't sure. He was capable of many things, but he still wasn't much of a fist fighter.

"I'd have . . . hired car, no, a truck and run him down with it. Twice. Back and forth."

She turned and he could see she was amused.

"You wouldn't have just broken his nose again, like you did in college?"

"Oh. Well, maybe," he said, his brows rising thoughtfully. "I was pretty crazy that night. Actually, I'd forgotten all about that."

"Not me," she said, moving to the next picture, painted from a sketch he'd made of a majestic waterfall in northern California. "I'd never seen you like that before, it scared me." She paused. "Impressed the hell out me, too, as I recall."

"Huh. Now you tell me."

"But I also remember being ashamed."

"Of what?"

"Of letting you worry like that. I knew you would. I knew I should have called. But I didn't."

He felt compelled to ask why.

"I was angry, I think," she said, turning to face him. "But I didn't know I was angry. I . . . I think now that I could feel us heading off in different directions, growing apart, choosing different lives. I was losing you and . . . I wanted to see if you'd care if I was gone. It wasn't a conscious thing at the time, but looking back . . . I think that's what happened."

Liberated men know that women aren't the only ones with intuition. Livy had an itinerary for the evening; he could feel it. It was as if she'd planned and rehearsed the entire event months ahead of time—long before she received his invitation. There were things she'd been saving up to say to him. He could sense her bulging with them, ready to burst.

"Looking back," he said, meeting her gaze. "I always cared, no matter where you were." They stood there looking at one another for a moment longer, with so much to say between them. He took a quick, uneven survey of the huge room, then reached for her hand once again. "Come on, Livy, let's get out of here."

They hadn't gone ten feet before he heard his name being called. The voice was unmistakable. Princeton-educated-Lower-East-Side-Manhattan, he called it. He was perfectly willing to keep on going; it was Livy who stopped and turned.

"Shit," he hissed under his breath, and before he could think of a new exit plan, or mutter another word, he was deep into the introductions being performed by his agent, Leo Faubus.

"Mr. and Mrs. Fennel are interested in your mural of the mountains, *Snowcaps*. They were wondering if it was an Alpine scene."

This was his cue to charm the pants off these two middle-aged, remarkably average-looking people who probably kept hundred dollar bills wadded up in their pockets as spare change. Vollini's people were actually handling all the business details, but Leo had flown in that afternoon to handle these particular Chicago contacts personally—so they had a ton of money somewhere.

"Actually, those are domestic mountains, grown right here in America," he said, glancing impatiently in Livy's direction. She was a polite step or two away but she wasn't trying to hide her interest in the conversation. She looked as eager to hear about the mountains as the Fennels. He wanted to kiss her. Hold her. Touch her. He looked back at the Fennels and his agent, wondering who the hell they were. "Have you, ah, are you familiar with the Cascades in Washington State?" he asked, distracted by the tingling numbness in his hands. "I thought the Rockies were spectacular, but the Cascades are not only breathtaking, they're charmed with a certain magic all their own. Very beautiful," he said, his eyes shifting back to Livy, who smiled at him.

He knew the familiar lurching in his chest from other pretty faces—knew it best, however, from long ago when Livy smiled in just this certain way.

The Fennels said something else that sounded vaguely like praise, and he hoped it was because he said "Thank you." His very shrewd agent, seeing that the sales pitch was, for all intents and purposes, essentially over, said something clever to the Fennels that took them wandering back to the mountain mural to wait for him.

"This must be the friend you were telling me about," he said, looking at Livy. "Have you really known this man since childhood? And is it true that he was an incredibly talented young artist even then?"

"Oh, yes. Very," she said, warming instantly to the humor in his eyes. "And so sweet and shy and humble. It's been an experience watching him grow up and transform himself into . . . this."

They laughed together and Brian tried to appear completely left out.

"I'm sure it's been quite an evolution."

"A metamorphosis," she said.

"I'm Leo Faubus, his agent."

"Oh. His agent?" She looked confused.

"I know. It is shocking that I'd take on someone with an ego the size of his, but the truth of the matter is, we get along amazingly well," Leo said, shaking her hand.

"Leo, this is Livy Hubbard. My first agent was prettier," Brian told Livy in a loud whisper near her ear. "She and Mr. Rogers liked me just the way I am, Leo."

"I am truly amazed," he said good-naturedly.

"As you should be," he said, enjoying the banter but impatient to have it end. "Now, if you'll excuse us, we were making our escape. Go earn your commission."

"You see how he treats me," Leo said, putting a hand up to wave them away.

"You're a saint, Leo," she said, walking half-backward, waving as Brian pulled her away. "It was good to meet you."

Outside the gallery he felt like an idiot in the tuxedo, and if the stares of the passersby were to be believed, he looked like one, too.

That's all he could think about as they walked down the street, their hands in their pockets and their eyes focused straight ahead. What an idiot he looked like. What an idiot he was. It was a nice night for a walk, barely autumn, with warm days and cool prefrost evenings. Lake Michigan wasn't far off; he'd seen it from the cab on the way over from the hotel. It was the only place in Chicago he knew to take her where they could be alone. Not that it mattered where they went; they didn't need a view, just needed to start talking.

In the end, it was Livy who broke the silent barrier between them.

"I was in New York last year. I met Eve and I saw your walls," she said. Livy broke things better than anyone else he knew.

"They're murals," he said, though he could have said any number of things instead. His mind was reeling.

"I know. But I saw your walls, too. The sketches. Of me. Of all the things you've seen, places you've been." She glanced at him. "I know what you've been through."

He knew exactly what she meant when she said it. What he didn't know was how he felt about her knowing. He'd planned to tell her, of course, but in his own way, in his own time, in his own words. He'd sworn his mother to secrecy. He'd wanted some good, solid, sober time behind him, some direction in his life and maybe a little success before he told her. He knew not to be ashamed of his disease. He was learning to live with it . . . still, this was Livy. He just wasn't sure if he was relieved that she knew, angry or shamed enough to crawl under a rock. He examined the sidewalk in front of each step he took, trying to decide.

"Please, don't be angry," she said, reaching inside him to pluck out the emotion she wanted least to surface. "It was . . . like what you said before, I didn't know what to say to you. I was too late to help you. I . . . felt useless to you."

"Why were you there? Why did you come?"

She gave a small ironic laugh. "To dump all my problems on you, of course," she said, her right hand falling from her pocket to fidget futilely at her side. "Like always. Like you didn't have any problems of your own." She paused. "Brian, I'm so sorry."

"For what? It wasn't your fault. It wasn't anyone's fault. It just happened."

"No, I know. I . . . I've been attending Al-Anon meetings." He looked at her. "Almost three months now. I wanted to understand. I thought, maybe, I should have seen that you were in trouble; I should have done something. I thought . . ."

"You thought you could have made me stop somehow," he said, finishing her sentence as he wrapped his pocket-warmed hand around the chilly fingers at her side.

She nodded. "Why didn't you tell me, Brian? No, don't answer that. I know why. You didn't think I'd care. I let you down . . . as a friend."

"Oh. Don't stop going to those meetings, Livy," he said, with a soft chuckle. "You're still taking way too much credit for my addiction. You don't have anything to feel guilty about—certainly not on my account. What happened . . . happened. It wasn't your fault and you couldn't have stopped it."

He drew her hand into the bend of his arm and held it there with his other hand to keep her close beside him. He couldn't believe how good it felt, how easy and natural it was to talk to her, unguarded, even after all this time. He could have been six years old again, spouting off anything and everything that came into his head. And you know what? It felt great.

There wasn't another person in the world he'd rather spout off to; none who would love him despite his faults and stupidity; no other who would stand by him no matter how wrong he was or how foolish he appeared.

"You're going to think this is insane," he heard himself saying, "but sometimes I'm glad it happened. Everything. Just the way it was, the way it turned out."

"Why is that?"

"It's hard to explain," he said, as if thinking out loud. "In recovery they make you give up your crutches and blow off all your excuses until . . . until you're forced to see yourself for what you are."

"And what are you?" Her voice was soft and caring, a fragile lifeline to that part of his soul which needed her specific understanding and acceptance.

He sighed, resigned and . . . almost content. "Turns out, I'm just a man."

Livy giggled, all day long, for two days straight. She was such a sap! And so excited. The ticket agent at the airlines must have thought her completely mad when she called to cancel her flight reservation to New York, two days after she made it, laughing and tittering as if . . . as if she had feathers in her shoes.

New. That's how she felt. As if she were new again, with all the mystery and excitement of loving and being loved and making love ahead of her. She was twenty-nine years old, skipping through her apartment, hugging herself, squealing suddenly and uncontrollably into the silence, terrorized by the possibility of a premenstrual pimple popping out on her chin.

Brian's invitation to the art show, alone, was enough to make her heart soar. She didn't need the fancy card to know it was a special occasion—he could have been displaying his work at . . . at a recycling center and it would have been just as wonderful.

It was the *implications* of the invitation that made her giddy, raised her feet off the ground, had her pulses racing. He was coming to *her*. She'd been on her way to see *him*, but this was better. He was ready to be with her, ready to talk to her. And she was ready for him.

She had a fresh, tentative grip on her life. Her divorce was final, and she was holding her head up in public again. She liked Chicago. She had a job at the Trib—The Chicago Tribune—reporting on local politics . . . well, mostly just the meetings of the Planning Commission so far, but she was working her way up to an assignment in Springfield, and after that . . . who knew?

She had hope in her life once more, dreams and a purpose. She was prepared to meet Brian on even ground again, scarred but battle proud and ready for more.

And there he was, in Vollini's Gallery. Tall and broad shouldered, throat-squeezing handsome in a tuxedo, his long dark hair thick and shiny and tied back with a sliver of black silk at the nape of his neck. He'd shaved, but he had one of those shadows that dark beards leave before and after five o'clock, no matter how frequently it's removed. Had he always been this good-looking? Potent? Virile? She couldn't stop staring at him—and the way he kept looking away self-consciously made her want to giggle again.

Seeing him again was like reading a book about Rome, and then going there. You could have all the facts and figures and history down pat, but it would have little impact until you were there seeing it, touching it, smelling it. Ancient was only a word until you held something so old it turned to dust between your fingers. Conversely, dust was just dust unless you knew where it came from.

Knowing and then seeing changed everything. Removed the guesswork and replaced it with the obvious. She might not have recognized the look in his eyes, might not have understood why he kept taking her hand in his, might have missed the way he studied her face when he thought she was looking elsewhere, if she didn't know about the love that existed between them. She might have thought him uncomfortable rather than eager; shy not clever, and a little too conspicuous instead of deliberate in his actions.

The friendship and deep abiding love were still there, had been there all along. But they were different people. Older. Wiser. It was as if they were meeting once again in Granddad's clover field, for that's where she suspected things began to go askew for them. Young and innocent. Unknowing. The power and magnitude of their love overwhelming and frightening . . . and misunderstood. They ran in different directions, ashamed of the thoughts their best instincts were generating, afraid of destroying what they had together, confused and wanting. They'd come back to that fork in the road as adults. No longer innocent. No longer unknowing. The strength and immensity of their love was still overwhelming—and a little bit frightening—but not at all misunderstood.

And so they walked toward the Outer Harbor, hand in hand, the cool breezes from the lake in their faces, the love and sexual tension between them as real as the sidewalk under their feet, and as vast as the starry, near-cloudless sky above them. It was getting darker by the second—they'd missed the sunset—and the streetlights were dissolving the oncoming night in patches along the sidewalk. She couldn't recall the street they'd taken from the gallery—Ontario perhaps or Ohio Street. And the buildings they'd passed were a blur. But she was intensely aware of their present position.

They were, by then, standing near a railing that overlooked Lake Michigan at one of the many parks scattered along Chicago's beachfront—Olive Park or Lake Shore, she hadn't lived there long enough to know which one it was—in fact the lake was pretty much just "the lake" to her still. But she could hear the water lapping and there were seagulls squalling somewhere—on the beach or in the air presumably, but she couldn't move her eyes from his face to look. Couldn't move a muscle. Didn't want to.

"I wish you would have stayed that day in New York," he said, toying with the fingers of her right hand, which he held close in the crook of his arm. "There's so many things I've wanted to tell you."

"I'm glad I didn't," she said, resting her cheek against his upper arm. "I've done a lot of growing up since then."

"The hard way, as usual." He laid her fingers across his, stroking the knuckles with the pad of his thumb. Her awareness of his idle caress, the deep resonance of his voice, the slow rhythm of his walk and his size were as sharp as ice crystals. She shivered inside with chills that repeated like waves and spread like water over a flat, sloping surface. "I wish I could have helped you. The one time you really need me and I'm . . . Someday, just once, I'd like you to ask me for something, and then be able to give it to you."

"Brian," she said softly, then shook her head. He'd given her so much already. "That day, in New York, I saw you from across the street. I waited for you to walk by and it was . . . I don't know, a comfort, I guess. And everything seemed so clear to me. I wasn't ready to talk to you. I would have cried on your shoulder and you'd have been frustrated because there was nothing you could have done. I'd have felt sorry for myself, a lot longer than I did. Now you'll think *I'm* insane because all I needed that day was to see you. After that, it was like . . ."

"Like I was with you all along?" he asked, a strange curiosity in his voice. "Through everything. Helping. Advising. Encouraging. Pushing me along to the next step."

"Me?"

He looked skyward and grinned. "What would a shrink call that? Internalizing? Incorporating?" He looked at her. In his eyes she saw the rest of her life, so much a part of his that it wasn't surprising that the words *me* and *you* and *I* seemed to be interchangeable. "I do know what you mean, though. In L.A., about the time of your wedding, I was in a car accident, broke a couple bones," he said, glossing it over—that was another story for another time. "I wasn't driving that time, thank God, but I was shit-faced when it happened. I remember . . . waking up from this dream, in the hospital . . . and my leg was hurting and I was all banged up . . . but this dream was so real . . . I even asked the nurse if I'd had a visitor and . . . it was you, in the dream. And you were so mad and so hurt by what I'd done to myself. And, of course, I kept trying to explain to you that it wasn't my fault, I hadn't been driving, but you weren't buying any of it. You just went on and on and on," he said and they both laughed. "And then I woke up. But I couldn't shake the dream. I thought about it for days, went over and over it in my head . . . until I finally figured it out."

"What. That your oldest friend is a harpy?"

"No. In the dream, I was seeing myself through your eyes. Your disappointment in me was like my own. Your anger was mine . . . at me, at myself. I saw what I'd done to myself through your eyes and . . . I didn't want to see you again. Couldn't face you again. Not until I looked okay . . . through my own eyes."

"I know," she said, and she did, exactly. "It was important for me, too, to know I could clean up my own mess and then meet you again . . . with a clean slate."

She hesitated briefly, tripping on the speech she'd been preparing for this moment. She was about to risk the most important relationship in her life on a wish and a prayer. She could put if off a little longer, but where was the sense in that? If you had to cross a river, and you knew the water was cold, it was best to simply jump in and get it over with.

"I need to say something to you, Livy," he said, before she could make her leap. There was a contagious urgency in his voice that made her uneasy.

"Oh, God. Don't say you're sorry for missing my wedding, because I don't care anymore. It turned out lousy anyway," she said, suddenly nervous, anticipating a moment that had been thirteen years—no, more like twenty-three years in the making. "Eve said it was one of those steps you had to take, but I forgave you a long time ago, I really did, and I wouldn't know what to say now anyway, so let's forget it."

By the time she finished, he had her by the shoulders. His eyes narrowed and his muscles grew taut as he prepared to speak.

"I hate it when you do that," he said finally, nowhere close to angry.

"What?"

"Act like you know what I'm thinking or what I'm about to say. You've done it since we were kids and I hate it."

"I'm sorry."

"Don't be. I love the way you irritate me." His eyes darted away and back again as if he had to listen to what he'd just said. "I do. But I don't want you second-guessing me this time. I need to tell you something, and I want you to be quiet and listen and understand."

"Okay."

"Not a word till I'm finished." He was dead-dog serious, not a trace of romance or whimsy in his eyes. She nodded. Her heart was in her throat, racing, cutting off her air, making her dizzy. He let go of her and took a step back, as if he couldn't touch her and think straight at the same time. "There's something I want you to know about me, something I've known for a long time and . . . didn't know how to tell you or what to do about it."

"Oh, Jesus. You're gay." It was out before she could stop it.

"What? God damn it, Livy," he shouted when she started to laugh.

"I'm sorry," she said, trying hard to straighten out her grin. "You're being so . . . serious. You're never serious. I . . ."

"I am serious. I'm very serious. Just this one time, can't you shut up and let me finish something . . . serious?" He stopped short, closed his eyes, and sucked air in through his nose. When he could, he opened his eyes and as calmly and deliberately as an IRS auditor said, "I am not gay. I am completely un-gay. All right?"

She nodded. She knew this.

He held out his hands for some compassion and understanding. "This involves you. It's something I want you to know about and . . . I'm really nervous about telling you. I don't want to . . . screw it up or ruin anything."

"Brian . . ."

"Not a word," he reminded her, then he frowned as if he'd lost his train of thought. "I can't be anybody's hero, Livy, I'm not the type. I can't make the world turn the way you want it to, and I don't have the power to give you everything you want. Hell, I'm probably not even the dream you wanted to come true." He shifted his weight nervously. "But I love you. I always have. I always will. Loving you is the only thing I'm really good at."

She laughed. She couldn't help it. It was either that or cry like a baby, she was so relieved.

"Sure. Laugh. I figured you would," he said, expelling a hopeless and defeated sigh that very nearly broke her heart and sobered her up in a hurry. With his devastation protected in a thin coat of anger, he said, "But I mean this. I don't want to be your friend anymore, Livy. I don't want to be the clown that comes around to amuse you. It's not enough anymore. I want it all. I want your friendship and your love. I want a life. I want kids. I'm sick of looking for you in other women. I want to be with you . . . always. Every day. In every way. I'm sick of pretending that I don't want you." He stopped suddenly, at the end of his list, apparently. "So, there it is. And this is it. All . . ." he cleared his throat nervously ". . . or nothing."

She let the next second drag out for a whole tick, then asked, "Can I say something now?"

He did and said nothing, but stood there like a tin soldier in front of a firing squad. He wasn't going to cry or beg, back down, or give up any secret information. He was prepared to die.

She closed the space between them with a step and placed her palms flat on the front of his pleated shirt. She felt the muscles in his chest tighten over the strong, steady beat of his heart, felt the physical strength, knew the courage deep inside.

"Remember how you used to say that I was the smart one and you were the talented one . . . and the good-looking one," she asked, adding the second attribute to lighten the mood and ease his tension. He didn't bat an eye. "Well, sometimes . . . not often, but sometimes, I was just faking it." She sighed loudly, glad to have it out in the open. "Sometimes, when I didn't know something . . . or didn't know for sure, I'd just start talking. About anything. I'd bluster my way through it and then . . . and then people would get tired of hearing me talking and . . . and they'd just start to agree with me. Just to shut me up." She waited for him to say something, but he didn't. Evidently he was aware of this. "So . . . technically, maybe I haven't always been so smart," she said, wondering how she was going to bluster her way through this one. "Maybe I didn't always understand everything. I . . . I'm pretty sure I haven't known as long as you have, how I really felt about you, in my head . . . consciously, but here in my heart I knew. All along."

"Say it, Livy."

She moved her hand from her chest back to his. "I love you, Brian. I've always loved you. I teased you and tortured you and . . . and tried to ignore you because I . . . well, because I was stupid. I didn't know it was okay to love you the way I do. I didn't know you loved me the same way. I didn't know . . . anything."

His gaze skipped over the face he'd adored for so long. "But now you do."

She nodded. "Now I do."

Instinct drew them closer, eyes locked, passions mounting. Their lips touched. The match-stick, poised to strike years earlier, slipped across the fine sandpaper of time and burst into flame, brighter, hotter, and more intense than either of them had ever imagined fire to be.

Shocked and amazed they looked at each other, liking what they were feeling. She kissed him again. And he let her.

"This is so strange," she murmured against his lips, a lovely numbness settling in her brain.

With great control, he set her at arms length. He did his best to conceal his disappointment, saying, "It's okay, Liv. We don't have to do this now. I know it's strange. I know it's going to take some adjusting and some getting used to and . . . it doesn't matter. Sex is important, but . . . but not as important as being together again. I love you. I just want to be with you, near you. We don't need to worry about this now. This can wait. I can wait."

"Well, I can't."

She let her actions scream out her heart's desire in ways words couldn't come close to conveying. She seduced him with her lips, offered him the vessel of her soul, and did finally cry when his arms came about her, perplexed and probationary at first, then with unleashed passion and puissance.

"Shit!" he said suddenly, cursing into her mouth before he covered it again with his own, his tongue laving and tickling at the roof, his lungs dragging away her breath. One hand on her buttock held her close to him, while the other slipped under her jacket to push her bra up and out of the way to fondle her breast.

"What?" she asked, when she could, nibbling at his earlobe with her teeth before she moved on to draw a groan of pleasure from deep in his throat as she strewed tiny sipping kisses up and down his throat. His cummerbund was . . . cumbersome, but pushing it down and his shirttail up and out gave her an entire arm length of warm, smooth skin to touch, a nipple to tease. With the palm of her hand against his breast, she could feel his heart pounding, fast and furious, like her own.

"What?" she gasped again, half afraid he'd answered already and the muddle in her mind had caused her to miss whatever it was he was trying to say.

"My hotel is halfway across town." He said it like *"I need a bathroom NOW!"* but she knew what he meant.

"My car. It's in the lot about a block from Vollini's." His mouth opened over hers once more. She had her back against the railing to keep from falling to the pavement.

"Too far. Taxi. Where do you live?"

It was a second or two before she had an opportunity to answer.

"Oak Park. Too far, too."

That settled it then, but several minutes later the problem came up again.

"Shit!" he said again, stepping away as if she'd burned him. "Okay. Think, think, think," he said, walking in a small circle in front of her.

She wasn't the only one feeling too young and immature to deal with her uncontrollable passions. Giggles bubbled in her throat and nervous laughter eased some of her tension. She was probably hysterical, but who cared? She liked the way it felt. She was crazy in love and she wanted to stay that way.

"Look," he said, turning to her suddenly, pointing at the city of Chicago. "Every other building's a hotel in this place. One of them is bound to have a room with a bed and door with a lock on it.

What do you think? Do you want to check into the first one we come to?"

She nodded, her greedy hands reaching for him. She had to touch him or the world would explode.

"Livy, I love you!" he shouted, bouncing his voice off the water and the buildings and the sky above. He grabbed her hand when it became clear that she wasn't capable of moving any great distance. He was laughing, too, as he led her along the sidewalk, kissing her at every opportunity.

These weren't practice kisses they were sharing, not like that first kiss in Granddad's clover field. These were grown-up kisses, masterfully executed—some patient, some not, all rendered with the intent of giving and receiving the maximum in delight.

"Oh-oh. Wait, wait, wait. Brian. My shoes. I can't go that fast."

"Not a problem," he said, looking at them. With no other warning, he bent low and sacked her like a bag of potatoes, over his shoulder. "I should have done this years ago. Just hit you on the head and toted you off to a hotel."

She cried out to stop him, but all that came out was more laughter, and by the time he set her down, two steps later, they were both so winded they could hardly stand.

"Say it," he said, surrendering to her slower pace. "Say it again. Say it over and over. Tell me when you first knew it for sure. Tell me again how frustrated you were and how stupid you felt."

"Are you kidding? I've already told you a thousand times that I love you. And I won't tell you again how stupid I've been. I knew that was a big mistake."

"You're right, it was." Now he was omniscient. "I've known since college."

Her heart twisted with empathy. She calculated the pain she might have endured watching him date other women, get married, establish a life that didn't involve her—had she known sooner how much she loved him. It was crushing.

"Brian, I'm sorry. I'm so sorry I hurt you that way."

He looked skyward, the suffering he remembered and the thoughts he'd collected were his own—and long gone by the time he looked at her again. He was smiling.

"That's in the past, Livy. But you know what hurts? Now? More than anything else before? More than I can say? More than anything I've ever imagined or been through before? Do you know what *really* hurts? I'll tell you what really hurts . . ."

"What?" She'd make it better. Somehow, someway, she'd make it better. He took a deep breath, as if to bolster his courage, as if the mere thought of speaking it was an agony. "Tell me. What is it?"

"Walking this damned slow," he said. A grin flashed across his face and he laughed, speeding up their pace. "It's killing me."

Flushed, breathless, and leaning on one another like a couple of varsity basketball players after "the big one," they burst through the front door of a Days Inn.

"We need a room, bad," Brian said to the clerk, a young man who appeared very nerdy and businesslike behind the desk.

"Please," Livy added. They laughed. The clerk raised his eyebrows over the dark rims of his glasses and leveled them an unamused stare.

"Of course," the young man said, placing a card and a pen in front of Brian. "If you'll just fill out the registration . . ."

"We'd like the honeymoon suite, please," Brian said, trying to keep a straight face as he scribbled on the card.

"I'm sorry, sir, we don't have a honeymoon suite, per se, but we have . . ."

"Then we'll take the presidential suite."

"Well, we don't have one of those either, per se, but we have . . ."

"We'll take your best room," he said, as if he were the last of the big spenders.

"Yes, sir, Mr. . . . ." —he looked at the card— ". . . Jones?"

Livy snorted through her nose, then turned away to laugh into the breast pocket of the tuxedo.

"Yes. Jones. I'm John. This is my wife, Judy," she heard Brian say. It didn't take much imagination to picture the clerk's face, but "yes, sir" was all he said.

"Com'mere, Judy," John Jones said softly, when the clerk turned away for a moment. He placed his fist under her chin, lifting her face from his chest to look into her eyes. "Have I told you yet that I love you?"

"Yes," she said, meeting his lips, soft and quick. "And I want you to keep on telling me. Tell me until I'm sick of hearing it."

"How will I know when to stop?"

She kissed him again. "I'll die."

"We have room 312, sir. It's very nice," the clerk said. Brian reached out blindly for the key but didn't get it. "And how will you be paying, sir? May we put it on your credit card?"

"You could if I had one," he said, taking several bills from his wallet and tossing them on the counter. "Is that enough?"

"Oh yes, sir, and then some. If you'll wait just one moment . . ."

"Keep it," Brian said, taking the key in one hand and Livy's elbow in the other, turning toward the elevators. "Send our luggage up when it gets here, will you?"

"Yes, sir."

"Our luggage?" she whispered, watching the elevator lights count backward to the first floor.

"Yeah," he said, wagging his head as the doors opened. They walked inside. "I didn't like that kid's attitude, did you?"

"He was very . . . serious."

"They're all very serious. I hate it when kids act older than I feel."

She laughed. "And how old do you feel?" she asked, holding his gaze as she slipped first the outside button, then the inner button at the top of his pants, and they listened together to the loud rasp of the zipper in the silence.

He grinned, his eyes sparkling with the promise of a thousand delights to come. He bent his head to concentrate on the two bottom buttons of her jacket. "Right this second, I feel like a really randy seventeen," he said.

The elevator doors opened to the third floor and, holding his pants up with one hand, he started to pull her out by the opened front of her jacket with the other. He bumped into an elderly couple getting in—he begged their pardon, then laughed large at the shock and censure on their faces.

With much ado, he dipped her back over his arm and kissed her hotly as the elevator doors closed.

"I can't believe this," he said, righting her at last. He kissed her again—because he could. "I feel like I'm about to commit, and get away with, the perfect crime. And I don't care if the whole world knows because no one can stop me."

The brains of his operation was quickly reading the room directions on the wall.

"It's this way," she said, releasing the last obnoxious button on the front of the stiff pleated shirt, and letting her hands run wild over his chest. "I'm afraid my parents are going to find out what we're doing and ground us forever. I expect to see them any minute now."

He chuckled.

"Can't you see my mother, 'You did *what* to Livy?' " he mimicked, his brows raised in horror and mortification.

She could, easily, and they laughed.

Spotting Room 312, he made a plunge for the door with the key, holding his pants, losing his shirt and jacket and tolerantly exposing himself to Livy's assault of kisses to his bare chest.

"Oh, God," he groaned weakly, fumbling with the lock.

The door sprang open and they staggered into the darkened

room, leaving the door to close on it own, to block out the light, to cut off all sound save their rapid, ragged respirations, their gasps of impatience, and the wall-rattling rhythm of their hearts beating.

Somewhere, she registered the sounds of a door locking and she marveled at his presence of mind—her own was spinning wildly out of control trying to decipher and categorize each shattering sensation as she felt it. Too many, too varied, too splendid to do more than enjoy each one as it surged through her. Instinct propelled her to an end, pushing at clothing, touching, searching, kissing.

In her memory she'd seen his young body a hundred times, wet and summer-tanned in swim suits; hot and perspiring, bare-chested in gym shorts and sneakers. In the dark, she felt a man's body. Broad and lean, all muscle and sinew, lithe and powerful. It excited her beyond reason.

She was pressed against a wall, pinned there as he suckled first one breast, then the other; nibbling gently at her sensitive nipples; his hands at her thighs, pulling, pressing, parting. His frenzied fingers were flustered by her pantyhose, and he snarled his frustration.

"Wait, wait," she rasped, her voice thick with passion as she tried to shimmy quickly out of her second skin of nylon.

Suddenly, there was light. A switch on the wall had turned on a low-glowing lamp at the bedside, casting their little corner of the room in a dim golden haze of light.

She must have looked as startled and self-conscious as she felt, because his smile was tender and reassuring.

"Come here, Livy," he said as she straightened, stepping out of her hosiery. His hungry eyes were all over her before he met her gaze and held out a hand to her. She began to tremble, inside and out.

The sexual knowledge in his expression far outdistanced hers. She sensed he knew things she didn't, had experienced things she never dreamed of—it frightened her. All the beautiful bodies he'd seen . . . and then there was hers. Ordinary. Average. Plain old Livy.

"Come here, Livy," he said again, his voice a deep rumble that sent chills up her spine.

She put her hand in his, but lowered her eyes, afraid that she might see the disappointment in his face, terrified that she wouldn't know how to please him. She took the single step that separated them, standing before him, the coarse hair on his chest tickling her breasts.

His warm hands scorched her upper arms as he stroked her, from shoulders to elbows. In the heart-stopping silence he unhooked the red lace bra from around her waist and let it fall to the floor with her jacket. He tugged on the skirt bunched about her waist until it straightened, then reaching behind her, unzipped it and pushed it to a pool at her feet.

While in the position, he slipped out of his briefs. His penis was thick and stiff with longing when he stood before her once more. She closed her eyes, wanting, wanting, wanting him.

"Look at me, Livy."

She did, her heart fluttering and jumping with anxiety and awareness. She raised her eyes to his flat stomach, his broad sparsely furred chest, his neck, and swallowing hard, finally found the courage to meet his gaze.

She'd never seen him in this state of . . . she wasn't sure what. Odds, perhaps. Pent up like a wild animal, and content. Consumed by fire, and calm. Impatient, with all the time in the world. Fiercely tender. Powerfully gentle. Devastating and brimming with love.

Through his eyes, she felt beautiful. Perfect. Unlike any woman he'd known before. She followed the focus of his vision as he lowered it to watch his hand palm her small firm breast with a reverence only an artist would have, an instinctive awe and admiration for the excellence of creation. It was as if she'd never been touched before, so unique and particular was his mark upon her. She drew in a tattered breath, feeling faint, and she closed her eyes. His fingers trailed down the center of her abdomen and she could feel tears pressing against the back of her eyes.

"Brian," she whispered, surprised by how helpless she sounded.

"I know," he murmured, his mouth close to hers as he folded her into the circle of his arm. His kiss was sweet and drugging. She gripped his shoulders when she felt his breath and then his lips, torrid and titillating at her neck. She exposed her throat to him, whimpering as he went lower and lower. She groped the air for something to hold onto and found the wall, leaning against it, scratching for a better grip as he spread her legs wide and commenced a trail of kisses up her thigh before tormenting her with an exquisite indulgence that had her delirious with delight.

He held her upright at her waist, pressed against the wall. She buried her fingers in his thick dark hair, holding him close, her mind grappling with a magnificent insanity.

Her impatience swelled inside her, fitful and defiant. Fisting her fingers in his hair, she forced him to stand. Her body was a flame, lapping at him. She lifted her leg, high on his hip as if trying to climb him, and he held her there, taunting her briefly before he impaled her, thrusting deep, taking her breath away, obstructing the cry in her throat.

He straddled her legs around his waist, forcing himself higher inside her. She wrapped her arms about his neck and shoulders, bowing her back against the wall as his mouth took her breast once again. The world had long since reeled out of existence, leaving only Brian to cling to. She felt cool linen beneath her and she opened her eyes. He covered her with his body, boring deep into her soul with his gaze, rapacious, voracious, and possessive.

She wanted to watch him, tried to keep her eyes open, but with each slow deliberate thrust of his hips, her eyelids grew heavier, with every gasping breath they saw less, until they closed on the euphoric pleasure-pain coming quicker and harder, driving her forward, upward, closer and closer to a shattering ecstacy.

He followed her into the bliss, repeating her name over and over as if it were a one-word prayer.

Twenty-three

LIVY MARRIED HIM on the last day of the last month of the first year of the new decade.

New Year's Eve day 1980.

It was a simple ceremony in Livy's parents' living room in Tolford. The mothers cried and waxed poetic about destiny and finding love in your own backyard—like in a Judy Garland movie, they said, then burst into fresh tears. Mr. Hubbard grinned a lot and poured champagne. Larry groused about Brian's haircut—or lack thereof. His sister, Beth, hummed the wedding march for them, before, during and long after the twenty-minute ceremony. And twice that day he caught his twelve-year-old brother picking his nose and eating the fruits of his labor.

Old friends—Debbie Richie, Jimmy and Lisa Lowe, the McDunns, Larry Estes, and others—all still living in Tolford, came to shake their heads and say they knew all along something like this would happen. Leo, everyone's favorite agent, arrived late but in time for the small reception that was catered by someone from Union City—his mother planned to sue if anyone got sick on the shrimp. Someone donated six hours of taped music from their own wedding, of which every fourth song was *You Light Up My Life*—Brian slipped the tape into the punch bowl early in the second hour.

And Livy? Livy was beautiful.

She wore a simple white dress with an embroidered jacket and there were red poinsettias everywhere, in her hair, in her bridal bouquet, and there were pots and pots of them around the house. Leave it to Livy to find some way to work red into a wedding.

But it wasn't the sights and the sounds of the day that left the greatest impression on him. It was the perception of standing on the edge of an edge, waiting to fall.

That damned Livy. She looked so cockeyed sure of herself. Her hands weren't trembling the way his were, and she was smiling and laughing easily, as if their marriage was just another childhood lark. She looked confident, as if happily ever after really existed, and it was hers at last.

Brian knew better. He'd been around. He'd been paying attention. He knew what married meant and that there were reasons for calling it an *institution*. It was racked with responsibilities. There was sickness and health, good times and bad—and if those didn't cover enough territory, there were also the unspoken obligations of keeping her plumbing unclogged; knowing when not to argue with her; sensing fears she'd never admit to and making her feel safe; allowing her space to fly and trusting she'd find her way home without him . . . stuff like that.

What if he screwed up again? It wasn't just his life anymore, it was theirs.

When she vowed to fulfill all the verbal and nonverbal demands of a good wife and partner, everyone believed her. When he promised, he imagined everyone—except maybe Livy—had a few reservations. And yet, for all her certainty at the time, she promptly and recurrently put him to the test.

"I can't stand this anymore," she said. "I have to do something."

"Okay." Pop quiz number 248 came in the fall of 1984. He'd seen it coming for weeks. Frankly, the only pop it had was that it had taken her so long to present it to him.

"I have a brain. I need to use it."

"Okay." He couldn't say he understood the ritual of debating foregone conclusions, but it seemed it had to be done—Rule 11 in the unwritten marriage code. Did inevitable choices never take place without a prior discussion? Apparently not.

"Not that I don't love this. I do. I love being a mom. I love my children. I love you. I love this part of my life, but . . . I need more."

"Okay."

"I've been giving it a lot of thought lately and I really feel it's for the best. For all of us. And it isn't like I'd be the only one doing it."

"Okay."

"In fact, the majority of women are doing it now. It's the way things are. Most families *need* two incomes just to get by."

"I know."

"We're luckier than most people our age. It's a choice for us. You're doing so well . . . Most people don't have to make this choice, you know. It's simply a foregone conclusion."

"I know." And he was . . . proud that it was a choice for them and not a necessity. His painting hadn't exactly made him an American icon yet, but it was selling pretty well, especially the murals. And there'd been some merchandising of them lately, posters and puzzles. They weren't swimming in money, they had a budget, but they were doing okay . . . *he* was doing okay, supporting his family.

"And we agreed, didn't we? In the beginning?"

"Yes."

She was on her hands and knees scrubbing the kitchen floor in the little house they were buying in Oak Park, a Chicago suburb— not far from Frank Lloyd Wright's home and studio, actually—not that that had anything to do with anything. His career being more portable than hers when they first got married, it had made sense for him to make the move from New York. She twisted around to look at him. He was sitting on a stool with his sketch pad, behind her, the light from the breakfast room window at his back.

"Are you listening to me?" she asked, not irritated, but weary.

"Yes," he said, not looking away from his work. "You want to go back to work and I think you should—if that's what you want."

"Don't you think I should?"

"If you want to, yes, I think you should."

"Why wouldn't I want to?"

"I don't know."

"Brian, look at me."

He tried, but he had to finish a small detail first. He leaned back for a semiobjective view, then turned his head to look at her. He smiled. She was darling there on the kitchen floor, her hands and knees wet and red from the detergent, her face flushed with exertion. He wondered what the brainiacs at Southwestern—renamed Rhodes College just that summer—would think if they could see her now.

"You missed a place there," he said, pointing with his pencil.

Compulsive as ever, she frowned over her work, found the unscrubbed spot, and made it shine. It was a warm, sunny afternoon in early fall; the leaves on the trees were still green. She was wearing shorts because she hated wet jean knees. Her butt in the air, and the little wiggle of it as she polished, were entirely too tempting.

"Did you hear what I said before?" she asked, turning back to him.

"Of course." He always heard every word she said. He heard most of the words she didn't say as well. "You want me to tell you that it's okay for you to go back to work. And it is, if that's what you want to do."

"Well, why wouldn't I want to? Scrubbing floors and toilets is honest work, but it's not much of a challenge. I need a challenge. Motherhood is challenging, sometimes, but . . . I need to do more with my life."

"I agree. And I think you should find a good challenge—if that's what you want."

"Will you stop saying that. Why wouldn't I want to?"

"I have no idea. You're the one discussing this. I'm saying you should do whatever you want to do." Without a doubt, she was still the easiest woman he knew to talk to . . . and still the biggest pain in the ass. "If you want to go to work, go to work. If you want to stay home, stay home. The choice is yours, Livy."

"No, it's not. *We* need to make this decision together." She said this as if her mind weren't already made up—she was almost convincing. "If I go back to work full time, who's going to do everything around here? Who's going to take care of my boys?"

"Our boys," he said. *They* were a two-part, comprehensive, trial-by-error investigation, demonstration, and analysis exam. He looked down at the sleeping child he'd been sketching.

Generally, they were simply "the boys" unless she was feeling particularly accountable for them . . . or if they were performing in some outstanding manner—then they were *her boys*. Or *his boys* if they woke each other up in the middle of the night—a simple system of gene identification. They'd waited a couple of years before trying to have any children, settling in, saving a few bucks . . . but when Livy decided it was time to quit her job at the Trib and make babies, they made babies. Arriving only sixteen months apart, they were so similar in their developmental stages (after the first six months) and appearance (his curly dark hair, her dark eyes), they could have been twins. And so, instead of going to all the trouble of saying Aaron (after his father) and Geoffrey (after her father), they had shortened it to "the boys."

"And what do I look like?" he asked. "Chopped liver? I went to college for two years. I should be able to manage at least half of what you do around here, don't you think?"

"You're going to paint, take care of the house, *and* tend to the boys?" She had on her highly skeptical, know-it-all face. He hated that face.

"You know," he said reflectively. "I think it's amazing how quickly liberated women forget things."

She lifted her Ms. Smarty Pants eyebrows. "Such as?"

"Such as how it felt when men thought women couldn't do anything but have babies and scrub floors. They call it reverse discrimination nowadays. A popular concept among Afro *hyphenated* Americans and now in the women's movement, I see."

She stuck her tongue in her cheek and regarded him passively, a shimmer of amusement in her eyes.

"What would happen if you were commissioned for another project and had to go to New York or Miami or someplace, to paint another mural? Will you pack the boys up and take them with you during the planning stages? Or would I need to take a leave of absence from my job?"

"It's not *if*, it's *when* I get another project, and we'll cross that bridge when we come to it. Maybe your folks or mine . . . or maybe Beth . . ."

They frowned simultaneously.

Well, probably not Beth. She was still a little shaky after a totally unexpected suicide attempt two years ago. No one had seen it coming. No one was ready for it. She'd gone so many years since her initial hospitalization as a teenager, functioning normally, distracted at times, but seeming to cope with school and the rest of her life. She was living at home—Larry preferred it that way—and she'd had a string of low-paying jobs she either forgot to show up for and got fired from, or couldn't perform well and got fired from, but until she slit her wrists in the bathroom one afternoon, she had resembled a happy, forgetful, light-minded sort of person without a care in the world. Perhaps she wasn't the most trustworthy person around to care for the boys.

"Geoffrey's so little still, not even a year yet," she said, as if thinking aloud, her eyes fixed on the port-a-crib where their youngest child lay sleeping. "He's crawling but everything will change when he starts to walk. Maybe I should wait till then, see how much worse two toddlers are compared to only one." She smiled wistfully. "I'm really not in any hurry to see him walk, not like I was with Aaron, remember? If Geoffy is our last baby, I want everything to go slowly, cherish every moment. . . ."

"Okay. I'll take pictures and movies." A better idea. "We'll set up a surveillance camera and you can watch every move they make at night after work. If Geoff turns out to be as active as Aaron, I'll tie them both to a doorknob or something while I work. I'll build 'em a big cage. Livy, you're the one looking for excuses here. I can handle things here. I can. If you want to go back to work, go. We'll manage."

She grimaced, tilting her head to one side. "But it feels wrong. Not going to work, that feels too right. If I don't go, I'm going to lose my mind. But . . . leaving them, even with you, feels like abandoning them. What kind of a mother does that?"

"My kind of mother, and I didn't turn out so bad . . . after a while."

"But you wished she was there. I remember. You thought my mama was really neat because she stayed home to take care of me."

"I'd have thought your dad was really neat, too, if he'd stayed home. There was no one at my house, Livy. At least the boys'll have me here. There are lots of kids now, growing up the way I did. With baby-sitters and day-care centers. But I'll be here. We'll have the best of both worlds. Two career-oriented parents, and home child care. What could be better?"

He supposed every young couple in the eighties had that same discussion, or one similar. At the time, he wasn't paying much attention.

It was hard to put a finger on the pulse of the eighties—especially *during* the eighties. Most people thought yuppies were the hallmark of that decade—condos, BMWs, investment portfolios, Chinese art collections. But for Brian, a truer sign of the times was the new generation, the nonbelievers—Generation X someone dubbed them—those who were born and raised in the craziness of the sixties and seventies. The generation between him and his sons. Flat tops, New Romantics, Goths, B-Boys, teddy boys, and rockabillies. Mods and rudies, skinheads, punk rockers, heavy-metal rockers, and psychedelics. He read about them, watched documentaries on them, talked to them in the park every chance he got—he was a father now and needed to know what kids needed. From all he could gather, they were a fragmented fragment of society looking for something to believe in, something to aspire to, something they could trust. They found not a single cause that could sustain their fervor, that could unify them, that was worth the effort of their convictions. They made Brian's heart ache.

No one believed anymore.

True American heroes were a thing of the past, it seemed. Well, even the heroes of the past weren't heroes anymore. He guessed that someone, somewhere, really wanted to know all the dirty little secrets—the truth about heroes like John Kennedy, and Patton, and J. Edgar Hoover. But he didn't. He didn't want to know that presidents cheated on their wives, fixed elections, ordered assassinations, and manipulated foreign government coup d'états. That money and power corrupt was a given, in the back of his mind he knew this, but he didn't really want to know who specifically it was happening to.

Childish? He supposed so, yes, but somehow he thought he might have preferred living in ignorance to giving up his faith.

That was the eighties for Brian. He was in his thirties and he had no faith. No heroes. No hope . . . except for that innate trust he saw in his boys' faces. It kept him going. He watched, he waited, he persevered because his children had expectations.

There was that word again. Expectations.

Expectation \ n 1: the act or state of expecting 2: prospect of the future 3 a: something expected 3 b: prospects of inheritance—even Webster wasn't too specific about them, where they came from, whose took precedent, which were unreasonable, which were a right of birth.

And what were his boys expecting to inherit from him, from the world, from the future? What great gifts were they anticipating?

He didn't know if he should laugh or cry the day he finally decided they were probably expecting the same exact things he'd always expected, the same things everyone expected—love and acceptance from those around them, peace and harmony in the world, a safe future. Nothing too outrageous, really.

Maybe . . . maybe his children would be wiser, more circumspect, less self-indulgent when their time came. They'd asked for the simple gifts of peace, love, and harmony, too, back in the sixties—but they pushed the pendulum too hard, swung it too far.

It would take someone far more omniscient than he to decide the righteousness of American participation in the Vietnam war. But he knew that the peace they'd demanded came at a great price—in lives lost and in national shame as Americans watched the fall of Saigon on television with the rest of the world. He'd squirmed in disgrace as everyone took another look at America—beaten, chaotic, corrupt, no longer an invincible superpower; no longer full of pride and glory.

As much as he had enjoyed it, the virtue of the free-love movement and the benefits of the sexual revolution were degenerating into an agar for a mysterious and deadly disease called AIDS. It brought about a sharp challenge to permissive thinking, and from that sprang the term *Born-again*—an obnoxious state of grace acquired by neophytes of fundamentalist Christianity—health-food fads, physical fitness mania, transcendental meditation and . . . Nike.

Living in harmony became an inward spiral of taking care of yourself and living the life of the young urban professional. Unanimity was achieved with indifference—the minding of your own business and leaving others to theirs. Unity was a reward for those who stayed in the main stream, professed political correctness, no matter which direction the changing currents flowed, and didn't make any waves.

Brian was no different from anyone else in the eighties. Self-absorption was his basic nature—giving into it was effortless. He let the scope of his world narrow to what affected his five senses, to what he could hear, see, feel, taste and smell—his wife, his children, his work.

"Hey, Larry, can I talk to Mom again, please? . . . I know I talked to her twenty minutes ago, but I need to talk to her again. . . . No, Aaron hasn't swallowed any more pennies. That was weeks and weeks ago, can we let it go? . . . No, my hair wasn't in my eyes when it happened—it just happened. He's fine. The money was recovered. No harm done. Can I talk to mom now, please? Aaron, no-no. Don't dig in mommy's plant. Remember what daddy said would happen if you did it again? Aaron! No! Hi, Mom. Can you hang on a second? . . . I'm back. What? . . . Of course, I didn't hit him. I put him in the playpen with Geoffy. He's indignant. The bleach didn't work . . . Yes, I used hot water and I double-rinsed. We still have pink underwear . . . I know you taught me better. Yes, I remember, but I didn't mean to throw the red shirt in there. Geoffy was crying and Aaron was—I don't even remember what he was doing that time but I wasn't paying attention. I admit it was dumb, but if Livy comes home and sees all this pink underwear, she'll kill me. What else can I do? I refuse to believe no woman has ever made this mistake, so there must be something else I can do. . . ."

"Hi, Mom. Did I wake you? . . . No, it's Geoffy. He has a fever. I called the doctor and he said to put him in a tepid bath but he won't stay in it and when I hold him down his teeth chatter and he screams blue blazes. . . . Yes, yes. I gave him the baby aspirin first. Aaron! God dammit! . . . I'm back. What? . . . He knows I'm not going to break his neck, Mom. Hell, I probably won't have to if he keeps climbing up the bookshelves and all over the counters, he'll break his own neck. . . . I'll say I'm sorry later. Right now, I need to get Geoffy's fever down and . . . She had a late assignment at the courthouse tonight. She should be back in an hour or so, but . . .

You mean get in with him? Aaron, too? But Aaron's fine. Oh—to make it seem like fun. Right. I guess it's worth a try. . . ."

"Bobby, let me talk to Mom. What do you mean she isn't home? Where is she? . . . Is Beth home? . . . Ask her if she knows what happens if you only put one egg in a cake mix instead of three. I only have one egg here . . . Never mind. I heard her. I'll go to the store. . . ."

"Mom! He stuffed a KIX up Geoffy's nose! . . . Well, how long does it take one to dissolve? Livy'll be home in half an hour . . ."

"Hi, Mom, how are you? . . . No, no. Everything's fine here. I just thought I'd call to see how things are there . . . Good, I'm glad. Say, I was wondering, did I—did Bobby ever play with himself? You know, down there, between his legs? That's a pretty normal thing for boys to do, isn't it? Livy doesn't see it as often as I do, so she doesn't think it means anything. I mean, it doesn't mean they're oversexed or . . . weird or perverted or anything. I mean, I don't think it's particularly weird but I was sort of wondering what— well, what the general consensus was . . ."

"If you called earlier, why didn't you leave a message on the machine, Mom? I would have returned your call . . . Because I couldn't talk earlier. I was, ah, busy . . . Does it matter? . . . Okay, I was sawing another rail out of the banister. . . . He did learn his lesson. This time Geoffy had to learn it. They teach each other everything else, why can't they figure out how not to make the same mistakes? . . . I did measure and they are regulation, no kid is supposed to be able to get their head through a space that small . . . Mom, it's like childproof caps. Only kids can figure out how they work . . ."

Unlike *some* people she knew, Livy knew that the ideals she'd taken to heart in her youth were far from accomplished. A setback here, a disappointment there, a devastating failure now and again were all to be expected when the stakes were so high.

Some people said she was born thinking that way, fighting to what should have been the bitter end, then regrouping and attacking again. Sometimes, *some* people thought she was crazy, and yet, he had a way of looking at her that told her he was proud of the way she was, that he admired her tenacity, that he loved her for it.

It was *some* people's opinion that it was the overexposure by the news media to everything from birth to sex to death and back again that caused the sullen discontent spreading like a virus through the county—the ambivalence, the indifference. He said nothing on television was shocking anymore. Nothing in the news surprised anyone—*especially* in Chicago—and he cited the investigation of the Roman Catholic Cardinal, John Cody, for having diverted some $1 million in church funds to a lifelong female friend—more a juicy scandal than a shock, really.

Some people were probably right in assessing America's general attitude toward its problems as *punch-drunk*. She'd laughed the first time he said it, but it was a true appraisal nonetheless. You hit people with enough bad news, often enough, they get numb— rummy like old prizefighters.

In the early eighties Chicago alone, with a large part of its workforce in manufacturing, was stung badly by the recession, registering one of the nation's highest unemployment rates. The school system and transit authority were nearly bankrupt, and dogged by a destructive cycle of increasing costs and decreasing services and fierce political antagonisms between center-city and suburban interests. Worries mounted about the decline in production of American steel. A shift in Chicago's power base from the various large, white ethnic wards to the black and Hispanic wards of the South and West Sides made it evident that droves of people were leaving the city for greener pastures. Not to mention the endemic corruption of the police force, which had been going on for decades, and the black-filled housing projects created by the Chicago housing authority under the Daley administration.

Well, if it's true that you are what you eat and all you're ever fed is bad news . . .

That's what *some* people thought, anyway, and to some extent she was as cynical as he was . . . but not completely. She looked hopefully at the new black mayor, Harold Washington, and the reform aldermen to undermine the old Daley power machine. She cheered Police Superintendent Richard Brzeczek as he waged war on his own army of police officers. She admired and supported the Reverend Mr. Jesse Jackson in his campaign to rid black Americans of what he called their welfare mentality and the assumption that racism was the sole reason for their low status in American society. *Some* people just needed to look for the silver linings, is all.

Maybe it was motherhood that fanned the cooling embers of her trust in mankind. It didn't make sense to her that miracles as precious and perfect and unblemished as her sons could occur in a world that was self-destructing. Her pediatrician had a framed poster in one of his exam rooms that said something like "each new born child is a message from God that He has not yet given up on mankind."

She liked that idea. She clung to it.

"Well?" She could remember Brian saying that word as if it were yesterday. He was pale and anxious. "What happened?"

She stood in the bathroom doorway like a zombie. "Nothing. Nothing happened. It didn't work." She held up a small test tube of yellow urine. "It doesn't matter. I know I'm pregnant."

"You're sure?"

"Yeah."

He met her halfway across the room, where they turned and sank down on the foot of the bed together, in shock. Having a baby had been a semiconscious decision. They'd expressed their desires to have one. They'd mutually agreed to stop using birth control. They started a college fund at a 5.2% interest rate. But to tell you the truth, neither one of them ever really believed it would happen.

"Jesus," he said, after a few minutes. "What the hell am I going to do with a baby?"

"We, Brian. What the hell are *we* going to do with a baby?"

"Yeah." A pause. "I feel like a baby. Like I'm a baby having a baby."

In a monotone, she explained, "If you were a baby having a baby you wouldn't be smart enough to worry about having a baby in the first place."

"Right. They don't know anything. You have to teach them everything. God, what'll I teach it?" Livy was wondering the same thing, about herself. "What if I fuck it up? What if I screw up it's head so bad it turns to drugs or gets manic depressive or kills itself."

In the silence that followed, his words seemed louder than they really were, as if he were screaming them from some horrible place in the pits of hell, though he was sitting numbly beside her on the bed. She turned her head to look at him.

"The emotional illness was in Beth's daddy's genes, not your daddy's. And it won't have any marks on it because mine isn't hereditary. And it won't turn to drugs because we'll teach it not to," she said. Slowly he turned his head to look at her. A tiny bubble of excitement popped inside her, then another. Then a slightly bigger bubble. They started coming a little faster. She smiled at Brian. "That's what we'll teach it. We'll teach it to take care of itself and to do what's right."

"And basketball."

"We'll teach it about racial equality. To be kind."

"Football, too, if it's big enough."

"We'll teach her about ecology and conservation. We'll tell her she can be anything she wants to be."

"It's a girl?"

"It could be."

"We'll teach her to be home by ten, then."

Aaron was so beautiful and so much fun, they had decided to have Geoffy right away.

"We can't just pack up and move away. Change takes time," she said in a loud whisper, half a heartbeat later, afraid of waking the boys. They were four and three respectively in 1986, and they were worse than the Bell System when it came to monopolizing conversation. At eight-thirty every night they were divided and put to bed. They talked to themselves in the dark until they fell asleep, and usually by nine, if they could still hold their eyes open, Brian and Livy could talk—if they were very quiet and if they didn't say anything interesting. Infractions against either of these regulations would have both boys up and chattering till midnight.

"There were slaves in this country before this country was a country," she said, thinking that she sounded like Aaron, but unable to think of a better way of saying it. "And for two hundred years after that, blacks weren't even treated like fourth-class citizens. *Now* the United States is putting economic sanctions on South Africa to protest apartheid; the Supreme Court is backing the IRS in denying tax exemptions to private schools that practice racial discrimination; most people don't think twice about eating or working or living alongside blacks . . . or inviting them to dinner or parties in their homes. And no one would dare try to stop them from voting. My God, Brian, don't you remember how it used to be?"

"Of course, I do." He dropped his denims to the floor and left them there—one of the advantages to being the housekeeper. "But it isn't dead, Livy. It's still out there, as strong as ever. And it isn't just a black problem, either. Look at all the gangs in this town. Black gangs. White gangs. Brown gangs. Yellow gangs. Purple gangs."

"Not in mixed neighborhoods. Mixed neighborhoods have mixed gangs."

"Well, that's just charming, but the hatred is still there."

Sitting on the bed he watched while she turned back the sheets on her side. She straightened up and put her hands on her hips to say, "Then it's important to teach our boys how to cope with it. If we move to a better neighborhood with better schools and a better police force, they'll grow up thinking that it isn't their problem, that they don't have to deal with injustice, they can just move away from it."

"Injustice? Livy," he said, exasperation thick in his voice. "Aaron's going to kindergarten next year. He'll be five years old. Should I pack a gun in his lunch box every day so he can cope with injustice? That's how the other kids deal with their problems now, you know. Heck, that's how everybody deals with them. You don't like Reagan or the Pope or John Lennon, you just shoot 'em."

She sank down on the bed facing him and released a huge sigh. For all her faith in mankind, for all the good accomplished over the past twenty years, for all her noble intentions, the world still sucked—big time.

Terrorist bombings and airline hijackings and the taking of American hostages in the Middle East were as common in daily newscasts as weather reports. Oil spills and toxic gas leaks barely raised an eyebrow anymore. The nuclear arms race was so hot and intense that no one talked about bomb shelters anymore—there wouldn't be anything left worth surviving for. Was that the world she expected Aaron to cope with?

"What should we do?" she asked, looking up to meet his gaze, discovering the same question in his eyes.

"I don't know," he said. "All I do know is that I want to protect him, and Geoffy, a little longer. I'm not ready to throw them out with the other dogs, to eat or be eaten. I don't want them growing up scared and suspicious. If they have to die before I do, I want them to die innocent, not in some shoot-out on the school playground. Does that make me a wimp?"

"No," she said, caressing his warm, rough cheek with her hand, smiling affectionately. "That makes you a dad."

"A lot of good that does. I still don't know what to do."

They sat in silence. Their eyes faltered. They looked away. There was no immediate answer.

"We still have a little time," she said, injecting a little hope into their bedtime story. He'd be awake all night fretting over monsters and boogie-people if there wasn't a light left on somewhere. "Maybe something will change." She crawled under the covers and turned out the lamp on her side of the bed. "They might wise up and offer me the White House assignment. We could find a place in rural Maryland or Virginia and I could commute into the city. Anything can happen in a year." She paused. "They don't actually issue semiautomatic weapons until first grade anyway, right?"

"Very funny," he said, scotting in beside her. "You know, you've been talking about changing things since the day we met, and every time something does change, it changes for the worse."

"That's not true," she said, turning on her side to face him. She'd bore him into sweet dreams if she had to. "Look what the women's movement has accomplished."

"The ERA lapsed without ratification."

"I know. But the awareness of equal rights is still there. We broke through. We changed things. Look at Sandra Day O'Connor, first female Supreme Court justice. And Sally Ride, first female American astronaut. And . . . oh, and Geraldine Ferraro, running for Vice President, the first female candidate on a major party ticket. None of those things would have or could have occurred twenty years ago." She paused. "Of course, she and Mondale won't win, but it's still cool, don't you think?" He yawned on cue. Nothing put him to sleep faster than current events. "People like Reagan, so they'll vote for him again. That's strange isn't it? I mean, he's not particularly a gung-ho sort of President, but he has a sort of charm about him. Joe Massari calls him the cheerleader. But maybe that's not so bad, huh? Having someone in the White House who doesn't have a closet full of skeletons, who's basically honest and still thinks America's the greatest nation on earth."

"War memorial," he muttered. His eyelids were getting heavy. She reached across him to turn off his lamp, cocooning them in safety and darkness. She put her arms around him and pressed her ear to his chest, taking her own comfort from the strong steady rhythm of his heart.

"That's right," she said, as if she were agreeing with some brilliant deduction by Aaron or Geoff. "He's turned things around for the vets. Helped them get some of the respect they deserve. Massari says there's a rumor going around that he was instrumental . . ." She yawned. ". . . in getting the out-of-court settlement for the vets who filed the class-action suit against those seven chemical companies relating to the use of agent orange in Vietnam." She went quiet to listen to his breathing. He wasn't snoring yet, but she knew how to fix that. "I also like his attitude on war," she said. "He's not real eager to start anything big, but he doesn't take any shit either. That mess with the air traffic controllers, he fired them all. You can only be so unreasonable with the guy, you know? El Salvador and Grenada were a little out of line, but he pulled right out after a little show of muscle. And he was really pissed when the CIA mined the Nicaraguan harbor." She chuckled softly. "And he yanked our guys right out of the international peacekeeping force in Beirut when the casualties started." She heard his first soft snore and yawned. "He'll probably do okay for the next four years . . . but a woman in office . . ." She sighed wistfully and fell asleep to dream about it.

Twenty-four

"I LOVE THIS GUY," she said in early June of 1988, her dark eyes shining with yet another I-told-you-so as she peered over the top of the newspaper at him. "Didn't I tell you Gorbachev was different? Younger. Smarter. Communism is a great idea, but it just doesn't work anywhere but on paper. He can see that. He'll open things up, get a little democracy working over there and . . ."

"Mauuum. Geoffy has his feet up again," Aaron whined from the back seat.

They were cruising along Interstate 30 toward Fort Wayne, Indiana, in their late-model minivan—American made, of course. Having adopted the Buy-American religion several years before, she was ardent and faithful as often as possible. Choosing a second-favorite dress over one she loved because it had Made in America on the label was a common occurrence.

"Put your feet down, Geoffy," she said, without turning to look behind her. "And he'll hang in there with us till we get rid of all the nuclear weapons. You see? This is real progress. This is real change . . . and it's nothing but good."

"So far," he said, ever the skeptic.

"Mauuum. Geoffy won't put his feet down. Can I hit him?"

"No. Geoffy, put you're feet down before I let Aaron hit you. What do you mean, so far?"

Brian smiled. She admired Mikhail Gorbachev's broad thinking and predilection toward democracy, but he suspected that at least part of her hero worship was rooted in the fact that he had a port-wine birthmark smack in the middle of his forehead. And there he was, out in front, the leader of men, the transformer of a nation. A marked man, leaving his mark on the world.

"I mean, the changes he's made look good *so far*, but the truth is in the pudding . . . and that takes a while to cook."

She looked at him for a second or two, then grinned. "Do you know that you never use sporting analogies?" He frowned, wondering if he should be insulted or not. "Milly Jarvis was complaining about her husband the other day. Apparently, he uses them . . . like three strikes and the kids are in time out, or she's gone all the way to the goal if she cooked a particularly fine supper, that sort of thing?"

"Mauuum. Geoffy's spitting on the front of his shirt."

"No spitting," she called. "Only that's all he ever uses, sports analogies. She said she's noticed that you never use them. I think she has a little crush on you anyway," she said as an aside. "But I was sort of surprised that I hadn't noticed it. I mean, I never paid much attention to your analogies."

"You mean . . ." He cast her an elaborate glance of deep pain and betrayal. "All this time . . . you've been taking my inventive analogies, homespun homilies, and snappy repartee . . . for granted?"

"Mauum. Aaron touched me."

"Maybe," she said, trying to muster a masque of repentance. "I think maybe I have. Did he touch you or hit you?" she asked, looking at the roof of the car, as if that position would automatically direct her words to the back seat. Which it apparently did.

"He touched me," Geoff said.

They could bicker all they wanted—they needed to release their feelings, Livy said—but hitting was absolutely not tolerated. They needed another way to deal with aggression and anger, according to Livy, and *touching* was on that microfine line between the two that attracted children like . . . like old people to day-old bread—pretty inventive analogy, huh?

"No touching, unless it's to hug. Understood?" she asked, and without waiting for an answer she picked up the trail of their conversation. "And I apologize, profusely."

"Profusely?" he asked. He cast her a warm look.

"Yes. Profusely. I . . . I have no excuse," she said, her lips twitching with humor. "If I promise to make it up to you later, will you forgive me? Will you . . ."

"Mauum. What's profusely?"

"A lot," she said. Then to Brian, "Will you promise not to stray toward Milly Jarvis just because she seems to appreciate you more than I do? Because she doesn't, you know."

"She doesn't?" he asked, blatantly fishing for praise.

"Mauuuuuuum! Mauuuuuum! Aaron's hugging my throat till I'm dead!"

Three- and four-way chatter-tattle-fests were also a common occurrence in their life. Livy could handle them with her tongue tied *and* order pizza over the phone at the same time.

"Sit on your hands, Aaron," she said—this being the punishment for excessive touching. "Ten minutes." The length of his sentence. Treating a six-year-old like a baby was a humiliating deterrent to sibling abuse—to paraphrase his wife. "And no, she doesn't," she said, back to him in the same breath. Was she an amazing woman or what? "*I'm* the one who appreciates you. *I'm* the one who knows what a sweet, gentle, loving, kind, understanding and tolerant man you are."

He nodded his head. "In other words, you want to stop again at the next gas station."

She smiled sweetly and spoke calmly through her even white teeth. "If I don't get out of this car pretty soon, we may as well turn around and go home because all our folks will be able to see by the time we get to Tolford will be three little dead bodies in the back seat."

He grinned and started looking for gas stations and rest stops.

Tolerance, as she noted before, was his gift, not hers. Still and all, when it came to the children, her supply was almost infinite. Almost.

He'd worried at first when she'd gotten pregnant again last year. Sent to bed for the last three months of her term due to a high blood-pressure problem, she was a little unused to being cooped up with the kids for long periods of time. But she'd handled it remarkably well . . . except for the staying-in-bed part.

He'd carried her everywhere that spring. To the bathroom. To the couch so she could "be where the action is" and back to bed if she looked the least bit tired or anxious or frustrated or out of patience with the boys. After the first three weeks, she spent most of her days on the living room couch, and the boys quickly adapted to the rule that they could play quietly with Mom or go outside. To curb their natural instincts to be loud and act like animals, simply to be in the same room with her, hadn't really surprised him. They adored her, as she did them.

Chloe Carowack—after no one they knew and with no middle name—wasn't the only good thing to come from what started as an "incarceration." In the evenings, while he made the family supper, Livy took to telling the boys long, involved, and detailed stories to keep them occupied. Stories like the ones she used to tell him when they were kids, only better. And the heroines *never* died in the end.

"Do me a favor," he said to her one night, after the boys were in bed. "Write down that story you were telling the boys earlier. Just the highlights of it. The one about the two brothers who rescue their little sister from the bridge." She was watching *Dallas*. J.R. threw a drink in Sue Ellen's face. He handed Livy a pen and a notebook. "I liked that story. It had a good moral to it."

"Thanks," she said, looking at the pen and notebook curiously. "You don't like the ones about the aliens as well, though, right?"

"No. They're good, too, but . . . Well, I was listening tonight and I got this idea that I could draw a few sketches or watercolors maybe, of these two little boys who look like our boys and, depending on what the new baby looks like, I could draw the sister and it might be a good way to teach them some of the things we want them to know."

"Such as . . ."

"Well, tonight's story. Those two boys were supposed to be watching the sister for their mother. They got involved with something else and weren't paying attention and the sister wanders off and puts herself in danger on the bridge . . . and they rescue her, which makes them heroes, *but* they also knew they were wrong for not watching her better. I thought that before the situation came up here, in real life, we could maybe teach them the lesson from a homemade book. Your story. My artwork." He shrugged. It wasn't a big deal, just a thought he'd had.

The sketches were a big hit and the boys named the characters—after themselves, big surprise. He redid them in watercolor. A bigger hit . . . but then, his family was conditioned to ooh and aah at his work. Shortly before Chloe was born, and after much badgering by his hugely pregnant, invalid wife, he sent her story and his pictures to Leo in New York, just to see what he thought of them.

Leo, in turn, had a friend who had a friend who knew a children's literature agent . . . who loved the pictures and the story and sent it to a publishing house . . . who, before Chloe was six months old, offered to purchase the work for publication . . . and they wanted more stories.

That was a year ago. Four more books of the brothers, Aaron and Geoffrey, who rescue their innocent and unknowing little sister, Chloe, were finished and Livy was loving the process.

"This is too wonderful. Too easy. Can you imagine *them* paying *me* to make up silly stories? God knows, it's your beautiful illustrations that sell the books, but can you believe that they're paying us to do this? Where were they thirty years ago when we were doing this? Isn't it weird? It's like we were always meant to do this. It's very bizarre, if you ask me."

He didn't have to ask her. He thought it was bizarre, too. And to it's being fated to happen . . . well, he'd heard of stranger things.

"Mauuum. Geoffy's smiling at me." Since Aaron was still sitting on his hands, everyone knew it wasn't a smile-smile but a neener-neener smile, whether they could see it or not.

"No smiling."

Suddenly, Geoff's face was in the front seat with them.

"Chloe went to sleep, Mom," he said, informing them of this event in a whispered voice.

"Then let's be real quiet so she doesn't wake up crabby, okay? You go back and get buckled in again."

There was silence in the car for exactly nineteen seconds.

"Mauuum. Do fish sleep?" Geoff hollered up his question.

"Sure."

"When?"

"At night, like you do."

"Is that why Granddad Larry takes us fishin' early in the morning? Cuz then they're hungry for their breakfast?"

"Yep. That's exactly why." And Geoff knew it. Larry had fed him that same dumb story since he was old enough to hold a fishing pole—he just liked to . . . rehear it.

"Do they stop swimmin' when they're sleepin'? Do they float on the top all night, like when they're dead? Or lay on the rocks on the bottom?"

"Um . . . I think they keep swimming, but very, very slowly."

"Do they close their eyes? Or keep them open so they don't bump into things?"

"Golly, I don't know, honey. Next time I sleep with a fish, I'll look. Okay?"

"Okay."

She twisted in her seat to look back at him, to see how long it would take him to get the joke. Brian could see in the rearview mirror that he was already grinning at her. Geoff was the joker in the family. Aaron was the more serious, definitive older brother.

"If Aunt Beth wants us to walk her cat again this time, I'm *not* going to do it." This wasn't the first time Aaron had made this declaration. "It's stupid. Nobody walks cats. Cats don't walk. They just go where they want to go."

"I'll walk Aunt Beth's cat," Geoff said. "She gives you candy to walk her cat."

"You're so dumb. She'll give you candy for sittin' on the kitchen stool and not talkin' for five whole minutes. You don't have to walk her dumb old cat. Nobody walks cats. It's stupid. Cats don't walk. They just go where they want to go."

"Hey," he said, talking to both of them via the rearview mirror. "Don't call your brother dumb. And if Aunt Beth asks you to walk her cat, you walk her cat. Understood?"

"But it's stupid, Dad. Nobody walks . . ."

"Aaron?" It was the tone of his voice that caught his oldest son's attention. "Don't you like Aunt Beth?"

"Sure. I like her."

"Does she ever make you feel uncomfortable?"

"No."

"Then you wouldn't want to hurt her feelings by letting her know that you think something she wants done is stupid, do you?"

It didn't take a psychiatrist to decipher the look on his face. If there were any other way of letting her know that walking cats was stupid, he'd do it. But he'd walk the damn cat before he hurt her feelings.

"I guess not."

Milly Jarvis was right about Brian being different than "most" men. She'd meant it as praise and Livy agreed with her, at the time.

He did possess his own roll of duct tape, but as a rule he fixed things "proper" when they were broken. It was part of his country upbringing, she suspected—or Larry's it's-cheaper-to-do-it-yourself influence. Whichever, he liked working with his hands. He was more of an after-sex cuddler than she was—so that was no problem. He didn't stick his hand down the front of his pants when he watched TV. And he didn't leave hair in the bathroom sink, most likely due to a housekeeping habit.

But be that as it may, he was not perfect. The man would pretend to read a Chinese road map and stay lost for days before he'd ask for directions while traveling. *And* he got very snippy if someone tried to tell him that he didn't know where he was going.

Take Interstate 30, for instance. They were lost. And she knew for a fact that it didn't go anywhere near Tennessee. In fact, it traversed the state of Indiana. East, not south.

Family outing was another definition for tension headache anyway. The boys had already asked a hundred million times how much longer the trip was going to take—just wait till they found out their dad was lost! Chloe woke up crabby from her nap when Geoff accidentally threw his shoe in her face. Everyone was hungry, despite their lunch an hour ago in Fort Wayne. Everyone was tired—from inactivity. Family outings were generally not the best time to gently offer suggestions, like "Let's stop and ask someone where we are."

Besides, she *knew* where they were.

"Oh, look there, kids. It says Welcome to Ohio on that sign," she said, looking pointedly at Brian. "This'll be a real treat for you. Ohio is miles and miles and miles of more farmland. A lot like Indiana was."

He was either ignoring her or he'd gone stone-deaf. He sat over in his captain's chair, sailing along as if he knew exactly where he was going, humming to the Fleetwood Mac *Rumours* tape he'd been playing since they left Chicago.

"Put in the *beat it* music, Dad," Geoff said, his little voice pleading. The music was getting on everyone's nerves, but if he put in that particular Michael Jackson tape, *she'd* beat it . . . and him.

"I hate that one." Good old Aaron. "Play *Thriller*, Dad."

Aaron!

"How about some . . . Steppenwolf?" he asked, rummaging through his box of select recordings.

"No!" It was unanimous.

"Stones?" This was his idea of introducing the children to "the classics." During his week to carpool to Little League, he had every kid in the neighborhood playing Name That Tune to the oldies station on the car radio, for boxes of fruit juice. They had Elvis, The Beatles, The Beach Boys, Neil Diamond, and Frankie Valli down pat. Jim Croce, The Mamas and Papas, and Johnny Mathis were all double box winners. If they recognized a Barry Manilow tune he playfully threatened to make them walk home.

"No Stones!"

"Boz Scaggs? Carly Simon?"

Maybe Carly . . . but the boys said no.

"Ricky Van Shelton?"

That was okay with the boys, but if she had to listen to country-western, she wanted George Strait. Country and blues music was something akin to church music, something *his* children should instinctively know was good for their souls.

"Bonnie Raitt, for Mom?"

"Yes," she said.

"NO!"

"Billy Joel?"

"Yuck," they said.

"What do you say, Mom? We're down to Michael Jackson or the farm report on the radio?"

"Fleetwood Mac," she said, beaten.

He laughed and slipped the Jackson tape into the player, turning the volume down and off in the front of the van, so they could barely hear it.

"Tired?" he asked. She wasn't as tired as he was lost, but she could see his concern—he did that quite often these days, watch her with concern. Chloe's birth had been long and difficult, for both of them, and she hadn't bounced back physically the way she had when the boys were born. She was fine now, but he still worried.

"A little," she said, closing her eyes for just a few seconds to rest them. Navigating for a lost captain was . . . tiring.

"Chloe's getting drowsy again. At the next rest stop the boys and I'll play some catch, shake off some jitterbugs, and you and the baby can take a little nap."

"Okay," she said. Whatever. "You do know you're lost, don't you?" Awareness of a problem was generally the first step to correcting it.

He chuckled. "I love you, Livy. You surprise me every day." She opened one eye to him. "I can't believe you waited so long to mention it. This new and improved self-control of yours is going to give you ulcers if you're not careful." Humph! She closed her eye again. "And I am not lost. I know exactly where we are."

Right. Was there a woman in the world who didn't know what that assertion really meant?

With a sigh and an obsequious nod of her head, she gave into the regular rhythm of the tires on the road and the—for now—low mutterings from the back seat and gave her mind permission to wander if it wanted to . . . which it didn't.

It immediately started to list and catalogue duties and chores and appointments she'd put off for the simple thrill of getting lost in Ohio for a three-day weekend.

Her obligations at the Tribune were becoming a burden . . . No, that wasn't exactly true. It was a good job, she liked it. Over the past four years she'd developed a network of contacts in both state and local government, and in many ways her position was actually eas-

ier than when she'd started. It wasn't the job. It was her. The job
hadn't changed. She'd changed. In her heart she wasn't any less enthusiastic. She was a freedom fighter, a righter of wrongs. But her
body was tired and her mind was battle weary. She'd swallow splin-
tered glass before she'd ever say it aloud, but she knew she was getting . . . old.

Well, certainly not old-old, but older, almost middle-aged if
you figured that was anywhere between thirty-five and sixty.

And time. Lord, there was never enough time anymore. Brian
was a terrific father and a great Mr. Mom. Before the boys started
school, he worked early in the morning before they got up, during
nap times, and late into the night while they slept. She hadn't heard
him complain once about having to go back to that routine since
Chloe was born. His gender-based internal compass was pretty
screwed up, but he loved her unfailingly, as she loved him. She
couldn't have asked for a better husband or a more generous partner. Still and all, there were things only the real mom could do for
her children; things a wife wanted to do for her husband; things a
woman should do for herself. And wayward of any scrupulous intentions she had or made or amended and remade, time conspired
against her.

And now the children's books, which were so much fun and a
wonderful family project with the boys choosing which stories they
liked best, voting on which to publish next, approving Brian's
sketches . . . it was the one-time consuming interest she had that
satisfied her as a woman, as a mother, and as a wife.

Torn characterized her these days. Pulled and stretched. She did
what she could to make time for everything, but she wasn't doing
anything as well as she would have liked it to be done. She was
quick, hurried, rushed. Neglecting one concern to tend another,
then counterbalancing or overcompensating. She was running on
ice. Anxiety was a constant in her life.

Was Brian getting enough time for himself? Was he happy and

fulfilled? How much would the new roof on the house cost? Was simply loving the children to distraction enough to make them feel safe? Had her parents had their cholesterol checked lately? Were the children mentally equipped to avoid the dangers in the perilous world around them? Were they eating right? What chance did that young, ambitious, smart-alecky Stone Watson have of taking her job? Were the children being disciplined correctly or was she screwing them up forever? Was she taking Brian for granted? Had she covered the issues of public school officials censoring student activities well enough? Or the civil rights bill in March that President Reagan vetoed and Congress—particularly *their* Congressmen— overrode? And what about Councilman Sandifer? Wasn't anyone reading her articles about him? And what about piano lessons for Aaron?

"What is this, Dad?" she heard Aaron asking. She must have fallen asleep; the car wasn't moving and the boys were getting out.

"A farm," Brian said from almost directly behind her. Not a rest stop? She opened her eyes. It was nearly dusk, the sun setting low in a broad, clear Ohio sky, melting golden light over the rolling fields of grain and corn. Inhaling deeply, she remembered the scents of long-ago summers, earthy and sweet.

From its resting place on the window, she lifted her head and looked around. With eyes still blurred with sleep and a head full of cobwebs she saw the drainage ditch, the three-acre field of still, green wheat, and a big old white farmhouse with a red barn beyond that. So familiar. So like a hundred thousand other farms in the Midwest. For a second or two, she thought it was her Granddad's place . . . in the next second, she knew it for sure.

Awash in a flood of happy, wonderful memories, she smiled as tears crowded to fill her eyes. Warm summer nights. Hanging by her knees from a limb in the big elm tree out front. The smell of fresh hay. Bare feet. Gramma's perennials by the back door. A Coke so cold you couldn't taste it . . . from a bottle. Watching cloud formations in the grass with Brian. Granddad's booming voice. Soft winds billowing lace curtains in the upstairs bedroom. Morning. Fields of clover. A hundred million gagillion stars in a black sky.

Aware that Brian was removing Chloe from her car seat, she was surprised when he popped the door open beside her.

"See there, Mrs. Know-it-all Carowack. I told you I wasn't lost."

She laughed softly, blinking at the tears as she stepped out of the van.

"Well, whose farm is it?" Aaron was asking.

"Oh, honey," she said, stepping to his side, automatically smoothing his wild head of dark curls before she put her arm around his small shoulders. "This used to be my Granddad's farm. Your great-granddad. Your Granddad Hubbard's daddy. We used to come here every summer when we were little, Daddy and me. See those doors on the barn, up on top? Well, sometimes there were big bales of hay stacked almost as high as those doors there, and Daddy and I would climb and climb and climb to the very top of them, or we'd jump out the door onto the bales and climb down . . . for hours and hours. Didn't we, Daddy?"

He was leaning against the van with Chloe sitting on one arm. "Yep. And we had chores to do and . . ."

"You had to mow all this?" Aaron was aghast, thinking fields were harvested much like his front yard at home was.

"No, no. They had big machines for that. But we fed the animals and . . ."

"What kind of animals? Did you have a dog?"

Livy laughed. "Granddad had a dog named Stinker."

"Stinker?" The boys were delighted with that one.

"Old Stinker had a fight with a skunk when he was pup and that's how he got his name. And there were cows and chickens and pigs and two horses . . ."

"And a wild cat in the barn that almost tore your mom to ribbons one summer," Brian said, chuckling.

"Like a lion?" asked Geoff.

"Nope. Like a regular old house cat, only she ran wild in the barn and wasn't very friendly."

"Do you think it's still in there?" Geoff asked, watching the barn suspiciously.

"Oh no," Livy said, though she wondered if some of the ferocious feline's great-grandchildren might not be. "That old cat is long gone. The people who live here now probably have a nice barn cat." She paused, wading knee deep in memories. "We thought this was the best place in the whole wide world, didn't we, Daddy?"

"Yep."

She looked at him, smiling, with love in her eyes. "This was a nice surprise. Thank you," she said softly, her throat thick and tight with adult emotions for a long-gone childhood.

"This isn't the surprise, Liv," he said, looking around Chloe to see her. "That is." He pointed in the opposite direction, down the fence line, to the start of the long graveled driveway that led to the house. With eyes not as sharp as they once were—it took her a second to see it—a sign that read *For Sale*. "I've had an agent down here watching the place for years. He called about a month ago to tell me it would be vacant soon." She looked at him, stunned and speechless. He looked really nervous. "I thought maybe we could spend the night in town, and come back tomorrow and look it over. I mean, if you want. If you think it's a lousy idea and don't want to stir up anything from the past or . . . anything like that, we can head out for Tolford, first thing tomorrow. Not come back at all."

"To look it over?" she asked. It was a bigger question than that, but those were the four words that came out.

He nodded, looking at her, his expression hopeful and wary of disappointment. "I thought maybe we could buy it. Maybe. I always wanted to, always have. And I know what it would mean to you and your job and what a big difference it would make in our lives and all, but we don't have to decide right away. It's not like people are killing each other for farmland these days. But, well, I thought we could come down and look the place over and . . . think about it. Maybe. If you want."

He wanted to—badly. She could see it in his eyes, in the overcasual way he was standing to hide his tension.

"If we buy it will we have to live here, Dad?" Aaron wanted to know, not particularly hot on the idea.

"If we buy it, we will. We won't have to chain Chompers up here. Dogs can run around all they want," he said, hoping the freedom of the family mutt would be some incentive. "And you can ride your bikes up and down the lane there. And later on we might be able to get a horse . . ."

"What about that barn, Daddy? Are there wild cats in it, you think?" Geoff asked.

"Don't know, Geoffy. We'll have to look."

"Now? It's gettin' dark."

"No. Tomorrow. In the daylight." He paused, looking at Livy, trying to gauge her reaction—which she wasn't having yet. "Anybody hungry? Stupid question. How about we go into town and get some supper and find someplace to sleep tonight and . . ."

"Like a hotel?" Aaron asked.

"With a pool?" Geoff asked.

They were both more excited about a hotel with a pool than some old farmhouse, she could see. But the decision wasn't up to them. Brian had already made his, so the decision was up to her.

"What do we know about farming?" she asked. It was the only clear thought that sprang to mind. "We can't handle a farm this size."

"I know. We'd have to hire it out. Or sell most of the land and keep the house and barn and a few acres. We'd have to decide that, too," he said, looking almost guilty for bringing it up at all. "But we don't have to decide anything now. We don't have to rush into anything we're not sure about. Okay?"

"Can we afford it?" The questions were coming a little faster and clearer. "There's more than one definition for 'bought the farm,' you know."

"Yeah. Yeah, I think we can," he said, turning to strap Chloe back into the child safety seat—with no little trouble, as she was sick of being tied down to one place. "Even without your income from the Trib. I think we can swing it."

"Get in, guys," she told the boys, who had discovered dirt-clod throwing already. "How long have you been working on this?"

"You mean, recently? Or long term?" he asked, backing out of the van and standing to face her.

"Yes."

He grinned. "Long term, I was figuring these people wouldn't live forever and I've been setting a little money aside here and there for when we could afford it. Recently, I agreed to do a mural in Venice, California, that'll more than cover the down payment."

The prospect of buying Granddad Hubbard's farm excited him. She could feel it in the air around them. It was like the time they'd turned in enough Coke bottles to buy three new comic books for her *and* a new sketch pad for him. He was this thrilled the day he bought that '57 Chevy he loved so much. Leo's calls to contract for a portrait or a mural or the sale of another painting had him squirming with the same delight and enthusiasm. The pleasure and satisfaction at the birth of each of his children never appeared before he knew, for sure, that she was going to be all right, but it looked very similar to the look in his eyes now.

"You really want to do this, don't you?"

"Don't you?"

Twenty-five

WHEN A forty-one-year-old man is madly in love with his wife after a lifetime of friendship, eleven years of marriage, and three children, wouldn't you expect that a little happily ever after was in order?

He did.

As a matter of fact, for several years in a row now, he thought he was living it. Happily ever after. Fra-la-la-la-la. What an idiot. He should have seen it coming.

But he didn't. He was living in a blur of time passing. His children were growing up strong and healthy and bright. On cold winter days they'd come in after an afternoon in the snow, laughing and chatting, their cheeks and noses rosy red; Livy would be wearing an apron sometimes, and feed them warm chocolate chip cookies and hot cocoa, and he'd sit with them, thinking all the while that he was living in a Norman Rockwell picture.

It never ceased to amaze him that his own work continued to do well in the market. Two years earlier, they'd taken the children out of school to make a family affair of his one-man show at some swanky art gallery in New York. His two-story mural inside the Hemlin Building in San Francisco was taking on the signs of being his mark on history. The director of the art department at Ohio State had asked him to speak to his students a couple of times—nerve-racking experiences, as he wasn't constructed for public speaking. . . . Which isn't to say he didn't blow them away in Memphis last year, at the College of Art and Design, when he announced that fine arts degrees were for teachers, not artists. Even Livy was a little pissed off about that one.

But not for very long.

Aside from getting married, moving to the farm was one of their better joint decisions. Livy, literally, bloomed.

As it happened, the people living on the farm before them weren't hands-on farmers either. They'd already sold a great deal of the acreage, so that painful decision had already been made for them. There were three hundred acres left, and they were farmed by an adjoining neighbor for half the profits. Their share more than paid the taxes and insurance on the land.

Basically, their involvement consisted of the house, the barn, a few other outbuildings, and several acres of grazing pasture. Eventually, they bought a cow and a horse for each child, a horse for Livy who enjoyed riding, and an aquarium of fish for himself . . . because he wanted one.

Livy tried homemaking again, but it only lasted till the kids went back to school that first fall. On the third day of school, she went into town to pick the children up from school—because the bus usually took too long bringing them home and she wasn't doing anything anyway—and came home with "the perfect job." She'd taken the political beat for the local bimonthly newspaper, which consisted primarily of choosing one or two regionally pertinent Associated Press articles to reprint in every issue, and covering the city council meetings that convened once during every month with an R in it.

During the second and third school year, she took the sleepy little farming community like Schwarzkopf took Kuwait and became PTA president. (By the way, she was an avid supporter of Desert Storm until the allied forces proved it to be what she called another financial war, for the oil only, by pulling out and leaving the Iraqi government to take its revenge on the Kurds. That made her angry.) She joined the League of Women Voters and manned the polls on election days, or drove all over the Ohio countryside to transport voters. He caught her planting flowers one spring and was informed that gardening was something she'd always wanted to do, but never had time for. She was president of the garden club two years later. Two afternoons a week she was involved in the literacy program at the library in town. She taught a fifty-six-year-old migrant worker to read one summer, and the next summer he gave her a handmade rocking chair that she cherished and named her lifetime achievement award.

Best of all, she was happy. She *looked* happy, and healthy and strong again. She was busy and involved, but she wasn't chasing her own tail as much. There was time to sit on the porch on a warm summer evening and listen to the children chasing one another in the yard. She'd climb to the top of the hay bales with them, and spend hours picking wildflowers and brushing Chloe's hair, and on scorching summer afternoons she'd strip them all down to their underwear and get them wet with her garden hose. She slept like a drunk at night, no tossing and turning, and when Chloe went off to kindergarten, they made love in the afternoons . . . anywhere they happened to be.

If life were a maze, he'd have said he took a few bad turns, hit a couple of dead ends in his time, but all in all, he was braving it and doing fine. He calculated the exit to be just around the next bend—finish raising the kids, get a little older, have a dignified death—and he was home free. When his life flashed before his eyes at the end, he could say he'd done a pretty fair job of it, and that that last leg of the game had been a cinch, a lark, the best and easiest part of the puzzle.

Oh yeah, he thought the rest his life was going to be a bowl of sweet, bright red Bing cherries—till Livy spit a pit in it.

"Yoo-hoo," she yodeled up the stairwell to his studio. "Is there an artist in the house?"

"Who wants to know?" If this was about painting the bathroom again, he was definitely not home.

"The mother of his children." Ugh. Low blow.

He set his brush and palette on the worktable and walked across the dusty, dirty floor to the stairs. When they remodeled the attic to be his studio, they'd put in skylights, finished the walls and ceiling, put in a desk and drafting board, and built in shelves, but he had insisted the floor remain unfinished—to keep him humble, he'd said, but mostly it was because he liked the paint-splattered look and didn't feel like constantly cleaning it.

He had space in the barn for bigger projects, but working out there made him lonely. He found that he missed the family noise he'd gotten so used to; hence, the renovations to the attic.

He peered over the railing at her. "What does she want?" he asked, ready to get another earful about the bathroom walls. The best thing about working in the attic was that the kids weren't allowed to come up uninvited—hearing them was enough—and Livy didn't like climbing all the way up there to bug him. She had an intercom installed "for phone calls and lowly invitations to family dinners." The horrible dying-leaf green on the bathroom walls was now a *serious* problem, if she was actually coming up.

"She wants him to read something," she said, smiling up at him. A book of paint samples? She looked excited, eager for his opinion, ready to make choices.

"Can she wait till lunchtime? My paint's drying."

Her smile drooped a little and she looked taken aback at his lack of enthusiasm. "Oh, sure. Of course. She can wait till lunch. No problem."

"Liv?" She looked back at him. "Is it something important?"

Her smile was back, no harm, no foul. "No. It can wait. I'm sorry I disturbed you."

"Livy?" She kept trying to leave, but something in him sensed something in her and he couldn't let her go. "What is it?"

"Nothing. Really. Just an article in this magazine. I wanted you to read it, to see what you thought about it. It can wait."

"Is it a short article or a long article?" It didn't really matter at this point.

"It's not too long. A page and a half."

"If I read it now, I'm going to want to get comfortable. I'll need a nice lap for my head."

She grinned. "Well, I just happen to have one with me. Isn't that a coincidence?" she asked, coming up the stairs.

"Wonders never cease," he said, grinning in a way she understood, leaning against the railing to watch her.

She almost always wore jeans now—no dresses or hair ribbons for her anymore—and they hugged her backside in the nicest way. You'd think a man his age would get over feeling like a gorilla in heat every time his wife's ass wiggled . . . it was another wonder that never ceased, he guessed—and he sure as hell wasn't going to complain about it.

Looking at her made his heart swell with joy and contentment. He couldn't help it, it emanated from her. She'd agreed to a truce with the tiny corner of the world she called her own. She was at peace with herself, with who and what she was. She'd cut her hair short because it was "convenient" and because she didn't care who saw the mark on her face anymore. It didn't matter anymore. She'd come to know herself as a woman of intelligence, strength, wit, and unlimited inner beauty, and to realize that most of her world saw her that way as well.

She topped the stairs, looking around, wrinkling her nose at the . . . disorder of his sanctuary.

"What a mess. No wonder the kids refuse to come up here without a garlic necklace, or a wooden stake in each hand. How do you find anything?"

"Do I complain about your office? Which, by the way and according to Geoffy's scout manual, is a fire hazard due to the inordinate amount of unbound, stacked paper. Not to mention all the electricity you waste, leaving your lights and computer on when you run into town on this or that errand."

"Well, if you'd care to enter the twentieth century anytime before we pass into the twenty-first, you'd know that it uses more electricity to shut it down and restart it than it does to leave it running."

"Yeah? Well. . . . So where's this article I have to drop everything to read?" He was still teasing her, but her eyes grew suddenly serious, and she frowned.

"You don't really have to . . ."

"You promised I could use your lap," he said, cutting her off with an acrylic-splattered finger to her lips. Looping an arm around her waist and pulling her close, he eliminated the short distance between them. "And I promised to read your article. After that," he wagged his brows lecherously, "all bets are off. It's every girl for herself . . . and you're on my turf, little girl."

God. After so many years, she actually got flustered and excited with anticipation, her lips smiling shyly, her eyes dancing with desire. He felt the familiar nuances of her body as it filled with expectation and longing, springing the locks on the cage of the wild, insatiable animal he kept pent up inside him.

With lips parted she pressed her mouth to his, tickling his teeth with her tongue, moving inside to tease and entice his inner beast. A groan of deep pleasure passed along his throat. She dropped sipping kisses from ear to ear across his neck. He framed her face in his hands, holding gently as he ravaged her with hot, devastating kisses. Wrapping her arms around his neck, she clung weakly—it was the sound of the magazine hitting the floor when it slipped from her fingers that disturbed their delicate concentration.

Forehead to forehead, they laughed softly and silently marveled at their love for one another, that was ever fresh and undiluted. He took her lower lip between his teeth and sucked tenderly. She hummed with happiness, and carefully pulled away.

"Okay. I give up. Where's the damn article?"

She laughed and bent to pick it up. Handing it to him, she did a fair double-gainer onto the secondhand couch in the corner, and patted her lap.

"It starts on page sixty-seven," she said, displaying an expression she'd bequeathed to Chloe. He called it the female-getting-what-she-wants look. It could be either very amusing or really, really annoying.

He settled in with his head on her lap, found the correct page, and started to read. After reading the first three words six times, he reached up to take her hand out of his hair. Weaving their fingers together, he read in earnest. A frown had formed on his face by the time he released her fingers to turn to the back of the magazine to finish the article, and after that, he didn't much care where she put her hands—he was numb.

"What is this?" he asked, not because it was a particularly complicated article, but because he could feel the world slipping off its axis or maybe it had begun to counter-rotate or perhaps it had stopped moving altogether. He wasn't sure. Something was terribly, terribly wrong, and it hadn't been before he read the article.

"It's complex, I know," she said, as if she wasn't aware of the danger they were in. "All that medical mumbo jumbo and lasers mixed together . . ." She laughed. ". . . I had to read it a couple of times before it made any sense to me. But the long and the short of it is, they now have a laser technique that can remove port-wine stains. I can have my birthmark removed."

He sat up, still confused, and asked again, "What is this? What does it mean?"

She laughed. He wasn't usually so dense. "I just told you. They have a laser now that can remove birthmarks like mine. I can have it removed."

"But why?"

"Why? Because I want it removed. I've always wanted it removed. Now they have the technology to do it and . . ."

"But why?" She was speaking coherently, but nothing she said made any sense to him. "Why, after all these years? Why would you want it removed? Why now?"

"Because now I can." She was frowning back at him. "You know, this isn't exactly the reaction I thought I'd get from you."

He wasn't ready for a calm discussion. He stood up.

"What were you expecting, Livy? Am I supposed to jump up and down with joy and say hell, yes, let's go to New York and burn that thing off your face?" He held his hands out at his sides. "I love your face. I've always loved your face. I don't want it to change."

"Oh, Brian," she said, laughing kindly at his fears. "It's not going to change my face. I'll look the same but without the mark. My face will match now, both sides will look the same."

He refused to believe what he was hearing. "No. This isn't right," he said. "What if they're wrong? What if something goes wrong and they make it look worse? What if it scars? I'd rather have the mark than scars . . . I mean . . . if it were me."

Her brows rose indignantly. "Well, first off, this isn't about you. It's about me. It's about what I want. And secondly, I wouldn't trade a disfigurement I'm used to for a new one. I'm sure they area-test first, like with carpet cleaners, to make sure it'll work and not leave scars. They wouldn't do it if it was going to make me look *worse* than I look already."

"But you don't look bad. Nobody sees it anymore. Nobody thinks twice about it," he said. Unreasonable fear is so . . . unreasonable. He couldn't say why he didn't want the mark removed; all he knew was that he was frightened beyond anything he'd known before. He could even understand her dreams of having the mark gone from her face, but he was terrified of what might happen if it was gone . . . and what was that? He had no idea. He ran a frustrated hand through his hair, saying, "My God, I thought you'd gotten over this nonsense years ago."

"Nonsense? You call this nonsense? Every morning for the past forty-one years, I've looked in the mirror and seen a purple blotch the size of a baseball on my face. That's not nonsense. All my life people have stared, taken second looks at me, wondered about me, teased me, called me names, asked me questions about it, and that's not nonsense either. How do you *get over* something like this, Brian?" she asked, pointing to the dark spot on her left cheek. "You grit you teeth and put up with it. You grin and bear it. You might even give up and accept it. But you never, ever get over it."

He knew she was right. He knew the pain she'd endured because of it, the shame and the embarrassment. He empathized with her. If the mark were on his face, he'd feel exactly the same. Still . . .

"Livy," he said slowly. "I think I can understand what you're feeling. I'm trying. I just . . . I just don't know why you think it's necessary now, after all these years. Do you think it'll make me love you more? Do you think it'll make the kids happier or make them love you more? Will it help you make more friends or get you better jobs? What will it change? What can you do without it that you haven't already done with it?"

She stared at him for a second, then lowered her eyes to her hands, laying palm to palm in her lap. It was as if she'd had a sudden realization and was looking for some way to share it with him. He was positive that when she finally spoke, she'd say he was right; that she'd been wishful thinking for so long, she'd gotten carried away; that it wasn't necessary at this stage of her life; that she'd already proven to the world how insignificant it was; that she didn't need to change anything in her life because she was completely happy and totally content.

"It isn't going to change anything," she said at last, shaking her head back and forth. She looked up and smiled at him reassuringly.

"Nothing is going to change, except that my birthmark will be gone."

"You're going to do it then? No matter how I feel about it?"

She nodded. "I'd like your support in this. I want you to want this with me. I'm hoping you can understand that I'm not wanting or expecting anything in our life to change because of it, that I love you and the children and our life together more than anything. I need you to know that I have to do this for me, and that it means nothing more to me than simply erasing a mistake."

She stood and was about to reach out to him for love and support, to comfort and console him, when he said, "No. I don't want you to do it. I forbid it."

Who was more shocked by his words, they'd never know. He had never, would ever in his right mind, forbid her anything . . . much less say it aloud, to her face. Man, he was way out on the twigs on this limb, and he was going to fall, hard.

It was Livy who recovered first, however, and her acrimonious, self-righteous, liberated-woman act wasn't the reaction that surfaced first. Instead, it was simply Livy, the little girl, the woman, the wife, the mother . . . and she was hurt.

"I'm sorry," she said.

She and Brian didn't discuss the pulsed-dye laser treatments—or anything else—for the next few weeks. They didn't argue, or snap at one another. Didn't glare or slam doors or throw anything. They tiptoed around as if the floors were covered with broken glass. They avoided one another whenever possible. And they spoke in civilized monosyllables.

"Eat up, Geoffy," she said, absently noting that he hadn't touched his fish yet as she filled her own fork with the tender white meat.

"No," he said, laying his fork down, refusing to even pretend he was eating.

"Why not? Does yours taste funny?" she asked, sniffing at her fork. "I thought you liked this butter-and-herb recipe."

"I do."

"Then what is it? Are you feeling a little sick again, like this morning before school? Would you like to be excused, honey?"

"No," he said, his eight-year-old face looking like that of a condemned convict. "I just wanna get it over with."

"What, sweetie? What is it?"

He looked across the table at Aaron, who was staring back at him with a rare display of brotherly sympathy. Whatever the problem was, they had discussed it and Geoff had accepted the fact that he was in a world of trouble.

She met Brian's gaze across the table. He shrugged, as uninformed and concerned as she was.

"Aaron? Do you know what this is about?"

He shook his head and lowered his eyes to his plate of barely eaten food.

She looked at Chloe, who was watching the proceedings with interest, but she was clearly as unenlightened as her parents. Being five and female put her out of her brothers' loop most of the time.

"Geoff? Would you rather go upstairs to talk about it?" she asked, thinking some privacy might help.

He shook his head no, then glanced from Brian to her and back again.

"I didn't mean to do it, Dad," he said, his dark eyes grave and fearful.

Brian leaned toward him on his arm. "You didn't mean to do what, Geoff?" he asked gently, always a sucker for a pathetic face.

"I don't know," he said. "But I musta done somethin' and I'm sorry."

"For what, son? I don't know what you think you've done."

"Me, neither," he said. "But Aaron never does nothin' wrong

and you never get mad at Chloe when she does somethin', so it's gotta be me you're mad it."

"I'm not mad."

"Yeah, you are. You and Mom are both mad, so go ahead and punish me and get it over with."

"Geoff, honey," Livy said, laughing a little nervously. "You haven't done anything wrong. We're not angry with you. We love you."

"Then who *are* you mad at?" he asked. If not him, who else? He was the mischievous child, the daring child, the more outspoken child, the child they cautioned and corrected most often, she supposed.

"We're not angry with anyone." She glanced at Brian. "We, Daddy and I, are . . . thinking. We have a serious decision to make and we're having a hard time agreeing. We're not mad. We're not even mad at each other, are we, Daddy?"

"No. Not even a little bit."

"If this is about the big-screen TV, I say we should vote on it," Aaron said. He got most of the political genes in the family, and he loved all the three-to-two votes his parents had so much difficulty vetoing.

Livy let Brian explain that it didn't have anything to do with the big-screen television, it gave her time to think. Maybe they should vote on it, as a family. It concerned them all, to a certain extent. It might affirm some of the doubts she was having—was it too selfish? was it an indulgence that was too frivolous? was it a boulder or a pebble she planned to throw into their tranquil pond, and what sort of a disturbance would it cause?

"Aaron's right, though," she said, waiting for the right time to inject her proposal. "This is a decision that will affect all of us in different ways, so maybe we should vote on it."

"Are you sure you want to do that?" Brian asked. It was hard to tell if he thought he had insider information or if he thought it too

private a matter to involve the children. Either way, he looked as interested as she felt in their opinions.

"I think so," she said, then addressing the children, she came
straight to the point. "I'm thinking of having this mark on my face
removed."

She went on to explain that as a child, it wasn't possible for her
to have the port-wine stain removed safely, meaning without scarring or changing the pigment or color of her skin—which would
simply be trading one problem for another. Since the 1960s, with
the advancement of technology and a couple of fine-tuned miracles, doctors had found a way to remove the birthmarks from children, saving them all sorts of psychological traumas growing up.

Refreshing their memories, as each had been curious and
asked, she explained again that blood vessels carry blood and oxygen to keep everything in the body alive, including skin. Port-wine
stains like hers were caused by an overgrowth of blood vessels under her skin. Either there were way too many or they were way too
big compared to the blood vessels in her normal skin, and all the
blood in the too-many or too-big blood vessels showed through,
making her skin a dark, dark red or even purple.

She wasn't sure how much information to impart about the
laser, other than the name, pulsed-dye laser, and that it converted
electrical energy into light energy. But the boys thought it was very
cool that she was going to get zapped with laser beams and they
wanted to know more. As a laser illiterate herself, she told them
what she thought was most interesting, the fact that the light energy from the laser was so specific that it corresponded to the ab-
normal blood vessels only—which meant that in most cases, the
top layer of skin was not injured as the underlying blood vessels
were destroyed; and that the light was delivered so quickly (450 mi-
croseconds, or 1/3,000th of a second) that there was almost no
chance for destruction or scarring of the surrounding skin.

"Will it hurt?" Aaron asked, torn between the fear and the thrill of it all.

"Yes. But only a little while they're doing it, and for only a few days afterward. It won't be any worse than when I burn a finger making cookies."

"They burn you?" Geoff asked, ready to cast a negative vote.

"Well, they say no, they don't burn anything, but they say it stings like a burn and looks like a burn when they're done . . . until it heals. Then it'll look more like the rest of my skin."

"Will you look different?" he asked.

"No," she said, covering the stain with her hand—covering the stain with her hand as she had a thousand times before, to make it disappear. "I'll look just the same, but without the mark." She turned her head to and fro. "What do you think? Better without? Or better with it?"

The boys actually gave it some thought, which surprised her. They were generally quick to judge and hasty making decisions.

"Mommy?" Chloe's voice was quiet and unsure.

"Yes?"

"If the mark goes away, can I still be your little girl?"

"Forever and always, sweetie. Nothing will ever change that. No matter what."

While she and Chloe sealed the deal with a little wet kiss, the boys consulted with their father.

"What do you think, Dad?" Aaron asked.

Brian shook his head. "I don't know, Aaron. I love Mom the way she is, but it's her face. I . . . don't see the need, but it's up to your mom."

Both boys took another long look at her.

"Will you be happier without it?" Aaron asked. The depth of his perceptions continually amazed her—this time he'd outdone himself.

"I'm very happy *with* it, Aaron. I already have you and Geoff and Chloe and Daddy and you make me happier than I've ever been in my whole life. I can't get happier than I am right this second . . . or luckier. Having this mark removed from my face isn't going to change anything, except how I feel about me. It's like . . . if you had a wart on the end of your nose . . ."

"An ugly one with hairs in it?"

"Exactly."

"Can I have one on my nose, too, Mommy?" Chloe asked, forever afraid of being left out.

"Sure. But you won't like it. People will look at you funny. You'll scare some people, and they won't want to talk to you. Some people will make fun of you, and laugh. You'll wish all the time you could take it off, but you can't. Then, one day, a fairy godmother comes along and she can wave her magic wand and make the wart on your nose go away . . . but that's all she can do. She can't make you prettier or smarter or richer or nicer. All she can do is take warts off noses." She looked at each of the four faces around her supper table. "Would you let her?"

The final vote was four pro-removal, and one stubborn abstention.

Twenty-six

SUMMER HAD ALWAYS BEEN his favorite season. If warm, sweet-smelling May evenings were an indication of the climates to come, he had the next few months to look forward to . . . and that was about it.

What did she want from him? Why did she have to keep messing with things? Why couldn't she ever leave well enough alone? He lit a cigarette and wished he had a frosty beer to go with it . . . a cold six-pack . . . hell, a half-frozen keg wouldn't be enough to dull the aching turmoil in his chest.

Let's change the social consciousness. Let's change the government. Let's change the local school system. Let's change this. Let's change that. Let's change our faces! Livy and her damn changes. Thirty-five years she'd been changing things. Didn't she ever get tired of it? Couldn't she overlook this one tiny flaw in her world and let it be?

All right. It wasn't a tiny flaw to her.

She wasn't even mad that he couldn't take to her scheme like a pit bull to chuck roast. She was disappointed. Again.

Well, he was very sorry, but show him a man who would remain silent and amenable while his wife rearranged her face after thirty-five years, and he'd show you a man who was deaf, dumb, and blind when they met.

"Hi," she said, pushing the screen door open enough to stick her head out. He wasn't entirely happy about being interrupted. He'd been painting blue streaks of resentment and trepidation into the rose and fuchsia sunset, and he wasn't near finished.

"Hi."

"Can I come out? Or is this a private swing session?"

He had a thing about swinging in the front-porch swing. She and the kids were welcome to join him, but it drove him nuts if they sat beside him and started swinging to their own rhythm. They had to let him swing his way, slow and steady, or sit elsewhere. And so, he told her, "You can come out, but *I'm* swinging."

"Fair enough," she said, smiling, letting the door quietly bump closed behind her. She picked her moment, midswing, to sit beside him, pulling her legs up on the seat to sit Indian style. "Nice night, huh?"

"Um-hum."

As far as he could tell, the only advantage to marrying someone you've known all your life is knowing all their tricks.

At supper, she'd talked the kids into thinking that she really needed to have her birthmark removed. She had them thinking of it as something to look forward to. What fun! If she got to keep the protective eye goggles she used during the treatments, the boys both wanted a pair. And Chloe went straight from the dining room table to her toy box, in search of all the pieces to her Fisher-Price doctor kit—she'd volunteered to nurse her mother back to health afterward.

And now—what a coincidence—Livy had come outside to enjoy a warm spring evening with him, like she usually did, as if nothing was wrong. Humph. She was as transparent as Glad Wrap.

She'd used this same strategy to get Chloe, he remembered. She'd patiently waited for him to relax into fatherhood, for his mind to wander because he believed he had a family and a career under a loose, pragmatic control and he was feeling relatively secure. Then, POW! when his guard was down, she had him readily agreeing to another baby. He frowned at the deepening purple hues of the twilight. Bad example. Chloe had turned out to be one of the brightest lights in his life.

Nevertheless, the principle was the same and the tactic was all

too familiar. He wished she did want another baby. He was good
with babies. He liked his kids. At least he was ready, prepared, for
the impact another child would have on his life. Altering the physical features of a beloved face was, once again, a phenomenon in his
life with unknown consequences.

Well, he was ready for her this time. This time he'd wait patiently for her to make her move, then POW! he'd shoot her down.
He was working on a plan. He had his thinking cap on. Somehow
he'd find a way to make her understand that her face was his lifeline; that he saw it in his dreams, looked for it everywhere; that the
sight of it soothed him, excited him, made everything seem okay
for him.

Any second now she'd start to pontificate on her theory of
changes that didn't change anything. He wondered if her phraseol-
ogy could be classified as an oxymoron, like government intelligence or female logic; or was it a paradox, like being cruel in order
to be kind; or was there some altogether different name for her
style of talking in circles?

Any second now. . . .

Changes that don't change anything. Can you imagine it? Saying such a thing to a man whose whole life once changed, between
heartbeats, when a little girl with black braids and red hair ribbons
punched some other kid in the nose. This to a man whose longest
and most solid relationships were with his mother and his wife—
and he'd only known one six years longer than the other. A fad
fighter, he was the last man he knew to wear, and then give up, his
bell-bottom jeans; he never learned to ride a skateboard; he'd flatly
refused to swallow any goldfish in college and he never once wore
polyester in the seventies as a matter of principle. Livy called his
paintings superrealistic, but the truth of the matter was, he was either afraid to or didn't have the imagination to or simply couldn't
muster the desire to change what he saw.

Any second now, he thought, flicking the butt of his cigarette high and far across the front lawn. He sensed she was preparing to launch her missiles. He watched the hot, glowing pinpoint until it went dark, then stared out at the graying dusk, aware of every slow, calm stir she made in his peripheral vision.

Any second now, she'd find some flimsy excuse to bring the subject up again. Chatter about it like a jaybird drunk on chinaberries—until *he* got the headache and the hangover.

Any second now. . . .

"I'm scared," he said, shattering the silence between them.

"I know," she answered quietly. "Me, too."

"You are the single most important person in the world to me, Livy."

"I know."

"I love you the way you are."

"I know."

"Your birthmark is so much of what you are."

No answer.

"I've watched you, all your life, react to it in one way or another. Both good and bad. It's made you a fighter, Liv. It taught you about empathy and fairness and the insanity of bigotry. It gave you strength; it spurred the development of you mind; it blinded you to your own beauty. Even your mannerisms . . . the way you automatically turn the left side of your face away when you meet people, and away from cameras; the way you rest your left cheek on your fist, not your right, when you're reading or thinking; you used to style you hair to cover it, slather it with make-up. I've seen you hide behind it like a shield and flaunt it like a weapon. It's been the single biggest influence in the building of your character that I can think of, and I . . . I'm afraid you'll change if it's gone. You won't be the same."

"It doesn't work like that," she said, notes of compassion and patience in her voice. She turned on the swing to face him. "Do you think that once I look like everyone else, I'll suddenly hate everyone who doesn't?"

"No, of course not," he said, wishing with all his heart that he wasn't such a coward, that he could anticipate changes as eagerly as she did. "It's just . . . I . . . did you ever read that Nathaniel Hawthorne story called *The Birthmark?* The one where this mad scientist insists on removing this tiny birthmark from the cheek of his otherwise perfect wife, and he kills her. She's sweet and wonderful and beautiful except for one tiny flaw, and when he removes it, it's as if he's removed her heart. That's what this feels like to me, Livy. It feels like we're messing with perfection, and I'm scared to death of losing who you are now . . . of taking away your heart."

She smiled. "You think I'm perfect?"

"For me. You've always been perfect."

The palm of her hand was warm and tender against his cheek. Her eyes were dark and warm with emotion, soft and beckoning, brimming with deep affection; her lips bowed gently with happiness and satisfaction—and he didn't need the porch light to see it so. He'd seen that same expression a thousand times across a room, over a table, beyond a child's shoulder, early in the morning, late at night, in a random glance, during their lovemaking.

"You are the sweetest, dearest old worry wart," she said, laughing faintly. "*You* are my heart, my darling. I gave it to you the day we met. Remember? For safe keeping? And for all these years, you've protected it, fed it innocence and beauty, gave it hope. So long as you're with me, my heart is in no danger."

He covered the back of her hand with his, turning his head to plant a kiss in it. God, how he'd missed her—living in the same house with her, pushing her so far away.

"Come here," he said, tugging lightly on her arm. Unfolding her legs to cross them both over one of his, she leaned into his embrace and cuddled close. They rocked in silence, the tension between them fading away as if it had never existed. A choir of night bugs hummed and buzzed and chirped a soothing melody, and for several long moments he forgot his fears.

"I suppose, I'm all that's holding up this procedure," he said finally, his voice softly harmonizing with the quiet country evening.

"I have an appointment, three weeks from Thursday. For tests."

He grinned, nodding. He should have known—which was why he wasn't angry, he supposed.

"How long will you be gone?"

"Overnight."

"Can I go with you?"

"The kids'll be out of school by then. They'll be worried. It might be better if you stayed with them. It's only for tests anyway."

"Okay."

He was agreeing to stay home with the children, not to having the procedure done. He couldn't do that, and she knew why. But part of loving Livy was trusting her—about ninety-five percent of it. The other five percent consisted primarily of hanging on tight and praying for the best.

"Thank you," she said, after a few more minutes had passed.

"For what?"

"For trying to understand. I know how hard this is for you. I know it's not going to get any easier for you." Truth be known, the only thing he even halfway understood was that he couldn't do anything to stop her. As for hard and easy, well, it was hard pretending to be angry with her. "At least until it's over. Until you can see for yourself that it's not going to change anything."

Here we go! Changes that don't change anything.

He waited for her oration to begin . . . and he waited. But she seemed content in the silence and darkness and didn't say a word. He smiled and sighed deeply, almost glad, as he realized talking-time was over. She'd slipped into her show-him mode and there was nothing left to say. Her decision was made and irreversible. Her heart was set. She was committed. Once more, it was his time to hang on and start praying.

"Yesterday, Chloe asked me where shadows go when the sun's not shining," she said after a long while.

"And did you tell her they stand behind trees and wait for the sun to come back?" They'd written a story about shadows a few years back. It was one of Livy's favorites.

"Sort of. I told her they didn't go anywhere. I said that just because you can't see something any longer, it doesn't mean it isn't still there."

Ugh! She'd ambushed him, stabbed him in the back with a single sentence.

She was having the port-wine stain removed from her face, but just because they wouldn't be able to see it any longer, it didn't mean it wasn't going to be there—inside, where the only person it ever really mattered to could still see it. People she hadn't met yet might never know she ever had the mark. People who knew her now and in the past might forget it ever existed. But deep within Livy, where her soul spoke and her heart listened, the shadows of the emotional pain she'd endured, of the lessons she'd learned, of the strengths and weaknesses she incorporated into who she was, wouldn't simply disappear when the sun was no longer shining. They would remain, stay on like night shadows, a darker darkness in the dark.

Elizabeth Kubler-Ross would have understood it. Anyone who'd had an abortion, or a diseased gallbladder surgically removed, or rhinoplasty, or voluntary sterilization for birth control knew about it—that sense of loss she was experiencing. She suspected it was extremely common and very human, but that didn't make her feel any less alone.

She was mourning a birth defect. Crazy. Totally nuts. But that was the only way she could describe what she was feeling.

The grieving began days before she left for New York. The second guessing. The third guessing. Looking in the mirror and wondering what had possessed her to take such a drastic step. It was maniacal. Excited one minute, terrified the next. A lifetime of wanting the mark removed had a cumulative effect on her; imagining herself without it had no tangible effect at all. It didn't seem possible. And the sadness. . . . My God, if she'd ever dreamed she'd be sad to see the hideous thing gone from her face, never to return, she might have had her head examined. But that's how it was, overwhelmingly sad.

It made no sense to her, either.

She kept telling herself it was like graduating from high school or your baby's first day of school—one of those unforgettable, pivotal moments in your life that is as sweet as it is sorrowful. An end that was a new beginning. Abdicating the familiar with great expectations for the unknown.

It was utterly foolish and illogical, and if she was correct, it was completely normal as well. She didn't discuss it with Brian. Any doubts or concerns on her part would have been magnified a thousand times in his mind, causing him just that much more anguish.

Perky party faces were what she wore for her family, promising the children New York souvenirs if they were good—she was a devout believer in the bribing of children—and dodging Brian's requests to go with her, citing state laws against the transporting of mother hens across state lines and ordinances against mollycoddling inside New York City limits and, of course, all the well-known hotel regulations pertaining to the quartering and maintenance of fuddy-duddies in one's room.

Still, when the nurse helped her adjust the blindfold over her eyes to protect them from the laser rays, she was desperately wishing she'd brought someone to hold onto—a husband, a mama, a teddy bear. She was alone, possibly mistaken and very much at risk. A flood of tears pressed hard against the back of her eyes when the hum-plunking sound of the laser began. For all she knew, the doctor could have been snapping at her cheek with a rubber band, the pain was so sharp and so quick. Over and over, until she was no longer surprised each time it happened but expecting it, now and now and now and now. They swore that nothing was burning, yet the stench of singed skin filled her nostrils and made her nauseous.

Squeezing her eyes tight against the urge to cry, the sudden realization of having gone too far to turn back inundated her. Maybe Brian was right all along. Maybe some things weren't meant to be changed. The words permanent and forever echoed through her mind. Maybe tampering with nature, with God's handiwork, wasn't such a great idea. Test-tube babies. Genetic engineering. Cloning. Organ transplanting. Suspended animation. It all fascinated her, but she'd never been too sure how free and loose man should be when messing with that sort of stuff. Second-guessing God couldn't be all that wise or prudent.

They uncovered her eyes and placed a cool, saline Telfa pad against her cheek before she could make up her mind to stop the procedure. It was done. For good or bad, better or worse, it was done. Her doctor and the nurse were pleased and encouraging. Only the heavy dull ache on the left side of her face and the fear of bursting into tears kept her from telling them that she felt they'd just made a profound mistake, that she wanted the procedure reversed, that she wanted her face to stay as it had always been—her face.

She could barely recall leaving the hospital or the cab ride back to the hotel. She was in shock, she supposed, because the next clear memory she had was of dropping her coat and purse on the floor, along with the gifts she'd bought the children on her way to the hospital that morning. She left them there, just inside the door of her room, and turned to the nearest mirror.

Holding her tears at bay any longer was impossible as she stared at her reflection, the white dressing on her cheek making her look . . . afflicted, damaged, hurt. Her hands shook as she gingerly pulled the tape from her skin, released the Telfa pad, and exposed the gory wound on her face.

Only half of the port-wine stain had been treated, as she and the doctor had agreed was best. That half looked like her worst nightmare. It was an ugly dark red with lots of spots as if burned repeatedly with the hot end of a cigarette. What had she done? She sobbed and closed her eyes, tormented by her own stupid vanity and pride. What had she done?

The loss of the soothing coolness and the exposure to the drying air separated the heavy, dull ache in her face from the real pain it had concealed, an intense stinging and throbbing as if she'd been branded with a hot iron.

"Oh, God," she cried, tears flowing freely as she pressed the cool pad to her check again. Frustrated and finding herself in a world of misery, she cursed whatever it was that had compelled her to tamper with anything and everything that touched her life. She'd survived forty-one years with a port-wine stain on her face; would another forty have been impossible? The pain had been tolerable before she removed the dressing; couldn't she have left it alone? She swallowed two extra-strength Tylenol, finished the entire glass of water, and stared at herself in the mirror once more. Couldn't she leave *anything* alone?

In a sight-blurring state of dolor and despair she began to undress. Unaware of the continued flow of tears, her body racked with sobs, she intended to crawl into bed and never get up again.

She ignored the first light tapping at the door. The damned housekeeping staff could just damn well wait till she was damned good and dead before they cleaned the damned room, changed the damned bed, and replaced the damned towels.

She was in her slip, struggling frantically to get out of her pantyhose, when the knocking came again, louder, more insistent. With no little effort, she focused her eyes on the door. She'd forgotten to chain it. If she didn't answer, wouldn't the maid simply let herself in?

Her whole body sagged with hopelessness, and she began to cry in earnest—dejected, defective, and defeated.

"Please go away," she called, praying that if this particular New Yorker couldn't speak English, she could at least understand the get-away-from-me tone in her voice.

"Livy?" Softly spoken, barely southern English? "It's Brian. Open the door."

In utter shame, but without hesitation, she turned the knob and opened the door. He'd told her so, but he'd never say it out loud, not as she would have, were the situation reversed. He was a good person. Kind and sweet and gentle. Not like her. Not stupid and willful and never satisfied.

"Aw God," he said, taking in her general condition without a blink. "Aw Liv, honey, come here," he said, his face filled with sympathy, his arms outstretched to receive her weak, trembling body.

He stepped into the room, leaving the door to close and lock on its own, and scooped her up against his body as he might Chloe after a spill on her bike. She wrapped her arms about his neck and buried face against his throat, saying over and over, "I'm sorry. I'm so sorry."

"Shhhh," he whispered, trying to soothe her as he carried her across the room to the bed. He sat down, holding her on his lap, cradling her in his arms. "Shhhh. Livy," he said, rocking her gently. "No, I'm sorry. Shhhh. I knew I should have been here with you. Why do we do this?" he asked, as if he'd asked himself the question before and hadn't found an answer. "We're not going off to suffer alone anymore. Not like this. Not like last time. Never again. We've nothing left to prove to each other, to anyone. Shhhh. I shouldn't have let you talk me out of it. I should have been here. *I'm* sorry."

He let her cry. For a little while she believed he was crying with her. What was that old adage? Something about friendship improving happiness and abating misery, by doubling the joy and dividing the grief. Funny thing about those adages, they couldn't live to be an old one unless they were true.

"It's too late to get my old face back," she muttered when she was too tired to cry anymore. "They said it didn't burn, but it smelled like burning and it looks burned and it hurts like a burn."

"Did they give you anything for the pain?"

"Tylenol."

"Did you take any?"

She nodded. "I'm so stupid. I don't know why I'm crying. I want the damn thing gone. I've always wanted it gone. And now I . . . I miss it. I want it back. The way it was." He didn't say anything, but continued to rock her and hold her close. "That's stupid, isn't it?"

"Yep."

She sighed, feeling a little better.

"Really, really stupid," she said, looking to feel a lot better.

"Yep."

"I'll get used to seeing my face without it. I'll like my face better without it. No more double takes. No more staring. No more explanations. I'll be another face in the crowd."

"Yep."

"I'm glad you came," she said, feeling anchored and safe, and getting sleepy. "I was scared . . . and sad."

"Me, too. So I came."

"Who's with the kids?"

"Mom and Larry. I called them after you left yesterday. I drove all night, hoping to get to the hospital on time, but . . . I'm sorry I wasn't there, Livy."

"You're here now." She sat up to face him. His gaze roamed over her face, warm and loving, unafraid of what he might see, accepting unconditionally who and what she was—and what she looked like. She caressed his whisker-roughened cheek with the backs of her fingers, wondering what she'd done so right to deserve a man so wonderful. "More than my husband, more than my lover, you are the best friend I've ever had, Brian Carowack."

He tipped his face toward hers, closed his eyes, and brushed his lips against hers. A feather-light touch, fashioned to convey his endless devotion and desire, and to cause her the least amount of pain at the same time. He smiled. "And don't you ever forget it," he said.

Twenty-seven

THERE WAS NO KEEPING the boy down on the farm after that. Every three months or so, after the blisters and scaling and itching had subsided, they returned to New York together for another laser treatment. Made a "thing" of it, actually, leaving a couple of days early to shop or see a play and eat great food. Even as the stain shrunk in size and faded in color, to something looking more like a small sleep blotch or an hour-old slap on the face, he refused to let her go it alone.

He couldn't stay in the treatment room. The smell and the thoughts of her pain drove him out to the waiting room—no surprise—he'd proven to have a weak stomach and a low pain threshold when the kids were born, too. But he was there when it was over, feeding her Tylenol, making her eat room-service food, letting her sleep and seeing she wasn't disturbed until she felt like going home again.

And though he may still have had misgivings about the changes her altered appearance might precipitate, he didn't let them show. Quite the opposite. He was delighted that she now looked like all the sketches and painting he'd done of her.

"Now when I paint you beautiful, no one can say I forgot your birthmark," he'd say. "It was probably something psychic. I must have known all along it wasn't going to be there forever."

Eighteen months and six treatments later, he stood behind her in the doctor's waiting room, holding her long, red wool coat for her to put on—not an unheard of gesture on his part but certainly not a common one. She smiled as she slid her arms into the sleeves, felt him lift it onto her shoulders, and then she buttoned it blindly with one hand.

We've come a long way, baby, she thought, half-listening to the nurse's final instructions, sliding the strap of her purse over her shoulder. *A lifetime . . . almost.*

Almost.

She turned to him, smiling, ready to leave, and reached out to take his hand. His expression was wary, as it usually was when they were finished with one adventure and preparing to move on to the next. It was the suspense that got to him, the unknown. But he always, as he did in that moment, took her hand with unwavering trust . . . and wasn't it a greater compliment to be trusted than to be loved?

They had indeed come a long way together . . . and they would go further, together, as friends . . . friendship being the greatest love, the greatest usefulness, the most open communication, the noblest suffering, the severest truth, the heartiest counsel, and the greatest union of minds of which men and women are capable, according to Jeremy Taylor—a seventh-century theologian who like most old adage vendors, she assumed, was a very wise and truthful man.

Be that as it may, their greatest moments together had never been planned; they were never right or wrong or wasted, they were . . . inevitable, fated, meant to be, she felt. It was their destiny, since before that first day on the Tolford Primary School playground, to face and survive history together.

History. What did Gibbon call it in *The Decline and Fall of the Roman Empire*? Little more than the register of the crimes, follies, and misfortunes of mankind? Maybe. But she preferred Bulwer's thinking, that there are two lives to each of us—the life of our actions and the life of our minds and hearts. He said that history revealed our deeds and our outward characters, but not our true selves. We each have a secret self that has its own life, its own history.

It was what she'd tried to explain to Brian before about changes—that times change, fashions change, values change, land formations change, everything changes, except that place inside everyone where, if you're very quiet and if you really want to hear them, ancient voices can be heard, and nothing ever changes. Not ever. Not from the day you're born till the day you die—and some people believe it's that part of you that lives on forever, for all time and eternity.

It's where memories live and lessons learned are stored. It's where convictions are formed and courage is stored in readiness. Your life's worth, your values and what you believe are gathered, piece by minuscule piece, and slowly put together, like a mosaic, to form the whole of who you are. And in that space, shards of pain are set beside gems of joy; dull, apathetic pebbles are inlaid next to ugly, nasty-looking rocks of greed, jealousy, and hate; and the crown jewels of love and friendship and truth, outshining all the others, are set and fixed.

It's where man himself—and woman—in their hopes, in their fears, and in their desires; in their thoughts and in their emotions remain the only unchanged things in the world.

"I want to go home," she said suddenly, breaking the relaxed, reflective silence in the cab. "Right now. Let's get our stuff and take the next plane back."

His brow furrowed with concern. "Why? Aren't you tired? Doesn't it hurt?"

"A little, but nothing like the other times and I . . . I want to be home."

"Why?"

"I feel like I should be there. I don't know why, I just do. It's been the strangest morning. I've been thinking . . . I don't know . . ." She turned sharply in the seat to face him. "Brian, do you

know how lucky we are? Do you ever think of all the chances we've
taken and the mistakes we've made and realize how lucky we are
that things turned out the way they did? How different things could
have been? Do you ever think about stuff like that?"

His smile was small and somber; the light in his eyes was warm
and introspective.

"All the time," he said.

"Doesn't it make you wonder why? Doesn't it make you sort
of . . . eager to see what'll happen next?"

"No."

She tsked her tongue at him and shook her head. "You're such
an old poop. Tell me you wouldn't kill for a crystal ball. Tell me you
aren't dying to find out what happens to us, what the kids will be
like, what the world will be like. . . ."

"I don't *need* a crystal ball for that. If the kids don't kill each
other before they reach adulthood, they'll all leave home, get married, have children, and move back in with us. And it's only a matter of time before you get bored sitting with the town council and
decide to run for mayor of the dinky but prodigious town of Ar-
baugh, Ohio. I'll be Madam Mayor's husband, Whats-his-name.
Ten years after that, I'll be the first First Gentleman in the White
House and everything I paint will sell like hotcakes in souvenir
shops across the nation. We'll write a book about our life together,
and some fool will turn it into a miniseries for television. We'll
watch our grandchildren become Republicans, sell the family farm,
and put us in a retirement home. We'll drop dead over a fast-paced
game of pachisi and that'll be the end of it."

After a brief moment of silent awe and disbelief, she shook her
head. "And I thought you had no vision."